T0363666

MEDICAL

Life and love in the world of modern medicine.

Hot Nights With The Arctic Doc

Luana DaRosa

Nurse's Keralan Temptation

Becky Wicks

MILLS & BOON

HOT NIGHTS WITH THE ARCTIC DOC
© 2025 by Luana DaRosa
Philippine Copyright 2025
Australian Copyright 2025
New Zealand Copyright 2025

First Published 2025
First Australian Paperback Edition 2025
ISBN 978 1 038 94052 0

NURSE'S KERALAN TEMPTATION
© 2025 by Becky Wicks
Philippine Copyright 2025
Australian Copyright 2025
New Zealand Copyright 2025

First Published 2025
First Australian Paperback Edition 2025
ISBN 978 1 038 94052 0

MIX
Paper | Supporting
responsible forestry
FSC® C001695
www.fsc.org

Published by
Harlequin Mills & Boon
An imprint of Harlequin Enterprises (Australia) Pty Limited
(ABN 47 001 180 918), a subsidiary of HarperCollins
Publishers Australia Pty Limited
(ABN 36 009 913 517)
Level 19, 201 Elizabeth Street
SYDNEY NSW 2000 AUSTRALIA

Printed and bound in Australia by McPherson's Printing Group

Hot Nights With The Arctic Doc

Luana DaRosa

MILLS & BOON

Once making her home in sunny Brazil, **Luana DaRosa** has since lived on three different continents—though her favourite romantic locations remain the tropical places of Latin America. When she's not typing away at her latest romance novel, or reading about love, Luana is either crocheting, buying yarn she doesn't need, or chasing her bunnies around the house. She lives with her partner in a cosy town in the south of England. Find her on X under the handle @LuDaRosaBooks.

Also by Luana DaRosa

A Therapy Pup to Reunite Them
Pregnancy Surprise with the Greek Surgeon

Amazon River Vets miniseries

The Vet's Convenient Bride
The Secret She Kept from Dr Delgado

Buenos Aires Docs miniseries

Surgeon's Brooding Brazilian Rival

Discover more at millsandboon.com.au.

For Becky—the first of hopefully many!

PROLOGUE

'HEY, CHECK THIS OUT.' The voice of Larissa's best friend, Ally, barely registered as she took a sip from her coffee, wincing at the taste. Considering a three-day-old muffin that had, on a previous visit, chipped her tooth and the porcelain dolls sitting on floating shelves along the wall, Larissa had no idea why Heaton Perk was their favourite coffee shop. Neither of them were particularly into regular dental emergencies or creepy dolls whose eyes followed you around no matter where you sat.

Ally nudged her knee under the table, bringing her attention back to the tablet in front of them. 'Larry, we have to make a plan.'

'Okay, for the last time—Larry is a name for a cat,' Larissa said, taking another sip of coffee that landed like cement in the bottom of her stomach.

Ally's lips parted in a sheepish grin, and she gave Larissa's knee another shove. 'And I told you this way our names sound like a pair. Larry and Ally! You are always so serious—unless I want to talk about the future.'

Larissa groaned, her head coming down onto the rickety table. 'Because I'm still in denial about our practice closing. We built this for the last five years, pouring endless hours and care into it. Now suddenly the trust decides that this community doesn't need our services anymore?'

They'd both woken up last week to the news that their clinic had lost its funding and would shut down at the end of the year. What a great way to celebrate Christmas—finding a new place to work when she'd just got comfortable down here in Frome, in the south of England. For someone like her, who preferred solitude and self-sufficiency above anything else, five years seemed like a fast timeline to get comfortable, if she was being honest.

Now, they would spend the rest of the month updating their patients on this recent development and then get all of their documentation in order so they could transfer things to the GP clinic in a different district.

Ally's face grew serious. 'I'm right there with you—it sucks. But we have to...move on.'

Larissa lifted her head at that, noticing the hesitation in her last words. Were they meant for her or Ally herself? God knew they both had their fair share of baggage they carried around.

'What if I don't want to work in a place without you?' she said, steering the conversation away from where she could see the clouds building. 'There's no Dr Costa without Nurse Spencer.'

Larissa almost sighed when the sheepish grin returned to the other woman's face. She tapped on the tablet again, drawing Larissa's attention to it. 'I thought about that, and I have a solution.'

Looking at the screen, Larissa narrowed her eyes. 'New Health Frontiers?'

'It's a non profit organisation that matches medical professionals with places who need their certain skills. There are tons of places looking for short-term GPs and nurses. What if we take this entire mess with the clinic and with Rachel—' Larissa couldn't stop the wince at the sound of her ex-girlfriend's name '—and my long over-due return to the dating pool…and go on an adventure?'

When her best friend looked at her with bright eyes, Larissa remained unconvinced. 'An adventure?'

'Yes, Larry. A solo adventure for each of us. It'll get us both out of this place and give us some distance—we'll gain some perspective. Plus, while we are away, we can message and call to make our plan about what to do next. Because in the long term, I don't want to work without you, either.'

Larissa looked down at the murky coffee, thinking it must have been extra-old, because somehow Ally was making sense with this proposal. Without work keeping her anchored, Larissa didn't know what to do with herself. Had nothing tying her down, occupying space inside her that, if left empty, would send her thoughts down a spiral. Work was how she kept her independence. Without it… Larissa didn't know herself well enough to be without her purpose. Maybe a trip would really help her gain some perspective about herself.

'I guess it would buy us some time to find a new clinic that'll take us both,' she conceded, and Ally clapped.

'I knew I could convince you. But we're not just there to work. It has to be an adventure,' Ally said again, and Larissa didn't like the conspiratorial glint in her friend's eyes.

'Isn't going to a new place an adventure enough?'

'No, because I know you, you will work non stop and not even take one day to explore your new surroundings. So I've come up with a dare—for old time's sake.' Ally was getting so animated, Larissa couldn't fight the smile spreading across her lips. When they'd met on Larissa's first day at the clinic, she'd had no interest in making any friends—until Ally had dared her she wouldn't join her at this exact coffee shop for a cup of coffee. With her competitive spirit ignited, Larissa had come to see Ally outside of work. And they had been friends ever since.

Ally remained her only friend, but that did not bother Larissa. She only needed one when she had already picked the best there was.

'I see, a dare. What do you dare me to do? Find a new best friend?' She crossed her arms in front of her chest, pushing her chin out in a playful challenge.

Ally rose to it, slapping her hand onto her chest in mock indignation. 'The audacity—don't you dare derail this conversation. For the new year, and in the spirit of embracing new things and getting rid of old stuff, I dare us both to have a no-strings-attached fling while we're away.'

CHAPTER ONE

GO TO THE Arctic Circle, they said. It'll be fun, they said.
Larissa was *not* having fun. Somehow, 'fun' had missed
the plane from Oslo to Svalbard. It had still been there
when she'd boarded the plane in London, and she'd definitely seen it as the captain had announced that they
would land in Oslo early enough for her to stretch her
legs before she needed to board another flight.

But then she'd stepped out of the plane, wrapped in
a thick jacket, an endlessly long scarf, and mittens Ally
claimed she had made—even though Larissa could tell
where the tag had been cut off—and ready to conquer
the cold. But what she experienced right this moment
wasn't cold. It didn't even live in the same postal code
as cold. Whatever slammed into her the moment she exited the airport towards taxis and buses that would shut-
tle everyone to Longyearbyen was an evolution so far
from anything she'd ever known, Larissa couldn't find
the right words to fit. All she knew was that she was
going to strangle her best friend the moment they were
back in England two months from now. This had been
her hare-brained idea, and she would let Ally know she
would never listen to her again.

Why had Larissa picked that place again? Right, because the population was so low, chances were high

she wouldn't have to cash in on that stupid dare she'd agreed on.

'Dr Costa?' Larissa perked up as her name rang through the night—or was it daytime? She flicked her wrist, but several layers of clothing covered her smartwatch. Without the sun ever rising, it would be hard to tell what time of day it currently was.

An older man stood a few paces away from the line of people waiting to get on the bus. He looked down at his phone, then back up at her, and waved. Leaving the line, she dragged her bag behind her and approached the man. He stuck out a gloved hand towards her and said, 'I'm Olav Fjell. My wife, daughter and I run the hotel that New Health Frontiers booked for you.'

Larissa took his hand in her own, giving it a squeeze she hoped could be felt through the thick mittens. 'Oh, nice to meet you. I was told one of my colleagues would pick me up,' she said, her eyes darting around.

'Yes, Erik Fjell? My son runs the hospital in Longyearbyen. He asked me to pick you up since an emergency came up at the clinic.' The bright smile turned into something else when he mentioned his son. Mischievous? Uh-oh. Was she about to learn that the hospital was actually just an igloo? Larissa's brain rotated through all of her worst case scenarios in a split second and decided that if the hospital was indeed an igloo, she would leave.

'Ah, I see. I appreciate you jumping in. Please call me Larissa,' she said, and didn't resist when Olav reached for her bags and led her towards his parked car. After she neatly tucked away her belongings in the boot, she circled around the car to the passenger side, only to bump into Olav.

'Oh...right. Other side,' she huffed out with a laugh,

and when the old man smiled at her this time, the warmth in it put her at ease.

The interior of the car was marginally warmer than the outside. No doubt because of the lack of wind batting against her. She was at least accustomed to the icy wind from her town in Somerset. But there was cold and then there was...*this*.

Olav squeezed in behind the wheel, and warm air poured out of the vents when he turned the key in the ignition. Larissa had to suppress a shiver of delight at something as simple as heat. But the old man seemed to notice anyway, for he chuckled.

'Welcome to Svalbard, Larissa. I'm sure you've read a lot about our little archipelago, but it's a whole different thing to experience it first hand,' he said as the car moved forward, taking the offramp leading away from the airport building.

'It really is. I appreciate you picking me up. Makes me feel like a VIP,' she replied, and dared to peel the mittens off her hands. Then she stretched out her fingers in front of the air vent, soaking up the warmth.

'You definitely are a special guest for the Fjell family. We rarely have people staying for more than a week or two. That's enough for tourists to experience Svalbard as an attraction,' he replied, and then he said something else, but Larissa didn't catch any of his words.

A field of white opened up as the car lights illuminated the path in front of them. Lights twinkled in the distance, few and far between. Some cottages stood at the side of the road, their windows lit and smoke billowing out of their chimneys.

Winter never ceased in Svalbard. Larissa had read that the ice might melt on certain parts of the island, but this close to the North Pole, they didn't have what she would call a summer. Hands now warm, she rummaged through several layers of clothing to find the pocket containing her phone. It powered on just in time for her to snap a picture of another cottage further off the road.

She turned to Olav and asked, 'How do people live in these far away cottages?'

Olav considered, never taking his eyes off the road. 'The same way people live in other countries. It's not all that often that the harsh conditions of Svalbard impede anything. We have a cinema, restaurants, a library and some basic hospital facilities, as you probably already know. You can also eat your meals at the hotel.'

She'd checked out the hotel information along with everything else when New Health Frontiers had sent the information package over. The family-run hotel included meals and also had a social aspect to it where current residents could eat, drink or just meet up in a cosy common area. Outside of work, that would be the most likely space where Larissa could actually meet people.

Not that she wanted to meet anyone. Before she'd met Ally, Larissa had led a good life by only relying on herself and not getting sucked up into any drama. Her best friend had turned out to be so low-key that Larissa had believed maybe her self-imposed solitude wasn't necessary. Maybe she could be part of a community. Then her ex-girlfriend Rachel had happened, and she soon realised that Ally was an anomaly and not the rule.

They neared the town, with Olav prattling on about life on the island and easing some of her tension.

This was her new life. A change of pace to figure out what she wanted to do next in her professional life. Because her private life was quite clear—she wouldn't change a single thing. Ally and *The Great British Bake Off* were the only things she needed to satisfy her social needs. Paul Hollywood completed the trio between her and Ally, whether he knew that was irrelevant. Anyone with such a strong opinion about doughnuts would be her friend. Even if he didn't know they were friends.

'Why did you accept the placement here?' Olav asked, as if reading her mind.

Because my ex-girlfriend, who convinced me we would be together forever despite my reluctance, cheated on me in our shared flat while I was working late to fund our lives. Plus, perpetual darkness sounded exactly like my mood. Those thoughts flashed through her mind as she said, 'The GP clinic I worked at lost its funding, so I was unexpectedly out of a job.'

Olav raised his brow, convincing Larissa that he knew he had received the overly simplified and sanitised version of why she was here in Svalbard.

'That's a shame,' he said with genuine sympathy shining in his eyes.

Larissa nodded, looking down at her phone as they entered the town of Longyearbyen. The low hum of the engine and the muffled sound of snow crunching beneath the tires underpinned the silence between them. She stared at the empty bars at the top right corner of her phone and smiled when they finally filled with two lines.

Time to find out how Ally was fairing in India on her assignment.

Larissa: About to arrive at the hotel, and the cold is already too much. How is the heat of Kerala treating you?

Larissa: Also, jealous that it's hot and I hate you.

She waited for her friend to reply, but the three little dots indicating an incoming message didn't appear. So she slipped her phone back into her pocket just as Olav pulled up in front of a charming wooden building. Its exterior was adorned with twinkling fairy lights and looked like someone had copied the building right out of some Nordic-themed romantic movie.

'We're here. Welcome to the Aurora Hotel,' he announced with no small amount of pride in his voice. Larissa recognised the tone because she'd sounded almost exactly the same whenever she had spoken about her GP practice.

Now she and Ally would need to start over somewhere new and build back up—if they could even find a placement in the same practice again. But that was a problem for future Larissa. Current Larissa was stuck on an ever-white island in the Arctic Circle, and desperately needed a shower after so many hours of travelling.

'See you tomorrow, Erik.' Ingrid, the hospital receptionist—and secretary, janitor and office manager—waved at Erik Fjell before trudging down the snow-covered sidewalk into town.

There was only one vehicle left in the car park of the hospital. His snowmobile. Snow crunched underneath his boots, a familiar sound that soothed his nerves as he unzipped the outer pocket of his heavy winter jacket to grab his keys.

Today had been uneventful, and a part of Erik suspected it was some cosmic joke. If he was being honest with himself, he would confess that almost every day at the Longyearbyen hospital was uneventful, and that's how everyone in the town liked it. With a population that never breached three thousand inhabitants, including researchers and tourists, there just wasn't much to do when it came to medical needs. But even though he usually handled the sniffles, different sprains, frostbite and the annual vaccine rounds, occasionally it could get more interesting than that. The population was small, but outside of the town, dangerous wildlife patrolled its territory, and accidents happened.

Today would have been a good day for that. Not because Erik wished bad things on anyone, but it would have distracted him from his new arrival—and what that meant for him. His GP on staff had left rather unexpectedly a few weeks ago, needing to go back to mainland Norway to take care of some personal matters. Though he understood things like that happened, the sudden departure had put him on the spot of finding a new GP on brief notice. Since the hospital ran on a skeleton crew only, there weren't any redundancies in his plan. If something was too big for his hospital, they would airlift the patient to Tromsø.

Erik had no choice but to look for a temporary placement with New Health Frontiers until he could get a permanent staff member. That temporary GP had arrived earlier today, and because the hospital was short-staffed, Erik didn't have the time to pick her up from the airport to welcome her to Svalbard. Instead, he'd had to ask his father to do that for him. Something he'd avoid under any normal circumstances if it hadn't been for the fact that his new temp GP was also staying at his family's hotel.

His mood darkened as he swung his leg over the seat of his snowmobile. He didn't know anything about the new doctor other than that she was a woman. Which was also enough for his parents to start meddling. There would no doubt be the same song and dance about pushing him toward violating his strict 'no dating outsiders' rule. Which was a subsection to his general 'no dating' rule. Being the only permanent doctor on the island, he didn't have much time to give, especially not to a relationship.

Sticking the key into the ignition, he checked the strap of the rifle slung across his back to ensure it was secured for the ride. Unlike most people, he stayed in a cottage outside the main village, which required him to be armed in case he happened upon a polar bear.

The streets of Longyearbyen were empty of any cars, but there were still plenty of people milling around town. Streetlights, placed a few metres apart, emitted a bright light, indicating that stores, restaurants, and cafés were still open. Most natives didn't need the reminder during their polar night season, but even though the sun wouldn't rise until February, some tourists still dared to come here in these dark months.

An older couple waved at him as he stopped at an intersection, and Erik raised his hand in greeting before zipping down the road. A ripple of tension rose inside him as the snowmobile ate the distance between him and his destination. Aurora Hotel had been in his family for generations, with the parents passing on the knowledge, the passion and eventually the entire operation to their children. Erik grew up in that hotel, spending many years helping with whatever tasks arose. Once school and homework had been done, he'd follow his father around to watch him do maintenance tasks or help with turndown service.

When he'd announced he wanted to attend medical school in Oslo, his parents hadn't been enthusiastic until they realised how much that path in life had meant to him.

Then their concern had flipped over to him working too much and not spending enough time with them. Or not having a family of his own.

Gentle glowing fairy lights covered the wooden building, pulsing as they changed colour from light yellow to a deep turquoise, emulating the northern lights their hotel was named after. He had to admit, this was a nice touch. Probably his sister's doing. Anna was the one who was dragging the hotel into the current century as she took over more of the responsibilities.

Shaking off the snow already gathering on his arms, Erik hopped off the snowmobile and took a deep breath as he pushed through the doors of the Aurora Hotel. The warmth meeting him inside was a stark contrast to the sub zero temperature outside, and he tore the mittens from his hands. As he unzipped his jacket, a familiar voice said, 'Welcome to... Erik, dear.'

He hung his jacket on the coat rack, stuffing his mittens in the corresponding sleeves before turning around to face the reception desk. He'd noticed the slightly eager tone as his mother, Hilde Fjell, stepped towards him and enveloped him in a hug.

'Your new colleague arrived earlier,' she said as she let go of him, and he pulled his lips up in what he hoped to be a convincing smile. The meddling was already starting.

'Thank Dad for picking her up,' he replied, then followed his mother as she led them deeper into the hotel. 'How is she?'

He knew next to nothing about Larissa Costa. Only that she came from England, that she had run her own GP practice there, and that she had been willing to move here as soon as possible. That had been enough information for Erik to agree to her placement. He'd been working double shifts ever since his GP left him. He didn't mind putting in extra hours, but the community of Longyearbyen deserved better than him running himself ragged—and potentially making mistakes.

'She came prepared, that's for sure. We watched her peel out of five layers. Every time we hung one piece of clothing, a new one appeared. Like an onion,' his mother said with a titter.

'I won't be long. Just want to welcome her and give her some information about tomorrow,' he said, hoping to get out of here in a few minutes. Then home to his cottage to eat whatever leftovers were in the fridge while cuddling up to his dog, Midnight.

'Your sister just informed her that dinner is almost ready. Why don't you join us, so we can all welcome her?' Hilde tilted her head towards the dining room.

'I don't think so, Mum. I'll just say hi to her and be on my way,' he replied, recognising the invitation for what it was: a way for his parents to, once again, push him towards some ill-conceived match because they thought everyone needed to be coupled up. Just like them.

'Are you sure? I think Larissa would really like it if you stayed. She's already asking so many questions.'

Erik was about to refuse again but paused when someone in the corner of his eye grabbed his attention.

At the base of the stairs stood a woman with rich, dark skin that seemed to glow under the warm light. Her cream-coloured sweater matched the rustic surroundings, giving her an aura as if she had always been here. A fact Erik knew to be false. He would have remembered the captivating iridescent light in those brown eyes. It drew him in like an open flame on one of the colder nights on the island.

Watching her required far more concentration than it should have, yet he didn't even care that all thoughts left his mind the moment her lips parted in an unsteady yet bright smile.

Something odd was happening in the dining room, and Larissa wasn't sure what it was. Olav's wife, Hilde, was hovering behind a man as she came down the stairs, her smile a similar brand of mischievous she'd seen on Olav earlier. What on earth was going on with this family?

It had something to do with the stranger, because as Larissa reached the bottom of the stairs, she saw Hilde's eyes meet her husband's, and they both grinned.

The newcomer, however… her eyes went to him. And stayed there.

Clear blue eyes framed by long lashes stared at her, rooting her to the spot. His features evoked an immediate response of familiarity inside her—along with something sharper, hotter that she instantly shoved away. Whatever that sensation was, it was Ally's fault. She'd been the one to dare them to find a fling during their placement. Seeing as her dating pool would be only a handful of people, Larissa doubted she would find anyone suitable.

Except this man stood in front of her, unmoving, his eyes dipping just below her chin before coming back up. He swallowed.

A flutter rippled through her chest, one Larissa ignored. Instead she spoke up as the silence between them stretched. Remembering that they were supposed to be colleagues for the next two months, she shook off her trance and stepped towards him with her hand outstretched.

'You're Dr Erik Fjell, yes?'

His name seemed to rouse the man. He blinked once, his eyes focusing, and for a second, he looked around in…confusion? Was he *not* Erik Fjell? Or did he simply not know where he was?

'Eh, yes… that's me. Dr Costa, I presume?' The first thing Larissa noticed about him was his accent. Similar to the accents of the other natives she'd interacted with, yet his hit her in a completely different region of her body. A lot lower. Then he grasped her hand, and her focus shifted from his voice to where they touched. Rough calluses scratched over the inside of her palms, fingers lingering just for a second before squeezing her hand and shaking it.

A zap shot up her arm, as if he'd transferred static electricity to her, but she knew that wasn't what had happened.

'Larissa,' she said as she took her hand back, her fingers still tingling from his touch.

A smile appeared on his lips, rather unexpectedly, and Larissa didn't like what it did to her stomach. How it summoned a fluttering out of nowhere. White teeth peeked out from his lips, his mouth surrounded by the bristles of a close-cropped beard the same sandy colour as his short hair.

'Erik. A pleasure to meet you. I just wanted to stop by to welcome you after I couldn't fetch you from the airport.'

'We were about to sit down for dinner, Erik. Please

join us,' Hilde piped up from behind Erik, and the sparkling smile on his lips faded. Then retreated into a thin line. The loss of it was instantaneous, with Larissa's own smile faltering.

'I'm afraid I can't stay,' he said with only a glance at his mother before those ice-blue eyes narrowed back on Larissa—making her stomach swoop again. 'Welcome to Svalbard. The hospital isn't far from here, only a ten-minute walk. But if you prefer to drive, I can pick you up in the morning.'

She didn't mind walking, and was actually looking forward to it. But that didn't stop the next words coming out. 'Thanks. I would love to ride with you.'

His brows rose ever so slightly. Had he not expected that? Larissa couldn't blame him. She didn't know why she had agreed, except that it maybe gave her a few moments alone with him before the everyday business of the hospital demanded all of her focus. Was that strange? Absolutely. Especially since she could hear Ally's voice whispering in her ear, telling her she could do with a quickie or a fling, and Larissa might well have found the only eligible bachelor on the island. Dang it. She'd picked this remote location so she *wouldn't* meet anyone.

Prompted by the thought, her eyes darted to his hand, and she bit her lip—both to stop a relieved smile from appearing and also just to remind her that this was *absolutely* not happening. She'd agreed with Ally to get her off her back and had zero intention of following through with their deal.

'I'll pick you up tomorrow, then. Six thirty sharp.' He

smiled again, a much dimmer version than the one she'd seen before, and didn't even nod at his mother standing behind him before vanishing through the door—leaving nothing but a few stray snowflakes behind.

CHAPTER TWO

'I DON'T KNOW how to explain it. It's just…odd,' Larissa said as she looked out of the window and into the darkness. Well, not complete darkness. The street lights had come on at five in the morning at a low glow. Larissa knew that because Ally had called her, shaking her out of her sleep with her own personalised ringtone. Apparently, Ally had forgotten that they had a four-hour time difference now, and she couldn't just call Larissa whenever she felt like it.

But Larissa was desperate enough that she'd shaken off sleep to talk to her. She'd wrapped her blanket around her shoulders, had dragged the comfy armchair in front of the window and had watched the lamps lining the streets go brighter with each passing minute. The mechanism—and its purpose—caught her attention. It had to be some sort of simulated daylight to keep everyone in town on track with their circadian rhythm.

Now it was almost six, and Larissa was all clued in on what had happened in India while she'd been en route to Svalbard.

'I mean, it gets pretty dark in winter in England, but I guess it's much more different when you see no sun,' Ally mused. On the video call, Larissa could see her friend pulling things out of her suitcase and stuffing them into a backpack. She'd told Larissa she was off to do a vaccine drive in a more remote location.

'It'll be an adjustment, but whatever.' A part of her still wasn't sure this had been a well-thought-out idea. No, that wasn't true. She *knew* she hadn't thought this out at all. The anger from her breakup compounded by the loss of her GP practice had driven her to make a rash decision. One that she now had to sit with for the next two months. In complete darkness. All on her own.

Well, except that there was Erik…

'Oh, don't sound so glum! Something about Svalbard spoke to you when we looked at the job postings. I'm sure you'll find that spark there. Just give it time. You've not even been to the hospital yet,' Ally said, and Larissa sighed. Ally had always been the more positive one in their friendship. The yin to her yang. There were times she really appreciated that. Today was not one of those days.

'I just… Okay, so. Erik Fjell, the person who runs the hospital. You remember him, right?'

Ally hummed before her eyes went wide. 'Oh yes, the Thor look alike.'

Larissa rolled her eyes. 'You're really comparing a Norwegian guy to Thor? Isn't that a bit cliché?'

Her friend waved a hand in front of her face. 'Whatever. What's he done already?'

'He couldn't pick me up from the airport because he was busy, so he sent his father. Turns out, they own the hotel I'm staying at. But he came by last night to welcome me—' Larissa pointedly ignored the 'aww' sound coming from her best friend '—and the vibes his parents were giving were off. They kept staring at him *and* at me with this weird energy.'

Whatever had happened in the dining room completely eluded Larissa. Probably because she didn't have parents in her life that could give off strange vibes.

Her own parents hardly factored into her life anymore at this point. While she was growing up, they'd been so busy with their own marital drama that they didn't devote as much time as they should have to raising her. They'd taught Larissa early on that she only had herself to rely on, and she guessed she owed them some gratitude for that.

A lesson she'd had to relearn with Rachel first crashing into and then out of her life in a spectacularly painful fashion when she'd found her ex-girlfriend interlocked with some other woman in their flat. Only for Rachel to blame it all on her. That if she hadn't worked so much or got used to leading such an independent life, she wouldn't have resorted to finding some closeness elsewhere.

Yeah, right.

'Oh really? So you waded into someone else's family drama. That's…healthy.'

'Oh, shut it,' Larissa grumbled, but she couldn't help the smile spreading over her lips. 'I'm not wading into anything. Just here to do my job.'

Ally raised her eyebrows high enough that they almost vanished in her hairline. 'And don't forget about our deal.'

'Yeah, about that…'

'Larry!' Ally shouted, glaring at her through the screen. Even with thousands of kilometres between them, she could feel her ire. 'You promised you would at least try.'

'The thing is… I didn't realise how small this place would be. Longyearbyen doesn't exactly have a thriving singles scene.' It was a harmless lie, though by the frown on Ally's face, she could tell her friend wasn't buying it.

The lights brightened again, and her eyes darted to the time on her phone. Erik would be here soon, and she wasn't even dressed yet. With a groan, she pushed herself off the chair and walked to her own luggage. Pulling out a few things, she draped them over her body, surveying them with a critical eye.

'What about Thor? You thought he was cute,' Ally said, not willing to let this go.

'His name's Erik.' Larissa pulled out a pair of jeans she knew made her butt look exquisite and rifled through her pile of clothes for a top—settling on a pastel pink cable-knitted jumper.

She presented herself to Ally as she tamed her hair into a manageable bun on top of her head. 'What do you think?'

Her best friend furrowed her brow. 'What do I think? About...your clothes? I thought you were going to work.'

Larissa raised an eyebrow. 'I am.'

'Then why do you care if you look cute?'

'What? That's not...' She paused, examining herself in the mirror. Why *was* she concerned about how she looked? She wanted to leave a good impression, of course. But not with Erik. With her patients. With her new co-workers. Though Larissa had no intention of keeping any of these people in her life—the whole point of going away to work for two months was so she didn't actually have to hassle with befriending anyone—somehow this strange struggle with her wardrobe told a different story.

An amused glint entered Ally's eyes. 'What did you say is Thor's name? I need to google him.'

'And that's my cue to hang up before you can get any

ideas. Love you, babes.' She picked up the phone, pressing her lips to the camera while making loud kissing noises. From the sounds coming from the phone's speakers, she knew Ally was doing the same thing. When she pulled back, she got a glimpse of her friend's smile before the call ended.

Why did she need anyone else in her life when she had Ally?

Fresh out of medical school, Larissa had accepted the first placement that would put a considerable distance between her and her parents, who still lived in the North East of England. It hadn't been anything personal, at least that was what Larissa had convinced herself of. Her parents were decent enough people. They were just terrible parents who thought having a child would save their marriage, but instead they just slipped further into their misery while sometimes forgetting they even had a child.

So Larissa had early on got used to cooking her own meals and doing her homework by herself, and just became comfortable with her own company.

But then she met Ally. With her welcoming smile and her sunny disposition, she had weaseled her way into her life in what Larissa could only describe as a war of attrition. Because in her mind, she had come down there to work. She had no interest in making friends or inviting people in—romantically or otherwise. Connections like that went against her highly self-contained life, where she didn't have to mind anyone else's feelings around anything.

Until Ally had popped up, not giving up until she had broken through Larissa's icy walls. So Larissa had made an exception. She could have one friend, but that was it.

Rachel had been another exception in her life when

she had met the woman at a Pride event where Larissa had volunteered to oversee the first aid tent. Letting Ally get close had lulled her into the sense that maybe other people could be okay, too. That maybe she didn't have to do it all on her own.

But that hadn't worked out. At all. And now Larissa knew better. The only person she needed was a best friend and no one else.

A faint sound coming from outside grabbed her attention, and she rushed over to the window, peering outside. The faint hum of an engine cut through the otherwise silent morning, and Larissa followed the vehicle with her eyes, watching as it grew larger and larger and eventually pulled into the hotel's parking lot.

'What the...' The streetlamp cast enough light onto the car park to make out the male figure, who just slung his leg over...a snowmobile? This couldn't be Erik, then, because he had offered her a ride to the hospital. That would only be possible in a car, right? Where would she even fit on a snowmobile? She scrutinised the narrow seat of the vehicle as the helmet-wearing figure stepped away. A second person could realistically sit there, if they were really close, like...her front flush against his back.

That thought triggered a spark at the base of her spine, shooting out and across her body in a star-shaped pattern.

Please don't be Erik, please don't be Erik. Gloved hands came down on either side of the helmet, one arm obscuring her view as he pulled it off. Sandy blond hair came into view first, and Larissa swallowed her groan as the rest of Erik's rugged face appeared.

Well, shit.

She should have walked.

* * *

Vice-like hands held on to Erik's jacket, pinning him into place on top of the snowmobile. He almost tripped trying to swing his leg over the seat, not expecting the resistance. Their helmets clanged against each other as he twisted, trying to catch her eye over his shoulder, but Larissa stubbornly held on to him as if her life depended on it.

The corners of his mouth twitched as he fought off the smile. Her discomfort was understandable, even if it was hard to grasp for him. He knew how to handle tourists—from both his time at the hotel and his work as a doctor. But Erik realised he never actually helped anyone get used to Svalbard. Not since Astrid, and even with her, he had failed. She hadn't wanted to stay here despite the promise to build a life together.

Sliding the visor of his helmet up, he said, 'You can let go now, Dr Costa.'

A muffled sound came from underneath the helmet he'd brought specifically for her.

'I can't hear you with the helmet on. You should let go and take it off.' Her fingers on him flexed, digging deeper into his covered ribs, and Erik pushed away the bubble of heat inflating in his chest. His body was reacting to unusual external stimuli, as he would expect. He could hardly remember the last time he gave someone a ride like this. It would have been with Astrid as well...

Erik stiffened as he caught the unwelcome thought, pushing it away. She was gone, had left him behind to seek her happiness elsewhere—away from this island and its community that had sucked so much of the joy out of her life. Away from him.

The grip around him relaxed, and Erik took the opportunity to fully twist so that she completely lost her hold on him. More muffled words tried to escape into the open, and he reached out, pulling the helmet from her head.

A cascade of tight, dark brown curls tumbled into sight, their shine glossy even in the streetlamp's light. Her lips parted, steam forming in front of her with every exhale. Her eyes were wide and pinned on Erik. The unease of his memories vanished as they remained looking at each other. The condensation of her breath caught in her eyelashes, forming ice crystals that surrounded her eyes. The rich bronze of her skin stood in contrast with the white snowflakes, giving her the aura of an otherworldly beauty.

'Larissa,' she said, snapping him out of his trance—one he only noticed he was in because she'd said something.

'Pardon?'

'You said, "Dr Costa." But I would prefer it if you called me Larissa. Dr Costa is my father.'

Erik raised his eyebrows. 'Your father is a doctor, too?'

'Um... no.' Now those eyebrows came down, bunching together as he scrutinised her. 'It was a joke. Not a very good one, I have to admit. I talk too much when I'm nervous.'

That caught Erik's attention. 'What's got you nervous?' he asked, his head tilting to the side.

Larissa took a deep breath, and the space between them was narrow enough that he felt the warmth drifting across to him even in air that was −13°C. Her eyes widened slightly, then dipped to where he still held her helmet in his hands. As if she, too, realised that they hadn't moved away from each other for this entire conversation.

Even through all the layers, he could see her swallow

from the way her jaw moved, and a part of him wanted to peel her scarf away to watch her throat work. Erik blinked at the randomness of that thought, but before he could shove anything away, Larissa said, 'I don't know if you noticed, but... the sun didn't rise today. It's freaking me out a bit because for thirty-three years, it's been right there with me when I get up.'

A smile spread over his lips before he could even think about stopping it. 'Did you forget to pack it?'

Larissa's lips twitched. 'I was sure I put it in my suitcase, but now I can't find it.'

'Ah, there is your mistake. Always pack the sun into your carry-on. If the people working at customs realise what this gigantic ball of gas in your luggage is, they might grow long fingers,' he said, leaning much further into the joke than he would have expected from himself. It was something about how her lips moved when she smiled. He wanted to observe it again.

But she didn't smile. Instead, her mouth rounded as a thin line appeared between her brows. 'Long fingers?'

'Does that idiom not exist in English? In Norwegian we say someone has *lange fingre* to say they're a thief. You know, longer fingers make it easier to steal things.' When the corners of her lips twitched again, a thrill went through him, and he added, 'Supposedly. My fingers are short and not at all thief-like.'

Erik stopped breathing when she threw her head back and laughed. The sound filtered through the cold air in all its clarity, winding its way through the many layers of his clothes and somehow skating across his skin— sending a shiver down his spine.

His own lips cracked into a grin, and he joined her laughter. He couldn't have stopped it even if he'd tried.

Something about her laugh compelled him to join in, immerse himself in the sound and feel of it.

'By the end of my stay, if you teach me, I will become well-versed in mistranslated Norwegian idioms,' Larissa huffed out as her laughter subsided, and then she blinked. Some crystals coating her lashes fell off, melting against the warmth of her cheeks.

Her eyes darted down to where he still clung to the helmet, their bodies almost as near as they had been during their ride. As if the sudden proximity had only sparked alive between them in this moment, both she and Erik reared back a bit. He let her swing her legs over the seat and take a few steps in the snow before he got off the snowmobile himself.

'I gather this was your first time on one of these?' he asked, wanting to diffuse whatever strange moment they had shared.

Had he been flirting with her? He didn't even know this woman. Didn't *want* to know her. She would be here for two months before leaving Svalbard. The island, its community of inhabitants, the places—they would all become nothing more to her than a fun story to tell.

Where was this sudden intensity even coming from? The two metres Larissa had put between them didn't feel like enough anymore, so Erik took a few steps towards the hospital entrance, vaguely waving his hands for her to follow him.

'Yes, I've never been anywhere cold enough to warrant a snowmobile. One of the many new experiences I'm about to have,' she said, her voice a lot softer than when they were joking—like she, too, realised their conversation had taken a turn neither of them could explain.

'We can get you some lessons if you want to try it out

yourself. Or we can get you a rental car, though some situations require a vehicle that can go off-road.' He pushed through the doors of the hospital, and a pleasant warmth enveloped him almost immediately.

Erik waved at the receptionist and waited for Larissa to step up to the desk. 'Ingrid, this is Dr Costa, the new GP that'll be with us for the next two months.'

The woman stood and extended her hand towards Larissa, and he watched with mounting amusement as the doctor struggled to peel off her thick gloves. As the seconds went on, his self-restraint grew thinner—to the point where he wrapped his fingers around her wrist and pulled the right glove off for her.

Electricity passed from her to him through the tiny sliver of skin he'd touched on her wrist, but it was enough to shoot up his arm, his fingers tingling where they had made contact.

Larissa's eyes widened as they locked into his, and she mumbled a thank you before turning to Ingrid and finally shaking the woman's hand.

CHAPTER THREE

AFTER THE STRANGE conversation when they'd arrived at the hospital and the even stranger moment involving his hand around her wrist, Larissa's day had calmed down significantly. So much so that she now wished there was a bit more *something* happening. As long as that *something* didn't involve Erik.

The phantom of his touch still lingered on that small patch of skin on her wrist, and she fought off the memory whenever things got too quiet.

'How can I help you today?' she asked, looking at the patient in front of her. An older gentleman with thin grey hair covering his head. He'd limped into her office not even ten seconds ago.

'Something's wrong with my toe on this side,' the patient, Martin according to the schedule Ingrid had given her, said, slapping his right thigh. 'It's been tender for a few weeks, but now I can barely get a shoe on to walk the dog in the morning.'

Like Erik's, Martin's words had an accent to them— one that identified all the local people. There were enough people at the hotel's dinner to suggest a decent number of visitors as well, though she had yet to meet anyone. Her dare with Ally floated around in her head and with it, memories of the snowmobile ride. How they had stood there staring at each other with only a hand span between their bodies.

Her worst trait—making strange jokes when nervous—had come out, but instead of backing off, Erik had leaned in. Had even joked with her. Larissa was sure that if she had peeled away the layers of clothing from her body, she would have been kept warm from the heat inside her.

'That's not good. Why don't you slip out of the shoe and let me have a look?' Larissa focused on Martin in front of her. They had booked her a full day of appointments for today, though the cases weren't necessarily what she'd expected. So far, she'd seen three sprained ankles, two swollen knees and five routine check-ups. The patients were nice, but there wasn't a lot of variety.

So when Larissa got a glimpse of Martin's red and swollen toe, something inside her jumped and pushed away the thoughts of Erik—of her dare with Ally—that she'd been batting away all morning.

'Could you lie down here so I can have a closer look?' She patted the exam bed beside her, then turned around and slipped into some gloves as the patient moved behind her.

Dragging the backless rolling chair closer to the bed, she looked over the foot. The cause of Martin's discomfort was staring right back at her. Skin was growing over his toe in unusual places, his flesh red where the nail extended into it. With a glance at the patient, she took the foot in her hand and turned it around, testing the ankle mobility before placing it back down.

'Seems like you got an ingrown nail there, Martin,' she said when she was confident that there was nothing else going on. 'But no worries. We can remove that right here.'

'Oh really? I won't have to make the trip to Tromsø?' His eyes widened, forehead bunching up.

'No, I can take care of such small things. No need to take you away from home longer than necessary.' Something in his voice gave her pause, and she looked at the toe again, playing back his words. Did he not like leaving Svalbard? She'd assumed everyone took trips to Norway on the regular, even if it was just for a change of scenery.

'Let me get everything necessary. The way it looks, we will only have to remove a part of the nail and then pack it. Do you have anyone who can walk your dog for a bit while you recover? You should really keep off your feet.' Larissa frowned when Martin shook his head. 'We'll find a solution for that, too,' she said as she got up and began rifling through the drawers to find an anaesthetic, forceps and a scalpel to get to work.

With the last patient out of the door, Larissa devoted the last hour of her shift to updating all the patient notes and getting to know tomorrow's list of patients. By the looks of the notes Ingrid had left on the appointments, she was looking forward to another day of general check-ups, flu-related symptoms and some random body aches. If this was what every day looked like, her time here in Svalbard would be easy enough.

Her gaze wandered from the screen to her phone, and she picked it up to text Ally.

Larissa: I had to ride on the back of Erik's snowmobile today. I think I left bruises on his ribs.

Ally: Oh dang.

Ally: Does he have nice ribs, though?

Larissa blinked at her phone as the last message popped up, her lips drawing down in a frown.

Larissa: Nice ribs? What on earth are you on about? They're ribs.

Ally: Just reminding you that nice ribs could be adventurous ;-)

Putting her phone down, Larissa rolled her eyes as the topic from this morning came back up. The dare she'd agreed to loomed over her, mingling with the moment she'd shared with Erik earlier. No part of their conversation had been suggestive, and yet somehow joking with him had sparked something inside her. A heat that had been chasing her all day.

Was she really considering Erik for her fling? She'd said no in her call with Ally, and she'd meant it then. He worked with her, and she lived in his parents' hotel. Talk about awkward when it came down to doing the deed. But her main reservation had been that he'd seemed the opposite of interested in her—or anyone. Erik had been polite but distant yesterday. Aloof.

But this morning, some of that frost had melted, giving her a glimpse of what she suspected was so much more than he let her see on the surface. Beneath the icy sheets, there flowed a lively river.

Larissa's eyes wandered towards the door, considering. He was still somewhere in the hospital. She doubted he'd have left without checking in on her, though where the confidence of that knowledge came from, she didn't know. He seemed to be in charge of the hospital. *Seemed*, because she wasn't actually sure. New Health Frontiers certainly made it seem like he was the one in charge. But Erik hadn't really shared any details about the hospital. He'd just sat her down in her GP clinic, showed her the computer system for the patient charts and told her their facilities were limited to regular GP stuff. Anything that required surgical intervention needed to be transported via helicopter to Tromsø.

With all her charts done and no more patients to see, Larissa clicked around the computer system while debating whether she should see what Erik was up to. Why was she even hesitating to seek him out? This had nothing to do with her dare. She just wanted to go talk to her colleague—one she would spend a lot of time with for the next two months. Which probably meant she shouldn't think about him in any way other than professionally. Then again…it was *only* two months. That was an ideal time frame for a no-strings affair with a willing participant.

Letting out a huff, Larissa pushed to her feet and grabbed her phone before leaving the office.

Larissa: You got in my head with that Erik thing, you witch.

Larissa: I'm going to see him now to… I don't know. But whatever the outcome, I'm blaming you.

Not waiting for a reply, she stuffed her phone in her pocket and went to search for Erik.

The hospital consisted of three different sections. The two smaller ones were general practitioner clinics with waiting areas for their patients. Larissa hadn't seen whether the other clinic had been open as well or if it served as a space to put in walk-in patients without an appointment. With how light her schedule had been today, she couldn't imagine having a second GP here.

The front desk was empty already. Ingrid had shown her around the hospital's staff area when Erik had been called away, and Larissa already appreciated the woman's sunny demeanour. She left the impression of being an important pillar of the community, knowing every single patient by name whenever Larissa had escorted them out.

The main building appeared as deserted as the front desk, with the only light coming from beneath the door that led to Erik's office. As far as she could tell, he was both leading the hospital and acting as the emergency physician during the daytime.

Finding the door slightly ajar, Larissa knocked and then pushed it open.

Erik sat behind his desk, sandy-blond hair tousled as if he'd spent most of the day running his fingers through it. It was probably soft. Those short strands would slide like silk through her fingers. Would it be an enticing contrast to the neatly trimmed beard covering his face, leaving her own skin rough and sensitised in just the right way?

Wait, what?

Larissa cleared her throat, willing the lewd thoughts into the back of her mind, and that was when Erik looked up—and the full force of his icy blue stare hit her. The intensity in his eyes was enough to wipe any trace of order from her brain. All she could focus on was his gaze on hers and how her heart beat against her chest as if it was trying to stage a breakout.

She pressed her hand to her chest as if to say *you stay right there.*

The corner of his lips twitched, as though he'd thought to smile but had then decided against it. 'Dr—Larissa. Please, have a seat. I was going to find you after finishing up here,' he said, pointing at the chair sitting across from his desk. With her brain still rebooting itself, she obeyed and used the time it took to seat herself to remember where she was—at her job. In front of the person who was *technically* her boss, even if it didn't feel that way.

The faux leather covering the backrest of the chair squeaked as she leaned back, crossing one leg over the other to project a sense of ease she didn't quite feel on the inside.

'Patient charts?' she asked, unable to identify the papers lying on his desk.

'Sort of. This hospital is part of the Norwegian healthcare system, so we have to submit papers about procedures at regular intervals,' he replied, tapping the pen on the stack of papers in a rhythmic beat. 'It's the most boring part of running this hospital.'

'I would offer to help you, but there are at least three letters on that page that I don't recognise.' Larissa knew the woes of government paperwork all too well. She'd spent many nights sitting on her couch, getting through it so it didn't eat into her time with the patients. On the really bad days, she and Ally had made a game out of it, rewarding each other with pieces of candy whenever they finished a report.

The corner of his lips twitched again, and she wondered if that was just his version of a smile. Or was he fighting off the smile?

'I will survive.' He glanced down again, the tapping of his pen the only noise as the silence settled between them. Larissa wasn't sure what had even brought her here. She didn't need a ride home. The hotel was down the road from the hospital. As was everything else in this town, really.

'How was your first day running the GP service? Anything you need?' he asked, and Larissa was glad he'd broken the silence. For some reason, she didn't want them to stop talking—but she could equally not come up with anything to say. Her brain was still in the process of starting up again, too distracted from how the hair and the beard and those deep, clear eyes seemed to trip something inside her.

'It was good. Uneventful…which I think is the desired state of a GP clinic, especially if more complex cases mean they have to be shipped all the way to Norway. That's a long way to travel for a broken toe. I once broke my toe, and my GP just told me to be careful without actually doing anything about it.' Because her brain was preoccupied, her mouth developed a will of its own, forming word after word without her involvement or her explicit consent.

Erik's mouth twitched for a third time in this conversation. It was then that Larissa realised maybe staring at his mouth kept tripping up her brain.

'They are actually transported via helicopter to the hospital in Tromsø. Not by ship,' he said.

She blinked at him. Was he saying nonsensical things to poke fun at her rambling? 'Oh… Yes, I know that. Ingrid explained it to me.'

A huff of air left his nose in a rush and...was that a chuckle? Whatever the sound was, it found its mark inside her body, sending a spray of glowing sparks down her spine. 'You said *shipped*, and I thought it prudent to make sure you don't think they are actually using a ship for transportation. That would be highly inefficient.'

The rate of her blinks increased until she could actually see her eyelids half of the time. Her mouth opened, searching for the right words to respond, but the echo of that huffed laugh still vibrated over her skin, as if trying to find a way inside her. Then it dawned on her. 'You're messing with me, aren't you?'

The reward for her keen observational skills was a laugh. A real one. Not a twitch of his lips or an exhale that could be interpreted as a chuckle. No, she got a full-throated laugh, deep and melodic, and it fuelled this ridiculous idea that had popped up this morning. That she wouldn't mind having a casual fling to make good on her dare if it was with Erik.

'My apologies. People say I have a rather...dry sense of humour,' he said, his laughter fading into a smile that did funny things to her stomach. 'I forget that it sometimes doesn't translate well.'

Larissa needed to get out of here. Because clearly Erik understood the devastating effects his smile had on people, and that was why he forced himself to keep it hidden. Even with the considerable amount of space between them—a whole desk—the surrounding air heated. Damn Ally and her dumb fling dare. It was all her fault, putting the idea of some closeness in Larissa's mind. Without it, she wouldn't have perceived Erik as anything except her coworker. But now...

She shoved her hand into the pocket of her lab coat,

looking for her phone, when her fingers brushed over a piece of paper. Fishing it out, she stared at the address scribbled on it. 'Oh, right. There is something you can help me with. Can you show me where this address is? I punched it into my maps app, but it didn't land any-where,' she said, holding the piece of paper out to him.

Erik took the paper, and a frown pulled at his lips as he scanned it. 'This is a cottage outside of Longyearbyen. Isn't that where Martin lives?'

Of course he knew whose address that was. 'Yes, that's right. I performed a nail avulsion on him and had to pack his toe because the area had got infected. He says he lives alone and can't walk his dog, so I offered to come by be-fore work to help with that.'

Erik shook his head, strands of hair falling onto his brow. 'You're not allowed to wander outside of the town limits without a rifle,' he said, and nodded towards a cor-ner of his office where a rifle leaned against the wall, just behind the door.

'A rifle? But why...' Her voice trailed off as parts of the instructional pamphlet she'd read on the plane came back to her.

'There is a saying here that we are just guests on Svalbard and must be mindful of the true inhabitants of the archipelago—polar bears,' Erik said, reminding her of quite the most important part of the information package.

Damn. That would not cut it. Martin was counting on her to walk his dog. If he put pressure on his toe, he might cause the infection to spread. If it hit his bloodstream, there were all manner of bad outcomes... Larissa eyed the gun again, then swallowed the lump in her throat as she asked, 'How can I get a rifle?'

* * *

Was this woman serious right now? 'What do you mean?'

Larissa tore her eyes from the rifle and levelled that dark brown gaze on him. He rolled his jaw as her eyes swept over him, assessing him as if she could see through his skin and into him. Which was, of course, a ridiculous overreaction. A random adrenaline spike was putting his body in a focused mode that picked up every little detail about her. From the texture of her hair right down to the dark lines crisscrossing through her irises, he had somehow memorised everything in the few minutes they'd been speaking to each other.

And had more than once wondered what her jawline would feel like if he slid his fingers over it. Or better yet—his mouth.

Erik batted the thought away. This wasn't just highly inappropriate. I t was actually stupid. This was his place of work. His responsibility to his community was the most important thing in his life. There was no space for any ideas of attraction. Not when he knew first hand how much of his focus those feelings demanded. Though his family served the community in their own way, his dedication to looking after his people had caused a rift between them that had never truly closed. The same dedication had ended his engagement to Astrid. When she'd put him in front of the choice of picking her or Svalbard, the choice had been simple. Hard but simple in the end.

'I mean, how do I get a rifle? Don't you think I should have one if I'm here to treat people?' She paused, looking at the weapon again and rearing back from it. 'What if I need to attend to a patient in one of the cottages?'

'You won't. If anything like this comes up, I will handle it.' He could almost see the discomfort around Larissa, her lips pressed into a tight line and her spine stiff. Erik had to give her credit, though—she was putting thoughts of their patients ahead of herself. With one last glance at the paperwork, he stood and rounded the table. He leaned his hip against it, glancing down to where Larissa was sitting at the edge of the chair. 'You already promised Martin you would do it?'

She sighed, her eyes dropping down to her feet. 'Yes, he's expecting me there tomorrow morning before work. I didn't know how else to keep him off his feet. When he said he lives by himself and needs to let his dog out, I knew he wouldn't take the bed rest order seriously unless he had someone to take care of his dog.'

Erik had no power over the smile that spread across his lips—not for the first time during their conversation. The quiet enjoyment he got from her presence was throwing him for a loop. He couldn't even explain how she did it when they had just met yesterday. The last woman who had sparked an interest in him, his ex-fiancée Astrid, had taken far longer to break through his shell. They'd met when she came into the hospital with frostbite, and even though they got along right away, he didn't understand she was interested in him *this* way until Anna pointed it out.

Not that Larissa was interested in him. And he *definitely* wasn't interested in anyone. His time and energy now all went into work—the one thing in life that he could do his very best for. His dedication had only redoubled when Astrid left him, complaining that she would always be second to his job. But what had she expected? Svalbard was his home and the people...they were his.

At least he knew Larissa understood that side of him. Promising Martin that she would stop by to walk his dog before work told him everything he needed to know about her dedication—and that he wanted to learn what she was like as a person.

Erik knew he should offer to walk the dog. He was already familiar with Martin's husky, Storm, as they often met when he was outside with Midnight. He would walk her anyway, so taking an additional dog along would be no big deal. That would be the most practical solution, leaving Larissa out of it, and yet he still said, 'How about we do it together? I'll pick you up in the morning before work, and we can do a round with his dog. If I accompany you with my rifle, that's enough to satisfy the law.'

Her head whipped up, tight curls flying around her, and her eyes widened. Her lips fell open in an O shape, and Erik's thoughts screeched to a halt when his eyes dipped to her mouth. Fantasies of that mouth came over him unbidden, and he swallowed the lump popping up in his throat.

'You would do that for me? Erik, that's—' She jumped to her feet before finishing her sentence, grasping one of his hands with both of hers and giving it a squeeze. 'Thank you so much.'

A smile spread across her face, slow and bright, as if she was here to replace the sun for the months that he hadn't seen it. The sight was intoxicating, the heat he'd banished to the pit of his stomach exploding through his body as her palm pressed against his. That small touch provoked all sorts of misguided thoughts in him, all of them involving both of their hands on various other parts of each other.

Erik opened his mouth, willing the words to push past his throat, but the spark of joy in her eyes robbed him of the breath required to say things. Which was good, because he wasn't sure if the *right* things would come out. He just had to keep himself in check until she let go of his hand. Any second now.

Except the seconds ticked along, and her hands remained wrapped around his. Her grip slackened somewhat, almost teasingly so, but she kept herself firmly planted in his space, looking up at him. His eyes dipped lower as she swallowed, the sound of it vibrating through the space between them.

Finally she said, 'I took this posting with New Health Frontiers because of my friend.'

Erik had no idea why she had said that, but he also didn't care. Because apparently he just liked it when she spoke. How words sounded when they left her full lips. It was the reason they'd stayed outside in the cold, talking about sunshine.

'Oh yeah? How come?'

She swallowed again, her gaze obscured by her dark lashes as she lowered her eyes. 'We worked together at a clinic. When we got the news that it had lost its funding and would need to close, Ally urged us both to be adventurous before we find another placement together.'

'I'm sorry to hear that,' he said, trying to stay grounded in the conversation when her soft palm was still lying against his.

Larissa swallowed again, his eyes tracking her throat. It was alarming how much he enjoyed that. 'I, um...'

Her voice trailed off as she lifted her gaze to look at him once more. What he saw in there sent a spear of heat through his chest, setting his nerve endings abuzz until he could feel the sparkling in his fingertips.

Erik couldn't help himself. Not when her scent drifted up his nose—vanilla and something intangible that was uniquely her. Not when his fingertips grazed over the back of her hand and he felt the shudder trickling through her deep in his bones. He leaned in, closing the already narrow gap even as his good sense was desperately trying to reach him.

The lights above their heads flickered, then went out completely—plunging them into darkness.

Larissa gasped. Then her hand released his, and he heard the sound of metal scraping over the linoleum floor as she no doubt collided with the chair behind her. Losing sight was like a bucket of ice water poured straight into his veins, clearing his head and saving him from the colossal mistake he had been about to make. A mistake because of a desire, and he wasn't even sure where the desire had come from.

Was he so touch-starved that he would feel such an intense need for a woman he had only met yesterday? It was so unlike him, Erik didn't recognise himself in that situation.

'This happens from time to time. Stay still so you don't hurt yourself.' Navigating the office by memory alone, Erik sat back down behind his desk, opening the drawer and taking out the heavy-duty torch inside.

Cool light illuminated his office as he flicked it on. Larissa stood at the door, and from her widened eyes, he could tell she had just played back the entire situation in her head and was as horrified as he was.

'What do you do when you're in the middle of a procedure?' she asked, her voice straining with an emotion he couldn't quite pinpoint.

'There are torches on the wall and in drawers everywhere. But we also have a backup generator.' He picked up his phone, looking at the time. 'I'll check on the generator, and then I can drop you off at the hotel.' Erik wasn't sure if having Larissa pressed against him even for the short ride to the hotel was a good idea, but he couldn't make her walk just because he was losing control of his senses.

She fished her phone out of her pocket, tapping on the screen for a few seconds, and then the bright light on the back of the phone turned on. 'No, it's okay. I...think I want to walk. But I'll see you tomorrow.'

She didn't give him a chance to say anything else, rushing out of his office and around the corner until he could only see the dim glow of her phone's torch. Erik slumped against his chair, burying his face in his hands.

What the hell had just happened between them?

CHAPTER FOUR

ALLY DIDN'T CALL her this morning, which was a shame because she would have found Larissa awake and ready to leave the hotel. Only she didn't want to leave the hotel, or even her room. She wanted to crawl straight back underneath the blanket and just will herself to England. If she closed her eyes and wished for it hard enough, it would happen. Right?

It hadn't happened, and now Larissa sat in a comfortable chair in the hotel lobby, watching the small flame in the fireplace dance around. She definitely *didn't* imagine what it would be like to be curled up naked in front of the fire with a certain Nordic god look alike, their skin sliding against each other's as she learned every peak and valley of his body.

Nope. This train of thought could absolutely not leave the station. Or could it? It was the back-and-forth that had robbed her of her sleep—when her mind wasn't replaying the moment in his office on loop.

Erik had leaned in, hadn't he? There was no way she'd made that up. Maybe she had?

No one would call her a relationship expert. Her parents' rocky marriage had taught her exactly one thing: that romantic love wasn't worth the trouble. A much younger Larissa had believed that doomed her to a lonesome life.

Until she'd discovered casual sex. Oddly enough with a woman she'd met in a mostly deserted library during her first year in med school. Men had quickly entered the mix—being more readily available than lesbian or bi women—so being attracted to both sexes had actually worked out rather well for her.

Until Rachel.

The chemistry between them had been instant when they met, and even though Larissa was familiar with sexual attraction, there was something deeper there. Something more elusive that she wanted to explore because it had been such a novel concept to her.

Her curiosity got the better of her. As she hung out with Rachel, she learned more about the woman, and each piece of knowledge only intrigued her more. Enough that she said yes when Rachel proposed something Larissa had never considered: dating.

Despite not liking people in her space, she had tried to make it fit—make *Rachel* fit into her life. But it hadn't been enough. Rachel had wanted more of her, more of her time, more of her life. And Larissa had been stupid enough to give all she had. Right up until the moment she learned Rachel had cheated on her.

At least the breakup had left her with another lesson. One that reinforced the experience of growing up self-sufficient. Larissa couldn't rely on anyone outside herself. Except for Ally. But she was an exception, not the norm.

Erik brought back that sense of curiosity and intrigue inside her, and that was a red flag fluttering right in front of her eyes. She should have been neither curious nor intrigued by the guy who was basically her boss. Even if that was in no way how she was perceiving their dynamic. With five staff members total, there wasn't really the space for a big boss ego.

The chime of the door floated through the otherwise quiet lobby, and Larissa tore her gaze away from the flickering fire just in time to watch Erik enter. His eyes fixed on her with an intensity that had her tensing up.

'Oh, Erik,' a female voice said, and they broke their eye contact, both looking over to the counter, where a young woman stood. Her long hair was tied into a braid down her back, and her eyes were the same blue Larissa had got lost in yesterday.

Erik approached the counter, and he and the woman exchanged a few words in Norwegian. Despite not knowing a single word of the language, Larissa tried to listen to their conversation anyway, wanting to get familiar with the sound of it. The woman—Larissa thought from the familiarity she must be the other Fjell child Olav had mentioned on the way here—sounded chipper, her voice dropping deep at times as she filled most of the conversation. Larissa realised she hadn't been here yesterday, so she hadn't officially met her.

Something about Erik's voice when he spoke Norwegian did funny things to her stomach.

She closed her eyes to focus on the conversation, Erik's low and lilting voice soon washing over her like she was listening to a podcast he had recorded just for her. The lack of sleep throughout the night caught up with her, weariness settling deep into her bones, and his voice… she could listen to it for the rest of her life and never tire of it.

A log cracked in the fireplace, and Larissa sank back into the chair, soaking in the warmth. Her limbs grew heavy, her thoughts drifting away as she kept listening, trying to hang on to the words she couldn't understand.

'Are you ready to go?' The words had transformed into something she could understand, the voice now closer to her. She just had to—

Larissa's eyes flew open, and she recoiled when two piercing blue eyes stared right at her—through her skin and into her soul. She blinked several times, trying to shake the disorientation spreading through her. She'd been sitting in a chair in the lobby waiting for Erik, and then...

'Coffee still kicking in?' Erik asked, and she blinked again, shaking her head.

'I haven't had coffee yet,' she said, prompting Erik to shake his head, too. The side of his mouth kicked up in a half smile that she didn't dare to inspect any closer. Not when his voice had just lulled her to sleep. He could never know that.

He turned to the woman again, saying something before turning back to Larissa. 'We'll bring some coffee on the walk with us.'

'Like in paper cups? Will the coffee even survive outside?' Her phone told her that the temperature today was −20°C. Her takeaway coffee turned lukewarm within two seconds of stepping out of the shop back in Frome, so there was no chance she could take a coffee with her unless she wanted a *very* iced coffee.

Erik huffed out a breath in a subdued laugh, and the memory of what his full laugh had done to her insides came rushing back at her.

'No, unless you want a coffee-flavoured popsicle instead. Though I'm not sure what that would do to the caffeine,' he said with the usual tug at the corners of his lips.

'I mean, have you tried it? It could be the revelation everyone in Longyearbyen has been waiting for.'

The fine lines around his eyes crinkled, becoming more pronounced and adding a breathtaking quality to his already handsome face.

Damn it, was she seriously considering coming on to him? That was a dumb idea for so many reasons. The main one was that they worked together, and if he rejected her, that would make the next two months awkward as hell. Or maybe he was into her, but they weren't sexually compatible—that had happened on enough of Larissa's one-night stands that she knew it was a thing—and they still needed to see each other every day.

Then there was the entire thing about her being way too curious about him and how those feelings were definitely not good for a no-strings-attached arrangement.

'In case it wasn't clear, the coffee comes with us in an insulation flask,' Erik said, bringing her back into the room. She blinked twice as he held up two travel mugs. Her contemplations had mentally dragged her far enough away that she had missed a few seconds of their interaction. She looked around just to catch a glimpse of Anna as she walked through the door to the back of the hotel.

'You ready to go?' he asked, reminding her of why she was even up at the crack of dawn.

Right. They had a dog to walk. That was why he was standing in front of her, pretending like nothing had happened yesterday. Well...nothing *had* happened yesterday, but a very loaded nothing, one that was pregnant with possibilities. If one more second had passed, that nothing could have transformed into *something*.

Larissa nodded, getting to her feet and following Erik outside. He stuffed the two travel mugs into one of the bags hanging from the side of the snowmobile, fastening the top of it, and then they were off—gliding through the snow in a direction she had yet to explore.

The area outside of Longyearbyen was similar to what Larissa had seen on her way from the airport. It was mostly snow and ice, but occasionally a little cottage stuck out from the snow, lights in the window illuminated and showing the residents inside starting their day. This far outside of town, there were no lights besides the ones lining the streets, and most of the cottages were visible only by the light coming from the houses themselves.

They passed three more before Erik swerved left, going off-road and up a small hill. The headlights of the snowmobile illuminated the great white expanse unfolding in front of them, and Larissa gasped when they came to a halt next to yet another small cottage. Fairy lights hung on the outside walls, giving off a warm and welcoming glow to anyone approaching. The big windows framing the door on each side, however, were dark.

'Do you think Martin is not awake yet?' Larissa asked as she approached the cottage, snow crunching beneath her feet.

'No, he is. I saw the lights on in his house,' Erik said while fiddling with something on the snowmobile. She turned to see him shoulder a messenger bag and slip their two travel mugs inside. He held an object in his other hand, and when he stepped closer, she identified it as a key ring.

'But this…' She glanced at the house behind her and then back at Erik.

He huffed—why was this sound always doing weird

things to her insides?—and came to stand next to her in front of the door. 'This is my place.'

The icy cold surrounding her somehow gave way to a sizzling heat. Larissa stared at him wide-eyed as he stuck the keys into the lock and opened the door. 'Wait... Your place? Why are we...'

Her voice trailed off as he pushed the door open. A small light trickled from the opening—enough to illuminate the floor but too weak to penetrate the blinds that Larissa could now see were drawn over the windows. A pitter-patter sound of clawed feet against a wooden floor drifted outside just as a gust of warm air hit her face.

The head of a white-grey husky appeared in the door, looking up at Erik. Then its eyes shifted to her and it cocked its head, a strangely inquisitive spark in its eyes.

'You have a dog, too?' Larissa whirled around, looking at Erik. He bent down, locking what she now realised was a long leash into the husky's collar and tugged it outside, closing the door behind its tail.

'This is Midnight. She and Storm are actually friends,' he said, rubbing the dog between the ears.

'How—Oh my God, Martin has convinced *you* to take care of his dog as well, hasn't he? And yet you made me think I was all soft and squishy for the plight of an old man.' She remembered the glint in his eyes when she'd confessed that she'd promised Martin to walk his dog. She'd thought it to be disapproval. Turned out there was a good chunk of amusement mixed into it.

'I can neither confirm nor deny,' he said, the corners of his eyes narrowing enough to hint at the smile behind the neck guard he had pulled over his mouth. Even with all the layers, puffs of condensation floated between them as the harsh weather froze every exhale.

Larissa crossed her arms in front of her. 'You can't tell me if you've ever looked after Martin's dog?'

'Doctor–patient confidentiality,' he said, his tone so serious she had to blink several times.

'I'm his doctor, too. You can't hide behind confidentiality.'

'Yes, but this happened before you joined.'

'Before I jo—Erik, I read his patient file. There is no retroactive confidentiality.'

Erik looked down at his dog, and Larissa caught him making a quick gesture with his finger. Midnight got onto her feet and bounded through the snow, the long leash unfurling from his hand as she moved. He turned to Larissa, shrugging his shoulders, but the humour sparkling in those blue eyes was apparent.

And Larissa couldn't help herself as she laughed, falling into a brisk step next to him as they walked towards a far away cottage that she could make out by the lights in the windows.

The cold conditions of Svalbard had never bothered Erik—not until today. Because as he walked down towards Martin's cottage with Larissa next to him, he really wanted to see her face. *Why* exactly he wanted to see it was beyond him, but if he had to name the need bubbling up in his chest, that would be it. This doctor from England had proved to be far more intriguing than he had expected. All he'd wanted from New Health Frontiers was a competent doctor to take some of the workload until he could decide on whether there was enough capacity to hire a permanent GP.

He hadn't imagined that he'd find himself on a walk with her, wanting to know what lay underneath the surface.

'Can I ask you something?' he said, even though he knew he shouldn't get to know her better. Whatever that thing between them had been last night was already too much.

It was the phantom brush of her fingers against his wrist that prompted him to ask. Maybe he couldn't get her out of his head because she was an unknown person in *his* space. He prided himself on knowing his community—in serving the people of Svalbard to the best of his abilities. They were *his* people. Of course he would want to know someone living among his community. Attributing anything more to it would be foolish.

Larissa shot him a sidelong glance, her dark lashes casting a shadow across her cheekbones. They both wore headlamps to illuminate the path ahead. Conveniently, it also prevented Erik from looking directly at her for fear of blinding her.

'You just did,' she said, and her huffed laugh sent clouds of condensation adrift between them. 'But I'm feeling generous, so you can ask me something else.'

His own chuckle appeared in white puffs in front of him, and he stared ahead to where Midnight bounded through the snow. 'What did you escape by coming here?' he asked, letting the question out without filter.

He knew her placement was temporary. From experience he knew people didn't come to Svalbard because they wanted to. They were always running from something.

Astrid had run from her boring life, wanting the change and thrill the archipelago offered. She had swept him up in her life, ripping him off his feet—and his world off-centre—before he could even understand what had happened. He'd wanted to believe that the slow life wouldn't bother her long-term. That she would see the value of the community they had here in Longyearbyen and appreciate it for what it was.

But then she'd left, telling him her life was bigger than this island. That she couldn't cope with his long hours or the calls in the middle of the night when they needed him for an emergency. But what had she expected? Sometimes he was the only physician on this island. The lives of his community—his people—sat on his shoulders. He hadn't turned away from that to satisfy his family's plans for him. He hadn't done it for her, either. Hadn't even wanted to try.

A low hum interrupted the steady crunching of snow underneath their feet. Larissa tilted her head upwards, causing the path in front of her to be plunged into darkness. 'And here I thought I could avoid any existential questions for a few more days,' she said, though Erik couldn't detect any apprehension in her voice.

The snow lit up again as she moved her head, and the quiet of the early morning snow settled in between them for several breaths. Then she continued, 'As I told you yesterday, my clinic back in England got shut down. When the trust funding the clinic reviewed their spending, they decided to close some of the GP services and re-direct them to other practices. My friend Ally is a nurse, and together we worked hard to bring out the best of our clinic. So having it shut down so unceremoniously was harsh to see.'

Erik looked at her from the corner of his eye. The need to study her facial expressions bubbled up in him. Why hadn't he initiated this conversation in a place where he could actually see her?

'That's a tough spot to be in. But there's a critical shortage of GPs where you are from, is there not? Why come here when you could have found a place closer to home?' Though he couldn't see much of her, some sense told him that wasn't the full story.

'How do you know England lacks GPs?'

He shrugged. 'Recruiters sometimes call me with job offerings. They are disproportionately UK-based, so I figured there definitely wasn't a lack of jobs.'

'I see...' Her voice trailed off, the silence once again reclaiming the space between them. Only Midnight's occasional pants broke through as she ran back, regarding Larissa with a modicum of curiosity, before leaping away and into the snow.

She was considering leaving it at that—a boundary Erik would respect, no matter how desperately he wanted to know more about her. But eventually, the light from her headlamp flickered across the snow as she shook her head with a sigh. 'Did you ever have your heart broken hard enough that you just needed to disappear into a different life?'

The snow under his feet crunched louder than usual as he almost lost his footing at the question—at how close to a target it hit inside his chest. He forced his gaze to remain on the path ahead. The answer to that question was way more personal than he'd planned on getting with Larissa. But it also revealed an even more intriguing side of her. Because the only reason she would ask was that she had experienced the same thing.

Was there any danger in letting her know? She was here for two months. There was no way she would become someone of great importance to him. If the demise of his engagement to Astrid had taught him anything, it was that he was incapable of forming such attachments. Too much of him belonged to the people on Svalbard, and no one would ever be happy with just a small sliver of him. They tended to want it all. Erik wasn't free to give all. A slice was all he had.

But a slice was enough for...other things.

'I have experienced that, yes,' he said, letting the truth come out for the first time in the icy landscape of his home.

He saw the deep breath she released more than he heard it. 'And where did you escape to?'

Erik lifted his hands, indicating their surroundings. 'Out here, where it is quiet.'

Larissa seemed to consider that, tilting her head to the side so she could shoot him a glance without blinding him. 'Well, I came here.'

'What happened?' The question was faster than his critical thinking skills, floating in the space between them like an overbearing sales person at a shop a customer had just entered.

'Well...' She sighed again, more condensation gathering around her. 'I didn't have an easy childhood and kind of just learned how to deal with life on my own. It's what's worked best for me, so I never saw a reason to change that until my...ex appeared in my life. It took us far too long to understand that we wanted different things from life, and we could have avoided a lot of hurt feelings if we had just worked through some of our stuff. Instead of being an adult, though, she decided the right way to resolve this was to bring some other person into our home and then blame me for the lack of attention I had paid her.'

Clouds billowed from her mouth again, though this time they came from a huff of laughter with a sharp edge to it. 'Jesus, why am I even telling you this? That's way too much to know about a coworker.'

This was definitely oversharing. With anyone else, that was what he would have called it. Yet somehow, with Larissa, it landed differently. It spoke to the desire within him to know her better. Though where that desire came from, he couldn't tell. She wasn't part of his community, so why did he care?

Midnight tugged on the lead, growing more excited as they drew closer to Martin's cottage. She knew she was about to see her friend Storm. With the exterior lights of the house illuminating their path, Erik flicked his light off so he could steal a glance at Larissa. Her eyes remained ahead, showing him only half of her face, but it was enough for him to see the thoughts tumbling around in her head. Had she never shared these thoughts with anyone else, and they had been sitting in her chest for so long that at the first opportunity, they'd come bursting out?

Her ex-partner was a woman? He hadn't misread the signs between them, had he? No. Making up something like that wasn't something he ever did. The taut tension, the stolen glances, and even this strange closeness swooping in with her confession were real.

Which was a problem. Because if his parents picked up even a whiff of the attraction between them, he wouldn't hear the end of it. After Astrid had left, they'd been relentless about finding him 'another shot at love.' Something as small as Larissa leaving by the end of February wouldn't deter them. But he knew asking someone to stay on the island wasn't an option. They needed to *want* to be here, not stay here for *him*.

'You risk nothing by telling me,' he said, hoping it would inspire her to keep on talking. 'I'm some guy you met on an island very far away from your actual home. What's the harm in letting some things out?'

They stopped in front of the cottage, and when Larissa reached up to turn off her light, she faced him. Her neck guard obscured half of her face, so all he had to go by were her eyes. The dark brown colour of her irises shone in the dim light while shadows brushed over her cheeks with each bat of her lashes. Her gaze was piercing, and even though he couldn't figure out the underlying emotion, the need to fidget itched in his fingers. Was she weighing his words? Trying to figure out if he was as harmless as he claimed he was? He'd meant what he said. If letting go of some things was what she needed, she'd come to the right place. Erik had never felt judged by the ice and snow.

'Are you saying you live in a little house outside of Longyearbyen because you're avoiding your ex?' she finally asked, eyes narrowing on him.

He let out a breath. She seemed to regret the glimpse of vulnerability she had granted him and wanted to make it even between them. Erik pressed his lips together, considering. If he was serious about him not being a risk to her, then she shouldn't be a risk to him, either. He should feel safe around her. If he let her see that tiny slice of him, maybe she would share one, too. To what end, Erik wasn't sure. A curiosity unlike anything he'd experienced compelled him—all wrapped up nicely in the safe knowledge that Larissa was only temporary.

'No, I lived there before I met her. Living outside the

town was more to gain a bit of distance from my family,' he said, focusing on those eyes to gauge her reaction. Bracing because he knew what question she would ask next. He had asked the same thing moments ago.

What happened?

But to his surprise, she didn't ask. Instead, she tilted her head to the side, her eyes sweeping up and down his entire frame. When they settled back on his face, she said, 'So that means you're not seeing anyone?'

His thoughts came to an abrupt halt. 'Seeing anyone?' The words came out as a question even though he hadn't meant to say anything out loud—the surprise had his lips moving before he could consider.

'Yes, like...*uninvolved.*' Larissa stressed the last word.

A shadow flitted across the illuminated window to their side, and they both turned their heads to see Martin's backlit silhouette waving at them. As one, they raised their hands and waved back.

'I, um, no. I'm not involved. There is no one.' He paused when the corners of her eyes creased. Was she smiling?

The door to the cottage opened, and Larissa climbed the three steps that led to the deck where the house was built. On the last step, she looked back at him over her shoulder. 'Good,' she said, amusement mingling with something else—something sharper—in her eyes before she turned back to Martin to greet him and Storm.

CHAPTER FIVE

'THERE IS NO way strawberries actually cost that much. What are they made of—solid gold?' Larissa stood inside Longyearbyen's only supermarket with her phone to her ear, staring at the fruit selection with a growing lump in her throat. People shuffled past her, some stopping and nodding at her in greeting before grabbing overpriced produce without even blinking and putting it in their baskets before moving on.

She shouldn't have been surprised. As a new face, she stuck out from the usual crowd. But two weeks in and not only did people already know her by name, she also knew some of them. Some she recognised from the clinic, while she'd seen others at the coffee shop she liked to visit when she was feeling particularly homesick.

'At least you have strawberries. I've been living off of oatmeal, lentil stew and prayers for the last two weeks,' Ally replied with an edge to her voice. Sounded like the ongoing work in Kerala required a lot of travelling from her friend.

Fragments of conversation hummed around her, some in English, others in Norwegian, and she could only imagine that they, too, were wondering how much they would have to tighten their belts to afford some strawberries. The store had printed new price tags for the strawberries, with hearts replacing the zeroes and the letters 'Valentinsdag Spesial' stuck next to it on a separate sign. Oh God, Valentine's Day was still a month away and they were already promoting it?

Today was Larissa's first day off since starting at the hospital—and she had no idea what to do with herself. After scrolling through TikTok for a solid hour while lying in bed, she could feel the brain rot setting in and realised she needed to move her body. It was an excellent tactic to avoid brain rot and also *other* thoughts she was trying to ignore.

Thoughts around Erik and the sound of his voice as he said, 'There is no one.' Heat stained her cheeks as she recalled that moment. The word *good* had formed on her lips as she embraced the dare she had made with Ally. One fling—for fun. Just because she let herself crave and indulge in some tender moments between the sheets didn't mean anything about her had to change. Larissa was done with dating, done trying to fit someone into her life who didn't *want* to fit. It took little imagination to see that anything more than a casual fling with Erik would cause a repeat of the disaster that had been her relationship with Rachel.

Good.

It *was* good. Except for the fact that they hadn't spoken about it since. He'd unpacked the travel mugs as they left Martin's cottage behind, and then Erik had spoken about the people living in this area just outside of town. He'd known every single inhabitant by name, telling her who to expect in the clinic and who was due for a checkup.

Had he changed the topic because he regretted the direction it had gone in? They rarely interacted at work, and half of the time when she went looking for him, Ingrid informed her he was attending to someone at their home.

'Okay, theoretically,' Larissa said to Ally, stressing the last word. '*If* I was interested in *maybe* banging a dude. No one specific, mind you.'

Ally gasped on the other side. 'You're going for Thor? Yas, queen!'

'No, I'm not. Stop even thinking about that.' Larissa wasn't sure why she was still pretending like it wasn't Erik when she was talking with Ally. Something about all of this remaining hypothetical just calmed her down. Like she could opt out at any time.

To her relief, Ally seemed okay to play along. 'I think the best way to go about it is to just tell this man of mystery. Did you already bat your eyelashes at him and touch his arm whenever you laugh?'

Images of their morning dog walks together fluttered through her mind. The distance between them as they marched through the snow had definitely diminished. So maybe not touching, but there were glances. The conversations had been pleasant. Fun, even. He'd introduced her to people as they returned to town, pointing out important and well-loved members of the community. Larissa had also learned more about the history of the hospital and how Erik spent most of his time there.

Through the conversations, one thing had become clear to her: Erik valued his community. And by how many people already had taken the time to get to know her, she could understand why.

'Okay, let me pose a scenario to you. You're hanging out with some cute guy, who shall remain unnamed, and then he tells you about—'

'Fancy meeting you here.' Larissa lurched backwards

at the sound of the familiar voice—which turned out to be a mistake. Because that put her firmly within Erik's personal space. He had apparently been somewhere behind her. His broad chest collided with her back, the contact enough to give her an idea of what lay beneath the layers of clothes. Thor indeed, she thought as a shudder raked through her.

'Ally, I'll call you back,' Larissa whisper-hissed. She lowered the phone from her ear while smashing the disconnect button. How much of the call had he heard?

Larissa winced at the thought that it might have been every single word. Time to do some damage control. They might have been vaguely flirty with each other at times, but she wasn't ready to move her hypotheticals into reality.

'Ally is having man trouble. She doesn't know how to talk to him about it. You know how it is,' she said.

Erik cocked his head. 'Not really.'

'You're telling me you are *not* an expert in propositioning men?' she asked, the familiarity between them far too comfortable after two weeks.

His eyebrow quirked up, and the beard hair surrounding his mouth twitched in one of his subdued smiles. 'Nope. Never been with one,' he said, and why did those words send another wave of heat through her? What he had or hadn't done with *anyone* was none of her business, yet the casual openness of his experience did something to her limbs—as if she had misplaced all of her bones.

'Damn, neither have I,' she said, and laughed when his other eyebrow joined the first one near his lush hairline.

He really did have perfect hair that she knew would feel like heaven between her fingers.

'You...' His voice trailed off, and Larissa burst into laughter.

'I'm kidding, okay? Though that look on your face...' She paused, her words trailing off when she thought of what she'd wanted to say. His expression had been one of shock for a reason. Was it because of disappointment? What did he have to be disappointed about? That she lacked experience? That implied he wanted something from her. Something more than just a casual acquaintance. Maybe a fling...

She knew how to agree to be passionate for one night. And she might not know how to do relationships, but the knowledge that this kind of human connection wasn't for her was comforting.

But a fling lay somewhere between a one-night stand and a relationship. A space unfamiliar to her.

Was his appearance here a sign that she should let her hypothetical thoughts become more real? Why did that thought send a thrill racing down her spine?

'That was amusing for you, yes?' His expression was deadpan, only making her laugh more. Maybe she was overthinking this and just needed to go with the flow. If he was interested, he would get it. Larissa was going to leave in a month and a half, and that alone should have signalled her only interest was in something temporary.

With her teeth sinking into her lower lip, Larissa took a breath and said, 'Maybe we can figure it out together? If we puzzle it out, I might be able to give Ally some better advice.'

There was a not-so-clear message woven through her

words, but by the widening and then narrowing of his eyes, she knew he'd picked up on it. Even through the noise around them, she heard Erik's exhale, felt it on her skin.

His eyes scanned around them, as if checking if anyone was watching, and then he stepped closer—putting himself squarely in her space. Their eyes locked, and the intensity in his ice-blue gaze was enough to make her breath stutter. Then he let his eyes wander down over her face to her neck, pausing as if to watch the rise and fall of her chest. But then his gaze dipped even lower, fixing on a point Larissa couldn't follow with her own eyes.

'What did you come here for?' he said, his unmovable frame and the scents of fresh laundry and snow the only things she could focus on.

'What? To...work?' Larissa wasn't sure why he was bringing it up, but by the playful eye roll, she knew he hadn't meant that.

'To the store.'

'Oh...' Now she looked down at her hand, too, inspecting the still empty shopping basket. 'I wanted some strawberries and something else for dinner. I was planning on sitting in my room and calling Ally back.'

Erik's feet remained planted firmly on the floor, but somehow he still got closer to her just by slightly leaning forward. 'Do you think Ally would be okay if I commandeer some of your time today? I'll take you to dinner, and we can workshop this particular question you have. Maybe even come up with some answers before you report back to her. Since you're so kind to help your friend.'

Larissa blinked, her throat suddenly dry. She coughed, willing the heat rising in her to slow. Thinking straight was a lot harder with Erik crowding up her space, yet she had no plans of telling him to back off.

Quite the opposite.

'Y-yeah, I think she will understand. It's her question, after all.' Understatement of the year. The moment she told her best friend that she was giving in to the lure that was Erik Fjell, Ally would punch her fists in the air like she had just won the Nobel Prize in medicine.

A smile spread across his lips. It was only the second or third time Larissa had got a glimpse of his teeth as he smiled, his amusement usually not showing more than a twitch of his beard around his mouth. She was glad for it, because the full effect of his smile wasn't anything she was prepared for in this moment. It shot through her body like a tiny, fiery meteor, colliding with everything it met and leaving smaller fragments in its wake in distant corners of her body.

Her knees wobbled, and she gripped the handle of the shopping basket tighter to stop herself from reaching out. Would his chest feel as solid as she imagined underneath her palm?

'Good.' He reached out instead, and Larissa's breath stuttered out of her when his fingers grazed her arm. But he didn't touch her. Instead, he grabbed something behind her. When his hand came back into view, he was holding a box of strawberries. 'Now we're ready to go.'

The pub buzzed with the low hum of conversation when Erik led her through the doors. Some eyes turned towards them as they walked in, and many people greeted him with smiles or a pat on the shoulder when they passed.

An unfamiliar warmth pricked the top of her scalp, trickling down through her body in a steady drip. Because when she glanced up at Erik, he was smiling back at the people, whispering a few words here and there before moving on. The smile was a more subdued version of the one she'd seen in the store, more familial and less...whatever it was brewing between them. The beginnings of this hare-brained idea of a fling? Larissa wasn't certain.

But from the brief seconds it took for them to cross the pub and find a small booth at the far end, she could tell that Erik was a pillar in his community. Everyone greeted him with a spark of kindness in their eyes, enough to send a pang of longing through her. She and Ally had joked that they couldn't go for a coffee or a night out in town without bumping into a patient. But she realised that she actually enjoyed those interactions, as brief as they were. Somehow, seeing that she was making a difference in people's lives—enough that they would recognise her outside the clinic—was gratifying in a way few things in her life were.

They stopped at the bar, ordering their drinks, and Larissa listened to the slew of Norwegian the person standing next to Erik directed at him when he recognised him. Erik kept on nodding, glancing her way now and then with an apologetic tilt of his head that she would have to let him know was completely unnecessary. Larissa could do with a break from these intense blue eyes trying to capture her soul. That was not on the table with them. Not that anything else *was* on the table. Not yet. Though she hoped this invitation was going the way she hoped it was...

Grabbing their drinks, Erik walked to a free booth, setting both glasses down as they slid in on opposite ends.

'Wow, you weren't kidding when you said you know everyone,' she said.

He huffed out a laugh, his voice vibrating through the space between them in a gentle hum. 'When the town you live in doesn't have more than three thousand inhabitants, you tend to get to know the people. Especially if you are the only doctor most of the time.'

Larissa nodded. 'Frome is much larger than Longyearbyen, but our clinic was in a smaller neighbourhood with a similar vibe to here.'

Erik took a drink from his beer. Larissa watched as the condensation from the glass clung to his fingers, slipping down in a random path across the grooves of his skin. '"Our clinic" being yours and Ally's?'

Larissa blinked at the question, not expecting it. 'Yeah...did I say "our"? That almost makes us sound like a couple.'

He shrugged as he looked at her over the rim of his glass. 'It's nice to have someone on your side, especially when you're running a medical service for a small community. That way you can observe trends and sometimes even forecast a particular illness going through the town.'

'The people here have been very welcoming to me, especially during the communal dinners at the hotel,' she said.

'It helps the long-term residents of the hotel to make some friends. Though those are rare. Anna hasn't mentioned anyone else staying there for longer.' Larissa had seen him interact with his sister each morning when they left. Just from their back-and-forth, it seemed she was teasing him about something, but Larissa hadn't had the courage to bring it up. His parents had acted similarly on the first night here, so there was *some* joke going on.

'Did you used to work at the hotel with the rest of your family?' she asked, hoping the question sounded innocent enough. She didn't want to run head first into a hornets' nest if there might be tension. That was more Ally's style of getting to know someone, or at least it was, before her boyfriend's death took that away from her. After that, she'd become more withdrawn and cautious about making new connections to the point where Larissa had seriously considered staging an intervention.

But even though she had spent two weeks with this man now and seriously considered giving in to the building attraction by just straight-up hitting on him, she knew little about him. Which should have been good, because knowing things about a partner was for people who wanted more than just sex.

There was the tiniest change to his expression, one she would have missed if she hadn't already been absolutely enthralled by his face. Just imagining tracing the lines of his jaw with her fingers—or lips—sent sparks flying through her.

'When I was younger, I used to help, yes. The Fjell family has looked after the Aurora for many generations. But after spending a summer volunteering at the hospital, I realised I wanted to do something else with my life. Serve my community,' he said, his voice dipping low enough for Larissa to feel it on her skin.

'And your parents didn't want that?' she asked.

'"Didn't want" is a strong way of putting it. They had expected something different from me, but they understood my passion. But now they are quite belligerent about my personal life since I "left the fold". Comments about how I don't visit enough or why I'm living by myself in the wilderness.' He paused, taking a drink from his bottle. 'They mean well, but I choose to live the way I do for a reason. It gets exhausting to keep on defending my choices. So I just stopped going by the hotel as much.'

Erik chuckled, his eye leaving the bottle and narrowing on her. 'You kind of forced my hand by moving in there.'

Heat flared in her cheeks, and Larissa swallowed the lump appearing in her throat. He chose isolation just like she had after Rachel. That hadn't been what she'd come to find out about Erik. No, her intention had been to continue the conversation they'd started at the grocery store, keeping things on the hot side of sexy. Somehow, they had landed in the warm region of closeness, sharing things about themselves—just like they had when they'd walked Martin's dog.

She shouldn't dig into this anymore. Knowing things about Erik was unnecessary for the deal she'd made— wasn't necessary to satisfy the pinch travelling from behind her belly-button further down her body whenever she saw him.

Yet she opened her mouth anyway, giving back a piece of herself after he had given one to her. It was only fair, wasn't it?

'My parents messed me up pretty bad. Since I remember, they've struggled with their marriage and relied on me to look after myself.'

The cold of the glass bit against Erik's palm, and he released his grip on it, forcing himself to relax. Easier said than done. He hadn't been more on edge since the moment Larissa Costa had walked into his life—had it really only been two weeks? Though they mainly worked on opposite sides of the building, they'd spent some time together early in the mornings as they walked Storm and

Midnight. After their first morning, all of their conversation had remained superficial. She hadn't granted him another glance beneath the surface, and neither had he. Had thought that maybe this was for the best. The last thing Erik needed in his life was an entanglement with the potential to get messy. He'd been there, done that, got the heartbreak that came free with it.

His life wasn't about that anymore.

But now she sat here, letting him peel off a layer and look at her with a fragile vulnerability that stole the breath from his lungs. A direct result of him oversharing just a few moments earlier. Was that what his words had signalled to her? That they had something inside themselves that made them the same outside of medicine? Erik hadn't even intended to share anything, but something in her eyes compelled him to seek closeness with her, even if he could only achieve it by being more personal.

'So, my parents are too involved in shaping my life, and yours were hardly there?' he asked.

Larissa's eyes drifted away from him—something he noticed with a pang in his chest—and scanned the gathered crowd in the pub. He didn't come out often, preferred to spend his time in the clinic in case someone needed him, but he'd lie if he said he didn't enjoy seeing everyone. It was the faces of these people that reminded him how crucial his role in Longyearbyen was. How he was unique in the way he could give back to all the people who had raised him alongside his parents. Give back to Martin, who had taught him how to handle a rifle. To Ingrid, who brought food to the cottage whenever he was sick and his parents couldn't look after him because of their guests. Or all the others who had so uniquely touched his life, tying him to this place on a molecular level.

'Maybe if they had met during our early years, they could have balanced each other out,' Larissa said, and her gaze darting back to him sent a thrill through his body. His fingers tightened around the glass again as he sought the cooling effect against the heat rising in him.

This conversation wasn't anything that should have him even near the state he was in. Her presence alone was enough to turn his head around, and Erik wasn't even sure where any of this was coming from. After the relationship with Astrid had collapsed in the fashion it had, Erik hadn't let himself think about any female attention, no matter how hard his parents tried to convince him. There wasn't much to begin with in Longyearbyen anyway, but he also couldn't afford the distraction. Didn't want to invite someone into his community—into his heart—only to learn that it would never be enough. Focusing on the people who needed him—the people of Svalbard—was easier than facing rejection again for something that was so intrinsic to his spirit, he didn't know if he could ever stop. Didn't want to think about it because he would not stop.

'So you learned how to look after yourself? Is that why you need to gather evidence before you can give your friend proper advice on her love life?' He purposefully brought the conversation back to what had got them talking to each other at the grocery store. The phone call he'd overheard had sent a buzz of electricity coursing through his veins, hoping that the guy mentioned was him despite Larissa's insistence that it was about her friend. He shouldn't want her attention in such a way. But the longer he spent time with her, the louder the voice got in his head, whispering one thing over and over again.

What's the harm?

Larissa was leaving by the end of February, and his life would go on as if she had never been there—except he might have found some closeness with someone who wasn't looking for more, either.

His words had the desired effect on Larissa. Her eyes flared wide, her hand around her glass slackening. Her cheeks flushed, the rich, dark colour deepening until it glowed from within. When her tongue darted out from between her lips to lick her lower lip, Erik swallowed the groan building in his throat. 'I'm not looking for anything serious. I tried that once. It didn't work,' she said when she found her words again.

'What a strange coincidence, because neither am I,' he said, fighting off the smirk tugging at his lips. Though he wanted to know more about her, wanted to dive deeper into who Larissa was behind the quick wit and stunning exterior, this was the type of conversation he felt more at ease in. These were the grounds on which he wanted to explore the attraction linking them—not the overly personal basis they were heading toward.

To his surprise, Larissa chuckled, head drooping down as she inspected the contents of her glass. 'What I'm trying to say is that I'm out of practice. After the breakup, I haven't really put myself out there. Not even in a casual way,' she said, her eyes only briefly darting up to him before she lowered them again.

That piece of information had him raising his eyebrow. 'Is that the ex you mentioned earlier in the week?' He could still remember her words, the rawness when she'd asked about his broken heart. They had found common ground in a place he hadn't meant to share—even though he'd been the one to ask that question.

For him, Larissa was somehow both push and pull, bringing him into her orbit no matter how ill-advised he knew it would be.

She nodded, something delicate in her eyes shuttering. Whatever had happened between them, she had no intention of speaking about it. What brief glimpse she had offered him was all there would be. Fair enough. Erik didn't plan on retreading old ground with her, either. It wasn't necessary for the thing he sensed swirling between them.

'You know so much about my heartbreak, and I haven't asked you anything about yours,' she said, taking the last sip of her beer before setting the glass down with a thunk.

Erik gave her a one-sided shrug. 'I don't think either of us is all that interested in knowing the other person's deepest wounds,' he replied, going out on a limb with that. A quiet part of him actually was interested, but he needed to convince himself that he wasn't interested in Larissa beyond anything physical.

She laughed again, shaking her head. 'I didn't flee here to confront my very complicated feelings. That sounds far too sane and stable for my taste.'

'So you're telling me you are neither sane nor stable?' Erik leaned forward, bracing his arms on the table between them. He noticed with a considerable amount of satisfaction that her eyes darted down briefly, taking in his forearms before her gaze came back up—and her throat worked in a swallow that sent a zap of electricity down his spine.

'Do you think sane and stable people come to Svalbard for a two-month placement in the middle of polar night?' she asked, and drew a chuckle from his lips.

'That was actually something Ingrid was concerned about when we spoke to New Health Frontiers. That there wouldn't be many people willing to spend two months of their lives in complete darkness.' Though the concept was easy to grasp in theory, it was a completely different thing to actually live through it.

'Well, there you go. I was basically your target demographic for this job posting.' A grin spread over her face, as if she was particularly pleased with having wrestled this concession from him.

'I'm glad it was you who took it.' He said the words without putting any thought into it and held his breath when a strange quiet spread between them. Ugh, that was the wrong thing to say to someone he wanted to be casual about. 'What I mean to say is—' he began to explain when a shout interrupted him.

Erik's name tore through the air with a sense of urgency that had Larissa on high alert. She joined him when he jumped to his feet and pushed his way through the crowd. Behind the bar, a middle-aged woman wearing a white chef's uniform waved her hand, pointing at something Larissa couldn't see on the floor.

The jovial chatter around them died when Erik knelt down behind the bar. Larissa rounded it a moment later, seeing the bartender on the floor clutching her hand to her chest. Blood already soaked her apron, staining the light grey fabric dark.

Her eyes darted around, taking in the details behind the counter. Shards of glittering glass covered the floor, with two large pieces standing out. One had bright red blood covering it while the other lay scattered in the doorway to the kitchen—where the chef hovered, worry lining her face.

Erik said something in Norwegian and then shushed the woman in a soothing tone as he peeled the hand away from her chest. The hint of an expression fluttered over his face before a calmness descended on him—one she was all too familiar with. It was the physician mask people in her care received. If patients got even a hint of what they were thinking as doctors, it would lead to panic that quickly spread all around them. They couldn't afford any of that, no matter how bad the injury might be.

'Can we stitch it up here?' Larissa asked, crouching down next to Erik. Now she could see the blood still seeping out of the wound, soaking the towel he pressed against her hand.

'The cut is deep. It would be better to move her to the hospital. I can't apply a lot of pressure to the wound without something to numb the pain,' he said to her. His eyes met hers for a few seconds. Then he looked over at a patron standing at the bar. 'Lars, call the ambulance to pick us up. We can give her a local anaesthetic and some pain relief while we head to the hospital.'

Larissa couldn't help her grateful smile as he kept all the conversation in English, with the villagers around them not seeming to mind. While Lars got on the phone, someone else began ushering the throng of people away from the door, so they had a clear path to transport the patient once the ambulance arrived.

Which, to Larissa's surprise, was in less than three minutes. Even in a small town like Frome, the system could get overloaded quickly, with the ambulance services needing to triage patients and send help where it was most pressingly needed. That was the upside of working in a small village where everyone knew each other's name. The medical emergencies were infrequent, and the system balanced itself well enough.

A nurse Larissa had seen at the hospital, Melanie, jogged into the pub while pushing a stretcher in front of her, and she went down on her knees next to the bartender. She said something to Erik, who nodded and then looked at Larissa. 'Mel and I will move her onto the stretcher. Can you keep pressure on Daniela's hand while we move her? Make sure you don't grab too tight,' he said, and Larissa nodded.

Grabbing disposable latex gloves from the first aid kit already opened and spread out on the floor, she unwrapped the gauze from its packaging and nodded at Erik when she was ready. Just as Larissa pressed the gauze to the wound, he pulled the towel away so she was now applying pressure to the wound. When she had wrapped the gauze around the hand a few times, she signalled for them to lift Daniela onto the stretcher. They then packed her into the ambulance and headed towards the hospital.

CHAPTER SIX

IN THE END, Daniela needed quite a few stitches to close the wound on her hand. Erik had ordered her to sleep off all the meds they had given her before he'd let her out of the hospital, and even though he'd told Larissa that he had a grip on things if she wanted to leave, something inside her had compelled her to stay.

She didn't want to contemplate any further that this *something* had the shape of an almost two-metre–tall Nordic god, but no matter how hard she tried, Erik kept popping back into her thoughts. Their conversation at the pub had veered into territory Larissa hadn't realised she could even talk about. Not just about Rachel and that she had existed, but also her parents. How she had grown up learning to be self-sufficient because they were too wrapped up in their own drama to look after their child. She'd told him how that behaviour had shaped her and had influenced her relationship. Had led to heartbreak…

The most surprising thing Larissa had learned was that he, too, seemed to be running away. He was also hiding something of himself with thick walls that warned everyone not to come near him. She'd seen them after their first morning out with the dogs. He'd let her glimpse something on that first day, but all the subsequent days, that glimmer of what lay beyond the wall had disappeared, the barrier reinforced.

Which was fine. Totally fine. Larissa didn't *want* to know him like that. Sure, there was something unbelievably intriguing about him. She couldn't stop herself from picking away at the loose stones she encountered every so often—hoping there would be another gap for her to peer through.

Like when she'd seen him smile at everyone in the pub, so at ease with who he was around his community. Larissa had lost that feeling when they had closed the clinic down, with nothing but Ally left to tether her to Frome, to her life there. She'd felt comfortable enough to contemplate roots, to let Rachel in and see if they could somehow figure things out.

What a waste of time that had been. Rachel had wanted a completely different person from what Larissa could ever be, and it hadn't mattered how hard she'd tried, how much she had explained what *she* needed. It had never been enough.

It was easier not to try. Like right now, as she vowed not to get to know Erik better. She didn't need to know anything for their fling to become a reality.

Yet there was still this need bubbling right underneath her skin, demanding she peel away at him.

'You're still here?' As if her thoughts had summoned him, Erik appeared through the door of the office.

Her eyes glided over his body as he took off the lab coat, tossing it in a bin in the office's corner before turning back to look at her. A low thrum of energy went through her as the ice-blue gaze snagged on hers. There was some wariness in his eyes, maybe a result of the emergency that had cut short their...whatever that had been at the pub. Date? Meeting between colleagues? Those didn't sound right. Not when she thought about how close he'd been to her in the grocery store. How his breath had brushed over her flushed cheeks when he'd leaned in to invite her. The subtext of that interaction was more than clear—he was interested in something physical.

Larissa gave a casual shrug—or at least she hoped it looked casual—and said, 'It's not like I have anywhere else to be. My room is not that exciting, and I already binge-watched my entire Netflix list. It took me years to put show after show on there, and they all vanished in a week.'

Even through her nervous rambling, Erik seemed to pick up on what she was *really* trying to tell him. He crossed his arms in front of his chest, giving her an enticing view as they strained against the fabric of his shirt. The urge to trace the grooves of his muscles bubbled up in her, and Larissa swallowed hard.

His eyes flickered down to her throat, and that was enough to send a burst of liquid fire through her veins. When his gaze came back up to her, the blue of his eyes was darker. More intense. Daring her to get close enough to touch him.

'Let me show you something,' he said, his voice low enough that it vibrated over her skin, pushing the fire in her veins all the way to her core.

He stretched a hand out towards her, his fingers slightly curled in invitation. Larissa didn't have a choice but to slide her palm over his and let out a shaky breath when his hand closed around hers, tugging her to her feet and to a door at the other side of the office.

The door led to a small glass annex of the hospital.

Larissa blinked when he flicked the lights on, her eyes adjusting to the sudden brightness. A worn-out couch and a few equally aged armchairs stood strewn around in no particular pattern, along with a bookshelf against the only non-glass wall of the building.

'This looks comfy,' she said, and Erik shrugged.

'It was designed as a greenhouse, but the light needed to run it during polar night was deemed too expensive. So now it's a little extra room that doesn't really get used outside of the long-term staff,' he replied.

'You wanted to show me another staff room?'

He shook his head, his eyes glancing at his wrist-watch before coming back up to her. There was a spark of amusement in his gaze that sent a spray of warmth trickling down her spine. How on earth could he do that with just a glance?

'We haven't been at the hospital this late, and I just remembered that now is the perfect time to show you something. You probably already caught some glimpses of it, but this is quite the nice spot.' He still stood by the door, hand resting on the light switch. 'Are you ready?'

Larissa blinked. 'Ready for what?'

'I'll take that as a yes.' He grinned, then flipped the light switch, plunging them into darkness.

Except it wasn't dark. She could still make out Erik's shape, his pale skin glowing blue in the light of... the moon?

Larissa looked up and then gasped, her eyes going wide. Streaks of light green and blue interrupted the night sky, drowning out the moon and the stars with their own vibrant light. They pulsed in a steady wave, moving along the horizon as if they were sentient beings on a journey across the sky.

Larissa had seen glimpses of them, had even wondered if that was what she was really seeing. The northern lights.

They were even more breathtaking than any of the Instagram pictures she'd seen. Something about the vibrancy and the movement of the light just couldn't be captured by a camera.

Her eyes grew wider the longer she stared at the swirling ribbons of light, completely enthralled by beauty such as she'd never seen. 'Wow, this is...' Her voice trailed off as her words failed her. She'd seen glimpses of the northern lights on her way to the hotel, but they'd only ever been small fragments, disjointed. Not like this, where they unfurled across the sky in a celebration of colour and form.

'You get the best view of the lights after ten at night,' Erik said behind her, his voice right next to her ear.

She whirled around and there he was, standing right behind her, his face illuminated by the light of the aurora borealis. He'd stepped closer to her, only a hand span separating them, and Larissa tipped her head back to look him in the eyes. The sense of sudden proximity thundered through her, reminding her of what it had felt like when his fingers had wrapped around hers. Her touch-starved brain had extrapolated far too many scenarios from this small touch, all of them ending with their clothes on the floor of her room—or his house.

'I don't know what to say,' she breathed out, meaning both the lights and the intention she saw written in his gaze. Intention that rang through her like the chime of a bell, its vibrations winding her centre into a tight coil, ready to rupture. She swallowed the dryness in her mouth and almost whimpered when his eyes darted down to her throat again like a wild cat assessing its next move.

'We probably said enough,' he told her. Larissa didn't understand how his words were even remotely suggestive. On the surface they weren't, yet her knees shook. She nodded, not agreeing to what he had said, but to the gentle touch of his fingers as they skated up her arms until his fingertips rested on her neck.

Her heart leapt into her throat when Erik stepped forward. She was sure if she opened her mouth, her heart would leave her body entirely. His scent enveloped her, notes of pine and fresh fallen snow—a scent Larissa had only learned to really appreciate since coming here. It surrounded her whenever she stepped outside the hotel to get to work and reminded her so much of Erik that she wasn't sure she could ever think of anything else. Any*one* else.

A bolt of electricity went through her when the tip of his nose brushed against her, his face so near she could feel each breath skittering across her heated cheeks. Her eyes wanted to flutter closed so she could lose herself in this moment about to happen, but she didn't want to miss a single one of his movements, either.

'I don't know if this is a good idea,' he whispered, his mouth now so close to hers that the phantom of a kiss brushed over her lips. The fire inside her twisted at that, burning even higher. The need overrode any rational thought, any concerns about what-ifs melting away from just standing so close to Erik.

Instead of saying anything, Larissa slipped her hands up his back, pushing him even closer and sliding her mouth over his.

* * *

This kiss was a terrible idea. It was also the best idea Erik had ever had. The web of nerves winding through his body caught fire when Larissa's soft lips brushed over his. The singeing heat rendered him immobile for a heartbeat, unable to decide what his next move should be.

Then his body moved on its own, sliding his hands over her body and pressing her closer to him until their fronts were flush against each other. A shaky moan escaped her lips when his hand tangled into her hair, pulling back her head to deepen the kiss.

Her taste flooded his mouth, and it was exquisite. Exactly how he imagined she'd taste—and dear God, had he spent a lot of time daydreaming about this specific taste. About her and having her underneath him as she came undone.

The attraction clicking into place between them had been shocking from the first day. After everything had fallen apart around him and Astrid, he hadn't even contemplated anyone romantically. It just didn't work. Not when he'd dedicated his entire life to Svalbard and its community. Not when he had to be available 24/7 for any emergency pages or requests for medical attention. There were few such late-night requests, but they existed, and they were his responsibility. They would *always* come first, no matter the circumstances.

Only this wasn't romantic. They flirted and teased each other, but the conversation Larissa had with her friend said nothing about how to tell a guy about your feelings. She chose her words to fit her purpose, and that was physical. Larissa hadn't come here to start up a relationship with him when she would just end up leaving in a few weeks. No, she wanted something quick.

And all Erik wanted was her. Larissa.

He must have moaned her name, for she pulled her head back, looking at him with wide eyes. Her throat worked as she blinked. 'This is—' she began, and Erik cut her off by brushing another, softer kiss onto her lips.

'I think that's how you let a guy know,' he said when he drew back, earning himself another confused blink.

'What?'

'The answer to your friend's question. How you let a guy know you want to bang him. Pretty sure this is how you do it.'

Larissa's eyes went even wider, and the colour on her cheeks deepened enough that he could see it even under the blue light of the aurora borealis.

'And this is how you know he's interested, too,' he added as he slipped his hands into her hair and pulled her into another kiss. His tongue swept over her lips, and an involuntary groan left his throat when her taste clung to him again.

They were okay with just being in this moment, right? Should they talk about this? The last thing on Erik's mind was talking. Talking was for people who had things to figure out. They had nothing to figure out. No, this might actually be the most straightforward relationship in Erik's life.

The thoughts threatening to surface in his mind drained out of him when Larissa dragged her hand across his abdomen until she reached his waistband. There she hovered, her fingers dancing over the material and grazing his flesh every now and then. A small touch, barely anything in the grand scheme of things, but it lit him on fire from the inside out.

A growl he had never heard from himself escaped his throat, and he hauled her closer to him, their breaths mingling as he deepened the kiss. He took several steps backward while keeping Larissa close to him until the backs of his knees collided with the couch behind him. Larissa yelped as she tumbled on top of him, and Erik grabbed her by the hips until she settled in his lap—straddling him.

Her heat pressed against his rising length, pushing against him and creating an ache that drove him out of his mind. If he'd had any reservations going into this, they were now all gone. He could focus on nothing but where her body connected with his and how he needed more.

Though apparently he was alone with this thought. For Larissa tore herself from his mouth, lips puffy from making out. 'This is not where I saw the evening going,' she huffed out, her eyes heavy-lidded as she looked down at him.

'Really? You were talking to your friend hoping it *wouldn't* end up like this?' he said just as breathlessly.

Larissa bent down with a chuckle, putting her forehead against his while wrapping both hands around his face. He marvelled at her lashes when her eyes fluttered shut. 'No, this is definitely where I *wanted* to end up. I just didn't realise that feelings were this mutual,' she said, eyes still closed.

Erik tightened his grip around her hips and moved against her, drawing out a deep moan from her. 'This is how mutual things are,' he growled, and he tilted his chin so he could capture her mouth again.

'And when I say feelings, I of course mean pants feelings,' she said as she untangled her mouth from his again. 'Like… horny feelings.'

Erik let out a dark chuckle and slipped his hand underneath the hem of her sweater, exposing her bare back to his touch. The feel of her smooth skin against his rough palm was pure ecstasy. He didn't mean to, but his hips bucked into her with the need for release already gathering at the base of his spine.

'We will keep it strictly to pants feelings.' He whispered the words against her skin as he nuzzled her neck, his other hand joining the one already exploring her back. His fingers slid higher and higher until they found the clasp of her bra. A shaky breath left her mouth when he stopped there, and he sought out her eyes with his.

'This okay?' Erik's rough and low voice thundered through her like a lightning strike. Everything inside her buzzed, little fires erupting all over her body wherever she touched Erik. Her senses could make out nothing but him, where he touched her, how he smelled, how hard his body pressed against her—against the ache she needed him to satisfy.

Not in a million years would she have guessed that an inappropriate conversation with her best friend would lead her exactly to the position she wanted to be in. Erik was precisely the kind of distraction that she needed to make time in Svalbard go by faster. Especially since they both agreed on what this was supposed to be.

So she nodded, and a shiver crawled down her spine when the tension of her bra loosened around her chest. Erik pushed up the sweater, exposing her flesh to the chilly air as he pulled both items of clothing away from her. Her breath came out in a stutter when he leaned back, sinking further into the couch. His eyes roamed over her, drinking her in, and the rise and fall of his chest increased.

They were still, each one staring at the other. Then, ever so slowly, Erik traced his hand from her back over her ribs to her front, fingertips brushing against the underside of her breast. Her shaky breath turned into a gasp when he palmed her, squeezing softly. A word she couldn't understand slipped from him as he brushed his thumb over her taut nipple. Her back arched, pushing further into his touch, and the low groan filling the space between them set every nerve in her body on fire.

'What?' she asked, her words no more than a whisper.

Erik's gaze snapped up to her, the passion glazing his eyes drawing out a whimper of need. He blinked twice, as if he needed time to parse her question. 'What do you mean?'

'You said…' He didn't give her enough time to verbalise her thoughts. Larissa shuddered, breaking out in full-body goose flesh when his lips connected with the skin between her breasts. His tongue darted out, caressing her and creating a stark contrast between his warmth and the chill of the night air.

This was really happening. Her plan had been to treat herself to overly expensive strawberries and shut herself in her room for the entire weekend. Because the heat between them had already been climbing with each encounter, and what she had thought she desperately needed was a few days away from him so she could reset.

But there was no resetting this. Not as Erik closed his lips around her nipple, drawing it into his mouth and circling her tip with his tongue until her vision blurred.

She let out a pant, one that she knew would normally

embarrass her. Who panted like that on a featherlight touch? It wasn't like this was the first time anyone touched her like that. Except somehow it was. Something about the tenderness, the feverish glaze of his eyes as he looked up at her, threatened to undo Larissa before they had even shed all of their clothes.

Erik nuzzled the skin between her breasts again, his breath hot on her as he traced his lips down her stomach. Each lick of his tongue sent sparks flying from wherever he was touching her straight to her core—right where she ached for his touch.

Larissa clawed at his shirt, dragging the fabric up his back until her fingertips brushed over his skin, relishing the smooth warmth that met her there. Lean muscles worked under her fingers as he drew the shirt over his head. Larissa leaned back, drinking all of him in.

The blue-green light filtering through the glass roof bathed them, illuminating his skin in a similar glow to that surrounding them—as if someone had crafted him out of the northern lights. His broad chest moved up and down at a fast pace and increased when Larissa reached her hand out, tracing the hard lines of each pec. She shivered when she ran her fingers through his chest hair, following the trail down—all the way to his trousers. Larissa paused there, raising her gaze to his. Then she slipped two fingers underneath his waistband, brushing over the top of his straining manhood.

Another Norwegian word left his lips through tightly shut teeth, the hiss that followed one of pure arousal. She didn't need to understand the language to know what was happening—what the tiny words meant that he couldn't help but utter in his native tongue.

'Your trousers seem a bit tight,' she said, hardly rec-

ognising her own voice. It was so low, filled with a longing that she hadn't known she possessed within her. It
wasn't like she hadn't enjoyed sex or intimacy outside
of her one serious relationship. She had. Enough times
that she knew what she liked and what she didn't like to
get a quick release.

This should also be just a quick release and nothing
more. A fling between two colleagues who, at the end of
her contract, would become strangers again. Except they
hadn't done more than kiss—*for the first time today*—
and Larissa was already burning for more.

Erik huffed a laugh, his big hands coming to rest on
each side of her hips, his gaze heavy-lidded. 'This wasn't
how I saw this evening going,' he said, each word accompanied by a deep breath.

'You eavesdropped on my conversation, invited me
to drinks with you and didn't think that it would end in
sex?' He didn't need to know that she hadn't believed
that, either. Had thought she was making up this attraction zipping between them. She was so rusty in the seduction game that she had to ask Ally how to let him know
what she wanted. Never mind that she had ended up not
needing any help, after all.

'Well, I…' The last word morphed into a choked sound
when Larissa undid the button of his trousers with one
flick of her finger, the back of her hand pressing against
his length. 'The hook up culture isn't exactly thriving
here.'

Larissa pulled down his trousers' zipper, folding the
fabric to the side. His erection strained against his underwear, and her thighs clenched at the sight. Dear God,
it had been far too long since she'd actually had a good
orgasm that hadn't been her own handiwork.

'I can imagine it's far too easy to fall into a relationship dynamic if you have the choice out of three people,' she replied, her eyes fixed on him. His right hand still clung to her hip while his left one wandered to her front, drawing tiny circles on her skin as he went all the way to her waistband—repeating what she had done to him until his hand had access to where she wanted him to be. His fingers brushed over the apex of her thighs, sending a renewed shower of pure fire through her, making her jerk forward. She slid back on his thighs and braced her hands on his knees to bare herself more—give him access to what they both wanted.

The sound leaving Erik's throat could only be described as a growl. It skittered across her skin, igniting her from the inside out, just as his fingers swept over the elastic band of her underwear. He played with it for a few seconds, each touch slow and torturous as it ratcheted up the arousal within her. Then his fingers slipped over the fabric of her underwear and pushed down where the ache was the greatest.

Her fingers clenched around his knees. Her hips jerked, leaning into his touch as if his fingers were the only ones who could satisfy her. As if it was Erik—and not sex in general—that brought her this pleasure.

'*Faen*, Larissa…you are already soaked for me,' he whispered, his breath shaky as he exhaled. Larissa's inner walls clenched at the words, at the *need* for him to finally touch her.

Her breaths came in rapid bursts as his fingers kept working her through the fabric, teasing her with a phantom of what his touch could be like without any barrier between them—and keeping her release just outside of her grasp.

Gathering some hard-fought breath into her lungs, she bit out, 'Are we going to do this or what?'

They were fighting words, meant to challenge him as well as make it absolutely clear what she wanted—some low-stakes sex between two consenting adults.

Erik clicked his tongue, his thumb still brushing over her. 'I've been looking forward to this since the day you arrived,' he said, and leaned forward to brush his tongue against her nipple. 'I'm going to enjoy you.'

His voice was deep and filled with a promise of release that had her straining against his hand between her thighs. Had anyone ever said something this *hot* to her? If they had, Larissa had no recollection of it. She was at the point where she was certain no one had even touched her properly, because she would remember such an intense burn in her core. Would have sought it out if she'd known just how good it could be.

'I'm still around for six more weeks,' she huffed out. 'Plenty of time to enjoy me.'

His hand stilled. Had he thought of this as a one-time thing? Granted, they hadn't spoken about *any* of this at all, so Larissa had just blurted out what she wanted— a fling for the duration of her stay. She pushed off his knees, wanting to slide closer and look at him when his grip around her hip tightened.

'Then I guess I can take my time to learn what drives you wild,' he said. His fingers slipped beneath the waistband of her underwear.

Her mind emptied of any thoughts. Pure pleasure lanced through her, her body responding to the featherlight touch. Apparently, he didn't need to learn what drove her wild, because this was it.

'Right there,' she breathed out to underline the thoughts in her head.

Erik obliged, running his finger up and down her centre. Release gathered around her like an iridescent veil—ready to shatter. Her back bowed into his touch, and she completely shattered when his hot breath skated over her skin and his mouth closed around her nipple again. He didn't stop, kept drawing longer and lazier circles as the tension flowed out of her body. When she slumped forward, he wrapped his arms around her, holding her close. Her chest heaved big breaths as Larissa gathered herself from the edges of space where Erik's touch had put her. After she finally reached her own body again, a fresh wave of arousal crashed through her when his erection pressed against her.

A smile spread over her lips as she ground against him, and Erik let out a loud hiss, his head falling back against the couch. 'Sounds like we are both easy to figure out,' Larissa whispered against his ear as she flexed her hips again. Her mouth pressed against his and swallowed Erik's second groan.

Then she slipped off his lap, kneeling down in front of him—between his legs. She reached up to pull his trousers down when his hand wrapped around her wrist.

'I wouldn't offer if I didn't...' she began, but her voice trailed off when Erik's head tilted sideways, his eyes on the door.

Larissa flinched when he jumped to his feet, pulling his trousers back up as he did. 'Someone is coming,' he said, grabbing the pile of clothes on the floor and throwing her sweater—sans bra—at her. Then he pulled his own shirt over his head, and Larissa buttoned her trousers.

The second she patted down the hem of her sweater,

the door swung open with a tentative 'Erik?' from a fe-male voice. The lights flickered above them before turn-ing on, and Larissa winced at the sudden brightness, closing her eyes.

'I came to check on Daniela, and she told me—Why are you sitting in the dark?' Ingrid's voice filled the room.

Larissa didn't know what to say, hadn't even realised how easily accessible this part of the hospital was to any-one else. To think she had been about to...

'I was showing Larissa the aurora borealis,' Erik said, his words clipped. Apparently he wasn't happy about the interruption, either. 'Do you need me for something?'

'Yes, her mother asked me to bring over some of her things, and she's complaining about pain,' Ingrid said. Larissa had to blink a few more times before her eyes adjusted to the sudden brightness. When they did, she looked at the receptionist and gave her a tentative smile. The old woman didn't return it. Instead, her sharp gaze flicked between her and Erik, the line between her brows growing deeper.

Erik seemed to notice her inquisitive stare too, for he stepped towards Ingrid, grabbing her attention and ush-ering her out of the room. Larissa caught a few snippets of their hushed discussion in Norwegian before the door closed, leaving her alone in the annex.

CHAPTER SEVEN

'SO, HE FINGERED YOU, and then he just hasn't said anything ever since?' Ally asked in her ear, and even though Larissa was well used to her best friend's preferred language, she still cringed. Something about reducing what happened between her and Erik to *fingering* just felt wrong. Even though it really was what had happened.

Larissa had got home from another day of work half an hour ago to call Ally. Larissa had opened up about that night under the northern lights.

'Oh my God, can I see it?' Those had been the first words about all of this from Ally. Because Larissa couldn't deny her anything, she'd got dressed while they spoke and was now close to the otherwise dark hospital. She didn't see any of the lights, but it was still early. She'd hang out on that cursed couch, wondering where she went wrong that everything between her and Erik had run so off the rails, while Ally assured her it had nothing to do with her. That seemed like an evening spent well.

'Can we go back to talking about your close encounter in a dank cave? That seems more urgent,' Larissa said, suddenly unsure if she wanted to speak about Erik.

'Um, no. I was still clothed for that, so by hierarchy of nudeness, your topic is more pressing.' She said it as if the hierarchy of nudeness was a real concept.

Ugh, fine. She might as well get it over with. 'We haven't really spoken ever since this thing a week ago—which is weird. Even if we didn't work together, we kind of just…hung out?' Larissa said, burying her face in her scarf to ward off the chilly wind blowing across her. 'He probably regrets getting so close after I told him he would have weeks to enjoy me.' That memory summoned another cringe. Why was it that whenever she thought she was being some sort of sexy siren, she actually felt more like a hag who had never in her life learned how to flirt? Or was her total inexperience in casual flings showing? Until Rachel, she'd never seen anyone beyond one night.

She pushed thoughts of Rachel away the second they popped up, not letting them take root in her head. Nothing good could come of thinking about her.

'Maybe he's busy. Did you guys text much before all of this?' Ally asked, her voice a low hush. Probably to avoid waking anyone up. It was well past the evening hours for her.

'Not really? We hung out in the hospital, kind of just doing our own thing but…together? We had some morning walks where we would talk, but with Martin back on his feet, I'm no longer needed for dog walking duties.' It was strange—and concerning—how much she missed those morning walks. Larissa had thought she would be glad to sleep in a few more hours before her shift at the hospital, but as if to remind her something was missing, her body woke her up every morning to get ready. Now she spent her morning sitting downstairs, having coffee by the fire and scrolling through her phone until it was time to leave. Sometimes locals joined her for a coffee, knowing the hotel was the earliest place where they could buy it, and asked her about her time in Svalbard.

Those were the mornings Larissa enjoyed the most, filling her with a warm sense of something she couldn't name.

'You should start texting him. Set the precedent so he can follow it,' Ally said, and Larissa knew how desperate she was to talk to Erik, because she was considering her suggestion. Should she just message him? At this point, she was all but convinced that Erik was avoiding her. The only reason she could come up with for that avoidance was how deep the regret of what happened between them sat within him. How he wanted to just forget she'd ever existed. So much that he'd literally started working different hours. Larissa now worked at the same time as one of the more experienced nurses taking appointments that didn't need to be seen by a doctor.

It reminded her so much of how she and Ally had run their clinic that her heart ached inside her chest with longing for a time that was now forever gone.

'Isn't that like super desperate? I'm down for some fun, but I won't chase him if he doesn't want...well, me.' The words didn't feel right on her tongue, though she couldn't pinpoint why. Of course he didn't want *her*. That implied an emotional connection that far exceeded what they had. They were just attracted to each other.

'Mmm, you're right. Damn.' Ally hummed in her ear, and then she went on to present her next idea. Only Larissa didn't hear it. As she approached the front of the hospital, the door swung open, and Erik stepped out with a box under one arm and a duffel bag slung over the other.

She froze in her steps, staring at the man who had been eluding her for the better part of an entire week. The proof that he had indeed begun working late nights for the past week just to avoid her stung a lot more than she was willing to admit.

'Ally, I have to go,' Larissa whispered and heard rustling from the other side of the phone line as her friend sat up.

'What's going on?' she asked, her tone a lot more alert than it had been a few moments ago.

'Erik just walked out of the hospital.'

'Seriously?'

'Yes, seriously. What kind of question is that?' Larissa hissed, staring the figure down. He walked over to a parked car, opening the back and putting the box and duffel inside. He hadn't spotted her yet, but the moment he turned around, he would see her standing there, looking at him like some deranged stalker.

'I'll have to show you the northern lights later,' she said, and held her breath when Erik moved again, turning around to head back into the clinic. He turned fully, his eyes gliding over her, and Larissa thought maybe he hadn't seen her or thought she was just a pedestrian out on a stroll. But then he did a double-take, his head whipping back to her and staring across the distance. His head tipped slightly to the side, scanning her. Then he moved towards her.

'He's coming to talk to me,' she said, unsure why her heart was beating faster. 'Ally, hang up the phone.'

'What? Why do I have to hang up?'

'Because my phone is three layers down. I can't reach it.'

Ally made a whining noise. 'What if I'm really quiet?'

'Ally!'

'Fine, fine. Jeez. I expect an update at the first convenient moment.' The line went quiet as Ally hung up just in time for Erik to reach her.

He stopped a few paces away from her, his head still slightly tilted, as if she was some piece of art he needed to study from different angles to understand it.

'What are you doing here?' he asked, taking another step closer.

Larissa crossed her arms in front of her. 'I work here.'

She could see Erik's brows narrow. She knew that behind the scarf, there was a frown tugging at his lips. If that was how he was going to play it, she was more than happy to comply.

'Not at this hour,' he said, exactly how she'd hoped he would.

'Well, neither do you. Yet here you are with your mystery box and mystery...duffel bag.' She swallowed, unsure if the jab had landed as intended. Her words sounded more petulant than fierce in her ears, but she'd committed to this, so there was no going back.

Across the distance, she heard Erik snort. 'This is my hospital. I have to work whenever there's work. Sometimes that means moving mystery objects around, yes. I'll concede this much.'

Larissa's temper flared at the ease in his tone, the relaxed posture. If she hadn't known better, she could have sworn that he didn't have a single clue they hadn't seen each other in about a week. Was he *that* indifferent about her? He didn't even notice her absence when he was working different shifts? So much that joking around seemed appropriate? Maybe she really had misjudged the friendship they had developed over the early morning dog walks.

The thought stung despite her best attempts to not let it bother her.

Instead, she nodded towards the car. 'I've never seen you drive a car before,' she said, attempting to bring some kind of normalcy between them again. Why had she somehow forgotten how to talk to him? Oh right, because last time they had said anything to each other, he'd told her in how many different ways he would enjoy her for the next few weeks. That had been right before he'd vanished for the better part of a week.

'I have to go vaccinate some new arrivals at a research facility a few hours away.'

That caught Larissa's attention. 'What vaccine do people need when they arrive here?' she asked, her brow furrowed. She hadn't received any special vaccine upon arrival.

She heard Erik chuckle again, and she tried to hang on to her indignation as the sound vibrated through the night air and settled down in her core, warming her from the inside out.

'The yearly flu vaccine.'

Larissa blinked at him. 'The flu vaccine? You have to drive all the way there just to give them a vaccine?'

'Hey now, don't downplay the importance of the flu vaccine. They live in close quarters with each other, heightening the chance that if one person gets it, the others will catch it, too,' he said, and though his words were an admonishment, there was an amused twinkle in his eyes. It was the latter that drove her temper into a hotter territory.

'I know how important the flu vaccine is. You can't even imagine how much time I've spent sending my patients annoying emails and texts about the benefits and why they should come in and get their free jab. But isn't...'

Her voice trailed off as her thoughts stalled and she questioned her own knowledge of the situation.

Erik raised an eyebrow, the corner of his lip twitching. 'Isn't what?'

'Isn't it all ice here? If they don't leave the research centre, how would they even contract anything?' Of course, germs and bacteria could survive the ice in the right circumstances, but it didn't seem as likely.

'Ah, I see. It's mostly a precaution, but some of them come to Longyearbyen and mingle with locals and tourists. I go there every six months to do a physical and deliver any medicine they need and also some other things they asked for.' His eyes darted to the box he'd just put in the car. When she followed his gaze, she could see there were already other boxes in there.

'How far is the research centre?' she asked, as an idea began to gnaw at her.

'It's a three-hour drive, but it will take me most of the night and some of the day to get through everyone's physical. I probably won't be back until later tomorrow.' Erik shrugged, and she wasn't sure why he was telling her this. It wasn't like he had kept her abreast of his schedule this entire week and if he hadn't just presented her with a solid reason he needed to leave, she would have accused him of avoiding her.

He probably *was* avoiding her, anyway. So this was the best opportunity she had to figure out what went wrong between them. With her decision solidifying in her mind, Larissa stepped around Erik and walked over to the passenger door of the car.

Erik was there a heartbeat later, his hand coming down

on the window and holding the door closed. 'What are you doing?'

'I'm coming with you. If it'll take you all night to vaccinate and examine people, then one additional person should cut that in half,' she insisted, determined not to let him brush her off.

'It's not necessary. I can handle it by myself.'

'I know you can. And I'm telling you that you don't have to. I'm here to help. That's literally why I came to Svalbard.'

His eyes narrowed on her, but Larissa didn't back off, her hand still on the door handle. 'What if there's something needed at the hospital that requires a doctor?' he asked.

'It's Saturday tomorrow. There are no scheduled appointments, and Melanie is on call for any walk-ins that can be handled by a nurse. If anything minor comes through the door, Melanie will take care of it, while the major things will be stabilised and pushed to Tromsø. Though I highly doubt that tomorrow is the day when something catastrophic happens.' There hadn't been a single incident where they needed to call the medevac to transport someone to mainland Norway in the three weeks she'd been here. Sometimes she didn't even have an entire day full of people to see and instead passed her time by scrolling through her phone and sending Ally pictures of herself in random places in the hospital with the caption, 'Look at me having all of this adventure we talked about.'

'I...' Erik stalled, clearly looking for another excuse to push her away.

So she went on, 'Listen, I know after what happened the other night, we haven't really seen each other. I think we should…talk about it. I'm not asking for anything else. But we're still colleagues, so I'd rather figure it out before the next month gets super awkward.' She chuckled as she added, 'I can't run away again, even though that's my preferred way, so I guess I have to be mature about it.'

Erik huffed a laugh, clouds of condensation billowing up in the space between them. 'You're right,' he said with a sigh. Even though she had told herself that the outcome of the conversation didn't matter to her, something sharp wedged itself between her ribs at his sigh. In her mind, she had nursed the hope that he might have just been busy and that he hadn't been avoiding her. But the pained concession she'd just wrung from him confirmed he had.

He regretted what happened between them.

'We'll have to work through the night, though. The researchers were kind enough to adjust their schedule so we can keep the time away from the hospital to a minimum,' he said, and released his grip on the door.

He agreed they needed to talk. His tactic of avoiding Larissa had only brought him to the end of the week before she'd caught up with him. Erik really didn't know what he had expected. He'd known eventually everything would catch up to him, and he needed to make a decision. That was the tricky part—the thing that made him avoid her like some conflict-averse child. Because he knew very well what he wanted. That was the problem. He couldn't forget the night he had shown her the northern lights. Every time he closed his eyes, he could see her sitting on his lap, her hips moving against his fingers as he brought her to climax. How easy it had been, how right it had felt. Like he knew this woman inside out and what made her tick. What made her come.

Only that was, of course, nonsense. Erik knew so little about Larissa except the details she'd shared with him on their dog walks and the conversation they'd had in the pub. Though they saw each other at the hospital, their relationship existed mostly in companionable silence.

The tension snapping in place between them was palpable, enveloping everything around them as they sat in the car on their way to the research outpost northwards. They said they would talk, and that was Erik's intention. Only he did not know where to even start. He hadn't made up his own mind. The cautious part within him urged him to forget that one night had ever happened, that they couldn't go there again, no matter how temporary it would be. But then he remembered the feel of her around his fingers, how sweet her mouth tasted on his, and he couldn't give that up just yet.

From the corner of his eye, he saw Larissa's mane of curls bob, as if she was shaking her head. Then her strained laughter filled the air. He glanced at her before turning his head back to the road. 'What?' he asked when she continued to chuckle.

'I don't think we've ever been this tense before.'

Erik shrugged, trying his best to ignore the apparently quite obvious tension in his shoulders as he said, 'I'm not tense.'

'Um, yeah you are. I've known you for close to a month now, and in that time, you have remained unfazed. Up until this moment. Now that I know you better, you can't convince me otherwise.' She crossed her arms in front of her chest, levelling a stare at him. 'What's on your mind?'

Now that I know you better. Those words should have sent alarm bells ringing through him, urging him to pull the emergency brakes. They didn't need to know each other to work together. They didn't even need to know each other to have sex. It was probably better if they didn't. But although he understood all of this, the words still sparked a warmth inside his chest that radiated through his entire body.

He had no idea why he responded. Maybe because she might leave, or maybe because something about showing her another slice of him just felt right. 'It's been a while since I let anyone this close, and I get that what happened between us is just physical, but I guess—I'm comfortable by myself. And to the annoyance of my parents, I don't have the need to find anyone to have in my life permanently. My job is that thing for me. Svalbard holds that place in my heart.'

He paused, sorting through his thoughts to figure out what he wanted to say. Breathing out a sigh, he continued, 'I told you I knew what it was like to have my heart broken. When that happened to me, my parents had got themselves far too involved with my ex. She bridged some of the gap between us by getting involved in the hotel business, and they thought I finally found my missing piece.'

Erik looked straight ahead, watching the snow drift through the air as the tyres disrupted the powdery ice on the ground. 'I don't believe there is a missing piece. What they think is missing is just occupied by something other than romantic love. It's represented in that need inside of me to help my community.' He paused, daring a glance at her to see if she understood what he meant. If she had felt this specific thing inside her, too.

A small smile appeared on her lips, and she nodded. 'A calling. The compulsion to do the work that we do.'

He nodded, surprised that someone finally understood.

That she specifically understood. Erik couldn't point towards the reason why, but having her understanding set his stomach on a freefall.

'Familial obligations are a strange thing to navigate,' Larissa said, her tone wistful, and he turned his head again.

'You had them even though you basically raised yourself?' he asked, remembering the things she'd shared with him—and part of the reason he had let her see as much of him as he had.

'Mmm, I don't know.' She hummed, shifting in her seat again so she faced the window. Her hand came down on the glass, her fingers tracing what he assumed were the flurries of snow outside. Quiet settled in between them, underpinned by the steady rumbling of the car's engine. His eyes flickered to the clock on the dashboard and widened when he saw the time. They had already been driving for two and a half hours. Another half an hour and they would be at their destination.

'My parents only paid me attention when I got to my third year in med school, when things looked more serious. They were never really interested in anything I did if it didn't affect them. So their daughter suddenly being halfway through to becoming a physician suddenly caught their attention,' Larissa said, just as he thought her previous answer was all he would get.

'By that point, I didn't care anymore. Life by myself was just simpler to navigate. I already knew how to ensure I ate, slept and had clean laundry for school. That didn't change when I left my family home behind to go to med school. If I'm being honest, it probably helped me in some aspects. The only thing I'm unsure about is whether an eleven-year-old should need to learn these skills in the first place. But here we are.'

Larissa shared the struggles of her upbringing a lot more freely than he'd expected anyone carrying these things around with them would. Then again, he sensed something beneath all of that—something she kept close to her chest. Something that still hurt, unlike what had happened with her parents. Erik knew that because he was the same. And precisely for that reason, he knew he shouldn't go digging for it. They would be better off in the long run if he let the things inside her be. If he shared nothing from inside himself, either.

'And yet here you are, on the run from a heartbreak someone inflicted on you even though you learned to guard yourself so well.' The words struck him, even though he wasn't the target—even though *he* had said them. They were intended to get through to her, to show her he saw what was happening and that he understood.

Larissa's hand froze on the glass, then dropped slowly as she turned around to look at him. Then her eyes darted to where the vague shape of a building coalesced on the horizon. Wind whipped around them, far stronger than when they'd departed from Longyearbyen, obscuring some of the view ahead of them.

'Guess at least now I know what to avoid. You won't catch me being dumb enough to fall for someone.' He knew the tone in her voice all too well—the icy barb warning anyone from getting too close. In so many aspects, they were similar to each other. How could it have happened that they got so close without them even noticing? Of course Erik had realised his attraction to her the first day they'd met, and promptly kept his distance as much as possible while working with her. That vow lasted less than a day before he found her in his office and close enough that he could smell the fragrance of flowers she left in her wake.

'I don't intend this as criticism but rather an observation. The reason I didn't speak to you this week was that I needed to think about what happened and how it fits into everything I know about you,' he said, getting to the underlying point of his tension. They would work through the night, and it would turn out far too long if he didn't get this out now—even though a part of him wanted to forget it had ever happened. Because the craving flickering inside him burned far too bright already.

She remained quiet as they watched the building on the horizon grow taller. Then Larissa said, 'So, what do you want to do now? I'm not sure what it means when a guy tells me he would like to use the next four weeks to figure out what drives me wild just for him to spend an entire week ignoring me. Are you lacking clarity?'

Her words were blunt. Under any other circumstances, Erik knew he would have felt a stab of guilt. He probably did, except the need flaring hot and searing within him covered up his other emotions, burning away anything else that might have attempted to compete with this feeling inside of him.

'A lack of clarity is a good starting point. What I'm worried about is closeness.' He was already slipping down that path, scared of it enough that he'd retreated from her this week. It hadn't been the most mature thing to do, but he needed time to figure her out. Figure himself out.

Steering right, Erik left what little he could see of the main road and took the small snowy path to the research building. He pulled into an open parking bay, casting his eyes around. There were three more cars around them. Larissa seemed to notice as well, looking up at the building before her eyes landed on Erik. A shiver clawed through him as those brown eyes narrowed on him and visions of that night a week ago filled his mind. He knew exactly what her face looked like when she stood too close to the edge, how her breathing turned ragged and fast, panting until—

'You mean you are worried about feelings entering this?' He focused on the present, on the conversation they needed to have. Even though when he was this close to her, he wanted to do many things to her, and none of them involved much talking.

'That's...' His voice trailed off as he searched for the truth inside him. 'You asked me if I ever had my heart broken hard enough that I just needed to be elsewhere. I said I have, and my elsewhere is my work. My purpose in this community. There isn't much space for anything else outside of that. Even my family gave way.'

Erik couldn't tell what thoughts were rolling around behind her eyes. He kept staring at her, searching her expression for something to latch on to. Eventually, she shook her head, but a smile tugged at her lips. 'If we agree that this is what we want, then we should be fine. Just some fun while I'm here with no risks of getting attached. I'm down for that if you are.'

How was this simultaneously the answer he wanted and had feared? Because there was no way in hell he could say no to her. Not when he'd already had her above him, sighing his name as she clenched around his fingers. That was a sight he knew he would never tire of—which was why he feared slipping in too deep. He was already burning on the inside with the need to touch her.

His voice was rough when he said, 'I want things between us to be clear. My life is here, and nothing is going to change that.'

He'd not told her about Astrid—at least not in detail. But Erik wasn't naive. He knew that even if they went into this with the best intentions, things could happen. People developed feelings even when they swore they wouldn't. So he needed to be clear about where he stood so that even if something were to happen, his stance was crystal clear from the very beginning.

'I'm not planning on whisking you away to England by the end of my stint here. But I am planning on leaving.' She paused, her eyes drifting down to where his hand still gripped the gearshift. Slowly, she extended her hand, covering his with hers and prying his fingers open. When their hands intertwined, she looked back up at him and said, 'Let's make it clear what we want by discussing what happened in the past.'

Erik blinked, his head tilted to the side. 'What do you mean?'

Her hand squeezed his as she took a deep breath. 'I was happy to live my life alone—the way I had always done. Casual, one-night things were all I needed. Men more often than women because of how male-dominated the medical field is. Then I met Rachel, and she seemed to get me. She wouldn't complain when I spent hours at the clinic or if I was too tired to do something. It felt like she was trying her best to fit into the life I already had, so when things became more serious, she had helpful solutions at hand.' She raised her free hand, making air quotes around the word 'helpful'. 'Things like, "What if I moved in with you? That way it doesn't matter how late you come home." And because I saw her compromise, I thought I needed to do that, too. My parents had never compromised with each other, and their fights dragged out for days. I didn't want that in my life.'

Her voice was even, hardly betraying the emotional depth her words laid bare. Or was it because of the lack of any inflection in her voice that he could tell how deep this wound still ran? Erik remained quiet, not wanting to disrupt the moment building between them.

'Turns out all the helpful things she did were for the purpose of getting concessions out of me. She thought she could drag me over to her side if I let her come close enough. Even though she had said she understood my hours, soon came the snide remarks and the passive-aggressive cold dinner left on the table. I thought we had agreed on who we wanted to be together, but she changed her mind—and tried to force that change on me. And when I didn't change fast enough, she sought out other people while still pretending to be with me. Like the efforts I made for her were not enough to be loved or valued. I, once again, became secondary to her needs.'

His eyes widened as he realised the meaning of her earlier words. Sharing not necessarily for the sake of getting to know each other better, but to avoid the things that were still haunting them. He knew she had her own life—just like he had his—and that was the common ground they could meet on.

'Our stories are strangely similar,' he said, each word coming to him haltingly. Erik had never fully opened up about his struggles with Astrid. Who would he even have to talk to? His parents were too obsessed with the next person to enter his life. Too keen on recreating what they thought to be the ultimate goal in life: to find your other half.

His eyes drifted to Larissa, who still held his hand

wrapped in hers. Maybe that was a second thing they could do for each other. Hold space when they didn't have anyone to do that for them in their real lives. This wasn't real, so they could make up the rules as they wanted.

'Astrid came to Svalbard the way most people outside of tourists do. They are either looking for something or running away. She was the former, looking for something else in life. Something to fulfil her. She landed in my hospital on her second night in Longyearbyen with potential frostbite, and we just…clicked. I'd been so focused on my work for so long at this point that I didn't understand her interest in me until my sister pointed it out.' As time passed, it got harder to remember the reasons why he'd fallen for his ex-fiancée. The hurt had overwritten almost all of his memories of her, and when he'd moved on from the pain, little else to remind him of her remained.

But he could understand Larissa better now, knowing what she had told him. Could let himself sink a bit deeper into the thing that was their attraction without getting lost in it. Because he knew it was a dead end. She needed to know that about him, too.

'She stayed at the Aurora Hotel. After she left the hospital, I went there a few times for follow-up appointments, and I think what drew me in was how she could talk to me in a way that made me feel seen and understood— and, at the same time, do the same with my parents. She brought us into the same room, interacting with each other without even trying.'

A gust of wind rattled the windows, obscuring their vision with a flurry of snow. Larissa's eyes widened as even the building right in front of them became hazy with the ice rising around them. Something inside Erik shifted as he looked outside. Beyond the exterior lights from the building, he couldn't actually *see* anything, but his senses still picked up on something. A sixth sense he'd developed from years of living surrounded by snow and ice.

'We should go inside. I think there's a storm coming,' he said, even though a part of him hesitated to end their conversation prematurely. By the set of Larissa's jaw when he said that, he could tell that she didn't want to move either.

So he added, 'I will tell you everything once we're settled inside and have seen to the researchers. Okay?'

Her eyes narrowed at him, and he couldn't blame her. Whatever was happening between them was fresh. Fragile. He'd already tested the stability by ignoring her for a week straight. But then she nodded, and they worked in tandem to pick up everything from the car and hurry inside the building. Erik's sixth sense proved accurate, because hours later, as they neared completing their work, the storm still hadn't abated—and they wouldn't be leaving until it did.

CHAPTER EIGHT

'WHAT DO YOU do during your time off?' Larissa pressed the cotton ball against the tiny puncture wound the needle left on the researcher's arm, giving it a good squeeze to encourage the platelets to do their job before she slapped a plaster on it.

The researcher, Elsie, shrugged, as if no one had ever asked her that question. A common reaction, Larissa found, as she had asked every person who walked through that door and they all had a variation of a shrug, a contemplative scowl or just a shake of their heads.

'We have downtime if we want it, but I usually spend time in the lab anyway,' she said, her lips pulled into a frown. 'But now that I say it out loud, it sounds sad. Like I'm just spending my days in this building, looking at spreadsheets of different readings.'

Larissa chuckled at that. After securing the plaster to Elsie's skin, she grabbed the blood pressure cuff and wound it around the woman's upper arm, pressing on the mechanism to inflate it and holding the stethoscope against the crook of Elsie's arm.

'I always wondered how that works,' Elsie said when the cuff was fully deflated. The sound of Velcro filled the air as she took it off, setting it aside and noting down the blood pressure on the patient chart Erik had provided her.

She looked up from the piece of paper. 'How what works?'

'Measuring blood pressure with a stethoscope like that.'

'Oh...' Larissa's eyes darted towards the blood pressure cuff she had discarded on the worktable behind her. 'You know how your blood pressure comprises two numbers?'

Elsie nodded, and she continued, 'The first one is the systolic blood pressure—that's the pressure when the heart is beating. I slowly release the pressure on the cuff while listening for a whooshing or thumping sound. It's the pressure at which your blood flows again in the artery as the cuff pressure lowers.'

She picked up the pen, pointing at the numbers she'd written down. 'The other number is the diastolic pressure, which is the one in the arteries when the heart rests between beats. I figure that one out by deflating the cuff further and waiting for the sound to stop.'

Raising her hand, she tapped the point of the pen against the gauge on the cuff lying on the table. 'Then it's just a matter of writing the numbers down.'

Elsie looked at her with an appreciative smile. 'You did it so fast.'

It was Larissa's turn to shrug. 'I've done this more times than I can count. Now I don't even have to think about it anymore. I'm sure there are aspects of your work that are similar.'

The woman nodded, her eyes glazing over slightly as if she was diving for a specific memory to match it against what she had just heard. As much as Larissa enjoyed the people she'd met here, she couldn't listen to another science story without rolling her eyes. So before Elsie could say anything, she got to her feet, signalling that the examination was over.

'And that's you done with a clean bill of health,' Larissa said as she finished her notes, returning the smile Elsie gave her.

The woman waved as she opened the door and closed it behind her, leaving Larissa alone with her thoughts. Again. The regret of ushering the woman out as fast as she had whooshed through her. She contemplated how weird it would be if she ran after her, asking her what kinds of things had become second nature to her as she spent her days here at the research centre looking at snow. Or whatever else they did here.

Larissa's fried brain genuinely couldn't retain any information that wasn't medically relevant. But pretending to listen helped her ignore the mounting unease in her belly at what she had done in the car. How much of herself she had just put out there for everyone to see. And by everyone, she obviously meant Erik, though as far as Svalbard was concerned, he was already an enormous part of *everyone*.

Not for the first time since they had divided up the researchers to do their health checks, Larissa picked up her phone. Still zero bars. There was a Wi-Fi network attached to the research centre, but she'd felt too awkward to ask anyone for the password. *What colour was the urine you passed last? Oh, and also, what's the Wi-Fi password?*

She'd have to freak out at Ally later, which was totally fine. She was a functioning adult who didn't need her best friend to help her process her feelings. Larissa was a *doctor*, telling people all day about their health, both physically and mentally. Why was the thought of facing Erik after she had told him about Rachel so daunting?

Larissa didn't even know what had possessed her. For the most part, she had meant what she'd said. He'd been avoiding her because of some notion that his touch might have warped her brain enough for her to catch feelings for him. If the roles were reversed, she probably would have had the same concern. And because she didn't want him to keep having those thoughts, she shared what had happened between her and Rachel. Had let him into the ruins that this relationship had left in her.

But another part of her had wanted him to know be-cause… That was the part that had her freaking out. Be-cause she simply wanted him to know her. Wanted him to have a piece of her, even though all she had said to him pointed in the other direction.

A knock sounded on the door, and a second later, the cause of all her jumbled thoughts walked through it. Erik crossed half of the room before he stopped. She thought she spotted something akin to worry in his expression, but when he raised his eyes to look at her, she took in a sharp breath. His smouldering gaze heated the air be-tween them, emptying her brain of any thoughts that had kept her spinning a few seconds ago.

'All done?' he asked, still keeping his distance, but the way his eyes dipped below her face before coming back up sent a shiver through her.

'Nothing to report here. You?' She knew he was about to tell her something, and whatever that was had him in a mood similar to a week ago. The air between them had crackled back then, too.

'We're stuck here until the storm subsides. They think

it won't be longer than a few hours, but given that we worked throughout the night, they gave us a room.'

Larissa got off her chair, turning her head to look at the window. The pane was near black, the only interruption an occasional snow flurry pressing against the window as if trying to find a way inside. When the meaning of his words registered, she spun towards him. 'Wait, *room*, singular?'

His laugh was low and luxurious, skating over her skin like a warm caress. 'Space is tight here, so they don't have much when it comes to emergency housing.'

He pointedly looked around the room they had commandeered to do their physical exams. Someone had brought in a cot that she'd used as an exam table while ignoring the tables and rows of computers and other machines that she couldn't decipher. Whatever work usually went on in this room had to be paused for the research centre's annual health examination.

Larissa sighed, unwilling to give in to the heat pooling in the pit of her stomach just yet. They still needed to have that conversation. She wanted to know the things about him that he now knew about her, wanted to complete the picture of Erik that was becoming clearer by the day. But working through the night when she hadn't expected it had left her exhausted and struggling to think straight. Maybe a few hours of sleep would do her well, and then they could have that conversation on the way back.

And then…then they were free to act on the tension crackling between them.

'All right, lead the way,' she said, following on his heels as he ushered her down a corridor until they reached a non descript door among many non descript doors. Everything looked so much the same that she didn't quite know how he had the required certainty to push *this* exact door open.

But he did, and then he stepped back, letting her walk in first. A double bed stood against the wall, light grey sheets on the mattress, light gray cover on the duvet. Also singular, as Larissa noted. So they were either going to take turns sleeping, or—

Larissa turned around to face Erik, who had just closed the door. His hand still hovered on the door handle. She watched as his fingers slipped lower and tightened around the lock. The bolt slipped into place with a soft click, and somehow that sound was enough to release the tight grip Larissa had kept on her desire for Erik.

She surged towards him, and when he met her half-way, she realised he'd done the same. Fires erupted underneath her skin, sending heat coursing through her from head to toe.

His hand slipped over her back, his fingers dancing down her spine until he reached the hem of her shirt. She gasped into his mouth when his hand slid beneath the fabric and splayed over her ribs.

Then Erik tore his mouth from her, leaving her bereft of the sensation for a second before he pressed it against her neck. His beard scratched over her sensitive flesh, drawing another gasp that sounded more like a hiccup from her. Men were nothing new to her, but she'd forgotten what facial hair felt like. If her neck was already this sensitised after a brush of his lips, then what would happen to her once he—

'I'm so glad you joined me here,' he said as he trailed his tongue down her collarbone. His breath swept over her, sending shivers down her spine as she arched into his touch.

'You mean you're really glad I'm so bossy and pushed my way into this,' she replied, a huff between each other word.

Erik's chuckle skittered over her skin, finding the sensitive spots and burrowing inside her. He tugged at her shirt, and she gave him the space he needed to pull it over her head. Before he could gather her back into his arms, she placed her hands on his chest and began to unbutton his shirt.

She let out a shaky sigh when she folded the fabric back over his shoulders, revealing the expanse of his torso. Larissa normally leaned more towards women, but this was... 'Oh my God.'

When Erik laughed again, she realised she had said it out loud. 'It was absolute torture to get through this week,' he huffed into her ear, his lips grazing the shell and sending another shockwave through her.

His hands now trailed her exposed flesh, finding the clasp of her bra and opening it again in a mirror of the last time. Only this time, there would be no interruptions.

Not willing to wait even a second longer, Larissa's hands got to work on the button of his trousers, pushing them down just as he pulled her bra down her arms, then made short work of removing her jeans. With both of them standing in front of each other in their underwear, Larissa let her eyes wander down his body—and felt him do the same.

Tight muscles rippled underneath pale skin as Erik breathed in and out, his hand flexing as if not touching her cost him whatever self-restraint remained within him. She planned on shattering that control.

Reaching out between them, Larissa trailed her hand from his chest down over his abs, her fingers tangling with the fine hair that led from his navel downwards and vanished past the waistband of his underwear.

She paused there, her breath growing heavy and her heart pounding in her throat. This was not the moment to retreat, to overthink it. They had their agreement, and Larissa would make sure he would say his part when they were done here. What else were they to do during a snowstorm? Plenty of time to give in to this thing building between them and see where the path led her.

'Well, we're here now.' She closed the gap between them and pressed the heel of her palm against his length. Erik's groan was low, his eyes fluttering closed for a second, and she felt the sensation race down her own spine. Her thighs clenched at the sound, and she knew when he touched her, he'd find her ready.

He huffed out another breath when she pushed down again, her fingers grazing over him, still wrapped in the fabric of his underwear. His hands shot up her body, burying themselves in her hair and pulling her head back. Then his mouth crashed down on her again, his kiss filled with the promise of passion.

'Get on the bed,' he said, voice low and gravelly—leaving her no room to argue. Not that she wanted to argue. The bed was exactly where she wanted to be.

'I see you're trying on the bossy pants now,' she couldn't help but say, even as she complied and sat down at the edge of the bed.

She watched with a predator's eye as Erik bent down, picking up his trousers and sticking his hand into a pocket. He pulled out a square of foil. Larissa's eyes widened.

'How could you have possibly brought condoms when you didn't even know I would be inviting myself on this field trip?' Her eyes travelled down his body as she said that, following his hands as he pushed down his underwear—exposing himself to her.

Her mouth went dry, and swallowing became a lot harder. Her heart was beating in her throat as Erik stepped out of the clothes discarded on the floor, ripping the foil open and then rolling on the condom.

'Whenever I come up here, I pack things they need. Prescriptions, first aid materials, books, board games.' He kept listing things as he came closer and stopped right in front of her. Towering over her. His gaze was ablaze as he raked it over her, his breath coming out heavy and uneven.

Then it dawned on her what he was saying. 'You stole the condoms meant for the researchers?'

Erik chuckled. 'I stole *one* condom. And I don't think it's stealing when the hospital purchased them.'

His hand came down on her naked thigh. Larissa made to move back to give him space, but his grip tightened as he shook his head. Then he knelt down in front of her, his body broad enough to push her thighs open. Skating up her legs, his hands reached the waistband of her underwear. And then he stopped. His fingers curling around the band, Erik looked up at her. Searching her face for an answer.

Permission.

Just when Larissa had thought she couldn't get any more turned on, he went and did this. Her heart leapt into her throat as she nodded. Then his warm breath grazed her sensitive flesh as he pulled down her underwear.

The roughness of his beard against her legs drew a gasp from her lips as he pressed his mouth along her inner thigh, kissing up towards her in a deliciously slow motion. Right towards the ache that had been building for him for far too long. An ache she'd tried to ignore, tried to explain away the best she could. Of course she was horny. Who wouldn't be on an island that was mostly ice and polar bears? Especially when the one hot guy on the aforementioned island worked in close quarters with her. That didn't mean any feelings were involved. They'd been clear about that. This was just an additional pastime for them to pursue—like reading books or playing board games.

'I've been thinking about this for so long,' Erik whispered as his lips trailed upward some more. His breath swept over her exposed sex, and the thought that he was breathing her in had her shivering. That he had fantasised about this moment just as much as she had.

'Please.' The word came out as a strangled noise that she didn't recognise as her own voice. *Please let me find out if it's as good as I imagined.* That was the meaning she was putting in one word, hoping he would pick up on it.

His fingers tightened around her thighs as he caressed her, and Larissa was about to make another attempt at speech when his breath hit her in that spot—right before his tongue did.

Her head lolled back as sensation exploded through her, a pent-up release already gathering at her spine. If she had found his fingers skillful, then his mouth was… There were no words for what his mouth was. Not as his fingers joined it, pushing into her and finding all the right spots. As if Erik had found a map of her body and studied it in preparation for this moment.

Larissa's breaths turned into pants, her skin growing more sensitive as she got closer to that cliff. The fresh linens rubbed against her skin as she bowed into his touch, arching off the bed entirely when the sensation became almost too much to withstand. But Erik was relentless in his willingness to pleasure her, his arm wrapped tightly around her hips and pinning her down as he licked and sucked and kissed her towards that iridescent veil gathering around her vision.

He didn't let up, not as she shuddered, feeling the pressure building at the base of her spine, her entire focus on the places where his body touched hers, and then—

Stars exploded behind her closed eyelids as release rushed through her, a loud sob tearing from her throat.

Her mind in pieces, Larissa lay there, catching her breath. A small sigh left her when Erik retreated—a strange emptiness rushing into the space where he'd just been—but then he reappeared on top of her as he got into the bed, pulling her limp body with him.

Her heart skipped a beat when he looked down at her, not with the blazing fire she'd seen in his eyes as they'd stripped down, but with an unexpected tenderness. As if he'd hidden it beneath the layers of need. But now, as he came to draw her into another kiss, this part of him slipped out.

'Erik, you—' He pressed his mouth against her again, his tongue slipping between her lips, and she thought that the taste alone would shatter her all over again.

'That's another way I know how to pleasure you now,' he said, and a shiver clawed down her spine when his body settled between her legs—his length pressing against her with a delicious pressure.

He looked down at her with nothing but tenderness and affection in his eyes as he asked, 'Are you ready to find out still another way?'

A shiver raked through her as their hips pressed together. Larissa nodded, and then her head lolled back again as Erik filled her.

Feeling Larissa all around him was a revelation Erik hadn't been prepared for by any measure. Another person couldn't possibly feel this *right*—this meant to be—in his own body. Need had driven him to this point, had taken him all the way to the brink with Larissa, and a shudder had raked through his own body as he watched her lose herself in his pleasure—again.

But this—there was something entirely different to this. She reacted as he moved in her, adjusting to his size, to his touch, guiding him where to go and how to touch. Always with a gentle kindness and a burning desire shining in her eyes.

The second Larissa fluttered around him, the pressure at the base of his spine intensified, signalling his own release. Erik thrust harder, picking up the tempo as her gasps of pleasure underneath him grew louder and the tension within them grew tighter.

He knew she was close. Knew it because he could feel it, and he was ready to go with her—dive over that cliff again. Because he knew there could be nothing as exquisite as their connection right at this moment. There was no way this could ever be replicated in any form, and he would hang on to it as long as he dared. As long as she'd let him.

'Larissa…' He breathed out her name as the pressure within him sharpened, his head coming down next to hers. Her breath skated over him, each pant and moan a warm blast over his sweat-covered skin.

'Don't slow down. This is—' Erik swallowed the rest

of her words as he pressed his mouth against hers, drawing her into a kiss passionate enough to break him. His
hands intertwined with hers, pinning her arms above her
head as he thrust one more time, relishing the fluttering
around him as release barrelled through him.

This wasn't supposed to be a mind-altering experience.
They'd made it clear that whatever happened between
them would never be more than a casual fling designed
to end the moment Larissa stepped back on a plane—into
her old life. But as her hands gripped him tighter and he
slid off her to pull her into his arms, a quiet part of him
wasn't entirely sure how he could let her go even if he
knew he couldn't have her.

'Continue your story,' Larissa mumbled, her lips grazing
over the back of his hand as she spoke.

Outside of crawling under the duvet, they hadn't moved
much. Still naked, Erik had pulled her back flush against
his front, and it was ridiculous how perfectly she fit him.
Like some higher being had moulded her to sit right here
against his body.

'My story?' His fingers drifted up and down her side,
exploring every hill and valley of her and making a map
of all her reactions to his touch.

'We said we're going into this with full honesty. To
understand what happened so we don't fall into the same
traps again.' She somehow scooted closer, her butt pressing against him enough that his manhood stirred again.
There was no way he would ever have his fill of her.

'Right...' Working through all of his patients had been
a new form of torture for him. Normally, he enjoyed getting out of Longyearbyen for a few hours and chatting
with the researchers at this outpost. But after the con-

versation they'd had on the drive here, all he could think about was their discussion and what they'd agreed on, what he'd learned about Larissa.

The burn of indignity had been a constant companion to him throughout the consultations, and even now he couldn't wrap his head around why anyone would ever desire to change Larissa. How they could look at her and not see all the generosity and kindness and sweetness within her. He hadn't know her for long, and a growing part of him regretted that he wouldn't get the chance to know her better. Right next to him was a woman who, on her first day, had agreed to walk a sick patient's dog because she knew he couldn't. She knew nothing about Martin or his circumstances, yet she hadn't hesitated to do what was right to aid someone in his community—*her* community for as long as she remained.

To think someone had told her this wasn't enough was unfathomable. What terrified him about this entire thing was how he really wanted her to know him, too. Know how much he cared about his community and that by giving them as much of her as she had, she had found a way to touch his heart without realising it.

He took a deep breath and let it out slowly, thinking about where he'd left things off. 'My parents were thrilled to meet Astrid. Especially when she showed interest in the hotel. They never saw me much, and so for them, it was easy to assume I was some lonely hermit.'

Thinking back to the moment brought a dull pain with it, all wrapped up in his own naive outlook back then. 'I thought it was a sign. I liked her, could see myself growing to love her, and she seemed invested in Svalbard. I never thought I'd find someone who felt that way, which has always been the thing to stop me from getting close to anyone.'

Underneath his hand, Larissa shifted onto her back. Then she looked up at him, eyes alert but soft. 'So your parents seemed to value you more just because you were conforming with their idea of a happy life? That's a lot of pressure to put on someone.'

Erik snatched up her hand, pressing it against his mouth in a gentle kiss as her words kicked something loose inside him. The realisation that someone out there actually understood him.

Her.

She was right here, extracting the core of his complicated feelings in two sentences.

'With my parents as enthusiastic about her as they were, my mother soon slipped me the family heirloom engagement ring, and I just thought—this was another sign. Everything fit. My parents were happy for her to work at the hotel and to see me matched up, and I could serve the community in a way authentic to me—to who I am. We got engaged, and she moved into my cottage outside the village, and then...' His voice trailed off as the memories caught up with him.

Beside him, Larissa shifted, her hand coming down on his chest, gently pressing against his sternum. Her fingers curled into his hair there, the soft tugging reminding him she was here not to interrogate him but to hold space.

'Then she got bored. There's only so much that ever happens in Svalbard. I mean, you know the reality of what life is like here, and you're about to complete your first month here. It *is* boring if you lack an appreciation for the village and its people.' His greatest fear and the reason he'd never indulged in any serious relationship had come true in his life. He'd wanted to be wrong, wanted to be exposed as the cynic his family believed him to be. Astrid was meant to be that person who showed him he could have it all and still show up for his community the way he needed to.

His hand came up to where Larissa was stroking his skin, his fingers curling around hers. 'She wanted me to leave. Said that settling down in Svalbard had been a mistake, but that *I* wasn't. That I was the only right thing in her life, and that...' His voice faltered as he remembered that evening. The feeling of being torn in two directions at the same time still lingering in his soul. 'That if I loved her, I would consider moving away with her.'

Just like that, she'd put him in front of the choice he had never wanted to make. She had believed so deeply that he would choose her, even though he'd always been honest with her that if it somehow came to that, he wouldn't—*couldn't*—choose her. Because it wasn't who he was.

A rush of air leaving her nose was the only noise Larissa made while he spoke, her eyes fixed on where their fingers interlocked.

There it was. The truth that had only pushed him further to dedicate himself to work. Now Larissa knew to be wary of him when it came to attachment. Because whoever wanted to be with him needed to accept that his life—his heart—belonged in Svalbard, and there was nothing that would ever change that. This was his home, even if it hurt sometimes.

Eventually, Larissa stirred. She tilted her head upwards to look at him, and the way her eyes brightened in the dim light of the bedside lamp had the air rushing out of his lungs.

'Do you regret choosing the way you did?' she asked, getting to the heart of his entire story in a very Larissa way.

There was no hesitation as he shook his head. 'Not once. I have my regrets about how things unfolded—the paths I allowed myself to be led down. But I won't ever regret choosing my people.'

He burned to know what she thought, but her expression remained veiled, not letting him see beyond the surface. He wasn't sure *why* he wanted to know. There was no real opinion to be had. He'd told her his story.

'Thank you for telling me. Now that I know, I promise I will slink quietly back to England when my time is up without making any great declarations.' She looked up at him, and her smirk sent a shiver trickling down his spine. 'I promise I won't fall in love with you.'

His stomach bottomed out as he heard the words he wanted to hear. A wave of ice sloshed through his veins, reaching out to his limbs until his entire body was cold. His grip around Larissa tightened, pulling her closer into his body as if he could borrow her warmth.

'Good,' he whispered into her hair, the scent of her so intoxicating, he closed his eyes to ground himself. 'I promise I won't, either.'

CHAPTER NINE

THE EVER-DIM LIGHT of the hotel's common room hummed with the activity of a few scattered groups of people. Larissa paid them no mind as she stretched her legs out in front of her.

This was what cats had to feel like. They got to lounge around furniture all day and receive food as if magic conjured it up. Larissa didn't know because she'd never actually had a cat—or any other pet. With the time she spent at work in the past, she thought another human was too hard to accommodate, let alone an animal that couldn't even communicate with her in words. Granted, a lot of humans didn't do that, either, though that was mostly because of a lack of willingness.

Somehow she and Erik had figured out how to be honest with each other without descending into the chaos that was romantic feelings. Learning more about him, about the things he'd been through with his ex-fiancée, had unlocked a piece of the Erik puzzle that she'd been staring at since the moment she'd met him without understanding how to get closer to him.

'You need anything else, just let me know,' Hilde said as she set down the steaming cup next to Larissa on a small side table to the right of the armchair Larissa had claimed for herself.

'Thank you.' She smiled at the older woman and took a sip of the hot chocolate, her eyes fluttering shut as the taste flooded her mouth. It was absolutely divine and led Larissa to question her life choices not for the first time since she'd arrived here. Why had she and Ally put up with the sewage water that they served at Heaton Perk for so long when tastes like *this* existed?

Digging out her phone, Larissa took the mug into her hand and balanced it on her knee, right next to the book in her lap, and took a picture. Then she sent it to Ally without a caption. Her friend probably wouldn't see the picture until tomorrow. They'd agreed to read the same book over their time away, though the more involved Larissa got with Erik, the less time there was for reading. Surely Ally wouldn't mind...

Fairy lights on the inside had joined the ones on the outside of the house and wound their way across the beams on the ceiling. They blinked, the colour fading from white to pink to red. Vases with roses stood on the scattered tables. Coming down earlier, Larissa had spotted a poster announcing the activities for the residents of the Aurora Hotel for Valentine's Day.

Her stomach lurched at the thought. The day was coming up, and she had no plans. Of course she didn't, because she wasn't in a relationship. It would be weird if she spent the day with Erik, wouldn't it?

'Are you enjoying yourself?' The familiar female voice had her glancing up and into a face that looked so much like Erik's, Larissa lost her train of thought for a moment.

'Um... yes,' she said as Anna slid into the armchair across from her, smiling big enough to show a neat row of white teeth. 'I have the day off today. Well, not really. I'm on call, so I can't go far from the hospital. Not that

I could do that even if I wasn't on call. But I thought I'd come down here and find something to occupy my time while watching the pager.'

She lifted the book from her lap, showing Anna the title. The woman's smile grew even wider. '*A Court of Thorns and Roses*? Nice choice.'

'Did you read it?'

Anna nodded, a spark illuminating her eyes. 'Oh yeah, any of the new books here are mine. My father contributed all the cold war novels. I don't know how he can read them. It's always the same. Spy man on some spy mission to save the spy world from the brink of spy...something.'

'Spy something?' Larissa asked, barely containing her laughter.

'Ah, you know. Man saves the world. Boring.' She waved her hand in front of her, and Larissa couldn't help it—she instantly took a liking to Anna. Why hadn't she interacted much with the woman before?

Maybe because she looked so much like her brother, who Larissa had become so wrapped up in that she didn't really have the capacity for anyone else. No, that wasn't true. She was *not* wrapped up in Erik at all. Maybe in his sheets, but that was the maximum wrapping she would do to him.

It didn't matter if he might have a charming sister, and Larissa *definitely* didn't wonder how she figured into the entire difficult relationship dynamic he'd shared with her. Because they hadn't opened up to each other to get closer to one another. No, the sole purpose of the emotional striptease they'd gone through was purely research—so they could avoid making this something that it wasn't.

'Well, this is definitely *not* man saves the world.' Larissa wasn't sure what exactly this was, but she'd seen the title talked about often enough on TikTok that she and Ally had picked this one to tandem read.

Anna leaned across the space, and Larissa tilted the book towards her when prompted, so she could look at the page number. Her eyes widened. 'Ah, it's about to start,' she said with a conspiratorial twinkle before leaning back. 'It's nice to see you down here unwinding. Hope my brother isn't riding you too hard at the hospital.'

Larissa coughed, almost spitting hot chocolate all over the book. Setting the mug down on the side table, she tapped her hand against her sternum. 'Sorry, I, um, forgot which way liquids go. Turns out the oesophagus and not the windpipe,' she said, hoping she'd covered up what had *actually* made her cough.

'Ah, yes. I hear that happens a lot,' Anna replied, and the small smile spreading over her lips had Larissa wondering if Erik had told his sister anything.

'He usually lets me have the weekends off. Though today I'm on call until Erik is back, which should be any minute.' She lifted a pager covered in rhinestones from the side table, showing it off. 'Since I have to be dressed for any emergencies, I thought I might as well sit by the fire.'

'Good choice.' Anna eyed the pager, then looked back at her. 'Please tell me you glued these rhinestones on to piss my brother off.'

Larissa chuckled. 'Ingrid and I did it yesterday after two appointments were cancelled.' She turned the pager around in her hand. 'I think he'll love it.'

Anna nodded, amusement dancing in her eyes. 'Yes, if my brother loves anything, it's *definitely* change. Never met someone who dealt with it better.'

Putting the pager back down, she straightened in her

chair, trying not to be too obvious as she eyed the other woman. Even though they looked so much like each other, the auras around Erik and Anna were so different. Like they were polar opposites. She remembered when Erik had picked her up for her first day. He'd spoken to his sister, but they hadn't exchanged more than a few words. Back then, Larissa hadn't even thought of paying it any kind of attention. Neither of them had been more than strangers to her.

But now... Now she felt like she knew who Erik was. Not someone who wore his heart on his sleeve, but someone who valued the ties to his community and the people around him. Valued them so much that he was willing to give up large pieces of himself just to ensure he was keeping his people safe. That his fiancée had asked him to give it all up was...

'How could anyone ever get bored with this?' Larissa asked out loud, and Anna raised her eyebrows.

'Why do you ask...' Her voice trailed off, the amused sparkle in her eyes disappearing as she tilted her head to the side.

Oh no... Had that question revealed too much about what Erik had told her? 'What I mean is that—'

A figure appearing behind Anna's chair caught their attention, and Larissa swallowed a relieved sigh. Erik towered over them, brushing the snowflakes out of his hair. The twinkling lights wreathed him in a soft pink glow as a smile spread across his lips, and the paper hearts hanging from the ceiling looked like they were sprouting from his head. His expression changed from neutral to inquisitive as his gaze bounced between Larissa and his sister.

'What are you doing here?' Anna asked, glancing up at him.

A wave of awareness rushed over Larissa, and to keep herself busy, she reached for her mug, half hiding her face behind it. What *was* he doing here? She knew he'd arrive today, but had totally not been looking at her phone every few minutes to see if a message from him had appeared. That would be weird, and Larissa was definitely *not* weird. Nope.

'I just got back from a meeting in Norway. Thought I'd stop by,' he said with a casual shrug, then looked around before grabbing a nearby chair and pulling it towards them. When he peeled his jacket off, Anna sat up straighter.

'Blir du? Her?' Larissa blinked at the woman as she switched to Norwegian.

Erik sat down, draping one leg over the other and looking at his younger sister with a raised eyebrow. 'Yes,' he answered, and Larissa wasn't sure what underpinned his voice. Was he annoyed at the question? What had she asked?

Before Larissa could inquire, he added, 'That's not a problem, is it?'

Anna quickly shook her head. 'Not a problem at all,' she said, following his lead and sticking to English.

Larissa didn't have any siblings, so the dynamic between them had always seemed like a strange concept to her. Her friends had often complained about their brothers and sisters growing up, but her parents had decided one was enough. These days she was almost certain they had decided that even one was too much, and that had been the whole reason they'd been at each other's throats so much. Their relationship was so overwhelming that they didn't have space for something additional to it—including their own daughter.

But she knew enough about interpersonal relationships to sense something odd about the siblings' exchange. Like Anna either didn't want him here or...was she surprised? Erik had said that he didn't come to visit often. That didn't mean never. She'd seen him here before, had she not? The night she'd arrived, he came here to greet her. Maybe he never lingered around for long?

'How was the trip to Norway?' she asked when silence spread between them, the vibe more awkward than she was used to.

'Good. Needed to talk to some people at the health ministry to discuss funding and research for next year,' he said as he relaxed into the chair, his shoulders slowly drooping. From where Anna sat in her armchair, she was still studying her brother, though her expression didn't let Larissa guess what she might be thinking.

'Research?' Larissa asked. 'Like medical research?'

But Erik shook his head. 'Research like the facility we visited last week. I need to know how many people are sent to Svalbard for long-term research purposes so I can account for their medical needs,' he said, and Larissa nodded. 'Thanks for taking over my on-call shift.'

Larissa waved her hand in front of her dismissively. 'Oh, don't worry about it. I can't believe that all this time you were the one fielding *all* the on-call emergencies.'

'I can believe it. Erik has been running the off-hours medical support since they put him in charge of the hospital,' Anna muttered, earning herself a glare from her brother.

'Wait, really?' Larissa's eyes widened when the information sank in. 'You are the only doctor who is ever on call? *Ever?*'

Erik only shrugged, like this wasn't a big deal. She'd thought that he just didn't want her to do any on-call things since it might require her to leave the village. She opened her mouth to protest and point out that this might be really dangerous. What if he got a call late at night after a long day at the hospital? What if he was sleep-deprived?

But before she could say anything, he cut in, 'I assume there was no need for anything?'

'There were no calls outside of minor things that the nurse on shift could take care of,' Larissa said, picking up the now *very* sparkly pager.

Erik stared at it, slowly blinking a few times. 'What on earth is that?'

The reaction was exactly what Larissa had hoped for, and she couldn't fight the grin spreading over her face. Even Anna was trying—and failing—to contain her laughter as Erik pinned the object in her hand with his glare.

'Oh, the rhinestones? Yeah, they are an additional safety measure,' she said, taking a deep breath to swallow her amusement when his eyes narrowed.

'Safety measure?' he repeated, each word coming out after a beat of contemplation as if she was speaking a different language.

'That's right. If you dropped the pager in the snow, it was hard to find with a torch because it was matte. Now that it glitters, it's very easy to find when hit by a light source.' She twisted the pager in her hand, and the light of the fire caught in the rhinestones. A kaleidoscope of colourful dots of light bounced around the common room as she rotated her hand.

'You're messing with—' Erik stopped mid-sentence when the pager gave off a shrill sound, its vibrations shaking her hand.

Flipping it around, she looked at the message crawling across the screen. Her heart skipped a beat when it got to the end and looped around once more.

Emergency: Animal attack reported 2 km east of Longyearbyen near Glacier Point. Two victims, one unconscious. Incident reported by victim. Bear sighted in the area. Immediate medical assistance required. Evac helicopter notified.

She handed the pager to Erik, who only glanced at it for a second before jumping to his feet. Not even two minutes later, they sped away on his snowmobile towards Glacier Point.

The temptation to leave Larissa behind burned at the back of his neck as they approached Glacier Point. An active animal attack was a rare emergency to deal with, as most people understood the dangers of leaving Longyearbyen. Still, some believed the law that they had to be armed at any time to be a mere suggestion. Those people were almost always tourists with more bravery than brains to go around. No one actually living here would ever forget that they were mere guests on the island and that the polar bears and other wildlife were the true inhabitants of Svalbard.

The snowmobile's high beams revealed a large area of the snowfield, and he slowed down as they looked. The last thing they needed was to run head first into an already agitated polar bear. Erik would hate to have to use his rifle, but he knew he wouldn't hesitate for even a second. Her safety was the most important thing here.

Our safety, he corrected himself as he came to a halt and the arms clinging to him loosened. This was not about Larissa; it couldn't be. They had agreed what their fling would be like, and nothing would ever change his mind about needing to be here in Svalbard.

He knew that in his head, yet his chest still tightened thinking about letting her go—about putting her in dangerous situations such as this one. Would he have had similar qualms with someone else accompanying him for this incident?

Erik pushed the thought away, not liking the answer that awaited him in the depths of his heart.

'Take the torch and shine it around. See if you can find any tracks.' Larissa nodded and half turned before he snatched her wrist, closing his hand around it. 'Do not move even a step in any direction without me, okay?'

Larissa's eyes widened, her breath gathering in a big cloud in front of her, and the intensity of his voice took Erik aback. Clearly she had been taken aback, too. 'You're unarmed,' he added to soften his words.

'Okay,' she breathed out, underlining it with a nod, and then Erik let go of her arm—only for instant regret to flood him all over again. It was way too dangerous out here for her. What would he do if...

Again, he swatted the thoughts away. They were leading him down a path he couldn't walk. One where he couldn't think straight because he was too worried, too focused on the wrong thing.

'I think I see some footprints over there,' Larissa said beside him, pointing the powerful beam of her heavy-duty torch at a patch of snow further away.

Erik unslung the rifle from his back, one hand tightening around the stock while the other came up around the trigger, keeping his finger near the trigger guard with the barrel facing downward. 'Keep shining the light there and follow behind me,' he said, monitoring her as they walked towards the disturbance in the snow.

'Two sets of footprints,' he said as they stopped in front of them, and Larissa followed their trail with the light when—

'There they are!' She pointed with her free hand at a dark figure huddled over another one. After exchanging a quick glance, Erik nodded at her, and together they hurried over.

Larissa kneeled down beside the patient. Erik pulled the headlamp out of his jacket pocket, put it on and pushed the switch before turning in a circle. There was no trace of a bear, but there were some markings in the distance that could be footprints—or paw prints.

'What is your name?' Larissa addressed the person kneeling next to her, who seemed unharmed at first glance.

'Kaiden,' the man replied, his face almost as white as the surrounding snow. The woman's head was in his lap, her eyes pinched shut and her breath coming out in shallow pants.

'I'm Larissa, and this is Erik. We're doctors from the hospital. What happened here?'

Erik's eyes flicked around, monitoring their surroundings as Kaiden spoke.

'We went out with our tour guide last week, and Ashley, s-she wanted to take some more pictures before we leave tomorrow. We didn't mean to go far, just a few steps to catch some undisturbed snow, but then we got lost in the dark.' A low whimper drew Erik's attention downwards to the patient. The film of sweat on her scrunched-up brow was concerning.

Larissa nodded, working on identifying the patient's injuries.

'The distress call mentioned a potential animal attack,' Larissa said, following his line of thought unprompted. Something soft unfurled inside his chest, but he pushed it away. There would be plenty of time to figure *that* out later.

'We were just wandering around when our light went out. When we heard crunching in the snow and realised it was a bear, we ran, but she slipped, and she must have hurt her leg.' Kaiden kept his hands on her head as he spoke, looking down at her with the worry on his face growing.

Larissa kept her eyes on him, nodding him along his tale. When he'd finished, she examined the patient, her hands slowly working downwards with enough pressure to feel through the layers of clothing.

He watched as she paused and then shifted the patient's legs apart. The second she moved one leg a millimetre to the side, Ashley gasped before groaning into the quiet.

'Something wrong with her leg?' Erik asked, stepping closer to Larissa to give her more light.

Ashley groaned again when Larissa pushed her hands underneath the leg, carefully lifting it a finger-width off the ground and checking below. 'Potentially a break. We'd have to take off her clothes to inspect it. But I don't see any blood on the snow.'

Erik looked up at Ashley, whose stuttering breath showed her level of pain. A sprain wouldn't take someone out in such a way. A break was more likely.

Larissa gave Kaiden a reassuring smile before getting onto her feet and stepping closer to Erik. A flash of pride pulsed through him when her eyes darted around their environment the same way his had. She was behaving like a local.

'I can't tell the severity of the break like that,' she said as she pulled him a few steps away and out of earshot of Kaiden. 'It might still be an open fracture with how much pain she's in and how she reacts to being moved. Do we strip her even in these temperatures?'

Erik shook his head. 'Sometimes we do, but I'm comfortable being more conservative here. The medevac is already en route. Once she's in there, we can stabilise the break with the help of the evacuation team. It'll be warmer there.'

'But what if she is bleeding under the clothes and we just can't see it?'

Erik looked towards the patient, considering their options. They could wait for the helicopter. That would keep Ashley warm, though if she had a wound that needed attention, she could risk losing a lot of blood. Or they could cut off as much of her clothes as necessary for a proper examination and stabilise whatever damage they found. He had a few heat packs along with some blankets at the bottom of his backpack, but the risk of hypothermia would be so much higher than it already was.

'What did you feel?' he asked, hoping this would give him a clue on which way to lean. But Larissa only shook her head.

'Nothing that would lead me to believe there was a compound fracture. But I've never examined anyone wearing these gloves.' She held up her hands, showing off her heavy insulated gloves. 'Have you?'

He paused for a second before he nodded. Erik knew what she was going to suggest next, and it had been the thing he'd hoped to avoid.

'You examine her, then,' she said, and her brow creased when he didn't move.

'There might still be a polar bear around us.'

'I'll stay right beside you. Keep an eye out so that we don't get surprised. You know it won't charge at us out of nowhere.' Chances were unlikely that a polar bear would attack such a large group, but Erik had seen and heard weirder things happen. Especially if they were near its territory.

He wouldn't hesitate to inspect the patient if it was just him. If danger arose, he could get a shot out before it might be too late. But he had Larissa to worry about, and if she…

Erik squeezed his eyes shut. This was exactly the reason he shouldn't see people. Instead of thinking about the right thing to do for his patient, he was distracted, too worried about Larissa being in harm's way to act as he usually would.

'Okay, let me have a look,' he said, even though everything inside him protested against turning his back and lowering his weapon.

Before he could lose his nerve, he walked back towards the patient and took a knee while making sure the rifle stayed right by his side.

'We are evaluating our best options. The helicopter is already on the way to get you out of here, but we're not sure how to secure Ashley for the transport,' he said to Kaiden as he wrapped his hands around her leg and applied enough pressure that he could get some idea of what lay beneath her clothes.

'Ashley—she was in a lot of pain when she fell, but she grew quieter and... We need to get her out of here.' The edge of panic rang in Kaiden's voice, one Erik felt slicing through his chest. Suddenly, he knew such fear all too well.

'There are two things that might cause that. She might have broken her leg during her fall, which seems likely with how sensitive she is in that area. If it is a compound fracture, she might be bleeding.' Kaiden's eyes went wide. 'Or it might be hypothermia from lying motionless on the cold ground for a prolonged time. Either way—'

He paused when a faint sound caught his attention. 'I can hear the rescue helicopter.' Erik slid his hand further down, slowing when Ashley twitched with a painful groan. It was still hard to tell, but... 'I don't think it's a compound fracture. With the helicopter nearby, I say we'll wait for them to arrive. We will have an easier time stabilising her leg inside the helicopter.'

Kaiden nodded, and Erik slung his pack off his back, opening the top and digging through the supplies they had brought until he found the blankets and heat packs. 'Let's get her as warm as possible until they arrive, so when we—'

'Erik.' Larissa's voice was quiet, but the warning etched into his name was enough to freeze the blood in his veins.

His head whipped around, looking in the direction she was facing—and spotted the dark shadow moving towards them. All thoughts emptied out of his brain.

All he could see was Larissa in the direct path of the animal, frozen into place. Around them the helicopter noises grew louder, and through the frantic beating of his heart, Erik forced himself to remain calm. This was no different from any encounters he'd had with the wildlife here. Nothing he didn't know intimately already, except if Larissa got hurt... if he lost—

'We need to shoot up the flare gun so the helicopter can find us. Chances are the noise and brightness will be enough to scare the bear away,' Erik said, forcing himself to focus solely on the things he could control. His reaction and attachment to Larissa clearly weren't two of those things.

'What do you want me to do?' she asked, her voice steadier than he would have expected.

'Take a few steps back. But stay upright and as large as you can be. Don't crouch, and no sudden movements.' Erik stuck his hand into his pack again, finding the flare gun almost at the top and yanking it out. Then he stood, stepping around the patient and walking towards Larissa, who took slow and steady paces backwards with her arms raised. She kept facing forward, each step a loud crunch in the snow that echoed across the empty snow field.

'A few more steps and you'll be in my reach,' Erik said, his voice so strained he wasn't sure who he was trying to reassure: her or himself?

In the distance, the shadowy bear ambled towards them, its eyes lighting up when Erik's lamp caught them at the right angle. Just two more steps and then—

Erik raised the hand holding the flare over his head while he stretched out the other one towards Larissa. As his fingertips connected with her back, he squeezed the trigger of the flare. A glaring red light shot upwards with a loud bang, and underneath his hand, he felt Larissa flinch at the sound. But so did the bear, fully illuminated for a few seconds as the flare raced up into the sky. It reared back from the sound, stirring up a cloud of snow as it ran away into the distance.

The pressure in his chest eased instantly as the animal ran off. Before he could even think about doing differently, he hauled Larissa into his arms, pressing her against him. All the stress and anxiety of the last few minutes went into that hug, into holding her close until his terrified mind knew she was safe.

'I'm okay, Erik,' she said near his ear, mirroring the thoughts in his head.

She was fine. Safe. Yet his arms wouldn't let go. Not until the roaring of the helicopter was right above them.

'Help is here,' she said, and he nodded as he finally stepped away from her, the fear of losing her still clinging to him in a cold sweat.

Larissa was okay, but he wasn't sure if he would be after this moment—after seeing how deeply her safety affected him. How could he let her go at the end of her assignment?

CHAPTER TEN

'IT'S VALENTINE'S DAY.' Ally's familiar voice filtered out of the phone's speaker, filling the room.

'It sure is,' Larissa replied, looking between her friend's face and the view beyond her window. Like she could ever forget it was Valentine's Day when the entire hotel was decorated with roses, paper hearts and blinking lights.

'Two weeks and then we're back in England.'

'That's exactly right.'

Silence stretched between them, which wasn't unusual for them. They were at a point in their friendship where they could spend hours with each other and only exchange a few words. But that had been when they were closely working with each other and witnessing every moment of each other's lives. Now they were several thousand kilometres away from one another, and there were more than enough things they needed to discuss. Only Larissa didn't want to mention any of them because they involved Erik.

And she had an inkling that Ally was rather quiet for the same reasons.

Ever since they'd returned from the research centre, they'd been sneaking around—exclusively at the hospital after the other staff had gone home. With his parents being far too interested in his love life, they couldn't come here, and he hadn't invited her to his place. Though she tried not to dwell on that.

They weren't a couple, so she couldn't expect anything of him.

'Do we do our usual thing? Order food and watch an entire season of *The Great British Bake Off*?'

Ally frowned. 'I don't know if I can stream it from here. Getting messages through to you is sometimes a struggle. Anyway, I thought you'd have other plans?'

They fell quiet again, and Larissa stared at her friend, her own frown deepening. She would have to bring it up, wouldn't she? The last thing she wanted was to dive deep into whatever was happening between her and Erik.

No, she needed a different topic. So she blurted out the only other thing she could think of that they hadn't talked about. 'I almost got eaten by a bear.'

'Wait, what?' Ally's eyebrows rose. 'Your confession is not about Thor? I thought that's why you're being depresso espresso on Valentine's Day.'

'What? No, I'm not in love with Erik.' Heat rushed up her neck and into her face as she uttered her denial, and she ignored the tightness around her chest at those words. Of course she wasn't in love with Erik. That wasn't possible. They had both agreed that anything above a friendship with certain benefits would be far too complicated to navigate.

'So why are you moping around on Valentine's Day? Why aren't you lighting up the town with your Nordic god impersonator?' Ally crossed her arms in front of her chest, pushing out her chin in a defiant challenge. Like Larissa telling the truth about her feelings was somehow an affront to her friend.

'Light up the town? You mean go to one of the three bars that I've been to several times already and have a beer before slinking back to the hospital?' She paused, worried how nice the thought sounded. Though instead of going back to the hotel, Larissa would prefer to go to Erik's cabin, where they could have some alone time. Outside of a few stolen—and perilous—moments at the hospital, they hadn't really spent the night together since they'd returned from their trip to the research outpost.

'You talk about him *every day*,' Ally insisted, poking further into feelings Larissa would rather remain unexplored.

'Yeah, so? I talk about you every day. Doesn't mean I'm in love with you. Is that what you're suggesting? That you would totally move to a little island for someone you happen to talk about every day so that you could be together, even though that would put us several time zones away? And who even has the time to remain friends? Certainly not you when you are slipping deep into that new relationship energy.'

Ally tilted her head far enough that her ear touched her shoulder as she looked at Larissa through the screen of her phone. 'I didn't suggest any of this,' she said, brows high on her forehead. 'I think there is a rather curious dose of projection happening. You think staying in Svalbard would break our friendship? Because I can tell you I have never heard something this ridiculous in my life.'

'What? No. There's no projecting going on. I'm talking about hypotheticals.'

'Larry...'

'What I said wouldn't ever be true, because he doesn't want to leave Svalbard, and I could never move here. My life is in Frome. With you.' Was this woman seriously trying to make this about *him*? Because that was ridiculous. Her feelings for Erik didn't run any deeper than their casual fling allowed. She couldn't let herself go there.

'I don't think you're being honest with yourself,' Ally said, her voice soft, yet her words stung anyway as they rang familiar in her mind. They'd had a similar conversation before everything with Rachel had gone up in flames. She'd been right about her not wanting to see the truth back then, too.

'Okay, so, even if I were into him—which I'm still disputing—he is clearly not that hot on me. I mean, I'm sitting here all by myself on Valentine's Day, and he knows I'm not doing anything. Or anyone.'

Ally opened her mouth to reply, but a knock from the door interrupted her. Larissa looked between her friend and the door before calling out, 'Who is it?'

'It's Erik,' a deep voice said. Even though the door muffled the sound, she knew from the high-pitched squeal coming from her phone that Ally had heard it.

'He came to get you for V-Day,' her friend whispered, eyes wide enough that Larissa could see her irises changing into an obnoxious heart shape like a cartoon character's.

'I promise you he didn't,' Larissa replied, though a small and traitorous part inside her wondered the same thing. 'I'll call you back in a bit.'

Larissa hit the disconnect button just as her friend's face transformed with shock, and then stood up, opening the door to the man she had apparently manifested here by denying the depth of their connection. He leaned against the door-frame with his signature subdued smile that grew brighter as he saw her.

'You keep on coming to see me at the hotel. Either I

should feel very honoured or the nosiness of your family was overly dramatised,' she said, and then immediately regretted the words. How could she make light of something he'd told her in confidence? How would she feel if he made jokes about her dysfunctional family?

But Erik only huffed out a laugh as he righted himself. 'Their schedules are quite rigid. I know when I can sneak in without being seen,' he said, amusement lighting up his face.

'So I'm your secret?' Larissa tried her best to sound playful but didn't quite stick her landing. She winced when her words sounded far more needy than she meant to come across.

'In this scenario, *I'm* the secret,' he said, and then he took a step closer, putting himself squarely in her space.

Larissa had to look up to keep eye contact, though that didn't last all that long as Erik bent his head down to brush a kiss onto her lips.

'I just finished up at the hospital and wondered if you want to have dinner tonight?' he asked when their lips parted, though his face remained close to hers so that each of his breaths swept across her cheeks.

'Where do you want to go?' His scent enveloped her, making it so much harder to remember all the things she'd just assured Ally. They really shouldn't go on a date on Valentine's Day. That's what people who meant something to each other did.

'Let's pick up some things at the shop and go to my place. No chance of being overheard by certain people.' He angled his mouth over hers as he said that, dragging her into another kiss that had her knees trembling with the effort to keep her upright.

So this really was a date. Then she should definitely

say no. This would be far from appropriate and only prove Ally's point that she was in a relationship-type situation when she knew she wasn't.

'Plus, I want to show you something tomorrow morning. I had hoped it would happen today but... well, let's say the stars didn't align,' he added, breathing another kiss onto her lips.

Show her something? That was enough to poke at her curiosity and gave her a reason to ignore the cautious voice in her head telling her that if she spent Valentine's Day at his house, she would slip far too deep into this thing between them to find her way out again.

'What are you making me?'

There was something just right about seeing Larissa surrounded by his things. She lay on a plush carpet in front of the fire burning in his small fireplace, staring into the flames as if in a trance. And right next to her lay Midnight, her snout wedged underneath Larissa's hand and begging for ear scratches that she was all too willing to give.

'She will be insufferable with me now when you're not around,' Erik said as he rounded the couch and got onto the floor next to her.

Larissa gave Midnight another rub before turning around so she was facing him. A lazy smile spread over her lips, and Erik couldn't help it. He reached out and traced her lips with his thumb before touching her cheek.

'I was really worried about you out there when we responded to the animal attack,' he said, his fingers tangling into the stray strands of hair on her face.

'I know, but you prepared me well for the situation, Erik. I was fine and in no more danger than any of the others.' He knew that was true, saw the logic in it himself. But despite all of that, the fear that had gripped him was of a different kind altogether. Primal. And an indicator of how far he had let things go between them. How his feelings had taken over any rational thinking.

Even now, all he could think about was how he wanted her around in his cottage because, according to his brain, she was the missing piece in his life. Two hours in here and the place already *felt* different. Apparently, he'd been waiting for something—someone—very specific to appear and make it all fit. He'd tried so hard to do that with Astrid, had bent and broken himself to glue things together and give the illusion of wholeness.

'I enjoy seeing this,' he said, even though he didn't know why—or where he was heading with the observation. At the very least, he knew that they'd promised to be truthful with each other. But whether what he was about to say was a truth that needed to be said, he wasn't sure.

'You like seeing what? Your spoiled dog stealing all of my warmth?' Larissa replied, chuckling.

'Yes, I like that you're in her space and she's perfectly happy with that. I like...seeing you in my cottage. You fit right in here.' Erik had no idea what he was trying to accomplish other than letting her know him—know this new feeling inside his chest, even though they would only share the thing between them for a short two weeks.

Her lips parted as his words sank in. The words that sounded so much like a confession he was not ready to give. Would never be ready to give because their lives didn't align in such a way.

But lying down on the floor of his cottage and holding her close to him, he could no longer deny how she made his heart soar to new heights. How genuine terror had gripped him when he'd thought she was in danger and when he'd played out the thought of losing her so soon. That was a dark place he didn't want to return to.

Despite all of his best efforts to keep her away from the soft part inside his chest, Larissa had wiggled her way past his defences, and he was now at her mercy—in love with this woman he shouldn't want as much as he did.

'Erik, I... It's so beautiful here. When we came here to walk Martin's dog, I already wanted to know what it looks like in here.' She made a show of looking past him and around the small living room. 'It's much nicer than my hotel room—no offence to your birthright, of course,' she quickly added, and Erik laughed.

'No offence taken. They are cosy rooms but not really designed for full-time occupancy.' His hand drifted lower, grazing over her neck before slipping down her arm and relishing the goose pimples he left on her skin as his fingertips moved downwards. Then he said another thing he knew he should keep to himself, but something about her lying in his arms took him into places he promised himself he wouldn't go.

'Why don't you stay here? It'll be more comfortable for you, and I enjoy having you close.' To emphasise his point, he drew her closer and pressed a gentle kiss onto her lips.

This probably wasn't a good idea. His parents would notice that she hadn't been in her room for ages, and he would be the first suspect in her sudden disappearance. But he needed her close, regardless of what the rumours would be. This was ending in two weeks, and he would have every second of those.

Larissa hummed against his lips, a sound he'd grown to love. Like the pressure of his lips against hers was enough to send sparks of pleasure ricocheting through her—which was true for him, too. This connection was unlike anything he'd ever experienced. It made him wish that things were different. That he could be someone who left—or asked people to stay. But Erik was still Erik. Nothing had changed, so nothing *could* change between them.

Larissa huffed when they parted, her lips swollen and red from where his beard had rubbed against her face. The sight sent a flash of arousal racing down his spine, and he pushed himself closer to her.

Larissa gasped, shivering against his length now pressed between them. 'Are you asking me to stay here with you? Move in here with you?'

Her breath grazed his face, her scent enveloping him, making it hard to keep his thoughts straight. The softness pressing against him drained all the blood from his upper body, and his desire for her left no room for anything else.

Move in? Yes, that would make the rest of their arrangement far easier. What had her confused about that?

'Yes, stay here with me. If that's what you want, too.' To underline his words, he flexed his hips so he pushed against her again, and Larissa's eyes fluttered shut for a moment.

That Larissa would spend more time here changed nothing between them. She still wanted to leave and rebuild her life in England while he remained rooted to Svalbard. They both agreed that there was no way for them to live a life together that wasn't temporary. But if a temporary life was the only thing he could get, he still wanted to make the best of it.

'Wake up, beautiful.' Erik's low voice enveloped her, and Larissa sank deeper into the warmth that surrounded her.

This sleep had been the best in days—weeks even. There was no way she was going to pass up this time by waking up. No thanks.

The bed shook slightly, threatening to fully pull her out of her sleepy state, and then Erik's warm mouth pressed kisses on her bare shoulder and slowly travelled up her neck until he reached her ear. 'We need to get dressed. There's something I want to show you, remember?'

Larissa opened her eyes, but her lids were way too heavy, and gravity won this battle as she closed them again. Above her, Erik chuckled, his arms wrapping around her and pulling her into his solid front. Her body melded against his as if they'd been made for each other, her curves fitting perfectly into the dips and valleys that were Erik.

This moment was perfect, and she didn't want it to slip away.

'I promise you it's worth it. We can crawl straight into bed again afterwards. Unless someone pages with an emergency, I don't have any plans today.' His voice was low and soft and enveloped her with a different warmth. Her foggy mind reached out to his words, grasping at them, and with a sigh, she forced her eyes open again.

A warm light coming from an alarm clock on his bedside table lit up the small bedroom, and Larissa turned towards it. She squinted to make out the numbers on the display, and when the time of day clicked into place, she widened her eyes and sat up in bed.

'It's almost nine? How did I sleep so long?' Without the sun giving her any indication of when to get up, Larissa had developed the habit of getting up at six and starting her day by calling or texting Ally before heading over to the hospital. Even on the days she didn't need to go to work, her body now automatically woke up at the right time.

Erik sat up with her as he gave a shrug. 'My alarm clock lit up at six, but the light didn't seem to bother you.'

She glanced over at Erik, looking down at his exposed torso. On its own accord, her hand went up to smooth over the dark blond hair covering his chest. The coarse feeling sent a shiver down her spine and shook the last vestiges of sleep from her.

'Good morning,' he said as he bent over to brush a kiss over her lips. Larissa melted against him, soaking in the warmth of his body, and was all but ready to lose herself in his touch again when he grabbed her by the shoulders and pushed her away.

'If you don't get dressed now, we might miss it,' he said. Before she could reel him in again, he rolled out of bed and began collecting his clothes off the floor.

Bundled up in all the layers she usually put on for an excursion into the icy fields of Svalbard, Larissa sat on a bench on Erik's porch. A soft cloud of steam rose from the insulated mug in her hands whenever she opened the lid to take a sip. Erik sat next to her, his arm casually draped around her shoulders and pulling her into his warm body.

She'd been wrong earlier. *This* moment was perfect. It was messy and confusing, and she didn't really know what to think after last night. But despite all of that, this was exactly where she wanted to be right now. With Erik.

Because the thing she'd been fighting for, the emotions she'd denied having to Ally, were burning inside her chest right now. She was in love with Erik. Larissa wanted not just him, but *this* life here. Where people knew each other and cared for one another. Growing up by herself with only minimal help or attention from her parents from a far too early age, she didn't know what it was like to have an entire village at her side. Not until now, when she'd met and treated and formed connections with all the people in Svalbard. With Erik.

He'd asked her to stay. To move into his cabin. Her heart had nearly burst out of her chest as he'd said it, chipping away at her last defences and bringing her face-to-face with her feelings for Erik.

But he'd asked her to stay. Had told her that he *liked* seeing her entangled in his life. Somewhere between their time at the research centre and now, he had changed his mind. And she had changed hers, too.

Larissa would stay.

Because she'd been able to live her life exactly how she'd wanted. There was no hardship, no compromise. No attempts to change her. Things were different from the past, from Rachel.

Maybe now she could finally have it all.

'There, look at the horizon,' Erik said above her, and she shifted her eyes towards it. Erik had put a harness with light strips on Midnight and attached a long leash before letting her loose in the snow. She smiled as the dog jumped around in the snow, then focused back on the horizon.

The inky black was now a familiar sight, the stars so much brighter than she'd ever seen them in England. But slowly the darkness gave way, and a lighter blue mixed into the blackness. Larissa sat up as she noticed the gradual change, watching with wide eyes as for the first time in weeks, the sky changed colour—permitting a hint of a sunrise with the light blue haze covering the horizon.

When she turned to look up at Erik, his smile was broad and brilliant under the light of the stars. He was an amazing person, and she couldn't believe that chance had brought them together. Or that he felt the same way as she did.

'I thought you might like to see Svalbard's first official sunrise of the year.' He gestured towards the horizon.

Larissa smiled up at him, her chest so full she could hardly contain it. 'I'm keen to see what it's like when the sun comes up and never dips below the horizon.'

Erik tilted his head to the side, a fine line appearing between his brows. 'Are you planning to come back in a few months to see it?'

The warm glow in her chest winked out, letting the icy air surrounding them filter through her skin. 'No, I—' She paused, unsure what to say as her mind spun out of control. Because that question he'd asked made absolutely no sense. Of course she was going to be here. He'd *asked* her to…

'I thought I'd stay here. With you. Move in. That's what you said. To move in with you and stay here. Together.' Her voice strained against the words, suddenly fearful of saying them when just a few moments ago, the truth of her feelings for Erik had run so clearly through her. There was no way she had misinterpreted that moment.

He was leading her on.

Beside her, Erik stiffened, and when his arm fell away from her shoulder, Larissa realised that somehow they hadn't meant the same thing at all.

'That's not… Larissa, why are you saying this? We had an agreement about what this could and couldn't be. You can't do this to me now.' His voice was rough and so unlike anything she'd heard from him in the past few weeks. Ice gathered around her stomach as she sensed Erik slipping out of her grasp—and with him the future she'd only dared to envision yesterday.

'Do this to you?' Her defences kicked in at his phrasing. '*You* started this. You said last night how much you enjoyed seeing me in your cottage—in your life. It was you who asked me to stay. I thought you were saying—' The rest of her words died in her throat as all breath left her lungs at his shocked expression.

'That's not what I said.' He paused, and she could see the internal debate flickering over his expression as he, too, replayed last night in his head. 'I invited you to stay with me because we only have two weeks left, and I thought we both wanted to make the most of this. I never meant…'

His voice trailed off, and Larissa was grateful for the silence. She pushed herself off the bench, bringing some physical distance between them. Strange how this was the thing she wanted both most and least in this situation.

He hadn't meant any of it.

The realisation hit her like a ton of bricks, pushing any remaining vestiges of air out of her lungs. 'Oh my God, I feel so *stupid*. I was ready to let it all go, despite my growing feelings for you. I had convinced myself that it didn't matter and that I couldn't go back on my word. But then you showed up at my door, and you invited me over to your house. Not only that, but you told me you want me to stay, and dumb me thought you meant *forever*.'

Erik's gaze snapped to her, his eyes widening enough that she knew he had no idea about the depth of her feelings. So there was no way he reciprocated any of them. She was just some fun entertainment. Just like he said she would be. She should have believed him.

'Larissa, I'm sorry. This isn't—I couldn't...' His head drooped down, nervous fingers running through his still dishevelled hair. Hair she now knew to be so soft as it ran through her fingers. She wished she had never learned that, because missing him would be the hardest part about leaving.

'We haven't discussed forever. Didn't we both agree that this couldn't be anything more than that?' His voice wobbled. Or maybe Larissa just wished to hear that—to know that this was hard for him. 'I can't leave here.'

Larissa forced a breath down. 'I didn't ask you to leave, nor would I *ever* do that. Not after learning what happened to you and how you feel about Svalbard. You don't believe the people have grown on me, too?'

'I can't ask you to stay here. What if—'

She interrupted him. 'You're not asking. That's the whole point of this. I thought you were, but apparently that was all in my head. Our connection, our *emotions*. All made up.'

Erik surged to his feet. With one step he was halfway across to her, and his hands hovered in the air. But then they dropped back to his sides in tight fists. 'You'll change your mind. Living here is not as easy as you seem to think. You've been here six weeks. What makes you think you can even fathom what the rest of your life would be like here?'

She staggered back at his words. His lack of faith in her

conviction… 'You don't believe I know what I'm doing? That I know my own mind?'

He shook his head. 'I just don't believe love can conquer all.'

She flinched at that, his words hitting her right in the chest. 'In that case, let me say that while I appreciate the offer, I won't stay with you in the cottage. I'm afraid my feelings for you run a lot deeper than you're comfortable with, and so it's best we stop this now.' She forced the words out of her tight throat, swallowing the emotions trying to escape her. This was the right thing to do, no matter how wrong it felt.

'Larissa, I don't know how we got here. Please, I…' The genuine hurt in his voice urged her to rush over to him, wrap her arms around him and pull him close. She pushed that urge away.

'Please take me back home. I think we said everything we needed to say.' Erik stared at her, his mouth set in an almost defiant frown. Internally, she willed him to take it all back, to tell her he felt the same way and they could figure things out.

Her heart shattered when he let out a sigh and nodded as he untied Midnight's leash and reeled her back in.

This wasn't how they were supposed to end. Yet here they were.

The next two weeks would be tricky. But there was no way she would abandon her posting here, no matter how much she hurt. Because even though her feelings revolved around Erik, the people of this place still needed her. She hadn't taken this responsibility lightly, and that he would even insinuate she did sliced far deeper than she'd expected.

Though how she would go about working the next two

weeks without seeing him and deepening the wounds inside her, she had no clue. Larissa would just have to figure it out.

One day at a time.

CHAPTER ELEVEN

IT WAS DONE. Erik stared at the clock on his phone, then lifted the beer bottle to his lips and took a deep breath. Fragments of conversations from other patrons of the bar floated around him, but he didn't pay them any mind.

Her plane had officially left, and Larissa was out of his life forever. The two weeks he'd hoped to have—fourteen days he'd known would never be enough to satiate the need for her—had been cut short by her unexpected confession. And his hideous response to it. Just thinking about it sent a cringe through him, and he took another sip of his beer to chase the memory away.

He'd seen her at the hospital, going about her shifts like the professional he knew her to be, but somehow they had reached the silent agreement that they would stay out of each other's way. Or maybe the hurt he'd inflicted on her ran too deep for her to even see him. The problem was how badly he wanted to see her. How *desperately* he wanted to go back on his word and tell her the truth. Because the last two weeks had given him enough distance and perspective to understand how much Larissa had changed his life for the better.

And it was because of that knowledge that he couldn't let her stay here. Not when she might end up resenting him for making her move. What if she wasn't happy here?

They would end up at the same intersection again, where they would each have to bend in ways they couldn't just to accommodate the other.

'I think that's the first time I've seen you in here,' a familiar voice said, and he looked up just in time to watch his sister plop down on the opposite chair.

'I could say the same thing,' he replied, though he knew that was because he rarely went out to any of the bars in town. Not unless one of his patients was celebrating something important or there was a community event.

'That's because *you're* never here.' Anna reached over to grab his bottle and took a sip. She shook as she set it down, scrunching up her face. 'Ah, this still tastes awful.'

'Then don't drink it,' he replied, rolling his eyes at his sister.

Anna didn't reply, but instead reached across the table and touched his phone to reveal the time. She hummed as she tapped her finger against her cheek.

'What?'

'It's an unusual time for you to be here. It's not right after a shift at the hospital, which I think would be the natural time for you to be out.' She paused, levelling a stare at him that seemed vaguely familiar. It was the same look his mother had used on them growing up. Before he could say anything, she continued, 'Unless you wanted to be somewhere noisy and busy for a certain event. But what could that event be?'

Now it was his turn to level the same withering glare at her. 'If you have something to say, just come right out and say it.'

'You needed to be somewhere with people around you for when Larissa's flight departed.' There wasn't any smugness in her words like he'd expected, which had him looking up at her. Her expression was soft, as if she not only knew how he was feeling, but she also understood.

He said nothing to that. Didn't really know what to say. That he had let the woman he loved slip out of his grasp? That he flip-flopped between regret and emptiness whenever he thought about his life without her? Admitting that to himself was already far too much of a challenge. He couldn't possibly tell his sister. Even though she was sitting right there, urging him to go on.

'We got close during her time here. It shouldn't be surprising to feel something about her departure,' he said, hedging his words carefully.

By the frown appearing on his sister's face, he knew she wasn't going to let this go. 'I admit I've let you take the easy way out far too often. To the point where you don't really have to confront any of the tension around you.'

Erik bristled at that. 'The easy way out? I don't think—'

'I get that our parents can be overbearing, especially when a significant other is involved. Believe me, they never shut up about me finding someone and settling down, either. I get it. So when the whole thing with Astrid happened, I said nothing. I did nothing, either. That's probably on me.' Anna sighed as she shook her head, ignoring what Erik had been about to say. 'She wasn't good for you anyway, so I have limited regrets there. But with Larissa... You came to the hotel. *Unprompted.*'

He had. After avoiding the hotel ever since his breakup with Astrid two years ago, he had stopped going there because he had no reason to be there. They were too nosy, too obsessed with the next match that might come in and turn his life upside down. He just couldn't deal with the consistent comments, so he'd stopped going all together.

But when he'd come back from Norway after not seeing Larissa for a few days, he hadn't hesitated to seek her out at his parents' hotel. In fact, her whereabouts hadn't even factored into his thinking at all. He'd just wanted to see her.

Just like he wanted to see her now. Or any time of the day.

'She said she wants to move here,' he whispered on an exhale.

'I figured as much when she hardly left the hotel for her last fourteen days here. I also imagine you told her she couldn't possibly mean that and subsequently pushed her away.' She reached across the table again, and Erik looked up when she rested her hand on top of his clenched fist.

'She doesn't know what it means to live here. What she would give up.' That was at the heart of the problem. How could he accept her sacrifice when he knew she would come to regret it eventually?

'That's not really for you to decide,' Anna said, giving his hand a squeeze for emphasis.

Erik opened his mouth to protest, but the words died in his throat. He had no real argument for that. Or against that. Though he was loath to hear it, his sister had a point. Larissa had not only made the choice to come here in the first place, but she had also sought the company of the people in the village. Had even gone so far as to walk Martin's dog when he couldn't. And during the incident with the polar bear, she hadn't needed any of his guidance. She'd known how to act because she had paid attention to the people around her and how to live a life on Svalbard.

'What if she regrets coming here? What if love isn't enough?' he said so quietly, Anna had to lean forward.

The last fourteen days had been torture, and he was at the point where he had to admit to himself that Larissa owned his entire heart.

He loved her.

She squeezed his hand again and said, 'What if it is, though?'

Erik stilled at the question. It tripped up something inside him simply because he had never asked that question. All of his thoughts had revolved around the sacrifices she would have to make and the regret that would follow. That's how it had happened with Astrid. But had she ever really fit in the way Larissa had? He couldn't imagine Astrid ever offering to walk someone's dog.

'That's a lot riding on what-if,' Erik said, even as he felt himself slipping—let himself consider whether the what-if his sister posed could be true. What would life be like if Larissa was here with him, running the hospital and then going back home with him every night?

It would be the best version of his life he could imagine. If she were to give him this gift—and she had—he would be foolish not to grasp it with both hands.

The clarity of his thoughts must have been easy to read, for a grin spread over Anna's face. 'You're a doctor *and* you grew up in this family. So you know that when things don't work out, you deal with it when it happens. You don't overthink what *could* happen in some hypothetical scenario. I'd hate for you to lose out on something great just because it *might* not work out.' She paused, withdrawing her hand from his. 'What happened with Astrid was messed up. I know that her leaving felt like you would never be able to have something like this again. But give Larissa some credit. She might know what she wants. Don't let a hypothetical get in the way of your own happiness.'

His own happiness? Was it absurd that until this point, he had never contemplated it? For the longest time, he'd believed that the ideas of his parents were the most important thing in his life, and when he'd defied their wishes, he'd felt it every single day. Then the only way of making this sacrifice worth it was to ensure he had done it for the greater good. To help his community.

Asking Larissa to stay here with him would only be for him. Because he loved her. She needed to know that, in case his actions hadn't made that clear. And of course they hadn't, because like the idiot he was, he'd pushed her away in fear of history repeating itself. But how could it when things were so fundamentally different? When he hadn't even hesitated to part ways with Astrid, but the thought of Larissa now being out of his reach squeezed all the air from his lungs?

Anna nodded as if she'd been following his thoughts. 'Great. Now that we sorted this out, I have a present for you.'

Erik furrowed his brow. A present? 'I don't have time for that. I need to figure out what to do about Larissa. I told her to leave, let her believe I didn't feel the same way about her.' What a foolish thing he'd done. He'd been wrapped up in his own drama and hadn't even seen what was clear in front of him—how much he loved Larissa and that his life would be so much less without her.

Would she even give him a chance to speak to her again? He couldn't fault her if she was done with him for good. Erik hadn't really left any wiggle room.

'Well, I happen to know that someone didn't check out this morning. It seems like she moved her flight to next week and booked another week at the hotel.' Anna smiled as she said that, then grabbed his beer bottle to take another sip that made her shudder in disgust.

'Wait… She's still here?' Was that what she was trying to tell him? That Larissa hadn't left on the flight today? Erik was on his feet before he even had the chance to think differently.

'Go grovel and get her back. Going by all the ice cream containers in her bin, you'll need to do a lot of grovelling,' his sister said, but Erik was only half listening as he pocketed his phone and left the bar.

Some strange twist of fate had granted him one more chance to tell her how he felt. He would not let it slip through his fingers this time.

'Here is a suggestion—instead of watching another season of *The Great British Bake Off*, why don't you go talk to Thor and tell him you're not taking no for an answer?' Ally said with a surprisingly straight face.

Larissa looked into her half-empty tub of ice cream and then down at the oversized tee and equally large sweatpants she'd been living in for two days now. There were some clear advantages of being out of work, and not having to look presentable was definitely one of them.

'Mmm, pass,' she said as she speared her spoon into the tub once more to retrieve another mouthful of ice cream.

After their disastrous Valentine's Day date, Larissa had to keep it together and professional for an entire two weeks. Two weeks of seeing him at the hospital and wondering how she had got it so wrong. Though she knew she'd kept her cool at work, the pain following her around had been near overwhelming.

Ally sighed, hanging her head in defeat. 'Why not?'

'Because he basically told me to pack it and leave him alone,' Larissa said, pointing her smudged spoon at her best friend. Even in sub zero temperatures, ice cream remained the saddest and most calming of foods.

When Ally frowned, Larissa added, 'There is no other way to slice it, Ally. I told him I wanted to stay, and he said he didn't mean to suggest that, so I left. That was the sensible thing to do in this situation.'

'You're not supposed to do the sensible thing when in love. No, you do the crazy things, the scary things. The things that are living inside your heart and just about ready to burst.' Ally waved her arms around as she said that, painting an overdrawn picture that was almost enough to make Larissa smile and feel normal again.

Though she doubted she would ever fully feel like herself again. Not when Erik had forever rearranged things inside her. She'd come here convinced that her life would be about her work, about always watching love and connections unfold from the outside without ever getting to be a part of it. Because her parents hadn't taught her these skills, she would forever miss out on them. Rachel had supplied her with proof that she couldn't be with someone the way books and movies had taught her, and now Erik... The way she had misread his intentions just showed that she couldn't do it.

Larissa was flawed, and there was no way out of it.

'I know this face. Stop doom-spiralling and thinking you are somehow broken inside. You are *not*. People get it wrong all the time.' She paused at the end of the sentence, and now it was Larissa's turn to roll her eyes.

'I'm just saying that I spent two months here getting to know the locals through my work at the hospital, and

I've grown to like them. I thought they'd grown to like me too, and it's bumming me out that I was wrong about this.' Erik's rejection had hit her far harder than she'd expected, and it taught her again not to trust her heart.

'That's not accurate, though. Erik didn't say that he loves you, but neither did you. So I don't think you can really judge him on that. There is no way a guy shows you the first sunrise of the year and doesn't want it to be a romantic gesture. But even if it's accurate, that doesn't mean everyone else rejected you, too.' Ally's stare bore into her even through the screen and thousands of kilometres between them. 'Hasn't Anna been supplying you with ice cream for two weeks? Does she know what went on between you two?'

She had. After coming home from the hospital one day, Larissa had found a mini-freezer next to her fridge and upon opening it had found it stacked up with different ice cream flavours that must have cost a fortune.

'I don't think so. Maybe? She saw us together at the hotel before Valentine's Day, but we weren't too obvious, I hope. She just knows I'm sad for some reason, and ice cream is the saddest food out there.'

Come to think of it, even though nobody *should* have known what happened between her and Erik, Anna hadn't been the only one to check in. Larissa knew that any kind of news in the community spread fast. However, because they'd never been a real couple, she'd thought no one would notice the tension between her and Erik.

But every day at work, Ingrid had checked in with her, sometimes even warning her of Erik's schedule and where he might be at certain times. Martin had also appeared at the hotel, offering her his and Storm's company if she wanted to go out.

Despite owing her no loyalty and only knowing her for two months, the community of Longyearbyen had shown up for her. Even through all the hurt, her heart squeezed at the thought, longing to remain a part of this. Except Erik didn't want her here.

'It doesn't matter. After what happened between us, there is no way I can just stay here. He's the head of the hospital I would need to work at, and I don't think he's well-inclined to hire me.' She paused, following the thoughts all the way to the end. This wasn't the first time in the last two weeks that Larissa had contemplated staying and wondered what would happen if she did. It scared her how much that thought enticed her.

So she quickly added, 'Plus, you're not here, and that's a non-negotiable for me.'

Ally shook her head. 'Oh no, no, no. Do not put this on me. I'm not letting you hide behind that flimsy excuse. We've made things work long-distance already. You're my ride or die, Larry. No amount of distance will ever change that.'

With her last excuse gone, Larissa had no choice but to look inward and confront the feelings that had been brewing for the last two weeks. She wanted to be with Erik far more than she could have ever expected when they'd started their fling. But even more, she felt a genuine connection to Longyearbyen and her place in it. She didn't want to leave, and a part of her had already known that when she'd moved her flight.

Leaving now, while everything had been unravelling round her, had just been too much for her. Because even though the fling with Erik was over, something inside her balked at the thought of leaving. At some point over the last eight weeks, this town had become her home. She couldn't just up and leave all of this behind, could she?

But how could she consider staying when her relationship with Erik was now so fraught? Would it even be possible when her ability to work hinged on him? He needed another doctor at the hospital, and her placement with New Health Frontiers showed he had trouble finding staff.

But did she really want to subject herself to seeing him every day?

'So you think I should stay? Even though I would have to work with my ex...something day in and day out?' It sounded like the worst idea she'd ever had, so why was her heart fluttering at the idea?

'I can't tell you what to do, but I can say that I've never seen you this involved outside of our friendship. Even if you take Erik out of it, I've seen a change in you. I think you'd be silly not to explore it.' Ally shrugged. 'And even if it doesn't end up working out, you can always come back. What do you have to lose at this point?'

Larissa snorted at that because the answer was clear— precious little. Her heart was already battered and bruised. What was one more round of that if it meant some closure for her?

She groaned as she pushed herself to her feet, stashing the half-eaten ice cream in her freezer. 'You're really annoying. I hope you know that,' she said with a grumble. But Ally was right. The deep sorrow she'd experienced in the last two weeks was connected to Erik, yes. But it was also connected to the people she'd met along the way and a sense of belonging almost foreign to her.

It was worth a fight, even if she got hurt all over again. If he told her to get lost, she would accept it—but she would tell him she planned on staying with or without him. This had become her home, too.

'So what are you going to do now?' Ally asked, sitting up straight.

'I'm going to go talk to him. Because you're bullying me to do that. I would be happy to just come back and forget this ever happened, but you need me to go through some personal growth.'

Ally laughed at that, the sound burrowing through her chest and straight into her heart—filling her with a glowing warmth. 'I'm proud of you, Larry. I know something great is waiting for you down that road, even if it is a struggle to get there.'

Larissa swallowed the tightness building in her throat, then said her goodbyes to Ally after getting dressed and getting the okay from her best friend that she looked presentable enough to confront the man she was in love with one last time.

When she picked up the phone and opened his message thread to send him a text, she froze in place. A new message from him had appeared.

Erik: I'm coming over. Please open the door. I need to talk to you before you leave.

Her heart beat in her throat as she read those words and absorbed the urgency in them. Her fingers hovered over the keyboard on the phone screen, trying to squeeze the right words out of her brain. Was he coming to see her off? To tell her he'd made a mistake? Or did he somehow know she wanted to stay, and he was coming over to stake a claim on Svalbard?

She'd typed out, I'm still at the hotel. Are you—when

a knock sounded on her door. She almost dropped her phone as her heart leapt into her throat.

Hand shaking, she reached for the handle and pulled the door open. Erik stood in the door-frame, as tall and handsome as she remembered him. Her heart ached for her to reach out and touch him. Sink into the touch she had not felt in so long.

'I didn't leave.' She blurted out the first words coming to her mind and then cringed when she heard them. Of course she hadn't left. She was standing right here in front of him.

'I know,' he said with a lopsided grin, and some of the tension eased out of her at the pearly flash of teeth. He was smiling. Not as brightly as he used to, but he *was* smiling.

'Funny thing, I was about to text you when your message came up.' His eyebrows shot up at her words, his head tilting to the side enough that the top of his head brushed against the door-frame. The smile he flashed her was tentative, and she had to resist being sucked into his orbit straight away. She needed to talk to him first.

'I'm considering staying here. On Svalbard.' Surprise rippled over his face when she added, 'For good.'

'Is that why you didn't fly out today? You want to stay?' Larissa stilled at that. He knew her flight would have been today?

'I… No. Or maybe yes. I don't know.' His eyes were alight with a familiar spark, and she took a step back as his gaze threatened to undo her composure. 'My feelings about you haven't changed, but what I realised in the last two weeks is that I built something here. Something that I cherish. I want to share this with you, I really do. But I need you to know that I'm staying, no matter what.'

Larissa let out a deep breath as the words flowed out of her and she told him what she needed him to know. What she hadn't understood two weeks ago when everything happened. Erik was a big part of why this place had become her home, and her heart would ache if he didn't choose her. But he had to understand that his choice wasn't between her and his community. Regardless, she wasn't going anywhere.

Erik's expression slackened, and the lightness in his eyes—the spark of vulnerability—made her knees weak. Her eyes dipped down to his throat as he swallowed. His chest heaved as he took a deep breath and released it in a measured exhale.

'I owe you an apology, Larissa. I freaked out. *Hard.* Because I've never had someone be this important to me.' He paused to take another breath. 'I pushed you away because when you said you couldn't wait to see the midnight sun with me, I could picture it. With every blink, the image of you being here forever formed in my mind, burned itself into my heart. But I... I've been in this moment before, and I was scared that this time I wouldn't survive losing the woman I love if I let myself sink into this relationship too deep.'

Larissa's breath caught in her throat. 'The woman you love?' Had he really just said those words?

He let out a thin laugh. 'Yeah, something I should have had the courage to say sooner. I love you, Larissa. When we were in bed and I was watching you slowly wake up, I thought I wanted to see this happen a thousand times over. Wanted to learn all the different ways you can wake up. It hit at that moment that if you asked me for something—*anything*—I would have done everything within my power to give it to you. That scared me to my bones, and so when you said you wanted to stay, I panicked.'

Erik lifted his hand but stopped just before he touched her. 'Please forgive me. I've been living alone for a long time, and I won't always know the right way to go about things. But I want to try. For you, I want to learn.' He let out a huff of laughter. 'I came here to tell you we can figure this out. As long as you take me back, I don't care how we do things. Because I love you, and I want you in my life in whatever form you're willing to give me.'

Larissa had stopped breathing halfway through his speech, and only as he finished did she remember to fill her lungs with air. 'I was crushed and thought about leaving immediately. After what happened with Rachel, I thought I would never let myself feel this way again. The risks were just not worth it. But you somehow slipped in, right under my skin.'

She brushed her hand over her arm, tracing over her skin as she paused, casting her eyes down as she searched for the right words. 'I don't want to repeat mistakes either. And maybe I did by making assumptions about your intentions without bringing it up. I heard what I wanted to hear and just ran with it. What is different now from where we both were before we met?'

'We are different. What *we* have is different. Unique.' His voice dropped low, sliding over her skin and through her pores. The air grew thick around them as he stepped close enough that she could count his eyelashes. 'I haven't felt this way about anyone, ever. And yes, it's mad, but I *know* I need you in my life, however you are willing to let me be in yours.'

Her throat was thick, and words refused to form in her voice box. So instead, she reached out to where his hand hovered in the air between them and took it into hers. Then she pulled him closer, over the threshold of her room and into her arms. 'I love you, Erik. And I'll make sure that we *are* different. Because you showed me things I didn't realise I could feel. This place.' She lifted her hand, indicating where they were but also so much beyond. 'This place taught me belonging on a level I've never experienced before. I want to be a part of this because it's already become a part of me.'

His shoulders slumped, and his weight sagged against her in a relief that was too stark for words. Not that they needed words when they had their hands and bodies and lips to express what they couldn't otherwise.

Larissa sighed when his arms came around her, pressing her close to him. She breathed in his scent and knew she had found what she hadn't realised she'd been looking for all this time.

'I'm home,' she whispered into his neck as he held her tight, and hoped this moment would last forever.

* * * * *

Nurse's Keralan Temptation
Becky Wicks

MILLS & BOON

Born in the UK, **Becky Wicks** has suffered interminable wanderlust from an early age. She's lived and worked all over the world, from London to Dubai, Sydney, Bali, NYC and Amsterdam. She's written for the likes of *GQ*, *Hello!*, *Fabulous* and *Time Out*, a host of YA romance, plus three travel memoirs—*Burqalicious*, *Balilicious* and *Latinalicious* (HarperCollins, Australia). Now she blends travel with romance for Mills & Boon and loves every minute! Find her on Substack: @beckywicks.

Also by Becky Wicks

Melting the Surgeon's Heart
A Marriage Healed in Hawaii
Tempted by the Outback Vet

Buenos Aires Docs miniseries

Daring to Fall for the Single Dad

Discover more at millsandboon.com.au.

Dedicated to Simon, Charley and the cats.

CHAPTER ONE

ALLY SWIPED THE mounting beads of sweat from her forehead, dragging her giant suitcase behind her through arrivals. Its front wheel hadn't been broken at Heathrow, but someone had obviously tossed it too hard onto the plane. Of course, her bag would embarrass her now, careening all around her like an obstinate shopping trolley.

'Where is she?' she muttered to herself, scanning the bustling crowd. Dr Anjali Kapur—the Indian physician who would soon be assigning her tasks on her two-month assignment with New Health Frontiers was supposed to be here to meet her.

Pulling to a stop by a vending machine, she fanned out her shirt at the neck, praying she wouldn't be stranded here. It was already a thousand degrees. Well, OK, maybe only twenty-eight, but the sweltering humidity of Kerala was so far a stark contrast to the cold and rainy home she'd left behind in Somerset.

'Alison Spencer?' A melodic voice called out from across the throng. Ally turned to see a striking woman with warm brown eyes and a big, welcoming smile heading towards her, waving a sign with her name on it that she had completely missed. For a qualified nurse she wasn't all that observant on the other end of the fifteen-hour flight from the UK to southern India. The four-hour layover in Doha hadn't helped. Due to a lack of seating, she'd flopped in a shisha lounge and politely declined offers from about three hopeful businessmen to indulge in a bubblegum-flavoured smoke-fest.

'Dr Kapur? Hi! Yes, I'm Ally.' Ally reached out for a sweaty handshake, which Anjali returned with a firm grip. Gosh, this woman was strong, she thought. And really quite striking in her fuchsia-pink lipstick. Anjali had the kind of thick black luscious hair usually seen in TikTok videos about hair-curling devices, and Ally was suddenly more than conscious of her own unbrushed auburn locks.

'Welcome to Kerala, Ally. Let's get you to base. The team can't wait to meet you.'

They walked together towards the car park. Ally couldn't help but admire Anjali's traditional Indian attire. The vibrant colours of her sari were mesmerising and almost seemed to dance around her with each step she took. In contrast, Ally felt painfully aware of her own 'very English' clothes—practical and plain, jeans and a white shirt, both now sticking uncomfortably to her skin in the heat.

'The weather can take some getting used to,' Anjali remarked, seeing her mop at her brow with the back of her hand. 'But don't worry, you'll adapt soon enough.'

'Thanks for the reassurance,' Ally replied with a wry smile, already imagining what colour sari she might buy, as soon as she located a market. She also couldn't help but wonder how Larissa was getting on, and bit back a laugh just imagining it. Larissa—or Larry as she liked to call her, seeing as it made them rhyme—had taken a similar assignment with New Health Frontiers, only in Svalbard, a Norwegian archipelago stuck like a fractured iceberg between mainland Norway and the North Pole. Calling it 'out of her comfort zone' didn't cut it.

'Ready for the drive to HQ?' Anjali asked as they approached the car. 'We have air conditioning.'

'Oh, that's music to my ears,' Ally responded, her worry momentarily put aside. She'd already decided that whatever challenges lay ahead she would face them head-on, just as she had done back home in Frome for her sister, Nora, and Oliver, and for herself. Or tried to, at least. After two years in the UK without so much as a weekend escape, she deserved this. She was owed the chance to do something different for herself, but it wasn't as though she didn't feel guilty at the same time. Nora couldn't go far, what with Oliver being in school, but she had been very encouraging about this opportunity, saying it was time at least one of them took some time out after what had happened. They'd helped each other out of the pit of grief after Matt and Albie died, leaving Nora a widow, Oliver without a dad, and herself without the most loving, loyal boyfriend she'd ever had.

Nora had said it would do her good to 'get out there and do something different'. So she'd agreed and dragged Larry along too. Well, to their respective placements in totally different places. Who knew what else they would've done anyway, after the clinic boarded up its doors? Five years of working there together. Five years of making it all but their second home and building a practice that their clients trusted. While Larry always had a Plan B, C, D and E to fall back on, the future without Matt had stretched out ahead of Ally as empty as the pizza box after their final staff party.

The drive to the NHF headquarters took roughly an hour. Ally struggled to make polite conversation when all she wanted to do was sleep. She couldn't help but think of Matt, either. He'd have liked it here. He'd wanted to visit India.

Two years…just over two years…since he and Albie took the boat out on what was meant to be the holiday of a lifetime in Sicily. Two years since she and Nora watched their boyfriend and husband respectively sail off on their lads' fishing trip. Two years since they discovered the boat had flipped, and their men were never coming home again.

Don't go there, Ally. You're here to focus on work.

Palm trees hung over the car most of the way. Horses and carts spoke of a life that was still semi-stuck somewhere in the eighteen hundreds, and the twinkling ocean, rising hills and vast watery landscapes soothed her mind at least.

The HQ building was much bigger than the local clinic she had worked at in Frome. It was modern and sleek, and it really stood out amongst the bustling city streets. Impressive, she thought. However, the moment she stepped through the doors of the New Health Frontiers headquarters, she got the distinct impression she'd just entered an entirely different world. The bustling facility was alive with sounds of people speaking multiple languages and the faint smell of disinfectant that reminded her of an overcrowded hospital. Medical supplies were stacked high on shelves, creating a maze through which staff seemed to navigate perfectly well despite the heat. Outside, Jeeps lined up like soldiers ready for their next mission.

'Everyone, this is Ally Spencer, our new community health nurse from England, who'll be with us till the end of February,' Anjali announced, leading Ally towards a group huddled around a table strewn with maps and documents. The small crowd looked up, offering welcoming nods and smiles, which she reciprocated.

'Meet Sameer, our logistics coordinator,' Anjali continued, pointing to a young man with a thick beard and round glasses. 'He makes sure everything runs smoothly.'

'Nice to meet you, Ally,' Sameer said warmly, extending his hand.

'This is Lila, our pharmacist,' Anjali continued. 'And Priya, one of our local translators.'

Ally followed behind Anjali, trying to memorise each person's name as they were introduced to her. There were actually more than her jet-lagged brain could handle. Dr Singh—head physician; Aryan—medical assistant; Rani—community outreach coordinator; Malik—lab technician... The list went on until, finally, Ally decided she would probably have to ask people to wear name badges the whole time, wherever she ended up. Still, as they walked through the headquarters, she soon felt excitement win out over her trepidation.

'Ah, yes. Ally, there's someone else I'd like you to meet,' Anjali said suddenly, stopping in front of a tall, striking, dark-skinned man who seemed to have appeared out of nowhere. Time ceased to tick as Ally took in his lean, muscular build and neat, short dark hair. His intense brown eyes conveyed a quiet intelligence that sucked her straight into some kind of vortex as he caught her gaze.

'Ally, this is Dev Chandran, one of our emergency medicine doctors,' Anjali introduced him with a smile. 'Dev, meet Ally Spencer.'

'Hi, Ally.' Dev extended his hand. 'Welcome to Kerala.'

He looked Indian himself, she thought, making a mental note of how his shirt was buttoned all the way to the top, as if he were afraid that people might forget to look him in the eyes if he revealed any more of that smooth, delicious mocha skin. Studious, yet sexy. And buff, too. When he wasn't being an emergency medic, she could tell he spent his time fending off wild elephants, flying over skyscrapers on motorbikes and sweeping women up in those sexy big brown arms. He looked good in those glasses too. *Good Lord*, this jet lag was kicking in hard.

'Hey, Dev,' she replied, trying to keep her voice steady as she shook his hand. His grip was firm, and something about the way he flashed a row of dazzling white teeth as he held her gaze made her heart race. He looked Indian sure enough, but did she detect an American accent? Canadian?

'Ally?' Dr Anjali Kapur's voice broke through her thoughts, and Ally blinked, realising she had been staring at Dev for quite a bit longer than was socially acceptable.

'Sorry,' she murmured, cheeks burning with embarrassment. She mumbled something about jet lag, wishing she had looked a bit nicer for these introductions.

'You must be tired,' Anjali replied, her tone gentle. 'It's been a long day already, and you've only just arrived.'

'Right.' Ally nodded, trying to focus on what her new colleague was saying. Dev was distracting her, and he wasn't even doing anything, just standing there looking great, looking at his phone. He frowned slightly as he read something and a line appeared in the middle of his forehead before he shoved it back into his pocket a little too hard. 'So, what's our assignment?' he asked now. 'You said Ally and I were on the first one together?'

Oh?

'Ah, yes,' Anjali began, turning to her. 'You and Dev

will be leading a two-week measles and rubella vaccination drive together in the Wayanad District.'

'Is that close by?' she asked hopefully, picturing a shopping trip to the market for something a little less suffocating to wear.

'No, it's pretty remote. You'll be living together in a modest camp for the first two weeks, working very closely in a small team. All experienced NHFers.'

'Sounds like an adventure.' Ally tried to sound enthusiastic because it actually did sound like an adventure, but the words 'modest camp' were a red flag. Still, at least she would get two weeks with Dev and his preppy shirts and muscles. Maybe he could even be her 'fun fling'. She bit back a smile at the dare she'd made with Larissa. They were both supposed to have a fun fling in their prospective placements—something juicy that they could discuss together over long-distance calls. Really, she'd suggested it more for Larry's benefit. Larry had been a bit down lately, following that messy break-up with Rachel.

Following Matt's death, Ally hadn't exactly been the centre of anyone's attention, nor had she wanted to be, especially not romantically. She hadn't even dated anyone else, and why would she have? Not only had she been grieving the loss of a loving three-year relationship with the man she swore she would have married, had he asked, she'd seen Nora's total and utter devastation, having been widowed at thirty-seven years old. Her sister and Albie had been married for only three years…she'd met Matt at their wedding!

It was all enough to put her off relationships for life. And yet, here she was, undeniably attracted to the drool-worthy Dev Chandran. Ugh. Well, no harm in a crush, she supposed. It wasn't likely to go anywhere, not with them living 'modestly' on a campsite for the next two weeks, and after that, who knew where she'd be sent elsewhere in the country?

Dr Kapur excused herself, telling them their Jeep was ready when they were. Ally offered a grateful smile as the physician walked away. Oh, so they *were* going *right* now? Dev must have caught her look of panic.

'She likes us to get straight into it,' he explained. 'You can shower when we get there. Shall we?' He gestured towards the exit, where one of the Jeeps was waiting to take them on their journey into wherever the Wayanad District was.

The car ride to the remote village was another flurry of vivid colours and bustling activity that whizzed by as Ally sat in the back seat beside Dev. She tried to take it all in as the scenery grew more expansive and hilly and remote, but her mind kept drifting back to that electric moment when Dev's dark eyes had met hers. That had been quite shocking, all things considered. She hadn't been aware she could still be surprised like that, or feel butterflies like that. Maybe she had been imagining it though. She was so tired.

'Your first time in India?' Dev's warm voice pulled her out of her reverie.

'Yes,' Ally said, fighting back another yawn. 'It's quite different from Frome, that's for sure.'

'Frome? That sounds…cosy.'

'Does it? Well, if you like being stuck inside when it rains all the time, I suppose it is,' she agreed. 'How about you? Where are you from?'

'Toronto, originally. My parents came over from Mumbai for my father's work before we were born,' Dev said, adjusting his glasses on his nose and leaning back in the seat. 'I've been all over the place with NHF.'

'Wow,' Ally breathed, genuinely impressed. 'You must have some incredible stories to tell.'

'I have a few,' Dev said.

'We? So you have siblings?'

'I have one brother, Romesh, and…' He stopped talking and turned away, his voice tinged with something she couldn't read, all of a sudden.

'And?'

'Just one brother,' he finished. There it was, the same look he'd had when she'd caught him staring at his phone earlier. He sighed and turned back to the window, and before she could probe him any further, her own phone buzzed. Larissa, checking in again from Svalbard:

About to arrive at the hotel, and the cold is already too much. How is the heat of Kerala treating you? Also, jealous that it's hot and I hate you.

Ally couldn't help but snicker at the photo. Larry was bundled up in so many layers it was a wonder she could even move. She couldn't wait for a proper catch-up video call, as soon as possible.

'Everything OK?' Dev asked, arching an eyebrow at her sudden laughter.

'Fine,' Ally replied, deciding that she'd update her friend later. She huffed another laugh to herself, picturing Larry huddled up in an ice hut clutching a club. What did natives use to fend off polar bears over there? Surely they didn't shoot them, being nearly extinct and all. Dev was looking at her, head tilted at an angle.

'Sorry… I was just wondering if my friend has seen a polar bear yet,' she said, by way of explanation.

'Did she go to the zoo today?'

Ally baulked. Then she snorted a laugh that lasted longer than she'd planned it to. Composing herself, she explained the assignment her friend had taken for the same organisation in Svalbard and did not miss the slight look of alarm cross Dev's face. She had to wonder, was he alarmed at an unprepared GP from Somerset being stuck three feet from the North Pole, or at the thought of being stuck here, in Kerala, with her?

'So, how did you two end up on opposite sides of the world?'

'Long story short,' Ally began. 'Our clinic in Frome was closing down, and we both had to take assignments elsewhere. We challenged each other to have an adventure while we figure out what's next—and also to…' She stopped herself. No need to tell him she was supposed to have a fling. It had been her idea, even though she wasn't entirely sure she was over Matt enough to go there with anyone else. She'd done it more in solidarity with Larissa, who was still reeling over her break-up and really needed something or someone else to distract her.

'So, you want an adventure?' Dev's laughter filled the car, and she realised it was quite a lovely sound. She could feel the vibrations of it, almost like tiny tremors in the air, resonating through her body. It was a warm and comforting sensation that lingered after he stopped and made her want more. She'd felt guilty every time she'd laughed, since the accident. Like, how dared she find amusement and joy in anything after what happened to her boyfriend, and Nora's husband?

'How's that working out for you so far?'

'Too soon to tell,' Ally replied. But before they could delve any deeper, the car came to a stop. She followed his eyes to the palm-fringed field with its mountainous background and a circle of modest beige tents. Several other members of their team were climbing out of their respective Jeeps and starting to lift boxes and supplies. So this would be their home while they worked the vaccination drive. It wasn't too bad, she supposed. Outside on muddy ground, Ally couldn't help but steal another glance at Dev as, finally, he released his throat from his collar and insisted on wheeling her suitcase for her, along with his. What a gentleman.

Maybe the dashing Dr Chandran would play a role in fulfilling her and Larry's challenge, she thought, training her eyes on his pert backside. Then she caught herself. There was much more at stake here than just a fleeting romantic encounter. This placement was probably going to test her in so many ways and, as Nora had said, she needed to do something that wasn't wallowing in what could have been if...

No.

With a deep breath, Ally squared her shoulders and followed Dev into the camp.

CHAPTER TWO

THE HUM OF activity at the vaccination camp was like a beehive in full swing, and holy shiz, was it hot here. Ally felt as if she'd mostly been conducting her work from behind a sheen of highly unattractive sweat for the past few days, though she'd been administering vaccine after vaccine to the locals for an hour and a half today already.

Despite the important nature of the work, the chatter from people around the camp, and the muggy heat that clung to her skin, her attention kept veering towards Dev. Each time she glanced over, catching him in the midst of a task, she couldn't help but think back to the prospect of a fling. Something about him made her quite shy, and nervous. He was definitely the exact opposite of Matt, who'd always seemed so approachable, and affable and comforting. Matt, who, as a data analyst for one of Britain's top banks, would not have known what to do with himself in an outdoor space without computers. She'd always secretly wished Matt could talk more with her about her line of work, but she supposed it had always been nicer for him to come home and switch off from work talk completely.

Dev's tall, lean figure was bent attentively over a patient now, his thick dark hair falling forward as he worked. Even through the chaos, Ally couldn't help but note how the light caught the subtle contours of his muscles under his shirt. *Mmm.* Then, as though sensing his eyes on her from across the camp, he looked up, and caught her staring.

Oops.

'Next,' Ally called automatically as her current patient moved away, refusing to let her eyes wander back to Dev, where they would inevitably hover and embarrass her further. Mind you though, he did seem utterly focused on his work. She knew he was the kind of man she would trust if an emergency came up...as his previous role was as an emergency doctor. Here it was all hands on deck for the most part.

A little girl was talking to him now, showing him something she'd pulled from her pocket. Ally couldn't see what it was from here but the sight of him, so absorbed in his role and humouring the cute little girl, sent another unexpected and not so welcome flutter through her stomach. Every time it happened she had to wonder if it was him, or a burgeoning case of dysentery. You never knew in these remote locations, but so far it seemed to be just Dev causing it. She chastised herself silently.

Professionalism first, Ally.

With her water bottle running on empty for what felt like the tenth time already, Ally slipped away to the makeshift refreshment stand and filled it up, taking a giant swig and swiping at her brow. She could totally go for a nap after this round was done, the jet lag was still making her brain a little foggy, but she didn't think she'd get much sleep, even if she did lie down. The tightness of the camp meant privacy was a luxury. You could literally hear everything everyone did or said, thanks to the tents being packed so close together. Two more had appeared this morning for late arrivals, like mushrooms sprouting up after rain.

Her phone buzzed, and she yanked it from her skirt pocket under her white coat. Larissa!

Larissa had probably forgotten the four-hour time difference between them, but, to be fair, Ally had forgotten herself yesterday, calling her mid-afternoon. Svalbard was making her friend a bit glum, being so dark around the clock. Of course, she'd done her best to cheer her up thus far.

She answered the call, fanning herself with a napkin.

'Hey, you! Tell me everything. How's life in the dark? How is your Thor lookalike?' she said, thinking back to another text where she'd told her about a hot Norwegian guy. It felt as if she'd known Larissa her whole life already, but really it had only been five or six years. They balanced each other out, like yin and yang. Plus Larry had been a rock when they'd lost Matt and Albie on that vacation from hell. She'd been so sure Matt was the one, that they'd grow old together discussing *The Great British Bake Off* over mid-week biscuit binges. Bringing up two nutty kids in a three-bed semi with a fishpond in the garden. Planning the retirement cruise of their dreams.

What about the cruise? she'd wailed to Larissa in one particularly heavy bout of sobbing in the back room at the clinic.

I'll go with you, Larissa had promised. She would as well. Larry loved a bit of luxury. She also came over every week on cue for *Bake Off,* determined that it would be their tradition now Matt was gone.

Larry asked her if she'd spoken much to 'the hot guy from Canada you mentioned'. Ally sighed, and told her about last night's campfire dinner. They'd lined up for their meal of stewed meat and veggies, cooked in a giant pot in the makeshift kitchen area, and in the line, clutching their plates, they had had a brief conversation, where she'd asked him more about Toronto. She'd learned that Dev's father had been some kind of big-deal doctor in Mumbai, who had been relocated to Canada, and now he was working on leveraging his expertise in minimally invasive spinal surgeries by co-founding a startup focused on developing an AI-powered surgical navigation system.

She'd asked about his siblings again, seeing as he'd stopped short in the car after mentioning that, but he'd made it seem as though it was a difficult topic for some reason. Then they'd been separated and sat at opposite ends of the table in the mess hall, which Dev had actually helped to construct yesterday. She relayed how she'd watched his muscles bulge as he'd lifted, hammered and sweated, till the mess hall had been surrounded by giant mosquito nets. It must have tired him out. He'd gone to bed even earlier than she had.

Before Larissa could ask more, a male voice resonated outside. Someone was calling her name, looking for her.

Ending the call, Ally stepped out of her tent, the world started whirring around her again, and someone called her name again. It was Aryan, the medical assistant who'd set up his station next to hers, but it was Dev's eye she caught from across the way as she brushed a loose strand of auburn hair from her face, tucking it behind her ear as she hurried her pace. A man was sitting in the seat at her stand, bent over slightly, and he looked up as she approached. He was middle-aged, she could see now from the creased lines of worry etching his forehead.

'Hello, I'm Nurse Spencer,' she said, her tone professional yet as soothing as she could muster. 'How can I help you today?'

'I've been feeling a bit dizzy lately, Nurse,' the man replied, his voice tinged with an accent that spoke of the local soil. 'And now there's this rash on my arm. Your colleague said you might take a look?'

'Let me take a look,' Ally said, gently examining the inflamed skin. The heat was unrelenting, and beads of sweat formed at her temples, but her focus remained sharp on the task at hand, even as she felt Dev's eyes on her again. Maybe, as the emergency doctor here, he felt he should be involved in any impromptu examinations?

'Excuse me, Dr Chandran?' she called out to him, raising an arm in the air. Dev was only a few steps away, overseeing another vaccination station. His last client was just rolling down her shirt sleeve. 'Could you have a quick look here?'

Dev glanced up yet again, his intense brown eyes momentarily locking with hers before he pushed back his chair and walked over. The sunlight danced off his charcoal-black hair as he moved towards her, creating a halo-like effect that was hard to ignore. There was a gracefulness to his stride too. Very different from how Matt had walked. Matt had kind of…well…plodded, to put it kindly. Her mum had always said he was a sixty-year-old in a thirty-year-old's body, but he had been quirky, and kind, and he'd loved her.

Dev's tall, lean form moved with ease through the crowded campsite, dodging children playing in the dirt and other medical staff scurrying from place to place. How could he bear his collar being buttoned up? she wondered momentarily. It was so hot. Casual, professional, and hot in more ways than one—this was Dev. He knelt beside the patient, observing the rash with his trained eye. 'Have you been feeling nauseous or experiencing any headaches?' he asked, his voice calm and measured.

'A bit of both, yes,' the man admitted.

'It looks like heat exhaustion to me, more than measles,' Dev concluded after a brief consultation. 'We should get him hydrated and into a cooler environment,' he said to her. 'Some oral rehydration salts would do the trick, along with a rest in the shade.'

'I was waiting a long time, and I rode here on my horse,' the man explained, using a tissue she provided to mop his bald head.

'Right.' Ally nodded, impressed with how Dev had swiftly pinpointed the issue, and how he was now resting a hand sympathetically on the man's shoulder, encouraging him to stand with them. She could have treated him herself, really, but something about the way Dev had looked at her stepping out of her tent had made her want to close the gap between them. Together, they helped him towards a shaded area, one on each arm to assist him in his weariness, offering support with each step.

The man thanked them profusely, his gratitude for their joint efforts evident, despite the discomfort etched on his face, and the language barrier. Dev was translating everything, though body language spoke volumes in medical situations. Ally fetched the necessary supplies and handed them to their patient with instructions.

'Take care and make sure to drink plenty of fluids,' Ally told him, leaving him in her assistant Aryan's care, before catching Dev on the way back to his stand.

'Thank you for your valuable input,' she fibbed, her heart skipping briefly at the approval in his eyes.

'It wasn't the toughest case I've had to tend to,' he said,

and his mouth flipped up at one corner, as if he was suppressing an amused smirk.

'Well…it's always good to get a second opinion,' she retorted, fanning out her white coat over her shirt. His eyes travelled to her cleavage for half a second, and it made the blood zip about her body like a flock of mosquitoes. A new feeling completely, since Matt's death, and one she wasn't entirely sure what to do with: was this part of her she'd assumed to be dead still struggling for attention deep down somewhere? What to do with it? A fling…perhaps…just to see if her libido was still as alive as it was starting to seem?

For the next couple of hours, she watched Dev interact with his patients from across the camp, which included a couple of injuries, as well as administering the vaccines. Ally couldn't help but notice the tenderness in his touch as he saw to one of the young girls who'd been playing around the camp, the kid of a local volunteer. His large hands were careful and precise on her scraped knee, cleaning the wound with an expertise and a kindness that were fascinating and endearing to watch, even to her, an experienced nurse. There was something about the way he held the girl's gaze as she sniffled, reassuring her without words, that made Ally's chest tighten. As if he was lost somewhere in his head, at the same time as seeming entirely present. Who *was* Dev Chandran?

She had to get him alone and ask him more about himself. Maybe he would be fling material, but she'd have to crack him open a bit first. He seemed to hold a well of secrets beneath that cool, preppy and composed exterior. That much was evident by the way he'd fobbed her off when she'd asked about his siblings again yesterday. It made her wonder if he was involved in some kind of argument with a family member. People didn't work endless stints in random places with the NHF unless they were running away from something back home. She should know, she thought guiltily, thinking of Nora living out the same routine as usual, without her. Ally wasn't running exactly, but she had thought it might be nice to see a place Matt had wanted to see, and, at the same time, get away from all the stuff that still reminded her of him for a while. It wasn't as if she'd be gone for long…she would never. Nora needed her.

'How do you manage to make everyone feel so at ease when it's a thousand degrees out here?' she asked him later, when she met him at the water dispenser. The team were like elephants congregating around a spring, the amount of water they seemed to drink out here.

'You just get used to it,' Dev said, brushing off the compliment as he cleaned his hands with sanitiser. 'But I could say the same about you.'

'Oh, really,' Ally allowed, feeling her lips curving upwards as her mind raced with the fact that he'd clearly been watching her at work, too. 'But I still think you have a magic touch.'

Oh, God, was she flirting now?

She was terrible at it and should most definitely stop.

'Magic, huh?' Dev chuckled softly, a slight sparkle lighting his eyes again as she fanned her coat, almost inviting him to check out her cleavage again.

Ally, you are a traitor to yourself!

He refrained, anyway. Instead, he cleared his throat and looked at her face from under thick black eyelashes that should really be illegal on men due to the desperate unfairness of it. 'I'll have to remember that one.'

'Please do,' Ally replied as her heart continued to rev

up to top gear. OK, yes, she was flirting, apparently. She could almost imagine Larry egging her on. So why was she more nervous than excited, all of a sudden, feeling his curiosity pique around her and his eyes rove her breasts through her sweaty clothes? He held her gaze, amusement lighting his eyes, and she struggled to pinpoint why she found the prospect of being romantically involved with anyone for *any* amount of time so disconcerting. Matt was gone. He'd been gone for two years.

A flashback struck her. Herself and her devastated sister, collapsed in the driveway of their rented villa in Palermo in front of the Sicilian policemen. Oliver sobbing, both of them taking it in turns to comfort him, despite breaking apart themselves. Albie and Matt had been taken from them so suddenly, in the most tragic of ways. A dog walker had found their bloated bodies on a nearby beach and they'd heard the helicopters before the news. The broken boat had sunk half a mile from the shore. Just when they'd assumed their lives couldn't have been going better. You just never really got over something like that.

With a steadying breath, Ally turned to the supply tent. She needed more needles and gauze already…and air. A volunteer helped her locate what she needed, and she balanced a box on top of another. Why make two trips across camp when she could make one? She was just making her way back across the grass, three feet from the tent, when a sudden movement caught her eye over the top of the boxes. Smooth, sleek-furred, and undeniably feline, the creature padded quietly into her path, and promptly came to a stop in front of her.

Leopard.

Ally's heart thudded against her ribcage, the top box slipping from her limp fingers as she stifled a scream.

She took a shaky step backwards, her eyes locked on the agile, prowling cat in front of her. She had seen leopards on TV before, but never in person. And certainly not this close. She could make out every spot, every stroke of its fur. Its eyes were narrowed towards her, as if it were saying, *How dare this human cross my path?*

'Ally, freeze!' Dev's voice cut through the bustling noise of the campsite, sharp as a scalpel. 'It won't hurt you if you don't move. Keep eye contact, that's imperative.'

Ally could feel the sweat trickling down her back as she tried to stay completely still. *Oh, God...is this how I die?*

Time seemed to twist and stretch as every atom of her filled with dread. Her skin prickled with beads of sweat. Every frantic beat of her heart seemed to echo the tremor in her limbs as, from the corner of her eye, she saw Dev creep up slowly behind the cat, holding a long, pointed object. Was he serious? She saw him motion to the wide-eyed onlookers, but what he was telling them, she couldn't tell.

'Whatever you do, don't move an inch,' he instructed again, his tone a strange mixture of calm and urgency that somehow rooted her to the spot even more, even as her gaze stayed locked on the leopard's cold, unblinking eyes. The box she was still holding seemed to weigh a thousand tonnes. Every instinct screamed at her to run, but Ally knew the leopard's strike would be swifter than any movement she dared make. What was it even doing here? Was this normal?

The camp had gone eerily silent, all activity paused as eyes turned towards the human-versus-leopard stand-off. Dev was still creeping closer, and closer. He was holding a long wooden tent peg, she realised. He must have yanked it out of one of the tents. Suddenly, the leopard did a turn, making to face Dev and the crowd instead of her. She sucked in a breath and prepared for the worst as Dev threw his arms in the air, signalling for the on-lookers. Just then, everyone in the camp started yelling at the top of their lungs. Some were throwing sticks in the stunned creature's direction.

'Get out of here,' Dev commanded it, waving the tent peg with intent. She could finally move and darted side-ways as a shower of sticks landed around the creature. Then, miraculously, the huge cat finally seemed to think better about being here. It slunk away again into the un-derbrush, disappearing as quickly as it had appeared.

Ally's knees wobbled. She dropped the remaining box and stumbled backwards, only to be steadied by Dev's firm grip on her arm. The campsite seemed to exhale in collective relief, the sound rustling through the trees like a released breath. *What the heck just happened?*

'Are you OK?' Dev peered into her face. Those in-tense brown eyes shimmered with genuine concern and she forced herself to calm down, even though her heart was still a drum.

'Y-yes,' she stammered, trying to regain her compo-sure. 'Thanks to you.'

'Quick thinking,' a volunteer acknowledged, and in seconds Dev was receiving pats on the back from every-one who passed. He was only looking at her, however.

'I owe you my life. You just faced a leopard with a tent peg,' Ally said incredulously, her voice a whisper as the magnitude of what could have happened began to sink in. A look of strange determination crossed his face, mixed with something else she couldn't put her finger on.

'Let's get you sitting down for a moment,' he suggested, guiding her to a nearby chair. As she sat, the cool touch of his hand stayed on her shoulder, grounding her. Meeting his gaze, she tried to thank him, but then she saw a depth of caring on his face that went beyond the call of duty. It made her heart start to flutter all over again in a way that had nothing to do with fear. 'We lost a newborn baby to a leopard a few months ago in Nepal,' he told her.

'Oh, no, that's terrible. What happened?'

'Dragged it right out of the cradle. Lucky we didn't lose you, too,' he said, 'or anyone else here.'

Ally didn't miss how his hand remained on her shoulder and his eyes lingered on hers for a moment longer than he seemed to feel comfortable with, before he excused himself and walked back to his stand. He did cast a look back at her as he took his seat again, and as the adrenaline slowed its course through her body, she knew she probably owed Dev more than a fling, if she ever got up the courage to initiate anything. She might just owe him her life!

CHAPTER THREE

DEV STOOD BY the Jeep next to Ally as the schoolyard slowly filled with the children, pouring out of the classrooms to gape at the newcomers, their uniforms patched but clean. The school building where they were due to run today's vaccination drive was modest, as schools in most small towns out here in Kerala tended to be, painted a once-vibrant yellow that he knew would have been significantly dulled by the sun and time. In Toronto, this amount of chipped paint would probably be considered unsafe.

For a brief moment he thought of his nephew in Toronto: Romesh's son, Nikki. When was the last time he'd seen Nikki? The last time he'd gone home for that horrific family gathering three years ago, he thought guiltily.

Ally had a smile across her face as she started greeting them, humouring their curiosity.

'Looks like we're the main event here,' she quipped, her pale blue eyes twinkling with humour despite the early hour. He enjoyed how she seemed to find the humour in everything, even though it set him on edge. People who did that tended to be hiding something underneath, something they didn't want to face, or know *how* to face. He should know.

'Seems so,' he agreed, his attention briefly snagging on

her long, wavy auburn hair as it caught the golden glow of the morning sun. She was unquestionably pretty, with her milky white skin, despite the sun's capacity to burn its way across her slanted cheekbones. He'd caught himself watching her far too much all week, but it was lucky he'd been watching her when that leopard had crept up the other day. Otherwise...who knew?

They hadn't really talked much since. He'd been wanting to, but he knew she would ask him questions about his life, as she'd started to that first night in the line for dinner in their makeshift mess hall, and he wasn't about to get too personal, too soon. Especially not with someone as attractive as Ally.

The last time he'd got too personal with a co-worker on one of these assignments, it had ended with her fleeing the programme altogether, claiming she couldn't work with someone she was in love with, especially someone who didn't appear to love her back. Cassinda, the Brazilian-American, had done her best to dirty his reputation before and after leaving, even if no one had really given it much credit, thankfully, but he'd sworn not to get involved with a co-worker ever again. The last thing he needed was more guilt on top of the load he was always carrying. He was here to get away from that. Not that he ever escaped it, really. It just followed him.

A flicker of Roisin's smiling face crossed his mind for just a second. He should have gone home at Christmas, gone to her grave with the rest of his family, but he still couldn't bear it, knowing it was his fault his sister was dead; knowing they all knew it was his fault, even though they never said it.

The kids were upon them now, chattering in Malayalam, their smiles wide and welcoming as ever. He always enjoyed his stints in Kerala, but this one was proving more interesting already, purely because of this white woman with her funny English accent and high-pitched, infectious laugh. Ally crouched to their level effortlessly in her flowing blue skirt, responding with high fives. He had noticed this all week, how the kids around the campsite all responded to her warmth like flowers to the sun, basking in her attentiveness.

'Ally's got a knack with them, doesn't she?' Rani, their community outreach coordinator, noted from behind him, watching the scene unfold.

'Definitely,' Dev murmured, more to himself than to Rani. It was one thing to be good at your job, quite another to radiate care as naturally as breathing. Ally did both, without seeming to realise how rare that combination was. He had seen a lot throughout his time with NHF, a lot of people from a lot of places, and while he didn't really know why she was here, aside from her clinic back home closing down and forcing her out of a job, he had a feeling she wasn't the type to stay away from home for long. Just by looking at her, he could tell she probably had kids of her own, or at least in her family, that she was used to spending time with.

As for him, he'd been doing everything in his power *not* to go home and face his family. He thought a little guiltily back to his mother's email, still unanswered in his inbox. She'd asked what his plans were for Valentine's Day, aka Roisin's birthday. He would let her down gently, he decided, tell them he had a new assignment, even if he didn't. The annual get-together in honour of the love they'd had, and still had, for his little sister always got the what-ifs torturing him all over again. What if he hadn't let her ride with him in the passenger seat? What if he'd taken the usual route home instead of a shortcut?

He would let Mom down gently soon, he decided. Maybe when they stopped at the next place, when the Internet was better. *Always some excuse,* he thought as the guilt kicked in again.

The vaccination drive thankfully all went to plan in the shade of the trees outside the school. Dev found himself observing Ally when she wasn't looking. Her wide gestures and ebullient mannerisms made it hard not to. Twin boys, no older than six, seemed particularly taken with her ahead of their vaccines. They wore identical shorts and shirts, which meant they were impossible to tell apart. The fabric of their clothes was faded like the school building, washed and hung to dry in the sun too many times, but her jokes were making them giggle and nudge each other conspiratorially. He finished with his last patient, and his feet seemed to find their own way over to her somehow.

'OK, you two,' Ally was saying when he reached her side. 'Ready to be super brave for me?'

They nodded vigorously, apparently unaffected by any fear of needles.

'Braver than Superman?' Dev chimed in, hoping to share in the moment. Ally caught his eye and gave him a sideways smile from behind her hair, and he felt something tighten in his chest as he pulled at his collar in the heat.

'Braver than Spiderman!' one of the twins declared, puffing out his chest.

'I'm braver than both of them!' the other added, not to be outdone. Clearly they had been learning English at this school already, or they watched a lot of TV.

Ally laughed, ruffling their hair affectionately before instructing them to stay still, and administering the vaccines with a steady hand. The twins didn't flinch. In fact, their gazes were locked on Ally as if she'd woven a spell around them.

'See? You are superheroes. You didn't even feel it,' she praised, handing each of them a sticker.

'Thanks, Ally *chechi*!' they chorused. Dev felt his eyebrows rise. They were using the Malayalam term for older sister. It was rare people took to the volunteers as fast as this. The last time he'd been so impressed by someone's effortlessly easy-going nature was during the stint he'd done in Nepal, with Cassinda. He'd been so drawn to her and missing that vital flesh-to-flesh connection that resisting her powers of seduction late one night had been impossible. How was he to know she'd promptly fall in love with him and expect him to stop working for the NHF at the end of their fling, to go with her back to America, start a family?

As if he were ever going to stop moving. He'd thrown himself into it for the last seven years, thinking that by helping others in need, maybe he could somehow atone for the loss he'd caused his family. It hadn't worked yet. It would never work, and why would it? But each time he moved, he had a new chance to try…and another excuse not to go home and face the pain he'd caused his parents and Romesh.

That fling with Cassinda was definitely the *last* one he'd have on the job, though. These hook-ups never got him anywhere, and never made him feel anything other than guilt when they ended.

His thoughts flew from his head when he saw Ally.

'Good work, Nurse,' he said when she stood up, her face flushed with the joy of doing what she obviously loved.

'Thanks, Dev.' She brushed off her hands, unaware of the admiration she'd garnered. Least of all from him. She had a stunning body, he thought, wondering if that weird-sounding place she lived—Frome—had a good yoga studio, or whether she just got arms that toned from lifting other kinds of weights, like boxes and...babies?

Ally paused, locking eyes with him for a brief second, as if she might've caught a glimpse of his thoughts. 'What does *chechi* mean?' she asked.

He told her and she nodded, eyebrows hitched. 'I like to think I've been a good sister.' She paused. 'But then I think, if I *was* a good sister, would I really be all the way out here away from Nora?'

He frowned at her, her words going around in his head. He almost asked what she meant exactly but, by the look on her face, it seemed like one of those things that was best left unaddressed by a relative stranger such as himself. She almost looked sad. 'You have a sister?'

'Nora. We're close, but it doesn't exactly make me sibling of the year.'

'Well, I'm not exactly a great brother myself,' he heard himself say, thinking of Romesh, and she offered him a half-smile with questions in her own eyes. Then the moment passed, and Ally was swept away, leaving Dev with the echo of a brief connection he wasn't sure was safe to explore.

The vaccination drive was a whirlwind of activity again in the afternoon. The children wanted to show them everything.

'*Chechi, chechi*, come see!' the twins exclaimed. They'd been hovering around Ally all day and now she was allowing herself to be led across the schoolyard, her face reflecting wonder and delight every time she was shown something else: a ball, a toy, a drawing, and now...

'Look, the hummingbirds!' one of the twins pointed out, his small hand gesturing towards the flurry of wings suspended near a patch of wildflowers.

Dev rose from his seat. His nephew, Nikki, had loved the hummingbirds at the sanctuary in Toronto, last time he was home. Crossing the dusty forecourt, then the grass, he positioned himself just close enough to observe without intruding. The hummingbirds were a spectacle as they usually were, even more so in their natural habitat, he thought, all iridescent feathers glinting in the sunlight as they hovered and dipped with an elegance that defied the rapid beat of their wings. Ally's attention was fully on the birds as she knelt beside the boys, who were armed with paintbrushes and palettes of watercolours. So this was art class.

'You can paint them too, Ally *chechi*,' one boy said expectantly.

'Let's see about that—art was never my strongest subject,' she replied, her voice playful. Dev watched as she dipped a brush into a pool of cobalt blue and the twins leaned in, their eyes wide with amazement as colours bloomed onto the paper in the form of another hummingbird. She'd lied, she was actually a pretty good artist. And right now he kind of wanted to paint her too. Her hair was the colour of leaves in the fall; a special kind of red you found only in Canada. He sniffed, making her turn her head to him.

'Isn't it amazing how they just hang in the air?' she mused.

'Like magic,' one of the twins whispered.

'Exactly like magic,' she agreed, turning back to the boy, but not before Dev felt as if she'd seen something in his gaze that he wasn't entirely comfortable showing her. Yes, he would love to spend more time with Ally away from the camp and their work, but that kind of thinking wasn't going to do him any favours.

She carried on painting, and her laughter mingled with that of the twin boys, an infectious sound that brightened the entire schoolyard and brought more and more of the children over, all with paintbrushes of their own. He wondered what Nikki was doing now, as he often did. Did he ever think about his uncle all the way out here, or had he forgotten him by now?

'Dev, you're awfully quiet over there,' Ally called out. 'Everything OK?'

'Just thinking about logistics for tomorrow,' he lied smoothly.

'Right,' Ally said, not looking entirely convinced but letting it slide. She turned back to the twins, guiding their small hands as they attempted to mimic the iridescence of the hummingbirds on paper. But he didn't miss the way she kept turning back to him, looking at him when she didn't think he would notice.

Later that evening, as the flames from the campfire crackled, Dev found himself sitting beside Ally on a fallen log, the rest of their team scattered around.

'Can I ask you something?' Ally's voice was soft but carried a thread of determination. It made Dev brace himself internally.

'Go ahead,' he responded, watching as the flames consumed the wood with a fervour.

'Earlier today...with the boys, you seemed...distant. More than just tired. Is everything all right?'

Her pale blue eyes searched his face and Dev took a deep breath, feeling the warmth from the fire battling the chill that had nothing to do with the night air. 'It's just— seeing those twins today reminded me of my nephew, Nikki.' His admission hung between them like the smoke from the campfire, curling upwards and dissipating into the night sky. 'He looks just like my brother.'

'How old is he?' Ally prodded gently, probably sensing quite correctly that there was more he wasn't saying.

'He'll be nine soon. I haven't seen him in a long time. I don't go back to Canada often.' As the words exited his mouth he could almost hear them echoing the distance he felt.

'Why not?'

'Busy, I guess,' he said quickly. Then he felt bad for the lie. 'Well, maybe that's an excuse. Home is...not exactly my favourite place to be.'

Ally reached out, placing a hand on his arm, and her simple gesture felt laden with the kind of empathy that had drawn him to her before, when his feet had led him to her side of their own accord. 'I'm sorry to hear that, Dev,' she said.

He chewed his lip as they watched their co-workers chatting amongst themselves, swigging tea from tin cups. Ally was looking at him again. He could tell she wanted to ask why home was not his favourite place, and why he didn't go very often, but she didn't.

'I never thanked you properly for saving my life,' she told him.

'Yeah, you did,' he replied. 'But there's no need to thank me, really.' He poked a stick at the glowing embers, sending a shower of sparks up into the night. The firelight flickered across her face as she leaned forward. 'Most of the wildlife is more afraid of us than we are of them. We just have to keep our wits about us in the more remote locations.'

'Got it,' she said, smirking. 'As long as I don't see any snakes.'

'You will,' he assured her, and she winced. 'Snakes are great. I had a snake once in Toronto. A ball python called Monty.'

'You actually owned a snake?' She sounded horrified, and he bit back a smile at the look on her face. Mentioning Monty—a gift from his brother to keep him company during late study nights at med school—did tend to conjure images of serpents slithering through grass with evil intent.

'He was one of the gentlest creatures you could ever meet,' Dev continued.

'I never took you for a snake enthusiast,' Ally said, brushing her auburn hair back.

Dev shrugged. 'I've always been fascinated by them.'

'I suppose some animals rely on humans seeing beyond what scares them.'

'And sometimes humans need the same thing,' he found himself saying.

Ally nodded quietly. 'Speaking of animals, Nora—my sister—she has this cat,' she began, her voice softening. 'He's been such a comfort to her, especially...after Albie.'

'Albie?' Dev felt his brows furrow slightly.

'Her husband, my brother-in-law. We lost him two years ago,' Ally said, the words falling heavily between them. 'I've been living with her since then, helping with my eight-year-old nephew. It's been…a lot.' She drew in a sharp breath and hugged her knees.

'Ally, that's… I'm sorry to hear that,' he replied after a pause. 'How did he die, if you don't mind me asking?'

'He drowned.'

Oh. God.

Suddenly, the happy front she seemed to show the world became a lot more nuanced and it deepened his respect for her on the spot. But she shrugged off the weight of the memory quickly, as if she was regretting telling him already. 'We all carry something with us, don't we?' she said, forcing a small smile. 'Baggage.' The second she said it, she looked as if she wanted to kick herself.

'True,' he agreed, and for a second he almost told her about the accident that killed Roisin while he was beside her in the driver's seat, without so much as a scratch on him, but he kept his words to himself. The fewer people knew about that the better. At least out here he could simply be himself. People saw him just as Dev, instead of an extension of the tragedy, which was how he viewed himself most of the time.

'Speaking of baggage, that was some suitcase you arrived here with.' He nudged her and she chuckled, and they fell into silence, and the crackling of the fire punctuated his thoughts like hot rods, poking into his wounds. How could he not think about *Ally's* struggles now? She'd lost a family member, whereas he had distanced himself from his on purpose when they were all he had. As if he needed anything else to feel guilty about!

Quietly he excused himself and made his way to his tent, but he could feel Ally's eyes on his back the whole way there.

CHAPTER FOUR

ALLY STIFLED A yawn as the Jeep trundled along the rugged path, weaving through the lush landscape on the way back from the school to the campsite. Her gaze wandered outside the window, taking in the blur of greenery and wildflowers that lined the roadside. A rustic sign loomed ahead, its arrow pointing towards the Edakkal Caves.

'Look at that,' Dev said from behind the wheel. His voice yanked her attention back inside the vehicle instantly.

'Edakkal Caves,' Ally echoed, leaning forward to get a better view of the sign. 'I've noticed it before, but I've got no idea what's there, do you?'

'I don't know, caves, I guess,' he said with a shrug, and she smirked as his dark eyes briefly met hers before refocusing on the road. There was an ease about him at times, when he wasn't doing that dark, brooding thing, that Ally admired, a calmness that seemed to run as deep as his Indian roots. Still, he made her so hot. Dev was the perfect fling material. But aside from their few brief conversations, which had only left her wondering more about him, she still knew barely anything about the man.

She couldn't help but think back to when they'd sat around the campfire, and what he'd told her about not going home much. He'd said that home wasn't somewhere he enjoyed particularly. He'd seemed almost sad about it, as if he *couldn't* go home, for some reason. So mysterious.

Her own words echoed in her mind too. She'd told him how Albie died, and the consequent shadow it had cast over her family, but she hadn't been able to tell him Matt had died too, on the same day, in the same horrific accident.

If she'd started down that path, she would've had to offer details, but she was out here to be someone people could respect and have a fun time with, as well as rely on to get the job done. She was not here to invite glances and whispers over having a dead brother-in-law *and* a dead boyfriend. One of the trash mags had contacted her weeks after the accident, fishing for the 'shocking family story', offering four hundred quid. She'd told them to shove it. Then they'd had the audacity to contact Nora instead, who had also told them to shove it.

But she'd been moved by the sympathetic tilt of Dev's head, and how his brown eyes had held a universe of unspoken understanding. They'd barely known each other a fortnight but she'd dwelled on it afterwards in a call to Larissa. Larissa had of course told her to jump on him. She was meant to be having a fling, not looking for emotional connections! Not that *she* wasn't still holding herself back from pouncing on her Svalbard man, Thor, for one reason or another. Larissa said they'd been talking, and that she was kind of obsessed with his dog, called Midnight, but she'd also called Ally to ask how to tell him that she wanted to sleep with him! Maybe they were both a bit worried about developing feelings for someone?

'Can I ask you something?' Ally ventured, her fingers nervously twisting a lock of her hair. She was thinking she should ask Dev the same thing, but she wasn't as bold as she was pretending to be, obviously.

'Of course,' Dev replied, casting a quick glance in her direction.

'Do you think...?' She paused, unsure how to frame her thoughts without *sounding* insecure. 'Last night, when I told you about my brother-in-law, do you think it might seem like I'm running away from all my responsibilities back home? It only happened two years ago. Nora says she's OK but she's not. I know she's not.'

Dev considered her question, his eyes fixed on the winding road. For a moment, the only sound was the Jeep's tyres crunching over gravel and the distant call of a bird.

'Ally,' he said with gentle sincerity, 'it's not for me to judge why anyone takes a job this far from home.'

His words carried a hint of his own issues. He'd got up so fast last night, and exited their conversation before it had really got going. Ally had felt the intrigue building all night after that, her heart skipping a beat at the prospect of peeling back the layers of Dev, fixing her mouth to his on the pillow in his tent between his pouring out his deepest fears. Gosh, it was too hot and, thanks to Larissa, she was getting ahead of herself. *Way* ahead.

'Thanks,' she murmured, fanning out her top. He shot her a sideways glance and his mouth twitched in that way it did when he found her amusing.

'Sounds like it's been a heavy couple of years,' he said. 'Maybe you deserve some fun.'

Ally felt her next words catch in her throat. Had he read her mind, or had he been thinking about a little fling, too? The conversation around the campfire, while brief, had been unexpectedly intimate and here, in the daylight, this playful dance of attraction and intrigue going on between them was almost too obvious to deny. No wonder he was asking her.

'Shall we check out these caves, then?' he said, already signalling to turn off the main road.

Oh. OK. So that was what he meant by fun. He was a nerd at heart. Just as Matt had been. Only he was way better at the whole 'being intense and broody' thing, she thought. His eyes had been on her all day today, just like yesterday, and the day before. He hadn't been able to stop himself watching her, and she hadn't been able to stop herself staring at him either, or standing next to him every opportunity, under every guise: fetching water, fetching supplies, assisting an emergency he'd encountered with a young volunteer and an infected leg injury. But they were colleagues. They were professionals with an entire team around them. While it was intriguing to feel these things again, was it really a good idea to entertain them? She was already imagining pressing him against a rocky cave wall and devouring him.

Say no, stay professional, Ally! No way should you enter a cave with this man.

'Let's do it,' she said, a smile creeping onto her lips. What was one little adventure? Besides, Larry would kill her if she kept procrastinating over her mission—the whole fling thing had been *her* idea!

The Jeep veered off the main path, crunching over foliage as Dev steered towards the Edakkal Caves. Whatever they held was a mystery—how exciting. The lush Kerala landscape rolled by like an emerald sea. She loved how the towering trees brushed against the sky, their leaves whispering the secrets of their ancient history in a language they would never understand, maybe hiding

Dev's favourite pets—snakes. Ugh. But interesting. Not like the boring shrubbery and weeds back home. The air here was thick with the scent of damp earth and wildflowers and, with Dev beside her, she couldn't deny the excitement bubbling inside her already.

'So, you said you don't go home a lot,' she said, breaking the silence. Well, she couldn't help that he intrigued her. 'Why is that? Is Toronto just too boring now?' She could sense it was more than that, but she was trying to be polite.

'I don't know,' he said, wriggling his nose. 'Maybe *I'm* the one who's running away from my responsibilities.' There was a hint of self-reflection in his voice that made Ally turn to study his profile.

'What do you mean?' she ventured, thinking maybe it had something to do with his brother, Romesh. 'If you don't mind me saying, you seem a little...off...whenever you mention your brother. Is it because of him?'

Damn it, was that too many questions? She fanned her shirt again. Why could she never read a room and shut up?

'Kind of,' he said with a non-committal shrug. She looked at him apologetically, but the corner of his mouth twitched up and she could tell he didn't mind her questions really. It didn't mean he was going to answer any of them. 'It's complicated. Here we are, let's see what these caves are all about!'

Dev parked the Jeep in a clearing surrounded by a cluster of trees and they got out, the sounds of the forest enveloping them instantly. They followed a narrow path that snaked its way through the underbrush and led to the entrance of the caves. Ally couldn't help her own mouth gaping open at the sheer size of the gaping mouth of the cave before them, the way the rocky walls seemed to swallow the light.

'Whoa,' she breathed, her voice echoing into the cavernous space ahead and bouncing back around her ears. Another bird took flight somewhere close by.

'Right?' Dev agreed, his eyes lighting up with the same sense of wonder that Ally felt.

'There won't be any bats, will there?' she said, suddenly wary.

'I thought you'd love a superhero's lair,' he teased, and she rolled her eyes, secretly pleased he remembered what she'd been laughing about with those adorable twin boys. They entered the dark, dank space side by side, and the coolness of the cave wrapped around them like a secret cloak. The walls were rough to the touch, moist with condensation, and the farther they ventured in, the more the outside world seemed to fall away.

Ally could hear the measured cadence of her own breaths and the soft scuff of their shoes against the stone floor. The light faded the deeper they went, his silhouette a reassuring contrast against the dimly lit passages. Every so often, their arms brushed, and a jolt of electricity passed between them and made her skin buzz.

'Careful here,' he murmured as they approached a narrower section of the cave. His hand found the small of her back, guiding her gently. The touch was fleeting but intimate and Ally's pulse raced in response.

'I'm always careful,' she managed, her voice sounding small in the vastness of the enclosed space. The tension between them was a living thing that danced in the slivers of light that could still reach this secluded corner of...wherever they were! She wasn't quite sure how to navigate this cave, let alone this attraction. Wait till she told Larissa about this.

'Whoa, check it out!' She stepped forward, her eyes tracing the outlines of figures etched into the rock face. Dev was beside her in a heartbeat, following her pointed finger. The ancient petroglyphs were stretched across the walls like a storyboard of a time that no one alive now would ever know. In the dim light, the images seemed to move, as if the carvings and stories they told were coming to life before her.

'My nephew, Oliver, would lose his mind over this,' she said in awe, picturing the boy's face. She felt a pang of missing him, followed by the guilt over leaving him and Nora, but she snuffed it out. Nora had wanted her to come here, she'd encouraged it. Ally wasn't avoiding responsibilities. Or was she? Ugh, this was not the time to think about it.

'Look at this one,' Dev said softly, his voice bouncing off the stone and wrapping around her. He pointed to a cluster of shapes that Ally hadn't noticed, his fingers mere inches from the carvings.

'An animal of some sort?' she said, leaning closer to inspect the image. Her shoulder brushed against his arm, sending a subtle thrill through her.

'Maybe a hunting scene,' he proposed, his gaze following the lines and curves with an academic interest that was undercut by the wonder in his tone. It made her smile. He was such a nerd. 'See how the figures seem to be chasing it?'

Ally nodded. The excitement in his voice was infectious, the way his curiosity shone through drawing her in like an expeditioner discovering new frontiers or something. She moved to another section of the wall, her hand hovering over a series of intricate designs, careful not to touch. 'And these? Rituals, maybe?'

'Could be,' he agreed, peering at the petroglyphs. His closeness enveloped her, and for a moment she forgot about the drawings, acutely aware of Dev's proximity, the sound of his breath, and the weird but tangible mutual attraction in what would, with anyone else, be a horribly claustrophobic space. She hated small spaces. One time she'd got stuck in a changing room and had been so freaked out she'd called 999. She told this to Dev, and he laughed. He had such a nice laugh.

They walked on together, stopping at various markings that caught their eye. The cave air was cool, a stark contrast to the humidity outside, and it felt as though they were in another world.

'Amazing to think that, centuries ago, people stood right where we are now,' she said in awe, breaking a new, more comfortable silence.

'And that they left their stories behind for us to find,' Dev added, his tone reflective. 'It makes you wonder about the legacies we'll leave. If anyone will remember us at all.'

The weight of his words settled on Ally's shoulders like lead. 'I think you're a pretty memorable person,' she heard herself say. He said nothing, but when he turned to look at her, his brown eyes seemed even more intense in the shadowy light. It made her keep talking. 'And your legacy is that you help people. Your work—our work—it's important. Those months after Matt and Albie died, I threw myself into it. I suppose I felt a bit like, if I could take away someone else's pain, then maybe some of mine might disappear along with it. I suppose maybe I was right...well, I'm getting there at least.'

Dev had stopped looking at the wall. His eyes were on her now, with a frown that she realised was the result of her slip-up.

'Matt *and* Albie?' he said.

She swallowed, suddenly hot. She hadn't told him about Matt.

'Matt was my boyfriend,' she admitted, her voice suddenly small. There was no air in here. Dev said nothing, he just pressed a hand over hers, stepped closer. She couldn't quite breathe right all of a sudden, his eyes were just too sympathetic, too close, yet she couldn't look away.

'He died when Albie did, on the boat, they went fishing...' She trailed off, swallowing back the lump that wasn't so much the result of saying it out loud but the way he was looking at her. 'Sorry, I can't...'

'It's OK,' was all he said, covering her whole hand with one of his. Her fingers felt safe, consumed by his warm palm, and despite her confession a zing shot through her stomach, making her heart feel as though he'd plugged her directly into some invisible caveman socket. 'Ally, I'm so sorry.'

'Thank you,' she said, forcing herself to stand taller, but not moving her hand. 'Like I said, it was two years ago.'

'That's like...still fresh,' he said, still looking at her as if he expected her to crumble into pieces and float away. She dropped his hand. Her neck and her palms were sweatier than before. He looked as if he was going to say something, but he didn't and she was glad. She probably couldn't have found the words or the breath to reply, but as they continued deeper into the cave, Ally's mind churned. He must have questions for her, just as she did for him.

'Thank you for this,' she said finally. 'For suggesting we come here. It's amazing.'

Dev nodded, but the jovial mood was pretty dead by now. 'I'm glad you wanted to check it out. It's not every day you get to walk through history with someone who appreciates it as much as you do.'

The compliment landed softly in Ally's chest, and the zing she'd felt before settled into a mild buzz that seemed to lift her without threatening to short-circuit her heart. She hadn't intended to tell him about Matt back there, but the words had tumbled out anyway. Maybe it was a good thing? She hadn't exactly shared any of this with anyone except her sister and Larry, but the combination of being so far away and spreading the info out, dispersing it in different places, felt a little less like releasing something vital to her existence into the wild, and more like the start of setting herself free.

At the next petroglyph Dev turned to her, his expression unreadable in the shifting shadows. 'I really am sorry about your brother-in-law, Ally, and your boyfriend. You don't have to talk about it. But I wouldn't blame you at all if you were running away. Stuff like that is hard to handle. I mean, it's hard to know how.' His jaw shifted from side to side for a moment. He was speaking from experience, she could tell.

'So what about you? There's a story there, isn't there?' she prodded gently.

Dev shifted, directing her onwards, away from the walls and onto the path ahead. 'I don't usually talk about my life outside work,' he said, his tone guarded.

'OK,' Ally said, tilting her head as she followed him.

For a while, he walked in silence, stroking his big manly fingers softly over the walls as if the rocks could read him their history like brail. But his stance spoke volumes, as if he was weighing the cost of his secrecy against the trust she could feel building between them, slowly. Slowly, but irrefutably. Which was strange, considering...well... everything. His shoulders came up around his ears for a moment and he flinched before swiping a hand across his jaw, all with his back to her.

'I lost my sister, seven years ago,' he relented with a sigh, stopping in his tracks. 'In Toronto. I was the one driving. Roisin was in the passenger seat. The car hit her side, head-on. She died instantly.'

His sentences entered her ears like a bullet, shattering into separate words that splintered into even tinier fragments, all of which struck her heart like an explosion. For a moment, she was speechless. Her hand came up over her mouth, and the other reached for him, grappling a void for a second before she somehow found his hand.

'Oh, Dev.'

'I'm the reason we lost her.'

She sucked another breath in, willing the right words to form. They wouldn't. All she could feel was his pain, as if he were holding up a mirror at the top of a well, forcing her own emotions back to the surface in a giant bucket that threatened to spill at any moment. But he didn't ask for her sympathy; people rarely did. They just wanted to be heard and understood. She tightened her fingers around his, and their eyes met in the dark. He nodded at her, as though he somehow knew what she was saying, even though she wasn't really sure herself. She understood though, the core of it, the core of him. They were coming from the same place. His sister, in the passenger seat...she'd died right next to him.

They walked in silence for a moment. So this was his story. This was why he loathed going home. She knew that feeling. Everything she used to be comfortable around just reminded her of what she'd lost. Everything had a memory attached, like trying to forge a new path in a forest while the branches from the trees she flattened insisted on swinging back to slap her round the face.

She'd been the one in the driver's seat that day in Sicily, metaphorically speaking. She had waved the guys off, wished them a great fishing trip, told them she'd miss them, all the while planning a large glass of wine or three, a boutique shopping expedition and a gossip session with Nora. The what-ifs never stopped. They hit her when she least expected them, like now, in this cave! What if she'd suggested they listen to the boat-rental guys' warning about the choppy waves instead of agreeing that if they just stuck to the waters around the coast they'd be OK? What if she'd insisted they go tomorrow instead when the weather was due to be better? The guilt she felt, over saying none of those things, and causing Nora to lose her husband, had eaten her up. She would spend the rest of her life making sure Nora was never alone.

Ally was so caught up in her thoughts, she didn't notice the ground in front of her had roughened. Suddenly her foot slipped on the uneven ground, sending small rocks skittering across the cave floor.

'Careful!' Dev's voice came at her sharp as he reached out, his reflexes quick. His hands wrapped around her arms, steadying her before she could fall. The sudden contact sent the mild buzz back up to full-throttle electrifying shockwaves. 'We almost lost you there,' he said, his mouth hitching in one corner.

Pressed against his chest, she felt the steady thump of his heartbeat against her breasts, her lips mere inches from his. His breath came in warm waves against her skin, even warmer for the chill of the cave air, and it sent alarm bells and butterflies raging through her all at once. In that moment, everything else fell away—there was only Dev, the faint scent of soap and damp earth and mosquito repellent and this. Whatever this was.

'We didn't lose me, I'm OK,' she muttered, her voice barely audible over the pounding of her own heart. But she didn't move away, couldn't really, even as her mind screamed at her to put distance between them pronto. The closeness was too comfortable. Comfortably uncomfortable, she contemplated. It was weird and her brain would not compute. She'd placed her womanly cravings into a self-imposed isolation chamber months ago, determined to focus on herself and Nora and Oliver and her career and...and...and it was not enough. Not any more.

Dev's hands remained on her arms, not gripping, not claiming, just there—a silent vow of support that somehow meant more than any words could. She barely knew him, so why did his touch make her feel as she was feeling now? What was it about him?

The air between them crackled. Ally knew she should nip this thing in the bud before it wound any tighter around them and strangled any ounce of professionalism she had left, but then, she had promised Larissa, who apparently was figuring out a fling was also possible in polar climes... In fact, she was probably having freezing-cold sex in an igloo with Thor right at this very moment. Ally's heart was another caveman now, banging on a drum. Raw urgency hummed in the air, and she could almost feel the spirits of a thousand loincloth-wearing men carving a new story on the walls, cheering them on.

Curb your imagination, Ally.

'Ally,' he breathed. The imaginary cavemen went quiet as the slightest brush of his thumb along her forearm sent another pulse of electricity skittering under her skin. Every instinct in her body leaned into his touch.

'Tell me to stop.' Dev's voice was the kind of rough caress that might have come from a scene in an erotic movie. His words, and what they'd just shared, were charging the air between them, second by second.

The word was there, teetering on the edge of her tongue. *Stop.*

The simple command would end this before it went too far and sent her to a place she'd find it very difficult to return from. But because she had always been far too stubborn, even with her own conscience, the word would not come out. Instead, Ally swayed imperceptibly closer, her eyelids fluttering as though they were drawn by the most natural magnetism. For a fleeting second, she allowed herself to believe in the fantasy, that this was a cave of new beginnings! A cave where her delicious fling would begin.

Their breath mingled as Dev tilted his head, his intent clear in the softening of his deep brown gaze. He was waiting for her to say it. One hundred per cent, it was written all over his face, because right now, he didn't want to stop at all. This close in the half-light, she could see flecks of gold in his eyes, a world of warmth she hadn't noticed before that conversation, or maybe it had been an admission into the world he locked up tight inside his head. Right now it felt as though she could deep-dive into the ocean of Dev and yet never truly discover its depth. Goosebumps erupted across her skin. She submitted entirely to this yo-yo moment—breathless one second and full to bursting with brain-numbing desire the next. *Kiss me, then,* she willed him.

But he didn't.

So *she* would kiss *him*, she decided. Only, as their lips hovered a hair's breadth apart, the hurricane began. It blew in from the back door of her brain and completely decimated the haze of longing that had taken hold of her senses. First she saw her sister's grief-stricken face, pressed into the aeroplane window on the seemingly endless flight back from Sicily, two empty seats where Albie and Matt should've been. Then she heard the nothingness; the hollow echo of loss around Nora's too-quiet house, even as she moved all her stuff in—and she'd had a lot of stuff at the rental she'd shared with Matt. Then the sobbing late at night from the pantry, where Nora locked herself away amongst the tins and the plastic containers, where Oliver couldn't hear her scream. Then her own reflection in the patio doors as she stared at the shed Matt and Albie had put together, while she and Nora had sat there commenting on their work-to-tea-drinking ratio as if they'd had a deadline and were getting paid. Her face pale, her hair, raggedy and unwashed. Her heart, physically aching from her failure to smell Matt on the pillowcase any more. The last of him, the last piece of physical proof of him, gone.

It all surged up from nowhere, or maybe from where she'd stored it for moments like this. A rapid-fire round of harsh reminders came for her, one after the other. This would hurt so badly already, when it ended. With a gasp, Ally jerked back, breaking the spell. She stumbled slightly, her palm leaving the anchor of his chest as she forced the distance between them.

'I—I can't,' she stammered, her voice quivering with a cocktail of emotions that she couldn't fully decipher. 'I mean, stop. We have to stop.'

'We're stopping.' Dev held his hands up high, as though she'd threatened him with a pickaxe.

'Sorry,' she managed to squeeze out, wrapping her arms around herself as though she could hold together all the pieces inside her that felt as if they were about to shatter all over again. What the hell was wrong with her? 'I just—'

'I get it, it's OK,' Dev said, though he looked annoyed, more with himself than with her. His tone was devoid of any anger, which made her feel slightly better but no less ridiculous for overreacting, both to her memories and to that potential moment of physical connection. 'I got carried away...'

'There's no air in here, it just got to us,' she reasoned, even as the confusion mounted. She hadn't expected that at all, not the almost kiss, not the barrage of memories that had shot in and invoked the fear of God into her. So much for a fling! Maybe she wasn't ready. This attraction to Dev had come at her so suddenly it had thrown everything out of whack, but, realistically, was she even capable?

'We'll just forget all about it,' he said, cementing his own feelings. She tried not to feel disappointed.

Dev dismissed himself to his tent almost as soon as they were back and all night, from her place by the fire, Ally found herself watching his tent, wishing she could just unzip it and crawl inside and curl into him, or at least back into the moment where he'd seen her—all of her, the parts she usually hid away. They had the same pain babbling like a brook under the surface. He was dealing with it differently for sure, but he was still dealing with it. It had united them, created a bond that had turned physical in a heartbeat, it was that strong.

But that kind of pain could never lead to anything except more misery. Misery squared could never equal fun and flings, and she would never risk entering that kind of hellscape again if she could help it.

CHAPTER FIVE

THE AIR IN the coastal village near Kozhikode was as thick as soup, even as the lively Arabian Sea whispered promises of refreshment through the palm fronds. Children giggled in the distance and the less pleasant but ever-present buzz of mosquitoes made Ally scratch her leg on impulse, the second she stepped out of the Jeep after Dev. There was no time for swimming, they had work to do on a new anti-malaria mission. Not that Dev looked in the mood for swimming anyway.

He'd been glued to his phone the whole way here and had hardly uttered a word. Just who he'd been emailing so frantically she had no clue, but he'd worn that look of diligent concentration, almost verging on fiercely unapproachable, that told her she shouldn't ask. They'd barely spoken in over a week. She knew they were both trying to forget what had happened in that cave and all the stuff their admissions had sent shooting back to the surface, but with every day and night that passed they were finding new reasons not to stand or sit close, or to even talk, and it was starting to feel a bit lonely, honestly.

Larry had nothing to offer on it really. Apparently, she'd had a close encounter with Erik, aka Thor, and he'd been weird about it ever since. The compassionate side of Ally wanted to bring it up with Dev, despite the awkwardness of what had almost happened, but the part that didn't want her own backstory of depression and grief to haunt her forced her mouth shut and made her keep her own distance.

Every time she caught him staring off into the distance she wanted to crack a joke, or suggest they explore somewhere else, something new. She wanted the awestruck nerd back, the one who'd smiled and explored those ancient wonders with her, but she hadn't seen that side of Dev since. Almost as if he'd shut some door that she'd started cracking open. Just as she had.

Damn it! Ally smacked at her thigh. Another mosquito bite for the collection—great. Just over three weeks in already, she should be used to the mozzies by now, she thought as Dev shouldered his bag and strode on ahead of her, called by a member of their team, but the constant blotches on her legs were making her feel less human, more pizza, and there was no amount of mosquito repellent that would stop them feasting on her flesh, unfortunately.

Still, this was a different vibe from the vaccine drive. The air hung laden with salt and the tang of fish from the nearby market, and it mingled with the sweet scent of jasmine that was growing in wild abundance along the paths. She was trying to notice the little things now, rather than the big things she'd rather not address, like her mounting crush on the doctor she'd almost kissed in a cave, and the hollow chasm that had opened between them since it happened.

'Namaskaram.' A man with weathered skin and anxious eyes greeted them from a nearby ramshackle building, his hands clasped together in a gesture of respect and urgency. 'We are needing help. Many are sick.'

It struck Ally in this moment, a welcome interruption from her new thinking pattern, which was admittedly mostly about Dev, just how serious a malaria outbreak was with no medical staff or proper facilities. This was exactly why they'd been sent here.

Dev nodded solemnly to the local. His brown eyes swept over the scene, assessing the situation in that calm, methodical way of his that had been driving her crazy ever since she'd seen a glimmer of what must still be swirling underneath. He'd lost his sister. His sister had died a tragic death while *he* was behind the wheel. How could you unsee that, even seven years later? Surely it would haunt you?

'Show us where we can set up,' Dev said, his voice steady. Ally followed suit, trying not to think about the tension that had been building between them since that afternoon. She focused instead on the task at hand, letting the professional mask slide into place on her face, along with a second healthy slather of sunblock, as was becoming standard. They were here to work, she reminded herself, nothing more. Just forget the stupid fling thing. If only she could stop rewinding that magical moment in the cave…before she went and ruined it.

Together, they followed the locals through a maze of narrow lanes, sidestepping chickens and the occasional wandering goat until they reached an open space by the community centre. It was a clearing really, surrounded by houses with terracotta roofs and walls washed in cheery yellows and blues.

'This will do,' Ally declared, her nurse's eye appraising the area for its potential as their triage centre. Dr Anjali Kapur—the Indian physician who'd assigned them to both missions so far—had put her in charge, seeing as

staff for this one was limited. She was secretly pleased
Dev had been assigned too, though if he hadn't, it might
have made things less awkward.

'We need to get organised, fast,' she said, blocking out
the way he was still assessing the scene and occasionally
her when he didn't think she was looking. She turned to
the group from the NHF and directed them with a mix
of authority and camaraderie that made it clear she was
no stranger to crisis situations, if only they knew. She'd
always dreamed of having this much authority. In truth
she hadn't been quite sure she could handle it, being used
to operations on a smaller scale in Somerset, but this all-
hands-on-deck approach to fieldwork was always going
to challenge her, shake things up. Wasn't that a part of
why she'd applied?

'Let's set up stations for temperature checks here—'
she pointed to a shaded spot under a large banyan tree
'—and blood tests can be done inside the centre.'

'Right,' said one of the team members, a young lanky
guy whose name Ally couldn't quite remember, and he
hurried off to unpack the boxes of medical supplies from
the back of a second vehicle that had arrived moments
after theirs.

'Temperature checks, blood tests...what else?' asked
Sameer, their logistics guy, scribbling notes onto a clip-
board. Her iPad had died long ago, which reminded her
she'd need to source the plug adaptors too.

'Hydration station, rehydration salts...' Dev started.

'We need new mosquito nets, and a rest area for those
who've already been seen to,' Ally followed, looking at
Sameer now. 'And locate the plug adaptors if you can.'

'Got it,' Sameer replied, hurrying to follow his direc-
tives. Ally felt Dev's eyes on her again, but she straight-

ened her face. The fact that people were so willing to follow her caused a buzz of pride to thrill through her as she watched the site spring to life. Maybe she could do this. She rolled her eyes at herself then. She couldn't kiss a guy she was crushing on…but she could do *this*.

Dev was carrying a box, and he watched her over it for a moment with something like admiration flickering in his gaze. Then he masked it with his usual reserved expression, and she bit back a jolt of annoyance. They might not have discussed what happened in the cave but she knew he must still be thinking about it, as she was.

Suddenly a clatter from behind them stole her full attention. Dev dropped the box he was holding and sprinted towards the cause of the commotion: an elderly woman had stumbled and was crouched in a heap on the floor. Ally was beside him in a flash. 'What happened?'

'I don't know,' he said, speaking quickly to the lady in local dialect while they propped her up between them. 'Make some space, please!' he shouted at the people who were gathering around. Ally ran, retrieved the medical kit and set it down, assessing the scene alongside him.

'Looks like heat exhaustion and dehydration,' Ally diagnosed quickly, checking the woman's pulse, which was weak and rapid. 'Dev, we need to cool her down and rehydrate her immediately. Help me move her to the shade.'

Dev nodded, already positioning himself to assist her. Together they were able to relocate the woman to a cooler spot beneath one of the canopies, where Dev lifted her expertly onto a makeshift exam table. Ally gently tilted the woman's head back to open her airway and checked her breathing. It was shallow.

'We need to lower her body temperature quickly,' she said. As she positioned the woman on her back and elevated her legs on a pile of blankets to encourage blood flow to her vital organs, Dev retrieved a cold pack from the generator-run refrigerator and placed it on the woman's forehead. He then put another under her armpits, while Ally grabbed a third cold pack and pressed it to the back of her neck.

Her hand brushed his and stayed there as together they adjusted the pack under her head. When she caught his eye she swore she could see something burning for her underneath. It felt good to be helping someone with him, knowing they were a trusted team already. This was something she'd never been able to feel with Matt, something that came only from using her training with someone else in the medical field.

'I'll get some water and electrolyte solution ready,' Dev told her as she soothed their patient, who was already doing better for being in the shade, covered in ice packs.

As the woman took small sips of his carefully prepared drink, Dev set up a portable fan and directed it towards Ally, enhancing the cooling effect, and he watched her a moment, the way her hair was blowing around her face, even as she tried to plaster it back. She could feel his eyes on her as he lingered, awaiting more instruction, maybe? 'Her pulse is getting stronger,' she reported, after checking the woman's wrist again.

'Good,' Dev said, the relief evident in his deep voice.

'You go, I'll stay here, and monitor her vitals.'

'You sure?'

Suddenly she felt a little uncomfortable, as if they were back in that cave. 'Yes, I'm sure,' she told him, taking out a blood-pressure cuff and stethoscope from the kit, and busying herself. 'Blood pressure is stabilising, one-ten over seventy.'

Dev nodded approvingly. 'Let me know if you need anything else,' he said, and she purposely did not look at him. It would only make her heart beat harder for him than it already was.

Over the course of the week on site at the camp, Ally lost herself in the rhythm of work, telling her mind that the shared glances with Dev were purely professional as they moved around each other. Every patient who came through their makeshift triage area brought their own story—a grandmother who could barely stand, a father worried for his feverish son, a young woman cradling a listless baby.

Each time Ally's heart broke a little. It was so different here from the clinic, where she'd worked alongside Larissa for five whole years. What would she do after this? She couldn't exactly stay moving about on missions with the NHF—what about Nora, and Oliver? She wanted to go home, eventually.

Dev didn't, which was why he would be the perfect fling—think of all the things they could do around a place like this, all these magical locations to explore together! But no, no way. Her heart might have tugged in his direction for a brief moment but she wasn't cut out for a fling. Her heart loved too hard. And Nora's grief over losing her husband—someone she'd actually agreed to spend the rest of her life with—was etched like one of those petroglyphs in her memory, a chapter in her life that would scar all of them for as long as they remained breathing. Imagine losing a husband…worse than a boyfriend. Imagine taking those vows and then having them broken by a cruel twist of fate. It had put Ally off marriage too. Too much of a risk.

'Next,' she called out, signalling for the next patient as she readied her thermometer.

Ally wrapped a blood-pressure cuff around the arm of the middle-aged man who'd taken a seat. It was the same man who'd greeted them earlier, she realised. He had selflessly been letting everyone else go before him, till now. His skin was slick with sweat from fever. The line of villagers still waiting for medical attention seemed to be growing rather than shrinking.

'Started about two weeks ago,' the man murmured, his voice weak. 'First it was just a few cases. Then, before we knew it, everyone was falling sick. We sent word to NHF when we realised we couldn't manage alone.'

'Thank you for letting us know,' Ally replied soothingly. 'We're here to help, and we will, OK? As many people as we can.' She offered a reassuring smile, even as her mind raced with the gravity of the situation. If not contained, the outbreak could ravage the entire village. It seemed bad enough already.

Another commotion at the edge of their triage tent drew her attention. A young man had stumbled in, clutching his side and grimacing in pain. It wasn't malaria, she could tell that already. Dev shot her a look that said he'd deal with it, and she joined him after a few minutes, unable to ignore the cries of pain.

'Possible appendicitis,' Dev concluded after a quick assessment, his eyes meeting hers.

'Let's get him comfortable,' she said, already moving to fetch pain relievers and prepare an IV. Working alongside Dev, she found their movements fell into a familiar dance. It hadn't been long, working together like this in these remote locations, but somehow each step they took seemed to anticipate the other's needs. He was impressive, that much was for sure. She'd bet it almost destroyed him, when his sister died right next to him, knowing there was probably nothing he could have done. She had been a little selfish not bringing it up again, she thought now. He hadn't shared much, but that should have been enough!

Maybe she should try and talk to him again…

As Dev's hands skilfully guided the needle into the patient's vein, Ally caught herself watching him closely—his brow furrowed in concentration, a bead of sweat trailing down his temple. It reminded her of the vulnerability they had shared in that moment, right before their lips almost touched. He'd be an excellent kisser. The way he concentrated so deeply on everything he did.

She shook her head, refocusing on the task at hand. She would talk to him. That was all. No more kissing. Or getting close to kissing. It was not going to happen.

'Thank you,' their patient managed now through clenched teeth as the pain medication took effect.

'We need to get you to the hospital,' Dev told the young guy gently. 'You'll be OK.'

'I'm on it.' Ally made the call and Dev took over, his hands finding hers over the IV and sending a spark of adrenaline through her veins.

'They'll be here in half an hour. It's the best we can do from here,' she said.

Dev nodded sagely and asked her to bring some more water. She did so gladly. She would follow any instruction he gave her, she realised. They made a good team. The trust had been there from the start. Well, on a professional level anyway. She didn't trust the way her heart revved up every time they worked together like this or whenever else they were close.

Dev's eye for everyone else's well-being never faltered, and she wondered if he'd chosen this profession, or at least this constant string of assignments far away from Toronto, to somehow assuage his obvious guilt for whatever happened that night, with his sister. If he was helping other people, he was doing what he couldn't have done for his sister.

Just as she was doing what Matt would have been proud of *her* for doing, she thought with a pang. It was no longer a pang of missing him, she realised suddenly, eyes on Dev's broad back. More a pang of recognition that she was moving on, and that, since being here, things were undoubtedly brighter than they had been even a few months ago. Even if she still couldn't seem to kiss anyone, Well...specifically Dev, who was so much like her it was actually scary.

'Ally?' Someone's voice pulled her from her thoughts. 'Can you check on Mrs Kumar? I think she's ready for another round of antimalarials.'

The sun dipped lower and dazzled in the palm fronds as the last few patients were seen to. Ally's muscles ached from the continuous work, and her mosquito bites itched like mad, but at least the team were making a difference here, however small it might seem. Their appendicitis patient was doing fine in the hospital, and she found herself thinking about him as she stepped over the threshold of another temporary abode, hungry and exhausted. They'd worked fast, she and Dev, almost on autopilot. What would their kisses be like, if they could read each other this way?

The small house, which was serving as a guest house to herself and one other NHF worker who had yet to arrive, was a quaint structure with whitewashed walls and a terracotta-tiled roof. Her hosts, a middle-aged couple whose smiles were as warm as the chai they offered her, watched in amusement as she pushed strands of hair back behind her ears and let them show her to her room. It was unfortunate that they stayed only a few days in each place unless they were on a campsite, but the NHF didn't want to invade local communities for long, for various reasons, and at least she was meeting lots of lovely people.

'Your hair is like fire,' the hostess said as Ally put her bag down on the bed. 'Very funny!'

'Thanks, I think,' Ally replied, offering them a smile. She was used to standing out with her auburn hair, but the amusement it brought to others here in India never failed to amuse *her*.

The symphony of insects outside made a lulling melody as the hosts chatted to her in broken English. Ally was being polite. All she wanted to do was call Larry for an update on her own assignment and Thor, then pass out on the bed.

Her room was charmingly modest. A standing fan whirred rhythmically from one corner, sending a breeze across the four-poster bed, which thankfully had mosquito netting draped across its frame. Not that there was much room on her body for any more bites. A single bulb hanging from the ceiling cast warm shadows over three vibrant paintings depicting local life on the walls. One had a goat on it.

'Is that your doctor kit?' a small voice piped up from the doorway. A boy peered in with curiosity and was quickly introduced by her hosts as Anish, their young son. He had a mop of curly black hair and his big brown eyes widened with intrigue as he danced up to her and peered into her bag.

'Part of it, yes,' Ally answered, lowering it to show him properly, impressed by his English. The kids spoke it better than the adults. She pulled out a stethoscope, its metal parts gleaming in the soft light. 'This helps me listen to hearts.'

'Can I hear mine?' Anish asked.

'Sure.' She placed the ear tips gently into his ears and guided the chest piece to his left pectoral. 'Breathe normally.'

Anish's face lit up with wonder as the sound of his heartbeat filled his ears. His small chest swelled with pride, and Ally pictured eight-year-old Oliver again, the way his face always lit up when she walked into the house. She was glad every time she could bring a smile to his cute face, and sometimes wondered how many memories he'd retain of his dad, if any. He was only six when he passed. Still, he was a spirited kid. Oliver always puffed out his chest when he felt important and involved over something small, just as Anish was doing now.

'I want to help!'

'Maybe you can be my assistant later,' Ally teased. He was so cute, and his enthusiasm was endearing as she continued to unpack, arranging bandages, antimalarials and diagnostic tools on a nearby antique dresser, partly so she could double-check she'd have everything she might need for an emergency anywhere, any time, partly so Anish could feel involved.

Soon she heard the front door creaking open again, and her hosts greeting someone else. Then…oh, no.

Dev stopped at her door, his silhouette framed by the light from another low-hanging bulb, registering it was her immediately. Her heart started thudding like an old clock in her chest.

'Looks like we're neighbours,' he commented, his voice betraying nothing of the tension that hummed between them like one giant cloud of mosquitoes.

Of course, it would be you.

His dark hair was tousled, and there was a hint of weariness in the lines around his brown eyes that matched her own. They'd both been flat out all day.

'It's a cute place, isn't it?' she responded, letting her gaze flicker away as she busied herself with the equipment again. 'You must be exhausted.'

'Long day,' he said, simply.

She could feel his proximity like static in the air until he cleared his throat, shifting his weight from one foot to the other, his rucksack still slung over his shoulder. She almost asked if they could talk. They needed to talk, she felt so bad that they'd just left things like this, and so must he. But something stopped her.

'I'll just, uh, settle in next door, then,' he said.

'Right,' Ally murmured, her hands suddenly clumsy with the book she was holding. She didn't dare look up again. Eye contact would most definitely unravel the facade she'd somehow constructed. Thankfully Anish bounded over to him and asked if he could see his bag too. She soon heard the kid chatting in Hindi with Dev in the room next door. Dev sounded extra hot when he spoke Hindi.

Alone again, Ally released a massive breath she hadn't even realised she'd been holding in. The tightness in her chest eased a bit but underneath it all, the worry gnawed at her—they couldn't go on like this. And how the heck was she supposed to keep her calls to Larry about him quiet enough for Dev not to hear? As if reading her mind, her phone buzzed. She clutched at it.

'Larissa!'

'Hey, how's it going? Any news on Dev the delicious?'

Ally paused, then lowered her voice and told her she didn't think a fling was going to be possible, that there was just too much going on with the workload and the heat and her body full of mosquito bites. Larissa filled her in on the dog she'd been walking every morning, and how Thor had bought her some ridiculously expensive imported strawberries and how she really needed to start reading *A Court of Thorns and Roses*. Ally listened, still mentally going over her encounters with Dev 'the delicious'. She could barely even talk to the guy any more, so caught up in her head was she. And how was she meant to sleep at all, knowing he was in the bed right next door? This mission had just got a lot more complicated.

CHAPTER SIX

DEV PRESSED HIS back to the rickety headboard under the whirring ceiling fan. Another email with the emboldened subject line *Valentine's Day* glared up at him from his phone screen. His brother, Romesh, had written again this morning, after he'd failed to respond to Mom. They all wanted an answer. Was he coming home this year or not? Because he'd missed last year, and the one before, and they really wanted to do something special as a family in Roisin's memory. Neither had said what, but Mom was hinting that she'd tell him in a call. It was a ploy to get him to call her, and it sent the guilt into slasher mode inside his brain.

His thumb hovered over the keyboard as indecision gnawed at him from all angles. It wasn't the logistics holding him back from agreeing to fly back to Toronto; he could plan assignments with the NHF around anything and his role was well cemented now, enabling him to drop in and out of location-based projects wherever he liked. It was the thought of being sucked back into the maelstrom of regret and grief and guilt that made him reluctant even to answer these emails.

They'd never said it, but they all knew he'd taken a different route that night, and that he'd failed to persuade her to put the seat belt back on when Roisin had been tipsy and belligerent and had cheekily unbuckled it to try and reach for his bag in the back seat, where the bottle of rum from the party they'd just left had still been sloshing about. If he'd just ignored her drunken chiding and kept his eyes on the road…

Dev was deep in thought, rereading the message for the tenth time, just as a groan cut through the quiet house. He was on his feet before he even registered moving, instinct taking over as he strode down the hallway towards the sound. In seconds, another groan led him to young Anish. He was doubled over in the bathroom.

'Anish?' Dev knelt beside the boy quickly, touching a hand to his back. The child was obviously distressed, and sick.

Anish looked up, his face pale and sheened with sweat, his eyes glassy with pain. 'It hurts,' he gasped, clutching his stomach.

'Where does it hurt, buddy?' Dev coaxed him to lie down on the floor. Quickly but calmly he assessed the boy's abdomen, feeling for distension or abnormal rigidity. This had come on fast. It was possibly food poisoning.

'Here,' Anish moaned, pressing on his midsection.

Dev noted the signs—this seemingly acute onset of abdominal pain, the nausea, the cold clamminess of his skin. When Anish opened his mouth to groan again, Dev caught the sour scent of vomit, just as he saw it spattered on the toilet and floor. It all confirmed his suspicions. Gastroenteritis. It wasn't uncommon here, but in a child this young, it could turn dangerous fast without proper care.

'OK, Anish, don't worry, we're going to make this stop for you,' Dev said, mentally cataloguing the steps he'd need to take—hydration, electrolyte replacement, monitoring for signs of further dehydration. All doable, even here in the middle of the night. Luckily he and Ally had both brought their medical supplies from the camp. Ally, he thought with a frown. He'd have to wake her.

'Will you make it stop hurting?' Anish's voice was small but Dev caught a flicker of trust through the pain that sent his mind back to Nikki, the day his nephew had grazed both knees falling off a cannon at the play park's castle, and he'd patched him up. That was the last time he'd been home. He might be a decent uncle from time to time but, to Nikki and Romesh, it wasn't enough.

Suddenly his attention snapped from the groaning boy to the soft padding of footsteps. Ally emerged, her pale blue oversized T-shirt clinging to her in a way that was both innocent and inadvertently seductive. Oh, man. Dev's throat went dry on the spot, making him clear it louder than he'd intended. He quickly averted his eyes, hoping his professionalism covered the twist of attraction towards her inside him. It was still there, simmering between them like a watched pot that neither was allowing to boil over, and how could he, after she'd sprung away from him in the cave like that?

'Anish?' she whispered now, her voice thick with sleep and concern.

'Ally, could you—?' Dev began, but she was already moving past him, her nurse's instincts kicking in as she assessed the situation. He told her his suspicions and she agreed, racing for her supplies. She barely met his eyes though, and he couldn't help a glimmer of annoyance seeping in, maybe because he was so tired, maybe because she looked so hot in that T-shirt and he could do absolutely nothing about it.

Anish's mother was here now, looking concerned to say the least.

'Mrs Kapoor, why don't you rest in the sitting room? We'll look after Anish,' Ally suggested gently on her way back in. For a moment the boy's mother just hovered at the bathroom door, wringing her hands. But she allowed Ally to help her to the couch next door.

He watched her while he stilled the boy and pressed a damp towel to his head. Before that near kiss, Ally had been giving him all the signs, in fact, he'd been so certain she wanted it…but right at the last minute she'd thought better for some reason. Maybe she wasn't over her dead boyfriend. Probably for the best she stopped it, he thought, and had thought many times since. She was as damaged as he was, that much was evident. And she didn't even know that he had sworn he wouldn't go there with another team member after Cassinda. He'd almost broken his vow to himself.

Still, the tension that had lingered between them seemed to dissolve as they saw to Anish on the bathroom floor, where it was at least cool. They worked in tandem, Ally helping the boy to the toilet to be sick again, and cleaning him up, while Dev measured out an antiemetic.

'Small sips, Anish. It'll help with the nausea,' Dev coaxed, explaining what he was saying in Hindi instead of offering the kid English, as Ally had to. She watched him offering a spoonful of the medication to the boy's lips, and he didn't miss her T-shirt bunched up acciden-tally higher on one thigh as she bent across the bath to fetch another towel, revealing the soft white flesh speck-led with swollen red mounds from the insect bites.

'Thank you, Doctor,' Anish mumbled.

'This is my job, champ. Let's get you feeling better.'

* * *

As the hours crept by, they took turns wiping Anish's clammy forehead with a cool cloth and Ally told him stories in English, which made him smile through his fever. Eventually he felt OK about moving to the sitting room with his mother and Ally prepared the oral rehydration salts, showing Anish's mother how to do it, too.

'Looks like someone's finally turned a corner,' Ally said some time later as Anish's breathing evened out. The cramps that had racked his small body were indeed finally easing.

'Thanks for getting up in the middle of the night,' Dev said, catching her pale blue eyes in the dim light, forcing his eyes not to travel down her T-shirt to her bare legs and feet, or over the curve of her breasts. She nodded and he pretended he hadn't been glancing at her chest, because she wasn't wearing a bra.

Dawn crept up on them as they settled Anish back into bed. His mother was still fast asleep on the couch, exhausted from worry. Together, they tucked the sheets around the boy. Watching Ally smooth back Anish's hair, Dev couldn't help but think she'd make a great parent one day. He'd figured out by now of course that she was an aunt, not a mother, but her compassion and warmth shone through in the smallest actions, all day, everywhere they went, and he knew she'd be the kind of doting mother who would do anything for their child. Like his own, he thought with a pang.

Outside on the porch, only the chatter of insects and the melodic call of a lone koel filled the air. Dev leaned against the wooden railing, letting out a long, tired sigh, rubbing his eyes against the grittiness of sleep deprivation. Glancing back at the still house, he pondered over that email glowing on his phone's screen like an omen. The thought of re-entering that world twisted in his gut.

His parents had never moved house since arriving in Canada, so he'd have to take the small childhood bedroom he'd slept in next to Roisin's. Mom wouldn't dream of him staying in a hotel. She always wanted them all close for the occasion. Even Romesh and his wife and Nikki had to stay there, in an awkward set-up in his old bedroom, which was now an extension of his father's home office.

'Here.' Ally's voice cut through his reverie as she stepped outside into the dawn light that was now starting to spill onto the porch. She handed him a steaming mug of coffee.

'Thanks,' Dev managed, accepting it with a grateful nod. The warmth from the cup seeped into his hands, grounding him. 'You've changed.'

'No, I'm the same person.' Ally's mouth shifted to the side, as if she was judging whether to actually laugh at her own joke. She glanced down at herself in the comfortable top and shorts she'd swapped her oversized T-shirt for. 'Sorry. Yeah, I didn't think anyone needed to see any more of my sleepwear,' she said, and he stopped himself saying anything at all.

'I hope he's gonna be OK,' she said with a sigh, bobbing her head back towards the house and pressing the mug to her mouth. It took his mind right back to almost kissing her.

'He will.'

'And I hope it doesn't spread. He reminds me of Oliver when he's sick.' Ally perched herself on the edge of a wicker chair. 'He gets this little crease between his brows, just like Anish. Mind you, most kids remind me of Oliver.'

'Your nephew, right?' Dev questioned, despite knowing the answer.

'My nephew.' She smiled, though her eyes carried a twinge of pain that drew him closer to her instantly, like a magnet. 'Family's so important, you know?' She pulled a face in his direction. 'Oh, sorry, I didn't mean... I mean...'

'It's OK,' he said. As she spoke, Ally absent-mindedly scratched at her arms. The reddened welts from her mosquito bites stood out against her skin even in the soft light and Dev made a mental note; he had a remedy for that, or at least an old healer in the village did, not far from here. He'd met her on his first assignment several years ago, when she'd brought him several natural remedies he'd been unsure of at the start, all of which went on to help heal his patients in various ways. He'd take her there tomorrow.

'I miss my nephew too,' he admitted now. 'Nikki is my brother Romesh's first, and only.'

'Are you close with your brother?' she asked.

He shook his head slowly. 'Used to be. He, Roisin and I were inseparable growing up. Nikki was barely two when she died, so he didn't even get to know his aunt.'

Why was he telling her all this? Dev rolled his mug between his hands, feeling the warmth seep into his skin, allowing the bitter liquid to battle his fatigue. It wasn't worth going back to bed now. They had to be back at the site soon. He was grateful for the silence now, for the momentary peace it always offered before the world woke up, but Ally was still looking at him. He knew they should probably bring up what had happened between them just over a week ago, and he could tell she sort of wanted to, too.

'I had an email from my mother, and then one from my brother,' he found himself saying instead, on an exhale he hadn't known was building in his chest. 'Mom wants me to go home to Toronto. There's a family thing every year in honour of Roisin on her birthday. Feb fourteenth.'

'Valentine's Day.' Ally tilted her head, the soft curls of her auburn hair brushing against her shoulders. 'And you don't want to go, do you? Because of the memories.'

He turned to her, wondering what was making him divulge all this, suddenly. Maybe because he had no one else to talk to, and she was here. Maybe because she was the one person who might understand.

'I haven't been in three years. It's so selfish, isn't it?' he said, tracing the rim of the mug with his thumb. 'They say they all want me there, but I just don't know how that can be true...'

'Why? Why wouldn't that be true?' she asked, her eyebrows knitting together. She fixed him with that pale blue gaze that always seemed to see more of him than he wanted her to, all things considered. He shouldn't want this woman as much as he was starting to want her. She'd asked him to stop, and he'd stopped, but here he was, telling her all this.

The silence dragged on as they sipped their drinks, watching a hummingbird flit up to the feeder dangling on its string from the overhang.

'I felt the same around my sister for a while,' Ally said, after a beat. 'Like, maybe I shouldn't be there. Just seeing her swollen eyes and her red nose, and hearing her talking to Oliver, explaining why his dad wouldn't be coming back. I thought it was my fault. Like I could have done something to stop them from going out on that boat. We knew the weather was forecast to be bad…' She stopped herself, pressing her mug to her chest. 'If only I'd stopped them going. But how were we to know what would happen? They both *wanted* to go.'

'The boat capsized?' he asked gently, and she nodded softly as his heart started pounding at the thought of it. Her boyfriend, and her sister's husband. So tragic.

'They found them that same night. We were on holiday in Sicily, so nowhere near home. But…my point is, Nora felt the same as me. She also blamed herself for not stopping them. In the end, we could have spent our lives blaming ourselves, or band together and do what was best for Oliver. This is the first time I've left them.'

Dev felt the weight of her words settle over him like a blanket, warm but suffocating all at once. Without thinking, he reached out, briefly touching her arm. It was a simple gesture of solidarity, but it instantly took him back to that cave, and a hot whip lanced his stomach. He stepped back slightly, putting some distance between them. She did the same quickly, sipped on her coffee, then put her mug down and turned to him. Their eyes met and something unspoken passed between them—a recognition of these shared insecurities? It was so strange, the things that kept bringing them together. They still hadn't addressed the last time. Not with words. She stepped even closer, and he mirrored her, moving towards her again.

'Ally,' he began, setting his own cup down, realising his voice was barely louder than the hum of the insects now, 'what happened last week. I think—'

The words caught in his throat as she closed what was left of the space between them, and her lips found his. It started softly, a parting of their lips, a gentle brush, like a test. Then he went back for more, keeping his forehead pressed to hers a moment, running his tongue against hers, till a small groan made its way up his throat and into his mouth, sending her hands to his face, drawing him closer.

The next kiss was loaded with desire, all tongues and hands and heated breath from both, but as quickly as it started, Ally pulled back, training a finger across her lips, as if she was regretting it again. No. There was no way he was letting her do *that* again, not now he'd tasted this and felt her physical response to him and heard her say all that. He reached for her again and her arms looped around his back and shoulders as if refinding her place against his body was as natural as breathing. Something about her was so familiar, he couldn't even place it. Maybe he shouldn't try.

His hands found the curve of her waist through her clothes. 'Are you sure?' he whispered against her lips, just in case.

She pulled back slightly so her hips were barely brushing his, and pressed her palm to his cheek. 'It was just a kiss,' she said with an element of finality and determination that threw him off track for a moment. '*Just* a kiss.'

'If you say so.'

Her eyes narrowed, and she threw her gaze sideways, as if she was coming to some agreement with herself more than with him. 'I do. I do say so,' she said. 'But it doesn't mean I won't require more of them.'

He grinned, despite himself, finding her waist again. 'OK.'

The sound of Anish's mother stirring in the house caught his ears. Footsteps coming towards the porch made Ally jump backwards. 'More coffee?' the woman asked, looking between them, oblivious.

'No, thank you,' they said at the same time, and, with her head held high, Ally excused herself and headed past her, back to her room, leaving him reeling.

CHAPTER SEVEN

THE BUZZ OF conversation filled the local community centre. Ally stood at the front, scratching her arms, scanning the crowd of local leaders and residents who had gathered to receive the new supplies. Beside her, Dev's presence was a grounding force, his tall frame and dark, intent gaze adding weight to the gravity of this joint mission. She was probably on dangerous ground with her colleague after that kiss, but, as she'd said, it was just a kiss. Nothing to get hung up on. Nothing she would miss too much when it ended. Nothing that could ever cause her world to come crashing back down.

So why did her blood skitter to parts she wished it wouldn't, every time he looked at her? Before they'd left this morning, she'd sat at the table with Anish, who thankfully was doing much, much better, and Dev had sat opposite, brushing his foot against hers underneath it on purpose. She hadn't been able to look at him in case she gave the game away to Anish and his mother, who had been so lovely to them so far. It wouldn't do to come off as unprofessional, using her place for a casual hook-up. That wasn't what this was. Or was it? Her mind flickered back to the porch before they'd been interrupted, how he'd looked at her. A rush of warmth flooded her cheeks and she shoved the thought away, refocusing on the crowd.

'Good evening, everyone,' she started, making sure her voice was clear and steady. She was his colleague, someone he could rely on, above anything else, she reminded herself, forcing the thought of his lips on hers away yet again. She'd tasted that kiss all morning, taken a part of him into her bloodstream after learning all that about his family, too. 'We're going to show you the latest supplies, and hand out some mosquito nets. Please come forward if you need them, and, of course, feel free to ask us any questions!'

Dev translated, as he'd taken to doing when Priya, the actual translator, was busy with the patients elsewhere, which was most of the time. They were here to detail the risks posed by malaria and the facts they all really needed to know. As people approached for their nets and sprays, Dev chimed in with some statistics and personal anecdotes from his work in various other places, painting a vivid picture of some of the communities he'd visited on his travels during the last six or seven years he'd been with the NHF. Avoiding going home as much as possible.

After this morning, she was starting to understand a little more where he was coming from with that decision, but she'd pretty much gathered that he blamed himself for what had clearly been an accident. The details hadn't exactly been spelled out, but it was obvious. Her heart had practically spun upside down as she'd told him about herself and Nora, how they'd both blamed themselves for a while for what had happened with the guys. Sometimes, she still did, she thought, suddenly feeling far too far away from her sister again. But whether her point had sunk in, she couldn't tell. She'd been too busy throwing herself on him.

Every time Dev spoke, his deep voice resonated around

the crowd in a way that made her skin prickle for him, like a starved cactus calling for water. What had she started? He was talking about mosquito nets, for goodness' sake, and she *still* wanted to jump him.

But the people here were so grateful and kind, which filled her with pride for both herself and Dev. It was good to know their work here wasn't going unnoticed. Good to feel useful. A few people even approached the front, their arms extended with home-made treats and tokens of their gratitude, their smiles wide and genuine.

'Your being here is a blessing to our families,' one elder lady said to her when they'd called break time. Ally didn't quite know what to say as the woman placed a woven basket filled with ripe mangoes on the floor at her feet.

'Thank you,' she managed, her heart swelling on the spot. She glanced at Dev, catching him observing her with that unreadable expression he sometimes got stuck on his face. Was it admiration? Yes…she believed it was. It made her pulse quicken, even as she was swept away by someone else and their questions.

As the area slowly emptied of its occupants, the air buzzed with energised chatter and Ally caught Dev's gaze from across the room, where he was speaking with the elder who'd given them fruit. His eyes were on her again and she didn't miss a glint of something more than just professional admiration shimmering in their depths. Was he talking about her? She realised she had butter-flies, or maybe giant mosquitoes, in her belly. It was a look that said he saw her—not just Ally, the nurse, but Ally, the woman who had been through the same spin cycle of horror, devastation and guilt that he had…and whose lips still tingled and burned for more of the same connection. Even if a part of them knew they'd never forget what it was exactly that connected them so deeply. It wasn't the best foundation, but it meant something.

Oh, gosh, are you getting in over your head already? Calm down, Ally! You were determined for it to mean nothing.

'Looks like we have mangoes for life,' Dev said, approaching her once the last of the villagers had trickled out. She looked down to their gift and moved it to a nearby table to take back to the guest house, before finding her eyes drawn back to his lips.

It meant nothing, she reminded herself firmly, scratching a sudden itch above her knee. *It was just a kiss,* just as she'd told him.

She was here to have a fling. If only these damn mozzies would stop trying to eat her alive in the process.

'All we need is a blender. I make a mean smoothie. Oliver loves them,' she told him, forcing a smile to her face as she felt another pang for her sweet nephew. Was he missing her yet?

Dev stepped towards her, 'I don't have a blender. But I do have something else I think you'll appreciate.'

Ally forced her smile into a look that she hoped represented indifference and probably failed as her stomach lurched at his words. It felt like their secret was coming loose at the seams, leaving trails in the breeze for everyone to pick up. She tucked a loose strand of hair behind her ear.

'Come with me,' he said, his voice low and laced with a hint of intrigue that sent a ripple of anticipation down her spine.

She followed him, her curiosity piqued, as they navigated through the NHF workers clearing up and into a secluded alcove behind the community centre. The walls felt as though they were cocooning them in a world far away from their responsibilities and she couldn't suppress her grin as, without warning, Dev's hands cupped her cheeks, and he closed the distance between them. The kiss was a firestorm of suppressed longing breaking free and she gasped. His lips moved against hers with an urgency that made her pulse shoot straight to her groin, and the world faded into insignificance.

'I've been wanting to do that all day,' he breathed against her mouth, his fingers threading through her hair.

'Just another kiss?' she whispered, and she felt his smile spread under her lips.

'Just another kiss,' he replied, drawing her in as she grabbed him by the front of his shirt. He'd long given up on buttoning it up all the way to top, it was just too hot. Hot, hot, *hot*. Their attraction was magnetic, undeniable, she thought as their tongues danced and twirled together. She'd thrown up so many cautious walls around herself since Matt died and now she was coming back to life.

As long as she didn't get carried away. Her heart would not at any point get involved in whatever this was. Fun, it was fun, she reminded herself as Dev's arms wrapped around her harder, pulling her closer. This felt too good. Dangerously good. Her heart was dancing the samba as what felt like an hour later—but was probably only a couple of minutes later—he gently disentangled himself, his eyes sparkling with something mischievous that forced an internal groan to echo throughout her entire body.

'I almost forgot, I have a cure for those itchy mosquito bites you've been complaining about,' he said, a grin tugging at the corner of his mouth as she buffed up her hair. 'It involves a little diversion.'

'Is that so?' she replied, scepticism lacing her tone, though she couldn't suppress the flutter in her stomach. She should probably not take any diversions from her duties, neither big nor little, but then they were done for the day, besides the paperwork, which could be dealt with later.

'Trust me,' he said, leading her away from the community centre and onto a forest trail at the back. The funny thing was, she did. The idea of a little dalliance with Dev was exciting. And he'd thought about her mosquito bites too… Talk about a hero.

They hurried the last few steps to avoid being seen. The sunlight played peekaboo through the dense canopy above and the silence kicked in, nothing but their footsteps and the sounds of insects and birds. As they walked, he stopped occasionally, pulling her into his arms for another intoxicating kiss. Each one sent her heart into overdrive. Oh, my…she couldn't wait to tell Larissa how into it he was.

Ally felt giddy, like a schoolgirl with a secret crush, relishing the illicit thrill of this secret escapade. Larissa was going to melt. She was likely frozen in place, what with her current location…not that Thor, aka Erik, wasn't thawing her out being hotter than Iceland's volcanic craters. Good, Larry deserved some fun, too.

Soon they reached a clearing, and Ally felt her eyes widen at the sight of a small camp nestled unassumingly in the protection of the forest. A tent constructed of worn and faded canvas stood right in the centre, and an older woman with silver hair in braids emerged. She regarded them with knowing eyes that seemed to see right through Ally and, for some reason, Ally felt nervous.

'Um…' she started, but Dev was already approaching the woman, reaching out a hand.

'This is Amrita,' he introduced. Amrita looked to be about ninety-nine years old. In the light, Ally saw the lines of wisdom etched into her skin and she was instantly humbled. 'We met a few years ago on an assignment nearby.'

Inside her tent, the air was thick and stuffy in a good way with the scent of herbs and spices, all mingling with the unmistakable aroma of incense. It was more like a pharmacy and it was clear that this was no pop-up arrangement. Rows of glass bottles lined the shelves, filled with contents of every hue—amber liquids, powders in every shade imaginable, and more jars of unidentifiable balms.

'Everything is made from what's around here, what grows wild,' Dev explained, picking up a small vial that was filled with a vibrant green paste. 'This is made from neem leaves, for example—it's really good for skin irritations.'

Ally peered closer at a jar containing a honey-coloured syrup. How did he know all this stuff? 'And this one?'

'That's a cough remedy, I think, with wild honey and tulsi leaves.' He came up so close behind her that she could feel his breath on the back of her neck, and instantly she felt warmer herself. It was very impressive that he knew all this stuff. Amrita was chiming in, her eyes twinkling as Dev translated. 'She says it's especially good in the monsoon season.'

Each potion seemed more intriguing than the last, and Dev explained that Amrita was a healer, a keeper of ancient wisdom that transcended the modern medicine they both practised in the western world. Ally couldn't help but imagine this woman sitting in a wicker chair in the corner of her sterile clinic back in Frome, dishing out her little vials and jars.

'Here we are, here's what we came for,' Dev said now, offering Ally a tiny bottle that Amrita had given him. 'Try this. It's a blend of citronella and eucalyptus oils. A natural mosquito repellent. It's pretty strong, better than anything you'll get in the pharmacy back home.'

Ally expressed her thanks, taking the bottle, and she felt his eyes on her as she dabbed a bit of the oil onto her pulse points, inhaling the sharp, clean scent. He handed her another, told her to rub it on her bites, and the cool liquid on her skin tingled. The sense of relief was immediate, and she let out a long sigh, surprised to find her eyes were damp.

'I didn't even know how much I needed this. Thank you,' she whispered.

In this moment, the connection she felt to this place and these people stretched beyond the physical and into something far more. It felt a lot like something her soul had been needing, without her even knowing. She could picture Larissa standing in the tent doorway, saying something like, 'See, you wanted an adventure! How about this for an adventure?'

Desperate for more of the pleasant tingling to override the itching on her shoulder blade, she tried to reach a new itch. 'Let me help with that,' Dev offered. Dev's presence in the tent seemed to take up more space than physically possible all of a sudden, especially with Amrita looking on.

'Um, there's more light outside?' she managed, edging towards the doorway. Quickly she stepped back out into the sun, where she could breathe.

'Where?' he asked.

'You'll see it,' she replied, the word barely above a whisper, as she turned her back to him. She gathered her hair and swept it over one shoulder, exposing the nape of her neck and the expanse of skin down her back that she couldn't quite reach.

His fingers brushed against her skin as he uncapped the bottle, sending a shiver down her spine. The potion was cool as it touched her inflamed bites, but it was Dev's touch that ignited a roaring fire inside her. His hands were gentle yet firm, the movements deliberate as he spread the remedy across her skin. Ally closed her eyes, noting how the sensation of his touch was somehow both sooth-ing and intoxicating at the same time. Instantly she was picturing his hands going everywhere else, and she would let them, she realised, feeling wicked.

Opening her eyes, she saw Amrita had stepped out-side. She clenched her palms at her sides, so they wouldn't reach for Dev. She wouldn't touch him.

'Does that feel better?' he murmured close to her ear, his breath fanning over her shoulder.

'Much,' she managed to say.

'Good. Because it all feels good to me,' he said softly.

Oh, my goodness.

They could start a fire, she thought, swallowing back a retort before she landed herself in trouble.

'Your remedies are wonderful,' she said quickly to Amrita, willing the flush to vacate her cheeks. Did Am-rita hear the way Dev had just been flirting with her? She'd come here to work, she'd promised Nora and Oli-ver she would be working, not…having a good time?

Why couldn't she have a good time? Because the need to merely soldier onwards was all she'd known for way too long, and she didn't quite know how to live properly in the moment just yet, she realised. And also, she missed home.

The old woman studied Ally with eyes that seemed to pierce right through her. 'Child, there's a sadness around you,' she observed suddenly. Then she said something else in Hindi to Dev that for some reason made her heart start to rev like a rusty engine.

Dev translated, screwing the lid back on the potion. Half smiling, and sort of frowning, he turned to her. 'She said your sorrow is like clouds before the rain.'

Ally's heart jumped to the tip of her tongue. How could this near stranger see what was going on inside her head?

'She wants to know if we'll join her for a blessing ceremony,' Dev told her, letting the old woman squeeze his hands.

A what? she wanted to say, picturing herself in the back of that yin yoga class she'd dragged Larissa to not so long ago, when they'd had to sit on tennis balls with their hands in the heart position for so long she'd had a tennis-ball-sized bruise on her bum for two weeks after.

Dev was looking at her with that intent look he probably mastered at birth, probably noting her scepticism. She heard Larissa again in her head, reminding her she was here for adventure.

'OK,' Ally said. 'Sure, let's do it.'

Ally lay on the mat looking up at the sky. It was made of woven grass, and it was making her thighs itch more than the mosquito bites, but the earth beneath her was cool under the forest canopy, a much-needed respite from the heat of the sun. Hopefully someone was looking out for leopards.

The scent of incense curled through the air, mingling

with the musk of the fauna, and Amrita's rhythmic, soothing voice seemed to harmonise with the distant calls of the birds and the chirping bugs. If only Ally could bottle this and import it to Somerset, where the stench of cow manure and the sound of churning tractor wheels were prevalent over anything else, most of the time.

She closed her eyes as the ceremony—whatever it was supposed to achieve—began, letting the chant wash over her like a gentle wave. Dev lay on the mat beside her. She opened her eyes to look at him. Surprisingly, he was immersed in the moment. OK, then, maybe there was something in this, she thought. Maybe it wouldn't leave her jaded to all things spiritual as that tennis ball in the yin yoga class did.

The ritual turned out to be quite profound, involving a series of chants in Hindi and low mutterings in no language at all, the burning of herbs, and the laying of hands. As Amrita's palms hovered above her, Ally felt an unexpected warmth radiating through her belly, right around her heart. Confused, she opened her eyes again, but there was no fire, nothing hot at all. Weird.

The heat seeped deeper into her pores, and the longer she had her eyes shut, the more she felt it melting away some of the heaviness that had cocooned around her. She'd known it was there, of course, but somehow only now, as it dissipated, did she realise how much darkness had been there since Albie and Matt died, and...oh, gosh, poor Nora. If only Nora could be here, too, she thought.

Now it was as if each intonation untangled a knot inside her, unravelling the grief in some way and leaving room for breath, for life. She was surprised to find hot tears pricking the backs of her eyelids but, at the same time, Dev's mouth on hers sprang into her mind's eye again, stoking the fire she'd been snuffing out for too long, and she felt the strangest urge to smile.

Amidst it all, she sensed Dev's presence next to her, and when Amrita's strange but soothing chant lulled to a close, Ally took a deep breath, her chest expanding with a lightness she hadn't known she had been craving. Amazing! Opening her eyes, she turned to him, expecting to share a smile, some mutual relief, but instead, she found him staring into the canopy above. His face was etched with a vulnerability she had never seen before. It shocked her.

'Are you OK?' she whispered, reaching out to brush her fingers against his arm.

Dev's gaze drifted down to meet hers, and there was a slight tremor in his voice when he spoke. 'I didn't expect...that.'

'What?' she whispered back.

He closed his eyes and drew a breath before releasing it, kneading his eyes with the heels of his hands. Ally bit back her next question. He didn't need her to question him right now. It also didn't feel quite right to admit she'd rather enjoyed the whole thing. She didn't feel so much like 'clouds before the rain' as 'sunshine after a storm', and she had Dev to thank for it. And Amrita, of course.

'You released something though, didn't you?' she said softly, unable to resist. 'Something to do with your sister.' The words slipped out of her, and she expected him to confirm it, maybe offer her a smile even if he didn't speak, but his face clouded over, as if he'd taken on the storm she'd just shifted. He sat up slowly, rubbing the back of his neck.

'We should get back to the others,' he said, without looking at her.

Ally nodded, sitting up alongside him as her heart thrummed. 'How long have we been gone?'

'Too long,' he said, as if he were speaking from a different planet all of a sudden.

What happened? she wondered as they made their way back through the trees. This time, he didn't stop to kiss her at intervals, and she followed silently behind in a cloud of his melancholy. He was probably more affected by his past than he'd admitted, and it only made her want to know him more, but he wasn't going to talk about it with her, which was fine, she reminded herself. She wasn't emotionally attached, that would never be the case here. There was no need to know *everything* about him!

Liar, the voice in her head chided.

CHAPTER EIGHT

ALLY CLUTCHED HER PHONE, shaking her head in disbe-lief. She was trying not to let her laughter ring too loudly through the makeshift bamboo hut that was right now serving as her personal phone booth in the back of the community centre.

'Thor, the god of thunder, is sweeping away your cob-webs already,' Ally teased, imagining her friend's face at the other end of the line.

'He's definitely not a god, and he has his issues, but, let me tell you, he has a hammer that can cause quite the storm.'

Ally snorted. Her friend was sounding like a differ-ent person already, which was so nice to hear. Also, the absurdity of their conversation about her new life in the Arctic was a welcome break from the daily rigors of the camp, and reminding people why applying mosquito re-pellent, herbal or otherwise, might just save their life.

'Enough about me and my polar exploits,' Larissa said now, steering the topic elsewhere. 'Tell me about your healing session.'

Ally's smirk disappeared as she was thrown right back to the other day, lying on that mat.

'Believe it or not, it felt like something shifted inside me,' she confessed, hearing how her tone turned contemplative instead of portraying the usual jokes, which were admittedly a mask Larissa had learned to see through long ago. 'I've slept like a log ever since. Maybe there is something to this whole energy work thing.'

'Ooh, mystical Ally. Never thought I'd see the day a qualified nurse says something like that.' Larissa chuckled. 'And how are things with our handsome Dr Chandran? Done the deed yet?'

'No. And it's complicated.' Ally sighed, playing with a loose thread on the curtain by the door. 'I'm thinking it might be safer to stay friends.'

'Safer? Since when did you agree to play it safe?' Larissa probed.

'Since I met a man who makes me want to wrap him up in blankets and protect him from the world,' Ally admitted. She sighed again. 'He's...vulnerable, Larissa. And I'm tired of broken things.' Ally chewed her lip; the lie felt wrong, but if she didn't put a line under it, vocally, to her friend, she might go back on her word. The thought of getting entangled with another man who was all jagged edges inside made her hesitate. Wasn't she supposed to be the reckless one here? Not the healer! He had people in the jungle for that.

'Ally, if it's no-strings, what does a bit of baggage matter? Just live in the moment for once,' Larissa urged.

'Easy for you to say; you're shacking up with a Norse deity, with issues,' she retorted. Larissa hadn't seen Dev's face that day, after the ceremony. Ally and Dev hadn't spoken about it since, but she knew whatever had happened was still on his mind. 'Anyway, baggage is baggage and he has it.' She paused. 'Just like I do.'

Just then, a shadow blocked the sun streaming through

the doorway. She looked up, holding the phone away from her. It was Dev.

'Look, I gotta go,' she said to Larissa quickly. 'We'll talk later?'

'Sure thing. Stay out of trouble, and give Dev a chance to surprise you,' Larissa advised before ending the call.

'Who was that?' Dev asked as Ally pocketed the phone.

Oh, no, what did he hear?

'No one,' she said.

'Talking to yourself is the first sign of madness, you know.' He smirked.

'Or genius,' Ally shot back, recovering her composure as she turned to face him. 'I prefer to think I'm brainstorming with an expert.'

Dev nodded, and she knew he'd heard something. It was too late to pretend she hadn't been talking about him. 'Listen—' she began, but he cut her off.

'Ally, I've been meaning to talk to you.'

Uh-oh.

Dev knew he had to tell her. It had been playing on his mind ever since that ceremony. Whatever Amrita had done had brought back, not only the accident, but everything that happened after it, and, most notably, the way he'd buried himself in unsuspecting women to stop the guilt crashing back in. He was turning to Ally the closer he got to potentially going home to his family, and after what happened with Cassinda he had sworn never to hurt anyone else.

'There was someone else before—a co-worker,' he said now, and Ally crossed her arms, eyeing him with suspicion.

'OK,' she said.

'We were colleagues, as in she also worked for the NHF, and things got messy.' He might as well tell her the whole story, before she got any more ideas. 'She wanted more than I could give. She wanted me to settle down, stop moving, stop accepting assignments.' He ran a hand through his hair, picturing the way she'd blown up like a volcano in his face and started packing up her bags. 'I can't go through that again. I won't put anyone else through that...'

'Is that what you think this is?' Ally snorted. Dev looked up in surprise. 'Honestly, listen to yourself. You think I want to *trap* you?'

'No, I—' Dev faltered. This was not the reaction he'd expected. 'It's not about you,' he continued, lowering his voice as someone wheeled a cart through the community centre. They were separated by nothing but a flimsy bamboo wall. 'It's about me not wanting to hurt you—or anyone else.'

'Because you think I'm broken already,' she concluded. Behind her the colours of the sunrise were starting to paint the sky.

'No,' he said, 'but I literally just heard you say *you* were tired of broken things.'

Ally flushed and dragged her hands through her hair. 'I didn't necessarily mean that,' she countered.

'My baggage is carry-on size only, I assure you,' he quipped as she visibly squirmed. 'But I don't want to make promises I can't keep.'

Ally nodded, stepping back to put some distance between them again. She was touching her lips, feeling their future kisses disappear on the wind, probably. He did the same without thinking, mirroring her.

'I get it, Dev. Really, I do,' she said. 'And maybe I was

putting on a bit of an act for the sake of my friend, and…
to protect myself. But let's be realistic. I'm leaving at the
end of this. I have a home to get back to…a job!' She
paused then. 'Well, I *will* find another job, but my point
is, I know you're going to keep on moving. I know you
don't want to settle down. I know you don't want to go
home because you feel bad about how your family look at
you, even though I'm sure they love you, and miss you…'

Ouch. He felt his shoulders slump for a second as her
eyes widened in regret. 'I mean, oh, gosh, I'm sorry, but
it's true. Isn't it?'

He shook his head, feeling the shame wash over him
like an ice bath. It *was* true, and she was too observant,
and too honest. And it didn't make him want her any less.
He just couldn't bear the memories of Roisin everywhere
at home, his family reminding him what he'd lost.

*Keep on moving, keep working, keep helping other
people…nothing else matters, they'll understand. Won't
they?*

'Anyway, Dev, I'm not looking to get hurt any more
than you want to hurt me. We're both adults.' Ally
stepped closer, working her jaw side to side, as if conclud-
ing something in her head. 'If we were to continue this,
whatever it is, I would consider it more of an agreement.'

The tension that had knotted his shoulders began to
ease as he considered her words. She was offering him
an out, a chance to maintain their connection without the
weight of expectations. What happened with Cassinda
couldn't happen here, basically. 'An agreement,' he repeated.

'Look,' Ally said. The determination in her eyes
amused him suddenly. This woman was crazy, and he
liked it. 'A fling wouldn't be the end of the world, Dev.

I think we both know I'm not looking for promises. I'm not even sure if I'm ready for anything serious, maybe I never will be.' She bit her lip and diverted her gaze, as if she'd revealed a little too much.

OK, this wasn't what he'd expected either, not at all, but it *was* exactly what he needed to hear. Ally had always been straightforward, and he suspected her humour was a bit of a shield against everything she'd gone through herself, in Sicily, and back in Somerset, but now sincerity replaced sarcasm and he found himself drawn to her honesty. And the thought of more of those kisses...

Raking a hand through his hair, he searched her face for any last sign of uncertainty. He had to be sure she was being honest. His heart raced at the thought of being close to her. He'd been so damn lonely lately, and horny with all this heat, but there could be implications.

Ally crossed her arms in the other direction, and drummed her fingers. He noticed her mosquito bites had gone down a considerable amount. 'We're adults, and we know what this is. We know what it isn't. I'm not asking for more than you can give. I've got my own baggage, remember?'

He nodded slowly, watching her perfect lips, wanting to pull them gently between his teeth. She inched closer now, and he swore he caught a flicker of doubt cross her face before she snuffed it out and looked at him from under her eyelashes. 'Just don't fall for me, Doctor,' she said.

His body responded to her proximity before his mind could keep up. Dev pressed his mouth to hers, claiming her lips as if he had no other choice. Her magnetism was always going to win over his resolve. She moaned against his mouth, ramming her hands in his hair again, then down his back, digging her nails in, leaving her mark.

'OK, then,' he breathed, training a thumb over her bottom lip. 'Let's keep it simple.'

'Simple,' she echoed with a slight quirk of her lips. He couldn't fight the smile. A promise wrapped in a single word. An invitation. Without thinking any more, he swept a hand behind her head and closed the gap again. The kiss grew hotter and hotter and only when her hands began unbuttoning his shirt did he remember where they were. The community centre was bustling outside and she stifled a laugh, forcing herself backwards, smoothing down her hair.

'You're going to ruin me,' he growled, doing his shirt back up with a groan. Ally was watching him, lips swollen, eyes narrowed.

'Rule number one: No falling in love,' she said.

'Ha! As if,' he scoffed, his laughter a little too sharp. He caught the flicker of something in Ally's expression, the same vulnerability he'd seen when he'd learned how she and her sister had blamed themselves for what had happened, until deciding it was no one's fault. Different from what happened with Roisin, he thought, as a flash of darkness cast a fresh shadow on their conversation. That had been his fault, even if no one else had ever let him believe it.

Was this a good idea? What if she developed feelings and tried to pin him down, as Cassinda had, even after promising not to? Being in one place was dangerous—that was when you started letting people in, developing ties and emotions.

'Rule number two: We stop if it stops being fun,' she proposed next, her voice dropping to a more serious note.

'Fun,' he echoed, tasting the word. It sounded simple enough, yet the weight of a million potential complications bore down on him like baby elephants. They hadn't even slept together yet but this chemistry was crazy. It could keep him still, focused on her. The danger zone. It could put a real dent in his professional integrity, too.

'Or we could just stick to being plague-fighting buddies,' she added, lifting an eyebrow in a playful challenge.

'Plague-fighting buddies?' he repeated, unable to suppress a snort. 'Sounds like a bad comic-book duo.'

'Bad or brilliant?' Ally's grin was infectious, and Dev found his face stretching into a cat-like smile despite the tumult that was starting to feel a lot like a collective of crickets bouncing about in his abdomen. Some of the tension had lifted, at least. Before he could reply, she stepped towards him boldly and claimed the back of his neck with both hands.

Dev's hands roamed down her back and he couldn't help but feel a thrill at the way she all but melted into his arms, time and time again, as if she belonged there. It had been so long since he'd allowed himself to feel desired, wanted by someone who knew exactly how to touch him and make him feel like this...as if he was finally getting out of his own head.

Just as things started to get heated again, Dev pulled back abruptly, leaving Ally breathless. He'd been somewhere else entirely but he'd come here with another purpose.

'I actually came to tell you something else,' he said now, and, reluctantly, she released his crinkled shirt from her grip. 'We've all been invited to dinner,' he told her in a low voice, right into her ear. 'Time to act like we don't want to tear each other's clothes off.'

'Plenty of time for that later,' she responded, and it was all he could do to calm the bulge in his pants long enough to make an exit.

Ally's gaze wandered beyond the clinking glasses and animated faces, and rested on the lush tapestry of green cascading with the waterfall down the rolling hill. The elevated terrace where the NHF team had gathered for a special dinner to honour their last night on the malaria project was buzzing with the kind of warmth their Kerala hosts had quickly become known for throughout their posting. Their group were being treated to an array of local foods by the villagers, who were grateful for their work over the last week and were sorry to be seeing them go tomorrow, and Ally breathed it all in as she dug a fork into a chunk of spicy broccoli, feeling happy. Yes, that was it. She was happy. Content. It felt nice to be happy and content for once.

'I could get used to dinners like this.' Dev's voice brought her back to herself, his dark eyes reflecting the myriad lights. Dusk was settling over the landscape now and a soft glow from overhead lanterns dappled over the tables, casting an extra vibe of enchantment over the scene. 'Better than rice and peas.'

'Much—why is it always rice and peas lately?' she replied, her heart skipping a beat as memories of their last kiss sent a thrill down her spine. Tucking a stray strand of hair behind her ear, she lowered her voice. 'Maybe the food will be better when we move on tomorrow, to the maternal health camp. And maybe you won't ignore me there.'

'I have to ignore you. Because if I don't, I will kiss you in front of all these people,' he replied in a growl, trailing a hand over her knee with delicate fingers under the table. She suppressed a groan as it inched part way up her thigh, before she coughed and crossed her legs, essentially shooing him away. He was telling the truth. They'd been avoiding talking to each other since sitting down, even though they had purposely sat next to each other and the magnets were still doing their thing.

'Make it up to me later,' she told him. 'I dare you.' *Where is this confidence coming from?*

'That won't be a problem. In fact, let's seal that promise,' he said, raising his glass in a mock toast. Without even knowing what they were toasting, everyone at the table raised their glasses.

'To us,' Ally said, clinking a round of glasses. She couldn't help but laugh, but uh-oh. Was this being entirely unprofessional, and silly? she thought as laughter rippled between them, along with a fresh tangle of excitement and trepidation.Yes, it probably was silly. She'd entered that conversation with a certain amount of bravado in the heat of the moment, and even told him they should stop if it stopped being fun, but she already knew she was incapable of *not* developing feelings for a guy she was kissing at every occasion. His guilt over that ex-colleague, and his sister, coupled with her own propensity to unleash a maelstrom of emotion at any moment meant they shared a heavy load, but she just needed to keep reminding herself to be who he thought she was: fun, a functioning adult, perfectly capable of a meaningless fling.

'Stay out of your own head,' she muttered.

Dev smiled, as if to say, *Caught you talking to yourself again, weirdo.*

He started talking to someone else at the table, and Ally found herself in a conversation with their medical assistant, Aryan. Soon their chat was interrupted by a loud laugh that sounded far too smug for her liking. Ally turned her attention momentarily to the left, where Dev was still talking to another colleague, who might or might not have had too many beers. But that wasn't what held her attention. Dev's words floated over to her, clear and immediately jarring: 'Honestly, I'm single by choice. I can't imagine *anything* tying me down. I enjoy travelling too much.'

'Yeah, I'm the same, mate,' the guy agreed, clinking his beer can to Dev's glass of water.

A pang of annoyance pricked at Ally as she reached for her own drink, feeling her smile and happy buzz both faltering for a moment. It wasn't as though she expected declarations of love, far from it, but hearing Dev's cavalier dismissal of attachments literally hours after their last intimate encounter stung more than she cared to admit, especially after he'd so enthusiastically agreed on their… well…agreement. Was this for her benefit? She shot him a look of annoyance down her nose, but if he registered it, he didn't react.

'Man, that's the spirit,' one of the other doctors lauded now, clapping Dev on the back. 'Freedom to roam the world—that's living the dream.'

'Definitely,' a female volunteer chimed in, her admiration thinly veiled as she glanced Dev's way through her eyelashes.

Ally noted the mixed reactions—surprise flickering across some faces, nods of respect from others. She forced a laugh, aligning herself with the majority, while, inside, a quiet resolve took a stranglehold on her heart. If Dev's world had no room for anchors, she'd be wise to remember to ride the waves, so to speak, not sink beneath them. If Dev could enjoy these stolen moments for the fun they were, without looking back, so could she. In fact, she would initiate them. Lots of them. That was one way to stay in control, she reasoned.

But it wasn't just that bugging her, she realised later, when people were packing up for the night and she was smearing more of her magic anti-mosquito potion all over her legs. Dev was running away from things he needed to face, things with his family, if what he'd said was anything to go by. They missed him, surely, and, romances aside, he was doing all this 'travelling' in order to stay away from them, out of guilt for something he hadn't done. How infuriating that she was starting to know the real him, when everyone else saw only what he thought they wanted to see. But was it really her place to bring it up again?

As Ally and Dev made their way down the winding path back towards the guest house, the rumbles in the distance crept closer, until they were right above their heads.

'I think it's going to—' she started just as the sky opened up, releasing a torrent of heavy rain that felt as though someone in the treetops had upended a barrel of water over them, a proper downfall, not one of those bouts of measly drizzle she often encountered back home. This was real rain with a purpose. They ran, laughing as the downpour soaked through their clothes. Ally's dress was growing more transparent by the minute.

'Come on! You're too slow,' Dev called, grabbing her hand.

'You're taller than me—with those legs you're a gazelle compared to me!'

'Are you comparing me to a beast?' He laughed, pulling her into the shelter of a large banyan tree as the rain lashed at the ground all around them. His eyes sparkled with mischief, right before he kissed her. For a heartbeat, she sank completely into him, feeling his hands caressing her face, then her backside. His words at the dinner table charged back into her head, but what was the point of caring now?

He urged her closer with intent and deepened their kiss, his tongue dancing with hers as his hands roamed up her back to her hair, tugging gently on the strands, then harder. It was so erotic she could hardly stand it. He pushed himself deeper against her, and Ally let out another soft moan, her body melting into his as she responded to his touch by wrapping a leg around his middle. She could feel the rainwater dripping down her neck and back, her skin tingling from the sudden cold mixed with a thousand new sensations all hitting her at once. She'd never been this turned on, ever.

Their lips parted and they gasped for air before another kiss plunged them deeper into this entirely new world where she could not have stopped if she tried. His back was against the tree, her hips crushed to his. In an instant, the playful banter had shifted into something charged, something electric. Their laughter subsided into heavy breaths as they stood there kissing, the rain cascading around them with force. Ally could feel the desire emanating from his body mounting as his lips crashed against hers hungrily, and his hands hoisted the fabric of her wet dress up. She wrapped her arms around his neck and pulled him closer.

His lips worked like magic, sending shivers down her spine and making her dizzy with want. She pushed herself against him harder, arching her back to feel his hips pressed harder against hers.

The scent of wet earth swept her up with his cologne as they kissed desperately, hungrily, as if there were no tomorrow, and the world seemed to narrow down to the very space they occupied, to the sensation of his hands on her skin, the hardness of him pressed to her thigh.

'We should probably get out of these wet clothes before we both catch pneumonia,' he said against her lips. Somehow, even the word *pneumonia* sounded too sexy for her to resist pressing her mouth back to his again.

'Stay with me tonight,' Ally whispered, her fingers tracing the line of his jaw as she found her breath. She was panting, dizzy, and the words slipped out, so bold! Where was this raw desire coming from all of a sudden? A fight for control...because he wouldn't be sticking around?

Don't think about that!

All she cared about as he held her close was seizing this moment and exploring this connection before it slipped away. It was definitely going to slip away. He'd made that clear. And she was fine with it.

They dashed the remaining distance to the guest house.

CHAPTER NINE

ALLY'S BEDROOM DOOR clicked shut behind them, her shushes filling the space as Dev stumbled with her into the dimly lit room. The rain had completely soaked through their clothes, even more during the mad dash back to the guest house, and now, in Ally's warm room, in the dark and quiet, the reality of their entwined figures was setting every one of his nerve endings on fire. Whatever this was, it was too late to stop now, and it didn't seem as though either of them wanted to either.

Their mutual urgency was almost comical, hands grappling at damp fabric, tearing away every layer that separated skin from skin. The thud of wet clothes hitting the floor shot through the silence, and he held her naked frame to his chest from behind, letting his fingers trace the contours of her back, following the water droplets sliding over her shoulders. In truth he was trying to memorise the path of every curve without her clothes concealing her body, and she was perfect. So perfect, in fact, he was increasingly glad he'd made that announcement at the dinner table, about nothing tying him down.

His thoughts betrayed him as he turned her around and kissed her, flickering back to the phone call he'd overheard. 'He's…vulnerable, Larissa. And I'm tired of broken things.' She'd said it, and he'd heard it, taken it through to his core. He had vocally feigned indifference about relationships to keep her from seeing just how much her words had affected him once the thrill of their stolen kisses and the agreement had subsided slightly. How could he reveal the depth of his growing affection when she was right, he was carrying baggage, more than she deserved to try and carry along with him? Yet somehow he could not keep away.

'Dev,' she breathed out, pulling him onto the bed with her, and wrapping her legs around him. He'd been lost in the sensation of her kisses, and her fingers tangling in his wet hair. 'I want you.'

'Are you sure?'

'Do I look unsure?' she replied with a breathless laugh, tightening the grip of her thighs around his middle. Her eyes reflected a hunger that definitely matched his own, even though he was acutely aware of the vulnerability behind his facade. He should be anywhere but here, in Ally's bedroom, with her skin all radiant and flushed, and their rain-soaked clothes discarded all over the floor, but from the intensity that crackled between them like a live wire she was determined to live out this agreement and he wasn't going to retract everything he'd said either. They were adults, they knew their boundaries.

She reached for the foil packet on the nightstand, which he noticed she'd taken out of the drawer discreetly while they'd been making out. He searched her face for any sign of hesitation, any trace of doubt. He found none— only an affirmation that what they were doing felt right despite all the reasons it shouldn't.

'Promise me something?' Ally asked, drawing him closer.

'I thought you weren't looking for promises,' he replied. His heart thumped with anticipation and something else he couldn't quite name as he hovered above Ally.

'Let's just…let's just be here, now. No past, no future. Just us.'

She said it as if she was trying to convince herself of something. 'OK,' was all he could seem to say in response. For a moment, he allowed himself the luxury of being present, of feeling her beneath him, around him, a connection he hadn't expected to make.

'You love making deals, don't you?' he teased, running his hands along the smooth skin of her arms.

'I do.' She smiled, and her gaze said she wanted him more than her roving hands did.

Then, the shrill ring of her phone sliced through the thick air of the bedroom like a scalpel. He watched her eyes widen as she scrambled naked from beneath him to grab the device from the nightstand.

'Hello?' Her voice was breathless, and definitely carried more than a hint of what they'd just been about to do. He pulled the sheet around him and lay on his back, staring at the ceiling fan, catching his breath. The room was so quiet he could hear the voice on the other end of the line, even without her putting it on speakerphone.

'Ally? It's Nora. I need you; it's about Oliver…' The female voice was strained, edged with urgency, and Dev could feel the shift in the atmosphere, as if the temperature had suddenly dropped.

'Is he OK?' The concern in Ally's tone was palpable, and Dev found himself holding his breath, silently willing everything to be all right. It must be her sister. He recalled the name, Nora, and Oliver too. Her nephew.

'He's… It's just been a tough day, and he's asking for you. Can you talk to him?'

'Of course, put him on.' Ally glanced apologetically at Dev. Her eyes were clouded with worry. He nodded, mimed that she shouldn't worry about him.

'Hey, sweetie, what's up?' The transition from the passionate lover Ally had almost been just now to caring aunt was seamless, and Dev felt a twinge of something that might have been envy. She made it seem so easy. Should he go? He felt like a spare part suddenly, as if they'd physically entered the room and caught him naked.

'Can you read my story, Aunt Ally? I worked really hard on it,' came the small, hopeful voice that Dev assumed was Oliver's.

'Send it over, Ollie. I'll read it right now...oh, you want me to listen? Um...sure, I'd love to.'

She put her hand over the phone for a second. Sorry, she mouthed to him, already moving to sit at the small desk by the window, her wet clothes forgotten on the floor as she pulled a robe around her body.

'Take your time,' Dev replied, the words feeling hollow as he pushed himself off the bed. He grabbed a towel and wrapped it around his waist. An odd sense of displacement settled over him as he watched her switch gears so effortlessly.

He retrieved a glass of water from the bathroom, returning to find Ally absorbed in her nephew's story. The affectionate smile playing on her lips as she listened softened something inside him. It reminded him why he'd been drawn to her in the first place: she was fun and hardworking and kind... This nurturing spirit he was seeing now was so damn attractive in a woman. For a second, he could imagine her tucking a kid into bed, reading a story. For another second that surprised him he imagined himself bringing her a cup of tea while she was doing it, perching on the end of the bed.

'Listen to this bit, Dev,' Ally said, putting a hand over the receiver again as he sat down tentatively. 'And then the brave alien defender decided that no intergalactic monster was too big to fight if it meant protecting his family.' She repeated her nephew's words and laughed softly, and he could hear she was bursting with pride. 'He's got quite the imagination, our little Ollie. And such a good heart.'

'Sounds like someone else I know,' he mused, his thoughts drifting involuntarily to the email from his brother that he'd been dodging. The contrast between Ally's fierce loyalty to her family and his own strained ties didn't exactly make him feel all that great right now. In fact, all this was leaving him feeling exposed, as if she were unwittingly holding up a mirror, reflecting all his inadequacies. He cleared his throat, started gathering up his clothes from the floor, and she watched him, frowning down her nose.

'Just come back in ten minutes?' she said, holding her hand over the phone.

'I'm pretty tired,' he murmured, leaning in to drop a soft kiss to her forehead. She pulled away, shot him a look of surprise that might have been tinged with hurt, but he knew he'd killed the passion now, and he wasn't about to fake that it would just come back in ten minutes. Slowly, he crept out of the room with his clothes, and shut the door behind him.

Dev adjusted the straps of the medical supply bags slung over his shoulder as he took in the maternal health camp that the team had set up. The air was alive with a melting pot of languages. Healthcare professionals carried things between tents, while expectant mothers clustered in groups, some with wide-eyed children clinging to their colourful skirts.

The goal at this specific, and already far too humid, location was to help minimise complications and ensure a safe birthing environment for the women who would otherwise not have access to such care. But, as with all assignments, no one knew what kind of situations they might be asked to deal with in yet another small village tucked away between mountains and jungle.

And this thing with Ally was already another 'situation' Dev wasn't sure how to handle. Where did they stand after last night? She'd left the guest house early this morning and made her way here on another truck, without him. Tonight, they would all move as a group to new lodgings. Tents. Already he was dreading it; he never slept well in tents, and it was even harder to find any privacy on campsites.

At least he'd have another excuse for not having Wi-Fi, he thought before he could stop it. No...he would reply to his mother. And he would consider going home for Roisin's birthday. Ally had made him think, and truly take to heart what a terrible son and brother he was being. It stung more after last night.

'Over here,' she directed now, her voice cutting through the hum of conversations. Ally was standing ten feet across the site in her shorts and a shirt, her white coat loose over the top, and her red hair shining in the sun, piled high on the top of her head. Boxes of medical supplies bulged open by the table she was setting up under a canvas canopy, and the water dispenser was already half empty, as usual. The heat was more intense than

ever today, and already Dev could feel the sweat clinging to his neck under his collar. Together, they began to
unpack, setting up their workstations beside each other
without discussing it.

'How are you this morning?' she asked a little frost-
ily, without looking at him.

'Good. Ally, can we talk?' he asked after a moment.

She didn't meet his gaze and focused instead on adjusting the nearby incubator's settings. 'Not now, Dev.'

'Later, then.' His voice was steadier than he felt, but
he respected her evasion. The underlying current of de-
fensiveness in her tone was obvious.

'Later,' she agreed, though the word hung in the air
like a placeholder for a conversation he knew she didn't
particularly want to have.

He soon found himself seeing to a young expectant
mother with a standard check-up, and a little nutritional
advice; it wasn't doing her much good, only eating veg-
etables in accordance with her religious beliefs. She ran
the risk of becoming anaemic.

He felt Ally's eyes on him as a five-year-old girl wandered over, clutching her doll. Dev hunkered down to her
level with a warm smile. She introduced the doll as her
baby sister, a role-play they encouraged in these camps
to educate older siblings about newborn care. Soon he
was showing the girl how to support the doll's head, and
his gaze flitted once again to Ally. She was cradling an
infant in one arm, feeding him from a small bottle filled
with formula. Right until the bottle seemed to crack and
milk started spilling everywhere.

'Need a hand with that?' he asked, making his way to
her side as she put the child down gently and struggled

with a stubborn box of new bottles. They were here to provide essential medical care to expectant mothers and new mothers alike, and as such the team was prepared to offer all manner of prenatal care, postnatal check-ups and even childbirth if it came to it. But whoever he found himself talking to, his mind lagged behind, and his eyes wandered to Ally, replaying what had happened the night before. She was obviously still annoyed with him for just leaving.

'Got it, thanks,' she said, tearing the tape off a bit too quickly and almost causing the box to topple over.

He caught it deftly, and she smiled and muttered thanks, but it didn't quite reach her eyes. In minutes he was called away to attend to another patient, which he was glad about, considering her coldness was giving him frostbite despite it being a thousand degrees out. If only he could keep his mind from drifting back to her naked body exposed beneath him. They'd been so close. They would have kept that hook-up going all night, got zero sleep. Maybe it was better they'd been interrupted, he mused, swiping at his forehead. He was already feeling things he wasn't sure what to do with around her. Even her rejection just now grated at him in ways it shouldn't; usually he'd put his emotions completely aside and focus on the job.

Their silent dance of awkward coordination and stolen looks was disrupted when a local volunteer approached, calling for help. Straight away Dev abandoned his station again and crossed to where the guy was cradling a small form wrapped in a threadbare blanket. Dev's heart plummeted.

'Doctor,' the man called out again, his voice laced with

urgency. 'They must have known you were coming. They just left him here in the bushes! Can you look?'

Sensing the commotion, Ally's snapped her head up, and she crossed the distance in seconds. Dev watched as she gently took the baby into her arms before he could, uncovering the tiny, yellow-tinged face of the jaundiced infant. The baby's skin was pale and his body frail, and Dev's heart squeezed at the sight of it, the vulnerability... the look on Ally's face as she held it close.

'Malnourished, by the look of it, and abandoned,' he heard himself say, brushing Ally's fingers as they both went to touch the child. 'Tough start to life.'

'Let's run a check,' Ally murmured at him, already moving towards the incubator with the baby cradled close. She was handling the tot so carefully and calmly, but Dev could see the dogged determination in her face as Ally checked the baby's pulse, her fingers pressing delicately against the tiny wrist. His own hands moved seemingly of their own accord, prepping needles and drawing fluids for intravenous hydration.

'Likely hypoglycaemic,' he said quietly, focusing on measuring out a precise dose of dextrose. His gaze flickered to Ally as he handed her the syringe, her usually lively blue eyes clouded with concern. She took it from him with a nod, her hand steady as she found a vein and administered the solution. The baby cried out again and she shushed it, not leaving his side, even as Dev slipped off to see to a few other patients.

'All right, Sahil,' she whispered to the baby, when Dev returned to her side after several long minutes seeing to yet another pregnant teenager. They really needed to have a talk about contraception around here.

'Sahil?' He cocked an eyebrow.

'I named him. I had to,' she explained, and he watched the baby's tiny fingers curl around one of hers. Maybe it was a mistake to name him, he thought. Didn't that mean she'd grow attached? They should both know enough about the dangers of that by now, but how could he say that? Thankfully the baby seemed to have calmed down just a little under Ally's careful touch and attention. 'We need to get him on some nutritional supplements,' she told him, and this time she looked up, catching his eyes.

'He'll be OK,' he told her, needing to say something to reassure her. For now, they were a team. And having seen how maternal she was, at least with her nephew, Oliver, he knew it was important to her that they both do everything in their power to help this child... Sahil... get a better start than just being abandoned in a bush for anyone to discover.

Dev fetched the necessary equipment from the tent nearby. He returned with a small bottle filled with liquid vitamins and minerals prescribed for malnutrition cases like this one, and watched as Ally tried to feed the child. The baby seemed hesitant at first but eventually started suckling on it, his little body trembling with each gulp. Dev felt his heart expand and contract as her eyes reflected an ocean of compassion, the same look that always shifted something inside him. She extended her attention so effortlessly from her family to even the smallest, most forgotten lives, like this one. Her nurturing nature contrasted so sharply with the walls he'd built around his own heart, he might as well be wearing knives, and he'd barely even noticed how it had affected everything around him, till now.

His thoughts were interrupted by Sahil's soft cries. His tiny fists were clinging onto Ally's loose coat now, as if he were aware of their efforts to save him and was begging not to be abandoned again.

'We won't let any more harm come to you, sweet one,' Ally whispered, and Dev hoped they would be able to ensure that actually happened. 'We will, won't we?' she asked him now, quietly. There was so much hope in her eyes he couldn't stand it. If local organisations couldn't locate the child's birth mother, abandoned babies were often placed in orphanages or children's homes operated by the government or NGOs. He told her this, and she nodded thoughtfully. 'In some cases, babies like this are placed in foster care with temporary caregivers.'

'I know some people feel like they don't have a choice but to give up their child,' she said, brushing a thumb across the baby's soft cheek as he looked over her shoulder. 'I mean, how do you know what you'd do in any situation, if you came from a broken home, or you were too poor to care for it, I suppose...but I just... I couldn't.'

Dev stopped himself from putting a supportive hand on her shoulder. There didn't seem to be any words. He could tell by the look on her face how heartbreaking she was finding this, but in truth it wasn't the first abandoned baby he had seen across his missions with the NHF. Only now he was able to look at it through the lens of a woman he cared about, a woman who clearly had strong maternal instincts.

His own mother, who'd been nothing short of doting to her kids, growing up, must spend an awful lot of time wondering where he was...out here, flitting about, largely uncontactable, avoiding home because of the memories they themselves lived with every single day, in the very same house. Not for the first time, he saw his unforgivable distance through her eyes, and he didn't like himself very much for adding to his mother's trauma when she'd already lost one child.

'Excuse me,' he said to Ally now. 'I really have to go and make a call.'

CHAPTER TEN

ALLY'S BOOTS CRUNCHED on the underbrush as she and Dev trailed behind the chattering gaggle of local children, their chirpy voices weaving through the dense forest like sunlight between leaves. It was hot, as usual, and Ally was tired, what with the drama of doing everything in her power to ensure that poor baby Sahil was OK. He was doing much better than yesterday when they'd found him, thankfully, and he was now resting in the care of their local volunteers, but she was worried about his fate. There were so many children and worried parents and expectant mothers to see on this assignment. It was the most stressful one yet.

There was Dev, too, she thought, glancing back to find him trailing her, probably looking out for leopards and snakes and whatever else was waiting to eat her now that the mosquitos had finally grown tired of her taste. Dev's hot mouth and lingering kisses and eyes that could undo her were another reason for her skyrocketing stress levels and sleepless night last night. She'd lain awake, thinking about Oliver, and the fact that Dev had sneaked out of her room after they'd been about to do the deed. Charming! After today, all she wanted to do was head to their next campsite, locate her tent, and sleep. But these kids had seemed bursting with excitement to share something with their visitors from afar, and she couldn't exactly say no.

'*Anayude kulikkam kandu!*' one boy shouted over his shoulder now, wriggling his finger eagerly ahead.

Dev ambled up beside them, his tall, broad frame looking ridiculously good today in a T-shirt the colour of the leaves. 'They're excited for you to see the elephants bathing,' he explained, brushing a branch aside before she could walk into it. 'It's a tradition here.'

'Thank you, Dev,' Ally said, a little too coldly in light of all this wonderment around her. She had always been better than average at masking her feelings with humour, in fact, she was a pro at it, but in this moment, there was no need for a facade. He knew she was annoyed. That was why he'd tried to talk to her earlier. But the stubborn part of her was not going to let him off. He was scowling now, to himself, and she let out a frustrated sigh.

'Well, you just disappeared,' she said, keeping her voice low. 'I thought we were going to—'

'We *were* going to,' he finished, coming up beside her properly, making her nerve-endings fizz with the instant proximity. 'I'm sorry, OK, you just seemed busy.'

'Was that all it was?' she asked him. 'It seemed like I did something to scare you off.'

Dev went to reply, but stopped himself, chewing down on his lip, and she sighed again, pushing forward, forcing her shoulders to stay squared even as a palm branch swiped her round the face. If he wasn't going to talk to her, she wasn't going to force him. Maybe that agreement had been a stupid idea anyway. It was already more trouble than it was worth.

As they drew closer to the spring, the air grew even thicker with the symphony of nature's sounds. Ally was starting to recognise the calls of different exotic birds and enjoy the carefree laughter of the children at play. They seemed to live with the kind of simplicity that kids back home could probably never imagine. She couldn't help but be swept up in the infectious joy of it all, and soon she found herself forgetting her annoyance and fatigue and joining in their games, though she could feel Dev's eyes on her hair flying behind her as she chased the little ones through the jungle paths, laughing and ducking under low-hanging branches.

'Tag! You're it!' she called out, tapping a giggling girl on the back before darting away, pretending to trumpet like an elephant. The child squealed with delight and gave chase, her bare feet kicking up dirt as she followed the sun-speckled path. The heat clung to Ally like a second skin, sweat beading along her forehead. As she dodged behind what looked like a cabin in the undergrowth, shaded and almost hidden by vines, to evade her pursuer, a brief respite allowed her the space to breathe. But Dev rounded the corner in a flash and stopped right in front of her.

The feel of his kisses lodged in her mind, stubborn and intrusive as she ran her eyes over his, then down to his mouth. 'I see you found the kids' secret hideout,' he said, stepping closer, till he was obstructing her entire vision.

She pressed her back to the corrugated wall. 'What is this place?'

'It used to be a hunter's lodge,' he said, and she drew a breath, remembering the look on his face, how he had left her room so abruptly just as things were getting intimate.

'Does that make me your prey?' she whispered.

All she could think of was the warmth of skin on skin that had felt like nothing else she'd ever experienced, even with Matt. But as a result of those feelings, all swirling dangerously inside her, he'd also left her feeling rejected when he'd left last night, and hadn't even thought to come back as she'd asked.

'I'm sorry,' he said again, cupping her face. She leaned into his palm and closed her eyes, wishing she could stay angry. 'It wasn't that you did something to scare me off. Me leaving was not a reflection on you.'

Ally felt her jaw twitch. 'So what was it?' Why wouldn't he just talk to her?

'Ally, come on!' A small boy had run back for her, and was tugging at her hand, bringing her back to the present. She pulled herself away from the vine-covered wall, motioning for Dev to come, too. The laughter of the children up ahead by the spring mingled with the distant trumpet of an elephant and the sound felt like both a warning and a welcome.

Ally found a secluded, shady spot by the spring. There were four elephants here already.

'Are they dangerous?' Ally asked, her gaze following the gentle giants as they rolled and splashed in the late afternoon sun. Their hides, rough and weathered, glistened under the warm rays.

'Usually only if they're provoked,' Dev replied, sitting next to her as the children scattered along the water's edge, keeping a safe distance. Some produced sketchbooks and pencils. 'But it's best to respect their space.'

As the elephants bathed, there was a simplicity in their movements, a ritualistic grace that soothed Ally's restless thoughts. She let out a breath and allowed herself a moment just to be—to watch these animals, so ancient and wise, reclaiming something she supposed had been lost in human nature. How often did she just sit, and think, and be? It was tough to do that, what with all the thoughts that rushed back in every time she forgot to block them out.

Ally turned towards Dev, his profile cut against the backdrop of the forest. 'I'm sorry too, for being distant today,' she started, the words clumsy in her mouth. 'When you left last night... I guess I felt a little rejected. I haven't done...this...' she wiggled a finger between them both '...in a pretty long time. I know I always rush to talk to them whenever they call. It's a sense of duty, I suppose.'

Dev's expression was unreadable for a moment before he nodded slowly, understanding dawning in his brown eyes. 'That sense of duty is one of the things I admire about you,' he said. 'But it does make me reflect on how bad of a son, and brother, I am. That's why I left last night.' He brushed her shoulder on purpose with his, and goosebumps shot down her arm.

Ally bit her lip, considering. 'OK.'

'I've been avoiding giving my family an answer about my sister's birthday event.'

'Valentine's Day, right?'

'Yes. But I've told them I'll go now. Told them this morning.'

'Really?' Ally looked to him in surprise. She'd seen him on his phone today, with a look of consternation on his face. But if he was planning to return to Canada for Valentine's Day, it meant he'd be leaving in two weeks, or less, and before her. 'I mean, that's great, of course you should go home,' she said, doing her best not to sound concerned. 'Will you be back, afterwards?'

She watched a smile tug at his lips, and she realised she had sounded more hopeful about that than she'd intended. Dev just shrugged as she pulled her eyes away. 'Maybe, but usually if you leave an assignment early, you're just assigned a new one wherever they need you next. Especially as this one's so far from Canada.'

Ally felt his hand on hers, and the subtle gesture went some way to curbing the wild fluttering in her stomach. He could be gone so soon, and she'd probably never see this man again. 'Ally,' he said softly. The intimacy of the contact and the tone of his voice drew her gaze from the children's games to his face again. His eyes were pools of questions. He opened his mouth to speak, but she cut him off.

'Well, I guess that's it for us. Our agreement,' she said quickly, as rejection settled right back into the place he'd just removed it from. It wasn't fair, or right, to feel this way, but she couldn't help it.

'Neither of us entered into this thinking it would last,' he reminded her gently, running a thumb along the back of her hand. Ally's mind swam, even as she let her head fall softly against his shoulder.

'I know,' she said. 'It's just not easy for me, letting people in. Not any more,' she admitted. 'And I did it with you anyway, for some reason. Stupid of me, really.'

'Not stupid,' Dev said, and she could feel him choosing his words carefully. 'After what you've been through, I get why this whole thing was harder for you to initiate than you're making out. I do, Ally, don't think I don't see that.'

Ally felt her pulse throb. She drew her knees up to her chest, wrapping an arm around them. He could obviously tell she was watching their time together come to an end before it even had, because he exhaled long and hard. 'This is… We should just stop,' he said resolutely, though he didn't let go of her hand.

'We *should* stop,' she agreed, but the silence stretched on and she didn't let go of his hand either.

An elephant trumpeted, making the kids shriek, and Dev gave a flutter of a laugh that shook her head, making her lean into him more. Her other hand felt for his shirt, balling it in her fingers, drawing him closer still.

I'm scared, Ally wanted to confess suddenly. I am scared of stopping, and also of not stopping. I am scared of falling in love and then losing it all, all over again. Her other hand twitched beneath his, betraying the turmoil that was making a total mess of her insides. She couldn't say it, she couldn't even admit it to herself, that she was falling for a man she barely knew, a man she hadn't even slept with yet. And that she was going to miss him madly. She had promised herself, and him, that this wouldn't happen!

Dev's thumb was still drawing small circles on the back of her hand in a calming rhythm that anchored her to the moment. He looked away for a second, as if gathering his thoughts, before turning back to her.

'I don't want to complicate your life, Ally,' he began, his voice carrying a tremor she had never heard before.

'I know.'

He shook his head, squinting into the sun. 'After the car accident, everything changed. My relationship with Mom was pretty strained. She was always reaching out, and I gave her barely anything back. I think in some way I've been waiting for her to get mad, so she could direct her anger at me like I deserve. And dreading it, too.'

'You don't deserve anyone's anger, Dev,' she reminded him. 'And I bet no one is angry at you!'

He just set his mouth into a line, shook his head. 'I owe it to her to be the son she feels like she's lost,' he said. 'I need to be there for my family more, like you're there for yours.'

The silence stretched on. Ally drew a breath.

'So what happened, the night of the accident?' she asked softly, the word *accident* hanging in the air between them for what felt like an eternity. Dev stared at the elephants but kept the circles going on the back of her hand, as if she was grounding him.

'I took a different road that night. A shortcut. Roisin was drunk, distracting me...'

Ally listened, her heart aching at the raw honesty in his voice as he told her about the driver in the other car coming too fast in the other direction, how he tried to swerve but left it just a second too late. She pictured him, young and carefree, a life altered in an instant by a twist of fate. No one was immune to tragedy. The lump in her throat felt like a football, and she hesitated before voicing the question that had been nagging at her. 'But you want to keep on travelling, whatever happens with your family?'

Dev's gaze returned to hers, steadfast. 'Of course. There are still so many people out there who need help, and I can't imagine not being part of that. Working with NHF...it's part of who I am.'

'Even if it means leaving things—or people—behind?' she asked, a hint of uncertainty lacing her words.

'Even then,' he said, yet his fingers tightened around hers, suggesting he wasn't ready to sever this connection just yet. Then he looked at her sideways as if an idea was brewing in his head. 'What about you? Has this given you a taste for something else, a life on the move?'

Ally shook her head slowly, weighing it up. The thought of not returning to her sister, to the life she'd put on hold, didn't sit right and she felt it right through to her bones. Living the kind of life Dev lived wasn't an option for her. She had Nora and Oliver to think of. They needed her. And Larissa. Larissa was her best friend, and she needed her too. She was needed at home. And home was *home*, it always had been, even if she loved it here, even if she felt needed and useful in a way she hadn't at the clinic, amongst all these people who had no clue what it was like to have the facilities they enjoyed in other parts of the world but were, for the most part, happy and grateful and full of life!

Dev was looking at her intently, and she knew he was reading her mind. They were doomed. This agreement was already in ashes. They sat in silence for a moment, each lost in contemplation. Then, as if drawn by an invisible string, they turned their attention back to each other and, in seconds, Dev was kissing her again. Slowly at first, as if he were saying goodbye, but hidden from the children, in the shade of the trees, she was soon on her back, her legs wrapped around his middle, and he was hovering over her as though they were back in the bedroom, picking up where they'd left off.

She gasped as he started running his mouth along her lips and neck and chest in earnest, moaning her name, clutching her hand above her head as she reached for him with the other. She responded to every move hungrily, surprised at how her body was reacting to this cocktail of passion and torture. In the background she could hear the children playing by the spring, their laughter mingling with the sound of water splashing against rocks, the elephants, but they couldn't seem to let each other go.

'Come on,' Dev said suddenly, standing up and pulling her to her feet. 'Let's join them. I'm getting too hot.'

Ally looked up, breathless, smoothing herself down.

She couldn't even find the words. What was happening? Weren't they stopping…this?

Still, she laughed as she felt the cool water splash against her legs, her hand still firmly grasped in Dev's, the kids jumping and splashing around them, a safe distance from the elephants, who didn't look bothered by anything at all. The playfulness of the moment was infectious, and she gave herself permission to forget about the future, or whatever else she might lose. Doomed or not, maybe it was time she and Dev both learnt to live every day as if it could be their last, and not think about the fact that all this was leading nowhere fast.

CHAPTER ELEVEN

DEV ZIPPED THE tent flap closed, sealing away the wind that was kicking up outside in the cool early dawn. The space, lit by a single overhead lamp, seemed to shrink as he turned to face Ally. She was sitting cross-legged on her sleeping bag, and her face told him exactly how she was feeling, as usual.

'Hard to believe Sahil is gone,' he murmured, his voice low and heavy with the same emotion he saw etched into her pout. Why hide it, at this point? They'd shared everything this past week at the maternity camp, and not just their skill sets. He perched on the edge of her bed. The weight and intensity of their shared experiences here had been drawing him towards her both physically and emotionally this morning and now...here they were. It was still only six a.m. The foster family had arrived early to take baby Sahil away into their care, and he'd got the feeling that Ally didn't want to be alone.

Ally sat fiddling with the hem of her shirt sleeve. 'So strange,' she agreed, her throat tight. 'I'm going to miss him so much. Silly, really.'

'Not silly,' he assured her, reaching for her hand, and letting them fall into a companionable silence, the kind that was probably only shared, he thought now, by those who had to do things like this for a living, on pretty much a daily basis. A lot had happened in the week since they'd rescued the jaundiced, abandoned newborn. Ally and he had visited him in the makeshift nursery every day, either together or separately, and he knew she'd grown attached. They both had. Not just to the baby, but to each other. And now, five weeks into her stint in Kerala it felt more as though she'd been away, and with Dev, for years. The air between them was charged and electric with the potential for something more than they'd ever discussed, because it was completely illogical to even think about it.

Dev cleared his throat, glancing at Ally. Her auburn hair was spilling over her shoulders like a cascade of leaves and he liked her with no make-up like this. He liked her...he just liked her. Too much.

'You know...' he began tentatively, his heart pounding against his ribcage as if trying to break free, 'you would make a fantastic mother some day.' His words floated into the space between them, landing softly yet resoundingly in the quiet of the tent. He'd been thinking it every time he'd seen her with Sahil, and even before that. 'It's what you want, right? Eventually, one day, if you meet the right person?'

She lowered her gaze. 'I doubt it will happen now, so it doesn't matter what I want.'

'You could meet someone,' he said.

Ally's gaze darted away, and Dev kicked himself. What was he doing? He could see the muscles in her jaw tighten. He recognised the evasion. It was clear she didn't want to unravel the threads of this conversation, not when their time together was a ticking clock. Valentine's Day, and Roisin's memorial, was just a week away. Why did he ask that anyway? It wasn't any of his business, they weren't in anything serious, and right now, each second was marching them closer to an inevitable goodbye. Everything he did was for Roisin. He owed it to Roisin's memory to keep moving, keep doing good in the world...to make up for what he inadvertently did to his family.

Ally met his eyes again and, for a moment, Dev saw a spark of her usual fire flicker back to life. Then her lips curved into a soft smile that did funny things to his insides. 'We're not here to think about stuff like that, are we?' she said, pressing a hand to his thigh and squeezing it suggestively. 'We promised we would make the most of now.'

'*Now*, now?' he asked, as his body reacted instantly.

Their gazes stayed locked tight. Dev could hear Ally's breath hitch ever so slightly, the pull between them was mutual. 'Ally,' he whispered, the name feeling like a caress even as it passed his lips. The rest of the world seemed to fall away as their hands found each other, fingers intertwining naturally. He brushed a strand of her hair away from her face. How could he lose this—her smile, the sound of her laughter that could somehow make a day's worth of exhaustion evaporate?

Ask her to stay, the voice in his head urged, suddenly. He should just ask her...but wouldn't that prove his selfishness? His life was a series of departures and destinations strung together, fleeting connections. How could he even try and tether Ally to such a transient existence when she seemed so content with this being a two-month thing?

'Dev, make love to me,' she murmured now, the syllables heavy with an emotion he couldn't even name. He was hardly going to refuse. He peeled off her shirt, and she unbuttoned his, aching to feel her skin against his, as much as possible. He tugged at her lip softly with his teeth, making her moan and arch into him.

How many times had they done this now? He was losing track. Every night, every morning, whenever they could sneak away. Ally's presence was a balm to the part of him that felt perennially adrift and he was starting to need her and crave her. But the thought of anchoring himself to her, only to inevitably sail away again left him stuck. She wouldn't want him, or this life, after a while, and he'd be the one to suffer. Dev's heart thudded against his ribcage as Ally arched into his touch. His hands knew her now, his fingers were expert navigators already when it came to her body.

'Is this OK?' Dev found himself asking, though every fibre of his being screamed for him to close the distance even further.

'More than OK,' Ally replied, her voice a whisper that somehow filled the tent. Their lips were dancing their regular dance now, even as he fought his mind to stop dragging up the past. The air between them crackled with anticipation, their breath mingling in the small canvas space, all longing and zero restraint. He could see the pulse quicken at the base of her throat as she ran her tongue over her lips. She was so beautiful.

'I think I'm—'

'Shh,' she said, placing a finger gently against his lips, her touch setting off a cascade of goosebumps across his skin. 'Don't,' she urged, but there were tears pooling in her eyes as he pressed into her and they moved as one. What was happening to him? This kind of thing just... did not happen to him. This was what he had feared, that he'd start falling in love with her, and want to change his

entire lifestyle, when he'd sworn never to get this emotionally tangled again—no good could come of it. He
had work to do, people all over the world to help, and
how could he do that with integrity when his mind was
wandering elsewhere?

But the longer they spent together the world around
them—the canvas walls of the tent, the distant hum of
the insects—all his self-imposed limitations receded into
nothingness. There was only Ally: the curve of her waist
under his hands, the silkiness of her hair as his fingers
threaded through it, the press of her body against his,
her fingers tracing the line of his jaw before tangling in
his hair.

As they both reached the inevitable peak of pleasure,
Ally muffled her cries into his shoulder and silenced his
own with her hot mouth, and yet they still didn't stop.
He lay inside her, wrapped around her, lost in her, and
he was about to let out a laugh at the pure intensity, the
crazy, unthinkable words that had actually been on the
verge of tumbling out of his mouth, when suddenly, a
huge jolt shook the entire tent.

Ally almost fell from the bed. Dev caught her, pulling
her against him as the ground beneath them started to
shake violently, as though a giant had reached from the
sky, picked them up and dropped them again. The tremor
rippled through the tent and outside, the sound of heavy
objects crashing and frightened screams sending a bolt
of panic through him. 'Earthquake!' Ally yelled out in
unison, her voice laced with panic. She tried to jump off
the bed of her own accord but he stopped her.

'Wait, Ally, it might happen again.'

The chaos of the shaking world seemed to mirror the
utter strangeness and unpredictability of life he'd just

been musing on, the fact that his foundations were being truly shaken to the core by this woman. Was this some kind of cosmic joke?

'Are you all right?' he managed to ask over the din of rattling medical supplies and the distant cries of people in the vicinity who had just been rocked awake by the quake.

'Yes, yes, I'm fine,' Ally breathed out, blinking in shock. 'We have to make sure no one is hurt.'

They hurried to pull on their clothes and stumbled out of the tent as another aftershock from the earthquake pulsed through the earth under their feet. They had to get out, see who needed help. What if someone was trapped? Ally's grip on Dev's arm was vice-like, her knuckles white. One minute they'd been making love and he'd said...or almost said he loved her. Or had he? Nothing made sense right now.

She glanced around to see a member of the NHF team standing in the doorway of the next tent, looking shaken and sleepy, and now eyeing them with curiosity. The quake had subsided but now people, not just this guy, were seeing the two of them emerging from the same tent. But with the ground still threatening to split open at any moment, the potential for gossip was the least of Ally's concerns.

'Are you OK?' Dev called over, his voice steady despite the chaos erupting around them.

'I'm OK,' the guy said, swiping his brow. A quick ask-around confirmed no one was hurt. Ally could barely think straight.

'You OK?' Dev was looking at her again, concern written all over his face.

'Fine,' Ally managed to reply, though her voice trembled. She released his arm, suddenly conscious of how close they were standing together amidst the disarray.

As if on cue, the ground lurched beneath them again. 'Oh, God!' she squeaked, grabbing his arm again—who cared what anyone thought? A nearby table laden with medical supplies toppled over as the campsite descended into pandemonium. Glass vials shattered against the dirt, spilling their contents. A portable ultrasound machine crashed to the ground across the campsite, its screen flickering before going dark. Boxes of sterile gloves burst open, their contents scattering like bulky blue confetti. Ally's heart raced as she scanned the camp. A metal tray clanged loudly as it hit the floor, sending instruments skittering across the ground. The first-aid kits were up-ended, their bandages and antiseptics now covered in dust and debris. She heard something, coming from across the site. A person? Her heart lurched. Suddenly she was on her feet, heading for the noise.

'Watch out!' Dev called out sharply, yanking her back, just as the canvas roof of the nearby supply tent sagged dangerously, threatening to give way under the weight of a broken support beam.

'We need to see who's over there,' she cried, pointing to where she'd heard the noise. Her mind was spinning like a boat on the edge of a swirling vortex in the middle of the ocean, but she took several deep breaths, chan-nelling calm. This was no time for hesitation or doubt. People could be injured and there could be more after-shocks coming.

'If you heard something, we'll go, but be careful, go slowly,' he implored, his own experience kicking in. She trusted him, she realised. Implicitly. But whether or not she trusted the ground not to open up was a different story.

'We need to do another headcount,' Dev said, his brown eyes scanning the area with a practised calm that totally belied the adrenaline that must have been coursing through him as well. The last headcount was already insignificant—that last quake had been much more unsettling.

He gripped her hand as they made their way towards the nursery, her heart thudding wildly. Feeling his fingers curling into hers took her back to just now...which already felt like months ago. Had he really been about to confess something? He was either about to climax or tell her he was falling in love with her and the latter could hardly be true, this drifter, this nomad who'd been vocally adamant that he'd never fall in love for any reason. Why had she cut him off?

Another small sound pulled her focus back to the present. They needed to act fast. Nothing else mattered. Whatever almost-confessions had been on the brink of being shared before all this would have to wait. For now, there were lives at stake, and she still couldn't see further than a few feet in front of her without having to climb over something.

Dev stayed one step ahead as they neared the nursery. On the perimeter a few other people were trying to reach them, but he instructed them all to stand back for now. Their ex-jaundiced baby, Sahil, was safe in the hands of his foster carers but there were others inside. Ally was wracking her brain, trying to recall who had stayed in there this morning. One young mother, and a newborn, she remembered now.

'Oh, Dev.' Ally's heart hammered in her chest as the

high-pitched wails of infants cut through the clamour just
ahead. Dev moved a heavy unit from her path and, without a second thought, she dashed the rest of the way to
the nursery, her sneakers skidding on the dusty ground,
strewn with baby bottles and formula. Somehow she navigated through the disarray, sidestepping a fallen examination lamp and shoving aside a toppled IV stand. Her
mind briefly flashed to Dev's face just moments before
the quake, his lips parting, eyes so intense she could
barely stand it. It was so surreal, all of it.

A particularly loud cry snapped Ally back to reality.
There she was. The young mother, her dishevelled hair
clinging to her sweaty forehead, clutched her newborn
close to her chest. Both of their bodies were covered in
a thin layer of grey dust, making it difficult to tell where
their clothing ended and the dust began. Without hesitation, Ally scooped up a first-aid kit that had miraculously
fallen close by and approached them.

'Are you hurt?' she asked, and the woman shook her
head, holding out her baby now as if she wasn't actually
sure. Her baby, wrapped in a dirty cloth, had a head full
of wispy hair and his eyes were wide, just as Oliver's had
been, when he'd been born. She had fallen in love with
her nephew on the spot. They didn't seem hurt, thankfully, just scared.

'Come on, let's get you out of here,' she instructed, her
voice firm but gentle. She turned around, expecting Dev.
But he wasn't there. A knot formed in her stomach as she
looked again, hoping for a glimpse of his tall frame or
the familiar sight of his dark hair. Where had he gone?
Another voice met her ears.

'Ally?' It was Raj, a volunteer. She instructed him to
help her guide the mother and child outside, checking

for other people in the nursery on the way. They'd been so lucky that more people hadn't been in here! Outside, the knot in her belly wound tighter and tighter as she searched the campsite. People had straightened a lot of things out already, but there was an air of tension and mild shock amongst the locals, and she learned that some of their kids were not yet accounted for.

'Pritya, have you seen Dev?' she asked a nearby volunteer, who was busy securing a splint on someone's leg.

'No, sorry,' she replied, not looking up from her task.

'Has anyone seen Dev?' Ally called out, her voice barely cutting through the chaos. Each passing second without a sighting of him caused the knot to bind so tight she thought she might be ill and stop breathing altogether.

Forcing herself to focus, she saw to a minor cut on a young boy's leg, while she was informed that some people had gone to look for the missing children. He would have gone with them. She knew it. He had to be here somewhere. They needed all hands on deck, but more than that, she realised as she fought to keep the panic away, she needed him—his calmness, his expertise, his presence. She couldn't shake the fear that was latching onto her like a strangling device at the thought of him being hurt, or worse. *Not again, not again—please.*

'Ally!' A voice cut through the noise, strong and reassuring, instantly stilling her spiralling thoughts.

Oh, thank you, thank you.

It was Dev, emerging from around the tents that were still standing. A smear of dirt was streaked across his cheek but otherwise he seemed unharmed. Relief washed over Ally like a warm wave, and she almost laughed at the absurdity of feeling such profound gratitude, simply because he was OK. He wasn't Matt, he wasn't going to die on her...well, she hoped not anyway.

'Thank goodness you're OK.' She exhaled, not realising she'd been holding her breath.

'Of course I am,' he said, stepping closer. He almost wrapped his arms around her, she could see him itching to do it, just as she was, but she refrained. 'I see you got the mother and baby out... I was called off to help...'

'With the search, I know. Any luck?'

'Not yet. There are three of them. Rahul... Soman... Dinesh. They were last seen playing together right before the quake. They woke up early and said the dogs were acting weird, so they followed them outside. That's what their mothers told us.'

'Animals can sense these things coming,' she heard herself say, though her voice sounded as if it were coming from somewhere outside herself now. Those kids. What if they were hurt?

CHAPTER TWELVE

THE SEARCH WAS ON. The NHF workers and the locals split into groups. Ally and Dev took a road into the jungle, where they'd gone to see the elephants before. The kids often played around here and Ally could see the faint footprints of children and animals imprinted in the mud, leading in various directions. There was no sign of them though.

'It's so still. The birds have gone quiet,' she noted, and Dev nodded thoughtfully.

'So eerie.'

The road through the jungle was narrow and winding, surrounded by dense vegetation and towering trees. The leaves rustled in the wind, and rays of sunlight peeked through the canopy above them, now that it was after dawn. It would be hot again soon. The kids probably had no water, wherever they were. The occasional movement in the bushes made Ally's heart skip a beat, and another small tremor shook the ground beneath them, gently this time, though it still sent a ripple of panic through her belly, adding to the already tense atmosphere. Then... cries for help echoed out at them, sharp and desperate.

'Over there!' Dev was already on the move. She found herself praying as they raced towards the sound, the adrenaline fuelling their movements. Ally never prayed, but she could see the distress in Dev's eyes. Did he replay that night with his sister, in the car, every time there was an emergency situation like this? Every time there was a chance that he wouldn't be able to help?

He must carry every loss so deeply, as she did, as if it were his own. She might have gone some way to helping him see that he needed to let his family in, to stop inflicting more pain on them and himself by blocking them out of his life, but he still blamed himself for what had happened. It broke her heart that he did, but maybe it wasn't something you could just switch off after letting it rule your life for so long. It wasn't as if she could ever switch off her need to be near Nora and Oliver, not while they needed her.

An anguished scream suddenly pierced the air, halting them in their tracks. Dev spun around on the spot, holding a hand out in front of her to keep her quiet, and she strained her ears, listening for it again. 'Where are you?' he yelled out, and the seconds before they heard anything else seemed to last an eternity.

'Help!' It came again.

'I think I know where they are,' Ally said now, remembering the hunter's lodge from before. Dev seemed to read her mind, and she sprinted at his side through the dense brush, trying to force the thought of deadly creatures and big cat attacks from her mind.

The cabin was not the same place they'd been to before. At least it didn't look the same at all. Dev got on the radio to share the location while Ally got to her knees where the entrance used to be, near where Dev had found her that day when she'd been hiding from the kids. The metal structure had buckled and twisted under the force of the upheaval. Ragged sheets of corrugated iron had crumpled like tin foil and patches of rust were smudged with drifts of dirt and grit. The whole battered construct looked as if it had folded in on itself.

A sickening lump formed in her throat as she and Dev took in the wreckage. He crouched low, called the children's names, and they answered, giving whoops of joy that told her at least they weren't too hurt. But still, three young children were trapped inside this awful metallic carcass, their hopes pinned on her and Dev!

Just then, a small hand forced its way out from below the place the doorway used to be. Ally touched the boy's grubby fingers lightly. 'Hey, it's OK, we're here to help,' she said.

'Can you wiggle your fingers for me?' Dev asked. The children obeyed, and one by one they stuck their hands under, till a row of tiny digits wriggled in the dusty air. Relief washed over Ally. No crushed limbs—a very good sign.

'Can you tell me your names?' Dev added, looking to her. She knew he was trying to keep the children engaged while they worked out a plan. The narrow gap left after the collapse wasn't much more than a sliver but it was their only way in.

'It's Nurse Ally. I'm here with Dr Chandran,' she called into the dark recesses, keeping her voice steady despite the adrenaline coursing through her veins. 'We're going to get you out.'

She turned back to Dev, met his gaze a moment as her mind whirred. His brown eyes were hard with resolve. Without a word he started showing her what she should do to help, keeping his voice low or simply giving a nod here or there so as not to scare the kids inside. Together, they moved a lot of debris, communicating with silent movements that to anyone looking on, would make it pretty clear they'd been doing a lot more than just working professionally side by side recently.

They had become more than a team. As Dev lifted a plank, Ally supported it from the other end, the muscles in her arms protesting under the strain. Maybe it was the heat now forcing a trickle of sweat to slide down her back, maybe it was this unexpected disaster, but on top of knowing Dev was leaving her soon she couldn't help feeling far too emotional as they lifted, dug and extracted what they could from the scene.

'Ally, we need to move this section here—it's pinning down that corner,' Dev directed, indicating a twisted sheet of metal that had curled around a support beam like some kind of serpent.

'Push against my count,' he said, and she braced herself, thinking of the kids, ready to exert every ounce of strength she possessed. Dev's nose wrinkled up. 'One, two, three!' With a collective heave, they shifted the metal so there was just enough space to pull the children out. Only just as they moved it, another slab of metal crashed down, seemingly from nowhere. The kids all screeched, and it was all Ally could do not to scream herself.

'Are you hurt, Dev?'

'I'm OK.'

'Are you all OK in there?' she called out, resorting to prayers yet again inside her head. What was left of the roof sagged ominously, threatening to collapse further at any moment.

'We're good,' came the reply.

'I can't move this piece...can you work around me?' Dev said now.

'I'll try!'

In a feat that surely should have seen him donning some kind of superhero's cape first, Dev supported the heavy shard of metal on his back, his face taut with the weight of it, while Ally gently lifted one of the frightened children from beneath it. This was the eldest boy, Rahul. She recognised him.

'Can you hold it?' she asked Dev, frightened he would drop it at any moment. 'Careful with that—it looks jagged,' Ally warned, as she and Rahul both tried to help move it aside. It was no good, the thing was locked between Dev, more trees and obstinate branches.

'It's fine, keep them coming,' he urged them.

'Please, help my brother and my friend,' Rahul pleaded, but Ally was already reaching in carefully to try and get the next child out—a boy no older than seven. This was Soman.

'Come to me, sweetheart,' Ally coaxed, extending her arms. Soman hesitated before allowing himself to be guided into the tiny space. He was heavy despite his small size, and clearly couldn't hoist himself out as well as Rahul had, but together they managed to get him far enough through the new gap, as Dev grunted close by. 'You OK?' she checked in.

'Mmmph,' came his reply.

Oh, gosh, she had to move faster. Poor Dev.

The third child, a little younger but trying hard to be brave, clung to a tattered stuffed elephant. Ally reached for him with open arms. 'I'll take care of Mr Trunk too, Dinesh,' she promised, and the scared child let out a quivering breath that was almost but not quite a cry as he bravely let go, surrendering the toy to her care. As quickly as she could, Ally managed to extricate him. His small body was trembling all over, but thankfully he wasn't injured. It was a miracle these kids had only minor scratches, considering the state of the structure that had collapsed on them.

Just as Dev finally allowed what was left of the corrugated wall to drop to the ground, the crunch of leaves and debris behind them made them turn. Raj was here again, waving the radio. In the distance, the whine of a rescue truck told them more help was finally here. At last, they'd been able to get a vehicle around the debris.

'Everything's going to be fine. You were so brave,' she whispered, more to herself than to the children. The dust had caked onto all of their bodies, turning their torn clothes a ghostly grey. Scratches criss-crossed their skin, and now she realised that Rahul had a deep gash on his arm that he'd failed to mention before helping them rescue the others. Dev spotted it just as she did.

'Careful with that arm,' Dev warned in a hushed tone, and he got to his knees, checking for signs of fracture.

'I'm OK, Doctor,' the boy insisted, and Ally nodded, quickly disinfecting it with the kit she had thankfully brought from the nursery.

'You're a real hero, you know that,' she told him, casting her eyes to Dev right after. He could have been crushed just now, but he'd taken on the challenge willingly, put himself second.

'We heard there's a missing dog, still,' Raj said now.

'Boop ran away. He was scared.' The kid with the elephant sniffled, and Ally crossed to him again, brushed his dirty cheeks kindly with her equally dirty fingers. She felt a hot pang of missing Oliver. She would lose her mind, knowing something like this had happened to him and his friends.

'We'll keep looking for your dog,' she said, turning to Raj. 'Please inform their mothers they're safe.'

'He will,' Dev replied on his behalf. He was at her side now, and he took her hand, not caring, apparently, if Raj was literally standing in front of them. A small smirk of knowing crossed Raj's face, and, without a word, he led the kids away back towards the campsite.

'OK, let's think this through,' Dev said when the crunch of their shoes was out of ear shot. He looked terrible now, and so did she, probably. Hot, dirty, exhausted. 'If you were a dog, where would you go?'

'I'd go towards the camp,' she said, after a moment. 'Or to the village, where there's food and water.'

'He wasn't at the camp, we would have heard,' he said, leading her in the other direction.

Together they made their way in the hot sun towards the local village. It was about a mile from the campsite, but there were paths and trails a dog might have taken along the way if it was seeking shelter. Dev was exhausted and he knew his back must be black and blue under his shirt from holding that sheet up. He handed Ally a bottle of water he'd got from Raj and she drank from it thirstily, as if she'd never had water in her entire life. Dev called out for the missing dog, knowing full well there might be more people who needed help too. Who knew the extent of things in the village?

Today was crazy. This morning felt like a thousand years ago already. Did he really stop himself from saying he loved Ally, right as they'd been...well, making love? He'd been unpacking this ever since. The way his mouth had tripped up, followed by the pounding of knowing in his chest, and his swollen heart. Maybe she thought he'd been about to say something entirely different, he thought, realising what an idiot he would have been to tell her something like that in the heat of the moment. Even though he meant it. He had somehow fallen for this woman, one hundred per cent completely. But how could they have anything lasting? Was he even capable of it, even if she was? Life was different already with her in it, and it wasn't going to be easy to give up, but this was all unprecedented, and he still wasn't sure what to do.

Ally's hand gripped his as they took the path into the village and a pained cry hit their ears. It was coming from one of the small shacks that passed for houses. A woman.

'Over there!' Ally cried out, her legs already propelling her forward. Dev was at her side in an instant.

The air was thick with dust and panic as the harrowed cries led them to the tiny building. It was barely clinging to its definition of a home; the ceiling drooped threateningly like the shack they'd just pulled the kids from, and the surrounding walls were fractured mosaics of plaster and children's drawings.

'We're here,' Ally announced as she hurried ahead of him, sweeping aside a fallen chair to reveal the woman, cowering under a chipped wooden table. Her face was slick with sweat and contorted in pain. She couldn't have been more than sixteen, with a tumble of raven hair spread around her like a fan. Her dark eyes were wide with fear and they latched onto Dev's as they approached. The girl's body heaved with contractions, her hands clutching the tattered remnants of what must have been a colourful sari just an hour or so ago, but it was so dusty he could hardly make out any colours now.

Dev's heart jumped like a giant grasshopper in his throat as he navigated the fallen debris in the direction of the tap, his unsteady steps echoing out on the hard concrete floor. Quickly he refilled his water bottle and took it to the lady, instructing her to drink.

'We need to keep calm,' Ally was saying as he knelt beside the expectant mother who was grimacing in pain, sucking in huge breaths one after the other. 'Find whatever blankets and towels you can. Let's make her comfortable and prepare for delivery,' Ally said. 'The trucks won't be able to get here for a while. It took us long enough on foot.'

He followed her instructions, moving swiftly to a rickety wooden cabinet standing crooked in a corner and pulling open the drawers. His fingers wrapped around several fluffy towels folded neatly together. Some were small hand towels while others were larger bath sheets.

'Dev?' Ally was holding out her arms and he walked to her.

'Focus,' he murmured to himself, shaking off the memories and self-doubt. He realised his mind had flipped to a time at his grandma's house when he and Roisin had played hide and seek in the linen closet. He could picture her now with him; he and Roisin had been so close. If the dead really did watch over you, was she here now, cheering him on as he and Ally did everything in their power to ensure this baby's safe arrival into the world? What did she think of Ally? he wondered. Did she love her as much as he did?

He caught himself again, helping Ally disperse the sheets and blankets, creating a sort of bed to ease the woman's discomfort. This woman was throwing him into chaos, earthquake or not, and he'd almost told her he loved her this morning! Crazy. *But you have started to fall in love with her,* he thought, watching her holding the young woman's hand, encouraging deep, long breaths through another contraction. This kind of blossoming love had crept up slowly, born from respect and mutual understanding and, yes, the pain they had both had to endure before being thrown together like this. He would spend the rest of his life wondering what Ally was doing, and who with, if it wasn't him.

He saw the unwavering strength in her now, the same resilience that made her an anchor for her family back home. Ally was too rooted in her world to ever be swept up by his nomadic life. While his existence was a series of temporary stops in far-flung corners of the globe, Ally's soul was tethered to her loved ones, to Oliver, who adored her, to Nora, her sister, who relied on her. And he couldn't risk his life's work on a romance. It was too important; this was his legacy, in honour of Roisin. After he'd failed her and his family like that, he barely even deserved a great love anyway.

'Dev, it's going to happen, soon,' she said, barely flinching as the girl squeezed her hand till the colour drained right out. They had no oxygen for her, nothing.

The young mother whimpered, her face ashen with fear and exhaustion already. She looked impossibly young beneath the grime and sweat. Dust motes danced in the slanted light that was piercing through a crack in the wall. This would surely be all over the international news by now. Was his family worried about him? Did they ever worry they might lose him too, as they'd lost Roisin? Dev steadied himself as the young woman let out a wail that by all rights should have created another shockwave through the village. Somewhere in the distance a dog barked. Ally's eyes met his and he knew she was thinking the same thing. Was it the dog they'd come looking for? No time to look now.

'Can you imagine what Nora's thinking right now? Hearing about the earthquake on the news?' Ally's voice trembled slightly as the woman stilled between contractions. He frowned. Of course she had been thinking it too. 'She must be out of her mind with worry.'

'Let's give her some good news to hear about once we're out of here,' he replied, throwing a reassuring smile her way that he was sure didn't quite reach his eyes. Of course she was thinking about her sister—she was always thinking about her family. He was just selfish, he realised. That fact was undeniable. It hit him as if the roof had come down on him, and this time, he let himself be burdened with it, feeling it crush him slowly.

'You're doing great. Just focus on your breathing, all right?' he encouraged. Ally positioned herself behind the woman now, letting her lean back against her chest. She brushed damp strands of hair from her forehead, murmuring words of comfort as her breaths grew more ragged with exertion. He did not deserve this woman, for so many reasons, but their teamwork was seamless by now, a fluid exchange. What was he going to do, once she was back in the UK and he was…who knew?

'Dev, I need you to support her legs,' Ally instructed now. It was hot, getting hotter by the moment in this enclosed space, and in moments the baby was crowning. 'All right,' Ally continued, her blue eyes fixed on the emerging head of the baby. 'When I say push, you help her lift slightly, OK? On my count… One, two, three—push!'

Dev was as prepared as he could be as the woman, this terrified mother-to-be-any-moment-now, caught in the throes of labour, bore down with all her might, pushing her weight so far back into Ally she almost toppled over backwards. 'Good, good,' Ally encouraged anyway. 'Just a bit more.'

The supplies they had were meagre—a few clean cloths, a small bowl of water he'd brought from the tap in the corner, and the same basic first-aid kit they'd brought from camp, which seemed laughably inadequate for the task at hand, but if Ally was daunted by it all being so drastically different from what the midwives dealt with in Somerset she wasn't conveying that to this woman at all.

'Another push,' she instructed, signalling for him to switch places with her. After one more agonised cry from the woman, Ally gently cradled the newborn's head and shoulders, easing the tiny being into the world, slick and wailing right away, as if it...he, or she...was protesting already.

'You have a healthy baby girl.' Ally breathed out, a smile spreading across her face as she wrapped the baby carefully in a clean sheet. Pure adrenaline surged like lightning through his veins as he took the newborn from Ally's careful grip, feeling for the pulse at the tiny wrist, counting under his breath, relieved at the strong, regular rhythm. They would have to make do with palpation and observation in lieu of stethoscopes and monitors until they could get them to the hospital but so far, miraculously, everything seemed well.

'Good heart rate,' he murmured, more to himself than to Ally, who was sponging the woman's brow with cool water. Dev wrapped the baby again in another brightly coloured sari he'd found in the drawer, quickly repurposing it into a swaddling blanket.

He felt Ally's eyes on him as he did it, and when he

looked up, she was still watching. Her eyes held a different kind of light as she observed him with the baby, and for a second he wondered what she was thinking. Picturing him as a dad, as Cassinda had? The thought had all but turned his stomach back then. But now, for some reason, the thought didn't feel quite so alien. He'd done more difficult things in his time. Spending all that time with the abandoned baby, Sahil, had changed something, made him think that, with the right woman, maybe he could do this too one day. Of course, then the demons raced back in, reminding him otherwise.

Gently he handed the infant to her mother. His eyes met Ally's again over the tiny bundle, and something passed between them before she quickly looked away with a small harried sigh. In that moment, the pull towards Ally was almost impossible to ignore and suddenly he thought he might ask her to come to Canada with him. But then what? She hadn't specifically said she wanted marriage, kids, a man to settle down with, but she'd been planning all that with her ex who died, so it was written in her stars. Not for him though…not for him, never. He didn't deserve those things, at the end of the day, and his missions with the NHF were more important.

He leaned against the cool, cracked wall, radioed in what they'd done. Ally gently cleaned the mother's forehead again with a damp cloth while she cradled her baby, suddenly lost in wonder and joy. What a start in life, he thought. What a way to come into the world!

The air was still thick with the metallic scent of blood and he could hear the distant wail of sirens growing louder now. Help was coming. Just as he was about to help them both up to head outside, a noise from the doorway pulled his attention back.

'Oh, hi,' Ally said from behind him. 'Heard all the noise, did you?'

The dog was standing there, a scruffy caramel-coloured mutt with a patch of white fur over one eye. Dev was sure he recognised it—it was the dog they'd been looking for, the one belonging to the boys.

'So you found us before we could find you, huh, buddy?' he said with a sigh. Its tail wagged tentatively as it padded over the threshold and into the dishevelled room, nose twitching, dark eyes wide with curiosity. It paused for a moment, head cocked to one side as it assessed the situation. Dev watched as Ally stretched out a hand, inviting the dog to come closer for a sniff, and with her encouragement the dog finally took the last few steps and pressed its cold nose into Ally's open palm, right before nudging softly at the baby's foot, making the young mother laugh. They all laughed as its tail started wagging faster in excitement. Finally, a moment of normality in a morning that so far had been so surreal.

Things were going to be OK, he thought with relief. Thanks to Ally. Well, thanks to both of them, another kid had been given a fighting chance amidst a tragedy. It was just a shame that all this had cemented his own place in the world, a selfish man hiding out in the guise of a hero. An escape artist, playing the role of a stable lover and partner.

Ally deserved more. She might not realise it now, but when she came down from this high, she'd see that this agreement they'd made had some dangerous hidden clauses. Falling in love with Ally was ruining him already but he would only make things worse for both of them if they carried this on. From now on, he decided, he had to be less selfish in general, starting with letting her go.

CHAPTER THIRTEEN

THE STERILE WHITE cotton kept blurring in her vision as Ally folded the bandages. Of course, she was still thinking about the quake and everything they'd endured, but Dev had retreated emotionally. It was as if he'd already boarded that plane, in his head, and flown back to Canada. The base camp was like a buzzing beehive with the NHF volunteers all rushing about, but the echo of that young mother's relieved sobs and the baby's first cry after they'd helped it enter the world three whole days ago kept springing back to her mind, too, drowning out the commotion. She should have felt elated for having saved them, for finding those children and the dog, but a hollow unease had settled in her chest since. Nothing could get rid of it. And it was all because of Dev's sudden distance.

Ever since the team had been relocated back to base camp following the quake, he'd been someone else completely, as if he were pulling back the parts of himself he had given her piece by tiny piece, until she was left wondering if he'd ever given her anything at all. If she'd imagined it.

Grabbing her water bottle, she perched on the edge of the bench by the door, her eyes tracing the patterns of dust kicked up by all the passing feet. Zoning out. Since the earthquake, Dev had been like a ghost around her, his usual warm brown eyes somewhere far, far away. Someone had hung paper hearts around the place ahead of the party, or 'Celebration of Love', that was happening later tonight. Valentine's Day wasn't so much of a thing around here as it was back home, but the volunteers from their respective places around the world were throwing a little party early, anyway, before being assigned to the next mission. Everyone needed a break after the panic of the quake, and the clean-up. Would Dev even attend the party? she wondered. Or would he stay in his hotel room as he had the past few nights?

Ally couldn't help but wonder if his withdrawal was because of what had almost slipped out of his mouth that morning. The almost-confession still lingered between them. He probably hadn't meant it at all, he'd just been caught up in the moment...unless he *had* meant it, and he was just as freaked out by the implications as she was. A future was impossible, they both knew it. They wanted different things. Still, the knot tightened in her stomach as she considered the possibility of leaving Kerala without understanding where they stood.

'Ally?' Dev's voice sliced through the drone of conversation around them.

She glanced up to find him standing in front of her suddenly, his dark eyes brewing with an intensity that made her pulse quicken. His shirt was buttoned all the way to the top again, as it had been that first day. For some reason it irked her now, made him seem even more closed off to her, buttoning himself back up so she couldn't reach him.

'Are you going to this party later?' he asked her simply.

'I suppose so,' she replied. Her heart was stuttering,

even as she attempted to sound nonchalant. He nodded, but before he could say anything else, Dr Anjali Kapur diverted their attention. Her trademark flowing sari was a rainbow as usual and her smile was as enchanting as ever as she floated over to them.

'Spencer,' Anjali said, extending a piece of paper towards her. 'Your new assignment.'

Ally took the sheet, scanning the typed text. She was being sent to a small village in Rajasthan, where a waterborne disease outbreak needed urgent attention. Her role would be critical, leading health education efforts and supporting local nurses. Exciting. Challenging, probably. The perfect end to her mission in India...but what about Dev? Would he be assigned anything or was he still going to leave and fly back to Canada ahead of the real Valentine's Day, also Roisin's birthday, and the day of her memorial? The plans had all been thrown out of whack after the quake.

'Sounds interesting, thank you. I'm excited for this one,' she managed to say with a tight smile.

'Your expertise is needed there, Spencer. You leave first thing tomorrow.' She looked between them. 'I hope that won't be a problem?'

Oh, gosh. Anjali knew about them. Word had got back that something had been going on anyway. It was hardly a secret, not since everyone had seen them leaving the same tent that morning.

'Thank you, I won't let you down,' Ally said, but hadn't she let her down already, breaking focus all those moments to lose herself in Dev? She'd let herself down anyway. Excitement was the furthest thing from what she felt now. But she plastered a smile onto her face as Anjali turned to Dev next. There was no piece of paper for him.

'Chandran? I understand you won't be continuing this assignment, that you're heading back to Canada for a while?' she said.

Ally's stomach dropped into a sloshy puddle despite her smile as Dev nodded his head subtly. 'I leave tomorrow, yes. I'm not sure how long for. Not for long, hopefully.'

'Spending time with your family is important. Take as long as you need,' Anjali followed, and Ally didn't miss the quick glance in her direction, from both of them this time. Ugh. Dev was still bowing out early. He wasn't taking another position. Not here, not anywhere else in India. So with her also shipping out in the morning, she might never see him again after this.

'Excuse me,' Ally uttered, her voice barely above a whisper. She needed air, space, something to anchor the swirling thoughts threatening to capsize her composure in front of all these people. She stood to walk away and head for the door, but Dev called out.

'See you tonight, Ally?'

'I'll see you there,' she told him, without turning back. It would be their last goodbye.

Her hotel room felt smaller than usual as she sat on the faded bedspread, the phone pressed to her ear. Larissa's voice was a beam of sunlight that pulled her from the storm in her head, as it always had, even though she seemed to be having issues of her own with Thor. Ally could tell her friend was developing real feelings too, and denying them. All she could do, when pressed for details on Dev, was bite her tongue, as if she could bite back her own crazy thoughts, now forming a knot in her stomach. She couldn't say it, for some reason. She couldn't say she had fallen in love with Dev. Because then it would be real. He was leaving anyway, ironically before Valentine's Day—a date that up till now had held absolutely zero significance aside from a few bunches of supermarket flowers from Matt when he'd remembered, and maybe a card.

Ally couldn't believe how complicated things were getting for Larissa either, over there in the polar winds with her Viking. To think, they'd both come on this adventure looking for a simple no-strings fling, and now...well, who knew? They ended the call with a promise to keep each other updated and Ally's gaze drifted to the window. A hummingbird hovered near a cluster of bright flowers outside, and she watched its wings beat with a rapid, frantic energy that looked a lot like how she felt every time she thought about Dev. Restless. As if she were hovering on the edge of something that was just out of reach.

There was no denying the connection they had, fragile as it might be. Even when he was being distant, she could feel him still inside her, seeping into her blood like sugar into water. The thought of facing him tonight sent a ripple of anticipation through her. But it also struck her dizzy with a fear she couldn't shake off. She thought of Matt, the way they used to crack themselves up over stupid stuff, stuff that hadn't been funny to anyone else. Well, sometimes she'd been the only one laughing, but still...

OK, so maybe he hadn't been perfect, and maybe, now she really was being honest, she and Dev were a better match physically, and mentally too...but he'd loved her, and she'd loved him, so much so that she hadn't made room for so much as the thought of ever being with anyone else. This thing with Dev was stirring up some element of guilt too, the more she thought about it. Was she betraying Matt's memory? She definitely hadn't fallen for him as fast as she had apparently fallen for Dev.

Whatever it was that seemed to be simmering between them wasn't all stemming from the past. Not her past, and not his either, she was sure of it. It was its own entity—alive, unpredictable, and demanding to be acknowledged. Larry had tried to convince her that Nora and Oliver would be fine without her there. But Larry was wrong, they were not fine—how could they be fine? They did need her. They would always need her.

'Maybe he can visit me,' she whispered to the hummingbird, allowing the words to hang in the air like the creature. 'Visit me in Frome.' The idea sparked a flicker of hope, but she squeezed her eyes shut, laughing at herself. As if Dev would want to go to Frome!

But Larissa wouldn't forgive her if she didn't at least float the thought.

Ally felt his eyes on her the second she stepped from the palace terrace into the garden. How on earth they'd managed to secure such a venue was beyond her. It was literally fit for a king. The NHF had impressed some people over the last months, but right now, the only person she wanted to impress was Dev. He was talking to some other people and stayed in the conversation, but she felt his eyes trailing her as she clutched a single red rose and made her away around the garden towards her seat. The tables were illuminated by strings of fairy lights that cast a glow on the blooming flowers around the perimeter. The dark green foliage bent in the warm night breeze as if it were bowing to them and her heart drummed against her ribs as she stopped to talk to another volunteer.

'You look amazing, Ally, great dress. Red is your colour. Who's your rose for?'

'I don't know yet,' she replied. Ally cast her eyes sideways to Dev again. They had all been given a rose on the way in, and told to hand it to someone special. It didn't have to be anything romantic. Some people were laughing, handing them out to one another as friendly gestures, but Dev was still holding his to his side, just as she was.

'I think you do,' came the knowing reply, before the woman floated away, leaving Ally standing alone, rubbing her arms. Was it too late to back out? To head to her room and hide away? *No, chicken. Talk to him!*

Maybe she'd have one small glass of wine first, she thought, hoping it would calm her nerves. He was at the bar now anyway, talking to someone else. A woman. Jealousy flared in her chest for a moment before she reminded herself she was here with a mission. She had to be brave and talk to him. She was the one he'd been sleeping with, not this woman. There was no one else. It was just…everything else, getting in their way.

Ally's heart fluttered like one of the strung-up paper hearts as she approached the bar, trying to keep her cool. It was a beautiful set-up, trestle tables adorned with more flowers under the tree. But she barely noticed the decorations as she took a deep breath and walked over to them.

'Hey,' she greeted them both with a smile. Dev turned to her, his brown eyes widening in surprise. 'Ally! You look amazing.'

As if you didn't notice me before, she felt like saying. She felt herself blush at his compliment and smiled anyway. 'Thank you.'

The other woman excused herself, giving Ally and Dev some privacy. She couldn't help wonder if everyone here knew that something had been going on, following their exit from that tent together. With time running out though, she couldn't exactly afford to address the issue of her depleting professionalism right now.

'So, who's your rose for?' Dev asked, gesturing towards the red flower in her hand.

She hesitated for a moment before finally admitting, 'For you.'

He nodded slowly, a slight smirk on one side of his handsome face. He looked so good tonight in yet another shirt buttoned up to the top and navy-blue dress trousers that matched his tie. 'Who's yours for?' she dared.

He lowered his eyes, then looked up at her through ink-black eyelashes. 'Who do you think?' he said, offering it in one palm. She couldn't help smiling as they swapped roses, both ending up with an almost identical flower, just like everyone else in the vicinity. 'Happy almost Valentine's Day,' he said.

Her dress suddenly felt too tight. It wasn't quite Valentine's Day yet. Not quite his sister's birthday. Just thinking about him leaving tomorrow for Canada made her heart shrink inside her till she was left reaching for the jug on the bar, suddenly dying of thirst.

'I just wanted to talk to you,' she said, touching a finger to her wet lips.

He frowned and loosened his tie a little, looking everywhere but her. 'I know, me too.'

Ally swallowed a golf ball from her throat. She lowered her voice, stepped a little closer. 'What's going on, Dev? I've missed you.'

Her heart was pounding. She'd never felt so vulnerable in her life, but as his eyes landed on hers again, she felt the most powerful surge of emotions that she could hardly keep from showing on her face. This was bravery though, this was facing it, she told herself, when everything inside had been warning her to run, to keep the barriers up, just as he was doing. He wasn't Matt. Matt had had no choice but to leave her. Dev was choosing to leave without making any plans to ever see her again. And this time she needed proper closure, one way or the other.

Before she knew it, he was taking her arm gently, and leading her away from the bar. They passed the crowds, back into the palace, where Dev tried several doors only to find them locked. They soon found themselves in the cloakroom, complete with a golden chandelier that was wasted on the tiny room of hooks and lockers. Dev pulled the lock across the door behind them.

'Ally,' he said, turning to her. He opened his mouth to continue speaking but she interrupted him quickly.

'Can I ask you something?' Her voice was steady now, even if her heart was doing acrobatics inside her chest.

'Of course,' Dev replied, his hand tightening around the rose as he looked at her. All around them, scarves and shawls created an ocean of colour, but the room felt as if it were closing in.

'I know you have to go. I know that's probably why you've been distancing yourself, and I don't blame you, but would you consider…would you think about visiting me in the UK?' The words tumbled out of her, not as graceful as she had rehearsed in her head, but at least they were out.

Dev leaned back against the door, the surprise etched plainly across his features. It was as if she'd presented him with a puzzle, the pieces all scattered and uneven around them, and he'd been tasked with putting them together under the scrutiny of her hopeful gaze.

'Visit you?' he echoed, obviously buying himself time as he processed her request. Ally cringed. This was silly.

'Yes,' she said anyway, squeezing her rose so tight a thorn jabbed into her palm, making her drop it. She felt her fingers intertwining in a knot of anxious energy. 'I mean, no pressure. Just a visit. When I'm home, and you've spent some time with your family.'

She watched the play of emotions on his face—the furrow of his brow, the slight parting of his lips—as he weighed her words against whatever was going on in his head. She knew all too well the demons that danced in his mind, the fear of commitment that shadowed his every step since that thing with his colleague, Cassinda. His desire to remain untethered clashed with this undeniable connection that had grown between them, but he had to face it too, didn't he? Discuss it?

'Ally, that's…' Dev began, then paused, searching for the right words. 'It's a big step.'

Her heart sank. 'It's whatever it has to be, Dev.'

'I'll be taking the next assignment, wherever they send me,' he reminded her. She nodded, trying to steady her breathing and calm the storm of emotions that still threatened to spill over. It was as if every beat of her heart were tethered to his words now. He stepped forwards. 'And what will you do, Ally? Do you really still want to go back to England? It's not like you have to, you know. No one is forcing you. There's plenty of work with the NHF.'

His gaze pierced her, poking a hole in her armour. For a second she stared at him, floored. 'That's not part of the plan, Dev. My sister needs me. Oliver needs me. You know I have to go back. I don't have a choice.'

He shook his head slowly. 'I don't know if that's true.'

'It *is* true. Why wouldn't it be true?' she challenged.

What was with everyone insinuating her place was not with Nora, who still needed her? 'But there's a lot of work in England. We could find you something, we could both find…'

'That's not part of the plan,' he repeated. He shook his head resolutely. 'And anyway, I thought we *both* agreed that this was a bit of fun.'

Ouch.

Embarrassment threatened to short-circuit her entire system as she stood there in front of him, wishing she could disappear. For a second it looked as if he was about to reach for her, but he pulled back at the last second, swiped his hands into his hair.

'I just don't want to make the same mistakes again,' he admitted, his gaze not wavering from hers, even as she looked away, swiping at her wet eyes.

'I get it. I'm just another Cassinda.' She couldn't exactly help the snarky tone, but it didn't mirror her hurt either—how could it?

The moment lingered as Dev chewed on his lower lip, his forehead set in a deep frown. Voices chattered in the distance, a man laughed nearby, and somewhere, a bell tinkled. But for Ally, the whole world narrowed down to the man standing across from her. Right now, this one guy held her hopes and her heart in his hands.

'I get it, Dev. You want to be free and single for ever, floating around the world!'

'Ally, we had an agreement.'

Oh, gosh, this was humiliating. She had sworn she would never be in this position, yet here she was, and he was letting her down gently.

'I thought you were going to say you loved me, the other morning, before the earthquake,' she managed, doing her best to stand tall. 'You were, weren't you...? And then you just went all ice man on me, like nothing ever happened.'

'I'm sorry,' he said, his voice steadier than she felt.

'You're sorry,' she muttered, almost kicking the rose across the floor, then reining in her sudden fury. This was not how she'd expected this to go. 'I'm sorry, Dev. I am so very sorry. I clearly misread the situation.'

'Ally...we want different things.'

'I know, but I don't know. I've never done this before, but we could work something out. We've both lost people in our lives, Dev. I'm not ready to lose you. There, I said it.'

A pained look crossed his face for just a second. Enough time to see the guarded expression in his eyes, and the weight he still carried on his shoulders—the weight of a guilt that wasn't his to bear. She reached out finally, her hands finding his. She could already feel him slipping away.

'You don't have to keep running from what happened with your sister, you know, and you don't have to deny yourself happiness because you feel guilty. The accident wasn't your fault. Is that what this is about, really? You're just going to keep moving around, throwing yourself into danger zones, wherever they send you?'

'It's what I enjoy, Ally.'

'It's not going to bring her back!'

His jaw clenched, the muscle twitching with the effort of holding back. He looked away over her shoulder and she bit down hard on her cheeks. She had to tell him, even if he still rejected her. If she didn't, she would always wonder what if. 'Dev, after Matt died, I never thought I could feel anything like this again, for anyone. But then

I met you and everything changed. Everything! You reminded me of what it felt like to be happy and carefree… and I don't want to lose that. I don't want to lose someone else I love.'

Silence.

Still, nothing. She watched his face, the way his jaw tightened and his throat pulsed, as if he was swallowing something back that he didn't know how to say. Panic coiled in her belly. He wasn't saying anything. Gosh, she was being a total idiot. She was still waiting for him to say he loved her, that this fling had developed into something he couldn't lose, that he didn't want to lose her either.

'I don't feel the same,' he confessed instead.

Ally felt as if he'd slapped her. 'What?' she mumbled in shock, realising she was trembling, and cold. Goosebumps flared up her arms. 'But you almost said you lo—'

'No, I didn't,' he said, setting his mouth into a straight line, so unlike the way she'd had him memorised till now. Now, this was all she would remember. 'If I did, I was lost in the moment. Ally, we both got carried away. We agreed it would stop if it stopped being fun. So this is me, stopping it.'

With that, he turned around and fumbled with the door handle. In another second flat, he was gone, and Ally reached for her phone. She wouldn't break down, she would not. But she needed to call Larry immediately.

CHAPTER FOURTEEN

DEV'S NEPHEW, NIKKI, squealed in delight from his place on the couch next to him, his avatar leaping and ducking as the boy clutched the controller of the games console. On any other day, the playful shouts and laughter of his favourite kid in the whole world would have been contagious, but today, the joy seemed to ricochet off him. Not only was it Valentine's Day for real. A reminder of everything this family and this house had lost. He had ruined things with Ally and he just couldn't get her out of his head.

The delicious aroma of simmering spices wafted from the kitchen. His parents were preparing food for the memorial dinner and they were talking with each other, punctuating the air with the clatter of pots and pans ahead of the so-called celebration. All their friends were invited. Everyone who had ever known Roisin was invited to laugh and remember and cry, and the guests would arrive soon—friends, relatives, echoes of the past. He'd be forced to talk about her, and remember…everything.

'Uncle Dev, you just died again. Pay attention!' Nikki called out, pretending to bash him with his controller.

'Sorry, buddy,' he said.

'Your uncle's just jet-lagged, that's all,' his brother Romesh said, dropping a bunch of knives and forks on the table. 'Hey, Dev, beer run?'

'Definitely,' Dev replied, ruffling his nephew's hair and jumping up from the couch. Despite his outward focus on his brother as they drove into town, his mind was miles away in Kerala, with Ally. The thought of her watery blue eyes on that last day, brimming with tears over his cruelty, broke his heart. The loss of her sent an ache through him. He could almost hear her cracking a joke, trying to mask the pain that had always lingered just beneath the surface. How was she feeling now that he'd stolen his affections away...forced her to think she'd lost him that he'd never loved her in the first place? He had taken his selfishness to new levels by lying but he'd been trying to set her free of him.

His brother cast a sidelong glance at him from behind the wheel. 'Spill it. You've been more ghost than man today.'

Dev chuckled, but it sounded hollow. 'Sorry. Just thinking about something. Someone,' he admitted.

'I knew it. Ally, huh?' Dev had mentioned her briefly on the drive back from the airport when Romesh had picked him up, but he'd found he couldn't quite talk about it all then. 'Come on, give me the dirt. What's got you so twisted up?'

Dev found himself clenching his fists, voicing thoughts he'd barely admitted to himself since storming out of that cloakroom and making his way back to the hotel. He'd left early the next morning, and spent the whole time in the departure lounge fighting the urge to turn back. 'I ended things. I didn't want to hold her back.'

'From what? Being happy with you?' His brother's teasing tone had shifted, edged with sincerity now.

'From her life in the UK. Her family needs her.' As he said it, he knew she would never change her mind about that. But he hadn't exactly done much to convince her that she had every right to stop holding herself back for the sake of everyone else. Just like him, perhaps?

Romesh's mouth formed a thin, hard line. 'Settling down hasn't really ever been your thing. We all know that.'

'Maybe not...but maybe she got me thinking about a few things,' Dev conceded, the words tasting bitter on his tongue. Fear had taken root deep inside his bones—a fear of falling for someone he could hurt or lose, a fear of failing someone else on the cusp of a life-or-death situation. But ever since he'd been home, his whole family had taken him in with open arms, his mother especially. He'd found her upstairs that first afternoon, looking through clothes in her wardrobe, and he'd walked up behind her, told her he was sorry. Sorry for hiding away, for being an emotionless black hole, for being so afraid of hearing her blame him that he'd stayed away longer than he should have. Slowly, she had turned to face him.

'Dev, I never wanted to hear you say that you thought I blamed you for the accident.' The words had tumbled out in a rush, and the dam had broken. His mother's composure had crumbled, and she'd sobbed, reaching for him. Dev had enveloped her in his arms, her tears dampening his shirt as he'd held her, and forced himself to let the guilt and shame wash over him until it was out of his system completely.

'Oh, my son,' she'd wept, 'I've never once blamed you. Not for a single moment.'

She'd talked about Roisin after that, brought up a hundred memories, and every time he'd felt only love. And in turn, his love for Ally had grown and grown till it felt as if it were strangling him from the inside. Why had it taken so long for him to process this...all of it?

'Look, Dev,' his brother said now as they pulled into the car park, 'no one's saying it's going to be easy. But I haven't seen you this down in a long time. You need to do something about it.'

'Ally doesn't want a life of constant upheaval,' Dev said as they made their way into the store. The chill of the air made him shiver; this was a world away from Kerala. 'I can't drag her around the world on my whims.'

'Is that what she told you? That she doesn't want adventure? Or are you still telling yourself you can't stop and settle down?' His brother's voice was gentle, almost coaxing.

'She has her life, her responsibilities in England.'

'So what's stopping you joining her there?'

'Bro, we were just messing around...until we weren't.'

To his surprise, his brother took his shoulders and stood in front of him, shaking him. 'Go to her. If she's not doing any more assignments with the NHF after this, she'll be home soon. Just go to her, Dev, and be honest this time.'

Dev flinched, as if the words 'be honest this time' were a blow. Romesh had a point. They paid for the beers and wine and walked to the car again in silence, but as the snowflakes started to swirl around the car, he couldn't help thinking he'd made the greatest mistake of his life, not being honest in the first place. He'd lost her trust, most of all, on top of the one person he would have talked to about this most, if she'd been here. Roisin. Squeezing his eyes shut, he pressed his back against the car door and fought a wall of emotions. Romesh was there in a

flash. He held him tight as the grief overwhelmed him.
'I miss her so much, bro.'

'Roisin?'

'Yes, Roisin!'

'We all do, Dev, but you can't bring her back, no matter how much you keep chasing this impossible salvation. You can get Ally back, though, if you want.'

'Maybe.' Dev swallowed hard. 'It's just...there's so much to do out there.'

'And your work is the most honourable of anyone I know, the way you go wherever you're needed,' Romesh said, squeezing his shoulder a little too hard. 'But don't forget to help yourself too, Dev. Don't let this fear and grief dictate your life. You deserve more. Maybe if you give her a chance you can figure something out.'

Dev nodded, then pulled a face. 'That's what she said, but I lied to her. I told her I didn't have feelings for her when—' Dev broke off, the admission sticking in his throat. 'When I did. And I still do.'

'Then go to her, man,' his brother urged, his deep brown eyes shining with the same earnestness that reminded him of Roisin. 'Tell her how you feel.'

Ally lingered on the path to her house, her shopping bag swaying at her hip. She'd found Oliver's favourite chicken nuggets, he'd be pleased, and these days she lived for little victories. A hint of lavender from the garden next door hit her nose amongst the smell of the rain-soaked Somerset soil, and she stopped for a moment, letting the early March weather ground her in the present moment. This was where she was now. Back where she belonged in sweat-free Somerset, with the people who needed her.

So why did she feel like a stranger impersonating her own life?

Shoving the vision of Dev from her head for the thousandth time that day, she was making her way up the driveway when she stopped short. A man she had never seen before was stepping out of her front door, onto the front step, pulling it closed behind him. Tall, dark hair, a loose denim jacket. He blinked in surprise when she met him halfway.

'Can I help you?' she asked, suspicion clear in her voice. For a moment he looked her up and down, and she clutched her shopping bag tighter, before he let out a laugh.

'You look just like her! She said that was the case. I'm Tim.'

He held out a hand and she stared at it, wracking her brains. Tim?

He must realise she had no clue who he was, because he retracted his hand slowly and dashed it awkwardly across his chin. 'Nora's friend,' he finished.

Ally drew a breath so sharp she almost sucked in the whole front garden. Nora had a new 'friend'? In what world…? Why had she not said anything? Ally had been home for almost a week!

'I um… I think you need to talk to your sister. Maybe I'll see you later. It's nice to finally meet you, Ally.'

She watched Tim walk away, his steps brisk and purposeful. She couldn't deny it, there was something rather likeable about him. Cute too. And there was also something about the way he carried himself that reminded her of Dev. She shook her head, banishing the thought. Dev was a million miles and a zillion emotions away, and there was no use dwelling on what could have been.

That was what she'd been telling herself anyway, since she'd finished her last assignment and flown home. The emptiness was unparalled, the feeling of rejection, and hurt, and stupidity for putting her heart on the line only to get it thrown back in her face. At least she'd told him though. At least she knew she was capable of doing things on her own, facing some of those fears she'd let control her life since Matt.

Stepping inside the familiar house, she set down her bag on the dining table, trying to shake off the odd sense of disquiet Tim had just caused.

'Ally?' It was Nora's voice, calling from the other room.

'In here!' Ally called back, mustering a smile.

Nora looked sheepish as she stepped through the doorway. 'I saw you through the window just now. I see you met Tim?'

'Aunt Ally!' Oliver's voice rang out before she could reply. He dashed across the room, his arms flung wide. She bent down just in time to catch him, lifting him into a tight embrace. His joy was infectious, and, for a moment, she forgot about this new Tim guy. Ally's life was here, in Frome, amongst the people and the places that needed her. But still, Dev wouldn't leave her head. Neither would all the people she had met with the NHF, all the things they'd done. A world away from all this.

'Guess what?' Oliver's voice was a conspiratorial whisper against her ear now.

'What?' Ally played along, squeezing him gently.

'Mummy has a new boyfriend!'

The news struck her like a bucket of cold water. So, Oliver knew too. That could only mean it was serious. She sent her nephew to the kitchen with the shopping bag, and looked up to find Nora leaning against the back of the couch, the same sheepish smile playing on her lips. Nora twiddled with the brown ponytail that hung over her shoulder, and it was only now that Ally saw the sparkle in her eyes. It hadn't been there in a very long time.

Nora explained how they'd met, shortly before Ally had left for India, how the relationship had developed into something more, that she couldn't have fought it even if she'd tried. How Oliver seemed to adore him. She hadn't wanted to tell her, she said, because she'd been so upset about Dev.

Ally felt the swell of emotions almost topple her. She was genuinely happy for Nora, delighted, in fact, to see her sister taking steps towards happiness again. But beneath the surface, a million more questions were bubbling up. 'Come sit,' Nora said, gesturing to the kitchen table. 'We need to talk. This guy in India... Canada, wherever...'

Ally watched as Nora folded her hands together, the lines of worry on her forehead smoothing out as she spoke. 'Ally, you've done so much for us, for Oliver and me. But it's time you started thinking about yourself again.'

'Thinking about myself?' Ally echoed, her heart thudding a little harder. She could sense where this conversation was heading.

'Yes,' Nora continued, her tone gentle but firm. 'You should call the NHF. Take another assignment. Live your life.'

Ally felt a pang of longing just hearing mention of the NHF and the work she had left behind. The *man* she had left behind. He didn't want her, but she wanted more for herself these days. The warm monsoon rains, the laughter of all those children, and everything they had to teach her. For a fleeting second, she let herself imagine returning to that world, throwing herself head first into all the challenges and total fulfilment it had offered her, and potentially still could.

Larissa was happy, it seemed. She'd found a perfect match in her Thor in the end, and was talking about moving there to live in his cabin, and learn to shoot guns! Of all the crazy things her friend could do, this was pretty much the craziest. Nothing was the same around here now, and it probably never would be. Maybe the only way forward was to venture back out on her own.

Being in the old English pub was like stepping back in time, and somehow just as he'd imagined as Dev took a wonky wooden seat at the bar. The walls were lined with more weathered wood, and the faint scent of ale from at least twenty decades stung his nose along with the bleach. The dim lighting cast shadows over an assortment of tables where locals murmured over pints, their laughter occasionally bubbling through the low hum of conversation.

'Can I help you?' The barman, a grizzled man with a salt-and-pepper beard, wiped his hands on a cloth as he eyed Dev's out-of-place attire, and the suitcase he'd wheeled in with him.

'Uh, yes,' Dev started. 'I'm looking for Ally Spencer. Could you...could you call her for me? I don't actually know where she lives. I'm a friend. Her sister is Nora, if you know—'

'I know them. Sure thing,' the barman replied with a nod, reaching for the phone behind the counter.

As he waited, Dev's gaze wandered across the quaint

pub, right in the heart of Frome. It was charming in its antiquity, and very different from anything in Toronto. His stomach knotted at the thought that maybe it was him, not this small place, that Ally needed space from now. Would she even hear him out if he found her?

Soon, though, the door swung open, pulling Dev's attention towards it sharply. Ally's figure appeared, framed by the doorway. Her wavy auburn hair tumbled around her shoulders, her eyes wide with disbelief as her gaze fell on him. He stood up quickly.

'Dev?' Her voice was barely audible over the clinking of glasses and chatter, though everyone stopped immediately to stare. This was probably the most exciting thing to have happened here in a long time.

'Nora told me someone was here to see me,' she stuttered, still in total shock. She paused halfway towards him, looking around her, as if expecting him to disappear again at any minute.

'Ally,' he breathed out in relief. He stepped towards her. 'I had to see you. I've been beating myself up over how I ended things.'

'So you...you came to Somerset?' She looked too shocked to laugh, or cry. In this moment he couldn't actually tell how she was feeling, but the distance between them was charging with electricity already. Dev felt his resolve harden; he was here now, and his family had all been rooting for him to do this, so he was not going to let them down. Thankfully she let him take her hands. She was dressed in jeans and boots, and a light jacket, so different from her array of summer dresses and NHF white coat. This was English Ally, and she was even more beautiful than he remembered.

His fingers brushed against hers as he reclaimed the

space between them. 'I've been doing a lot of thinking, you know? About us, about myself.' He paused, searching her face for any sign of what she might be feeling. 'I shouldn't have lied to you. I will always regret the way I hurt you because of my own issues.'

Ally frowned, looking down at their entwined fingers. 'Did you talk with your family?'

'A lot.' He nodded sagely. 'It helped. *You* helped.'

She kept her eyes fixed on his, listening intently as he explained everything, all the love and support he had found the second he'd gone home and given them all a chance to open up, talk, and grieve together. A little vulnerability had infinitely changed the course of his life, and Ally had pushed him to make those changes. This new peace of mind was down to her, but she was still the missing piece he needed.

'I don't expect things to go back to how they were, but...' Dev hesitated, choosing his words with care. 'I understand if Frome is where you need to be. Maybe we can make it work. I mean, I've been offered work here before, and this place is kind of...interesting from what I've seen so far.'

Ally's expression softened, and she pulled her bottom lip between her teeth. The silence stretched, but it wasn't heavy; it was thoughtful, contemplative, and something lifted inside him.

'Actually, there's been a few changes around here, too,' she admitted at last, her gaze dropping to their hands before meeting his again. 'Nora...she's doing OK, and she wants me to, well, to live my life. She doesn't need me any more, really, not to the extent that she did. I think maybe it's me who needs her.'

Dev watched as Ally straightened her shoulders. He

wanted to kiss her so badly, but people were still looking on. He ushered her to the corner, where he found his hands reaching for her, too. He pressed his lips to her warm forehead and felt her sigh, before she reached her arms up around his neck.

'I've been considering taking more assignments with the NHF,' she told him.

He pulled back, searched her face. 'Really?'

'I loved it. More than I thought, with or without you, believe it or not.'

Dev couldn't fight the laugh bubbling up his throat and out of his mouth. 'I can believe that. That sounds incredible, Ally.'

He meant it. She had come a long way, they both had, and for them to be here now together proved it. This was literally the last place on earth he'd expected to find himself, following an emotional reconnection with his family.

'Ally,' he began, the words tumbling out like a confession he'd been holding in since he'd abandoned her in that cloakroom, 'I've spent so much time running around that I forgot what it was like to feel… I don't know, anchored.' He paused, searching her eyes and finding the understanding he'd been praying for the whole way here on the plane.

She smiled. 'We don't have to be anchored though, Dev. We can go anywhere together first.'

'I want my next adventure to be different, with you.'

'So do I.' Her hand in his gave a reassuring squeeze, but Dev couldn't contain himself now. He brought his mouth to hers and kissed her, and the roar of the crowd in the pub made them both laugh so much they had to stop. Ally was flushed, and so was he, probably.

'I love you. And not just the idea of you, or the thrill

of the chase. I love the real you. Of course, I almost told you the day of the quake, and of course, I just freaked out, and lied…'

Tears brimmed in her eyes. It had always been a gamble, laying his heart bare after everything, but the look she gave him now told him it had been worth the risk. And the expensive flight.

'Dev, I…' Ally's voice broke, and she took a moment to compose herself. 'I do love you too. You've flown halfway across the world to tell me that, to show me that you're serious about us.' She kissed him again, and took his hands in hers. 'There is just one thing we really have to do though,' she said, swiping at her damp eyes.

'And what is that?'

'We have to tell Nora that you're staying with us for now. There's more to Somerset than this pub, you know.'

'Well, I've a feeling I have the best tour guide in town,' Dev said, feeling the corners of his eyes crinkling as he smiled. 'Unless your man Oliver wants to show me around?'

Ally laughed, and grabbed the handle of his suitcase. 'Let's go and ask him, shall we?'

Fifteen months later

The doors swung open, and Ally stepped into the hall. She was a bundle of nerves, clutching the bouquet of roses to her gown, but the venue was alive with the soft glow of twinkling lights woven through the rafters, casting warm, dancing patterns on the guests, who turned to gaze at the brides. There was so much love in this room.

Larissa grinned at her from beside her. Her dark curls were bouncy as ever, adorned with tiny white flowers that matched the details of her wedding dress, and Ally felt the click of a hundred phone cameras on them, capturing this moment. Their joint wedding day!

'I still can't believe we're getting married,' Ally whispered in awe, but Larry's eyes were on Erik now, waiting for her at the end of the aisle. He looked just as handsome as Dev, who found Ally's gaze and held it, anchoring her. They both looked the picture of a dashing, sexy groom in their navy-blue suits and ties, and as she found Dev's family in the crowd, sitting amongst their own, Ally knew she would always be grateful that people had flown from near and far to be here, in Somerset. Some of them had been surprised, considering the two couples no longer lived here, but home would always be home for her and Larissa.

The scent of roses and lilies hung in the air, stronger than the cow manure from the nearby field, for once, and she breathed in the subtle scent of beeswax from the candles. In the third row of seats she spotted Oliver whispering something to Dev's nephew, Nikki. Nora gave an eye roll and a shrug, which almost made Ally giggle into her bouquet. The kids were besties already. Last night, when they'd gathered in the meadow out back for a hog roast in the marquee, their families had all met properly, and they were like one big happy, crazy united bunch already. Even the ones from Svalbard seemed to be having a great time, not wearing a thousand layers of clothing for once. Early summer in Frome was delightfully...and quite surprisingly...warm.

'We are going to make the best wives in the world,' Larry told her now, almost as if she was trying to convince herself as much as Ally. 'Even if our husbands hate *Bake Off.*'

'*We* can still watch it together, on Zoom calls,' she whispered back, and they both had to stop their giggles. Larissa was moving to a cabin in the middle of the Arctic Circle, after all. But her friend had fallen in love with Svalbard and the people too, and it seemed as if they'd fallen in love with her. Who wouldn't? The thought of visiting her there soon and seeing the life Larissa had built with Erik and their dogs filled Ally with the kind of happiness she'd never dreamed she would ever find again.

She and Dev hadn't managed to visit them yet, seeing as they'd been travelling through Cambodia and North Korea on their NHF assignments, but they'd vowed to meet at home at least every six months, and visit one another abroad when they could. Maybe they'd even all meet for Christmas in Toronto; there was still a lot to plan. At least Larry knew how to fire a gun and wouldn't wind up getting eaten by a polar bear before Ally got to visit Svalbard, she thought, suppressing another giggle.

Both women wore stunning white dresses. Nora had helped her choose hers, while Tim had taken Oliver to the toy store to pick out a board game. Ally's gown hugged her figure, the exact fit she knew would make Dev look at her in the way that melted her from the inside out. Larissa's was equally elegant and strapless, and made her boobs look phenomenal.

The brush of her dress against the polished wooden floor grounded her as her eyes found Dev standing tall and looking at her so proudly it sent a lump to her throat. His gaze locked on hers again with a love so tangible it felt as though he were reaching out and enveloping her in his big arms. He took her hands as she took her place opposite him, just as Larry stopped before Erik.

You look beautiful, Dev mouthed, and she sniffed back a tear. Getting married, saying her vows next to her best friend, and knowing she would spend the rest of her adventurous life with the man of her dreams was almost too much, let alone the fact that they were starting this journey here—in this place!

It was hard to imagine that this hall used to be their clinic. The operation had moved to another town and the clinic space had been sold and reopened as a refitted event space she had sworn never to visit, but she and Larry had both been enchanted by it the second they'd stepped inside, just on the off chance that the perfect Somerset venue they'd been searching for could be this one. And what a way to celebrate their friendship, too. This was something they'd remember for ever, both marrying their partners in the very place where they had first become friends.

'Ready?' Larissa whispered now, squeezing Ally's hand.

'Ready if you are,' she answered with a smile.

* * * * *

MEDICAL

Life and love in the world of modern medicine.

Available Next Month

Best Friend To Husband? Louisa Heaton
Finding A Family Next Door Louisa Heaton

The GP's Seaside Reunion Annie Claydon
A Kiss With The Irish Surgeon Kristine Lynn

Nurse's Baby Bombshell Charlotte Hawkes
The Single Dad's Secret Zoey Gomez

Keep reading for an excerpt of a new title
from the Modern Amore series,
ENGAGED TO THE BILLIONAIRE by Cara Colter

CHAPTER ONE

DISASTER HAD STRUCK.

Jolie Cavaletti had been back in Canada for three whole hours, and her sense of impending doom had proved entirely correct.

She stared down into the white elegant rectangular box. It appeared to be entirely filled with pale peach-colored ruffles.

"Isn't it, literally, so beautiful?" her sister, Sabrina, breathed.

Jolie was fairly certain she heard a stifled laugh from at least two of the other members of the small gathering of the bridal party. She shot a look at Sabrina's old friends from high school, Jacqui and Gillian, or Jack and Jill as Jolie liked to refer to them.

It's only a dress, Jolie told herself. *In the course of human history, a dress can hardly rate as a disaster.*

Holding out faint hope that the bridesmaid dress her sister had chosen for her might look better out of the box, she buried her hands deep into the fluffy fabric and yanked.

The dress unfolded in all its ghastly glory. It was frilly and huge, like a peach-colored tent. The ruffles were attached to a silky under sheath, with a faint pattern on it. Snakes? Who chose a bridesmaid dress with snakes on it?

Oh, wait, on closer inspection, they weren't snakes. Vines. No sense of relief accompanied that discovery.

Jolie did feel relieved, however, when she contemplated

the fact her sister might be playing a joke on her. The feeling was short-lived. When she cast her sister a look, Sabrina was beaming at the dress with all the pride of a mother who had chosen the best outfit ever for her firstborn child entering kindergarten.

Jolie glanced again at Jack and Jill, who were choking back laughter. She shot them a warning glance, and they both straightened and regarded the dress solemnly.

Inwardly, she closed her eyes and sighed at how quickly one could be transported back to a place they thought they had left behind.

Her sister, by design, or by the simple human desire to form a community based on similarities, had always surrounded herself with friends who were astonishingly like her. Sabrina took after their mother, tiny, willowy, blonde, blue-eyed, bubbly.

Beth, Jack and Jill, all of them with their blond locks scraped back into identical ponytails, seemed barely changed in the ten years that had passed since Jolie had last seen them. They were like variations on a theme: Beth shorter, Jill blonder, Jack's eyes a different shade of blue, but any of them could have passed for Sabrina's sister.

The odd man out, the one who could not have passed for Sabrina's sister, was Jolie. She took after her Italian father and was tall and curvy, had dark brown eyes, an olive complexion and masses of unruly, dark curls.

Maybe it explained, at least in part, her and her sister's lifelong prickliness with one another, a sense of being on different teams.

"Do you like it?" Sabrina asked.

"It looks, er, a little too big."

Jolie would, in that dress, walk down the aisle and stand at the altar with the rest of the bridal party, looking like Gulliver in the land of Lilliputians.

"Well," Sabrina said, accusingly, "that's what you get for being in Italy both when I chose the dresses, and when we had the fittings."

This was said as if Jolie had opted for a frivolous vacation at an inconvenient time, when in fact she lived in Italy, going there directly after high school, attending university, earning her doctorate in anthropology and never leaving.

"It will look better on," Beth, Jolie's favorite of all Sabrina's friends, said kindly. "I didn't like mine at first, either."

"You didn't?" Sabrina said, a bit of an edge to her voice. Jolie looked at her sister more closely, and saw that premarital nerves, right below the surface, were raw.

Well, why wouldn't they be? Sabrina and Troy had been married before. A wedding that Jolie had not been invited to, not that she planned to dwell on that.

It had, according to Sabrina in way of excuse for not inviting her own sister to her nuptials, been a spur-of-the-moment thing, basically held on the front steps of city hall.

Jolie, more careful in nature than her sister, did not think a spur-of-the-moment wedding was the best idea.

Though she had not felt the least bit vindicated when things did not go well. Jolie had lived far enough away from the newly married couple that she had been spared most of the details, but her mother had reported on a year of spectacular fights before the divorce. The fights, according to Mom, who spoke of them in hushed tones that did not hide her relish in the drama, had continued, unabated, after the split.

"It reminds me of your father and me," she had confided in Jolie.

A psychiatrist could have a heyday with her sister choosing the same kind of dysfunctional relationship Jolie and Sabrina had endured throughout their childhood. Her father and mother had a volatile and unpredictable relationship, punctuated with her father's finding someone new, and her mother begging him to come back.

All that ongoing angst had made Jolie try to become invisible, hiding in books and her schoolwork, which she'd excelled at. Somehow, she had hoped she could be "good enough" to repair it all, but she never had been.

She shook off these most unwelcome thoughts. She had hoped she'd spent long enough—and been far enough— away not to be dragged back into the kind of turmoil her childhood had been immersed in.

But here Sabrina was, determined to try the marriage thing all over again, convinced that if she did the wedding entirely differently this time, the result would also be different.

A part of Jolie, which she didn't even want to acknowledge existed, might have been ever so slightly put out that her sister was having a second wedding when Jolie had not even had a first.

She had come oh-so close! If things had gone according to plan, she would be married right now. Sabrina would have been *her* bridesmaid. She could have tortured her sister with unsuitable dresses. Not that she would have. She would have picked a beautiful dress for her sister. No, better, she would have let her sister pick her own dress.

Thankfully, they had not gotten as far as the selection of wedding party dresses.

Though no one knew this, not her mother or her sister, Jolie had purchased her own wedding gown, purposely not involving her family.

Because they somehow thought she was *this* horrible peach confection.

Her wedding dress, in fact, had been the opposite of the peach-colored extravaganza she now held. It had been simplicity itself. Beautifully cut floor-length white silk, sleeveless, with a deep V at the neck that had hugged all her curves—celebrated them—before flaring out just below the knee

Even though Jolie was thousands of miles—and a few months—from Anthony's betrayal, the pain suddenly felt like a fresh cut, probably brought on by exhaustive traveling, and now being thrust into bridal activities without being the bride.

How she had loved him! In hindsight she could see that she had been like a homeless puppy, delirious with joy at finally being picked, finally having a place where she would belong. Riding high on the wave of love, she had missed every sign that Anthony might not be quite as enthused, that her outpouring of devotion was not being reciprocated.

Her breakup was three months ago, her wedding would have been in early June, if Anthony—the man she had loved so thoroughly and unconditionally, who she had planned to have children with and build a life with—had not betrayed her.

With another woman.

Something else a psychiatrist would no doubt have a heyday with given the fact she had grown up with her father's indiscretions.

And so Jolie found herself single and determined not to be sad about it. To see it as not a near miss, but an opportunity.

To refocus on her career.

To celebrate independence.

To *never* be one of those women who begged to come first. Jolie's name on her birth certificate was Jolie, not Jolene, but she had not a single doubt her mother had named her after that song.

And also she never wanted to be, again, one of those women who *yearned*, not so much for a fairy-tale ending, as for a companion to deeply share the simple moments in life with.

Coffee in the morning.

A private joke. Maybe even a laugh over a dress like this one.

A look across the table.

Someday, children, running joyous and barefoot through a mountain meadow on holiday in the Italian Alps.

Jolie tried to shake off her sudden sensation of acute distress. She made herself take a deep breath and focus on the here and now at her sister's destination wedding.

The bridal party—Jolie, Sabrina and Sabrina's other three bridesmaids—were currently having a little pre–big day preview of the facilities, which had led to this tête-à-tête in the extremely posh ballroom of a mind-blowingly upscale winery in Naramata, deep in the heart of British Columbia's Okanagan Valley.

Jolie was all too aware she was in possession of the world's ugliest dress, and that it was somehow woven into the fabric of her sister's hopes and dreams.

Unlike Jolie, sworn off love forever, Sabrina was braver. Her sister still had hopes and dreams! She was going to give love another chance.

Which kind of added up for Jolie to *Suck it up, buttercup.*

She calculated in her head. It was Wednesday already in Italy, which made it Tuesday evening here. The wedding was Saturday. She only had to get through a few days.

Anybody could do anything for a couple of days. In the course of human history, it was nothing.

"I think I'll go try it on," Jolie announced.

"Yes, immediately!" Sabrina ordered, flushed with excitement that Jolie could see the unfortunate potential for hysteria in. "You're the only one who hasn't tried on your dress."

Reluctant to actually wear the dress, but eager to get away from her sister and the bridal party, Jolie gathered up the box.

She went into a nearby washroom—as posh as the ballroom—and entered one of the oversize stalls. She stripped down to her underwear, dropped her clothes onto the floor and pulled the dress over her head. It settled around her with a whoosh and a rustle.

She opened the door of the stall and stepped out, resigned to look at it in the full-length mirror that she was quite sorry had been provided.

It was as every bit as horrible as she had thought it would be, a fairy-tale dress gone terribly wrong, with too much volume, too many ruffles and way too many snakes. *Vines.*

A lesson in fairy tales, really.

The bridesmaid dress made Jolie feel like a paper-flower-festooned float in a parade welcoming the *carnevale* season to Italy.

Her sensible bra, chosen for comfort while traveling, did not go with the off-the-shoulder design of the dress, and in one last attempt to save something, she slipped it off and let it fall to the polished marble floor.

No improvement.

She fought the urge to burst into tears. She told herself the sudden desire to cry was not related to her own broken dreams.

It was because she had been home less than a few hours, and already she was *that* person all over again. Too big. Too awkward. Too *everything* to ever fit in here.

The exact kind of person a beloved fiancé—the man she would have trusted with her very life—had stepped out on.

A tear did escape then, and she brushed it away impatiently with her fist. She was just experiencing jet lag and it wasn't exactly home, she told herself firmly. Even though she was back in Canada for the first time since she had graduated from high school, Jolie was about a million miles from the Toronto neighborhood where she had grown up.

Her scholarly side insisted on pointing out it was two thousand eight hundred and seventy-nine miles, not a million.

It was that kind of thinking that had branded her a geek in all those painful growing up years. She had skipped ahead grades, and so she had always been the youngest—and most left out—in her school days. Her senior year—shared with her sister, Sabrina, two years her senior—had been the worst.

In fact, it may have been the most painful year of all.

Not counting this one.

See? Jolie could feel all the old insecurities brewing briskly right below the surface. Who wouldn't have their insecurities bubble to the surface in a dress this unflattering?

Privately, Jolie thought maybe since it was a second marriage—albeit to the same man—Sabrina could have toned it down a bit. But toned down was not Sabrina under any circumstances, which was probably why she was so eager to have a redo of the vows spoken on the city hall steps.

And really, all Jolie wanted was her sister's love of Troy to end in happiness. One of them should have a love like that!

And a more perfect location than this one would be hard to imagine, and that was from someone who had spent plenty of time in the wine country of Tuscany.

Taking a deep breath, reminding herself of her devotion to someone in the family getting their happy ending, Jolie picked as much of the dress as she could off the floor and headed back to the bridal party and braced herself for Jack and Jill's snickers, Beth's kindly pity, and her sister's enthusiasm.

But even her sister was not able to delude herself about the dress.

As she watched Jolie make her way across the ballroom to

the little cluster of the bridal party at one end of it, her mouth opened. And then her forehead crinkled. And then she burst into tears, and wailed. "It looks as if it has snakes on it!"

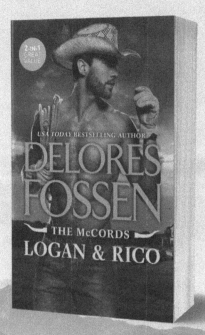